"I DARE YOU"

"You saying you won't give that little moan like you used to if I touch you?" Brodie took two steps toward her.

Laurel licked her parched lips. Didn't the man understand? Persisting in this folly could only lead to trouble.

"Should I find out, will your lips remain cold and lifeless?" He inched closer, narrowing the space between them more.

So close. A trickle of sweat slid down her back, soaking the tight waistband. The fragrance of leather and fresh cut hay tickled her nose. Heaven help her! His mouth pressed to hers would rekindle everything she wished to bury.

His lazy half-smile indicated enjoyment. He knew his nearness suffocated her thoughts.

"Convince me. For old time's sake?" He reached for a dark curl. "Show me I'm no longer in your blood. I dare you."

Redemption

LINDA BRODAY

LEISURE BOOKS   NEW YORK CITY

For Mom, who taught me courage above all else.

A LEISURE BOOK®

June 2005

Published by

Dorchester Publishing Co., Inc.
200 Madison Avenue
New York, NY 10016

ISBN 0-8439-5565-1

The name "Leisure Books" and the stylized "L" with design are trademarks of Dorchester Publishing Co., Inc.

Printed in the United States of America.

Visit us on the web at www.dorchesterpub.com.

Redemption

"When we cannot find contentment in ourselves it is useless to seek it elsewhere."

–Francois, Duc de la Rochefoucauld (1613-1680)

Chapter One

East Texas, 1869

When a man loses his soul, he has little choice except to try to find it again. Unless he wants to stay lost. An old Chinese proverb claims the journey of a thousand miles begins with the first step. Lord knows he'd found plenty of reasons to avoid taking that first one.

At the edge of town, Brodie straightened in the saddle. He squinted into the noonday sun and let his gaze drift to the wooden sign declaring the town Redemption, then to the row of establishments lining the main street.

White egrets flew overhead. In the distance, giant cypress stood in silence. The Spanish moss draping them gave an added ghostly quality to the massive trees. They cried in silent harmony—an army of unheard voices in the face of more death and destruction than he dared number.

He'd come home.

They say to become whole, a person must return to the beginning, to the place where his soul was born.

Redemption?

A one-in-a-million chance of that.

He sighed. He'd had worse odds, he reckoned as he gently nudged the big Appaloosa forward.

The town had doubled in his absence. That meant a lot of new folks. Old acquaintances likely wouldn't recognize him anyway. Eight years had a way of changing a man. War could do things to make you unrecognizable . . . even to yourself. The musketball, compliments of a Yankee soldier, had only shredded his leg. Other scars lay hidden, never to see the light of day.

Those he'd nurture until his dying breath.

The aroma of fresh-baked bread drifted past his nose. Mingling smells of home cooking originated from an untidy little restaurant that looked relatively new. His belly rumbled in acknowledgment. He should stop for nourishment.

Besides, he needed to plan what to say before he visited the house on State Street . . . if such words existed. In response to an unspoken command, Smokey turned and stopped at the hitching post in front of Ollie's Cafe.

A quick glance through the window revealed wall-to-wall patrons. The steamer tied at the pier probably accounted for a good many. He didn't miss the long stares from the cluster of men in front of the barbershop.

Brodie climbed from the horse and looped the reins over the wooden rail. He'd come to expect rude welcomes.

Maybe it was the devil's scorn that shadowed him or the deadly hiss of rattles from his hat that created such aversion. Or perhaps they spied the apparition that insisted on sharing his saddle.

Still, unwanted attention roused pinpricks. He adjusted the thin rawhide holster strip around his thigh and let his palm rest for a second on the polished walnut grip of his Army issue Navy Colt.

The gawkers gasped when he nodded toward them, but they didn't turn politely away. They never did.

He held the door for the couple who came out, stepped inside, and lifted off the old felt hat. A quick glance located the table the man and woman had probably vacated.

It hugged a wall in the far corner, perfect for needs requiring an unhindered view of the premises—where a man could blend in easily. This suited both counts. He moved unhurriedly, sweeping the room for trouble. He breathed a sight easier when he slid into a chair and dropped the hat at his elbow.

A woman well past the mourning of her youth jostled him as she cleared away dirty dishes left by the previous occupants. "What'll you have, mister?"

Before he could reply, a man yelled from the far side. "Hey, Ollie, where's my lunch? Did you hafta go butcher it first?"

"Son of a blue jacket! It'll be ready when it's ready and not a goldarn minute before." The rough talk put a grown boy to shame. Judging by unfazed customers, they likely got an earful on any given weekday.

"Can I count on that anytime soon?" the man persisted.

"If you don't like it, go home and cook your own!"

A most peculiar female, both in name and appearance. She'd evidently made someone mad as hell when they took a hatchet to the faded russet hair. What remained stood in short, uneven porky-spines all over her head. The good Lord must've squeezed in her nose and mouth at the last minute or she'd have wound up nothing but large eyes. Smoke curled from the corncob pipe clamped between her teeth. Except for the smoking apparatus, she could've passed for an organ grinder's monkey he'd seen in San Francisco.

Short, wiry females had a way of making him tread extra lightly. He'd rather tangle with a hardened mountain man.

The skinny termagant never spared him a glance. Her gaze flitted over the crowd the whole time she worked, as though expecting them to toss coins her way.

Yep, just like that trained monkey.

"Well, mister, I don't have all day."

He assumed she spoke to him, although she didn't even pause to look him in the eye. Her arms full of dishes, she turned toward the back.

"I'll have a steak. Biggest one you have." Brodie didn't know if she heard him. She didn't acknowledge the fact.

The monkey impersonator faded into the dark interior. He contemplated leaving . . . until a younger woman strolled from the kitchen.

Sweet damnation! Of all the luck.

Her image haunted his dreams much too frequently for forgetting. He'd lost count of the nights when memory jerked him from a sound sleep. And days when familiar yearning pulled deep in his gut, leaving a chest full of misery and bleary eyes.

From across the crowded cafe the violet-eyed beauty still made him pray for impossible things, promising each desire could come true despite the meager coins in his pocket.

Strange how she wound up here in Texas. He'd never thought to see her again after leaving St. Louis.

She blew away a strand of fallen hair, struggling under the load of plates piled with food. She concentrated on her footing and aimed for the complaining patron's table. With his griping satisfied, she went back for more. She carried one armload after another without noticing him. He doubted she'd recognize him after so long anyway.

The years had treated her kindly. She'd changed in small

ways—all of them favorable. A mature woman with rounded curves stood in place of the slender young girl she'd once been.

His throat clogged when she came close enough to touch.

Tiny lines hugged the lush mouth that once invited, daring him to resist. A block of stone might've. He bore no kinship with rock. In him she'd found a randy soldier who liked to taste.

Ahhh, those kisses. More an angel's than flesh and blood.

Brodie would stake good money she could make him believe he held the key to her heart even now.

He wouldn't make that mistake twice. Still . . .

A crooked smile formed when he considered his good fortune.

Laurel sent the clock a silent cussing. She swore it hadn't moved in the last hour. Her feet and back paid no heed that impatient customers waited for their lunch.

She lifted a plate containing a large cut of beef and strode for the dining room of the cafe, ever mindful of her purpose. Marriage to Murphy Yates offered answers to her dream.

The devil take anyone who stood in the way! She clenched her jaw. She'd worked too hard.

Miles of ground lay between Missouri and Texas. Trouble wouldn't find this town at swamp's edge.

"Let the last day of your past be the first day of your future." Olivia, or Ollie as she preferred, had given the first of much advice the night she sprang her from that hellhole.

The dear woman had seen something worth saving. The chance to make a new life would come just once. Laurel gripped the plate tighter. She meant to grab hold and ride until someone pulled her, kicking and screaming, from the saddle.

A dull ache between her shoulder blades reminded her what she stood to lose. She weaved between the tables, sidestepping sweaty cowboys and their heavy boots.

She'd do whatever was necessary to keep her secret buried.

In the midst of noon madness, someone grabbed her arm, sending the plate crashing to the floor. "Spit and thunder! Now look what you've done."

"Don't worry none about that, sweet thing."

A man pulled her onto a buckskin lap. She found herself staring into the cold disdain of young Jeb Prater.

"What do you think you're doing? Let me go!" Dear God, she'd thought to rid herself of this. The pounding in her head reminded her of bad things she'd tried to blot out.

"When I get good an' ready." Jeb squeezed her waist. Lust glittered in his stare.

"I think you're ready now, boy." The dark warning tore through the room like scattershot, instantly muting clanking forks, conversation, and noisy chewing.

Laurel struggled to see the owner of the bold voice.

"What's *good* for you is letting her go." The stranger spoke again, the threat in his low drawl making the gooseflesh rise on her arm. She strained for a better view.

A shadowed corner beyond reach of lamplight hid his face. But not the long, lean legs propped out before him. The way he lounged so easily in the chair stirred embers of someone she knew long ago. Like this one, his quiet bearing had carried much weight.

Jeb shot to his feet, upending her. His mouth flew open, then snapped shut in disbelief. Laurel scrambled to safer territory, clutching the back of a spindly chair.

"You're not from these parts, so I reckon you don't rightly know who you're dealin' with, stranger."

"I recognize a mealy-mouthed swamp rat when I see one." The man straightened, lifting the felt hat from the table. The deadly hiss of snake rattles filled the silence. Slowly, he angled it on his head. "I've crossed paths with far too many."

Only one man wore a hat banded with snakeskin from which diamondback rattlers dangled off the back. He leaned forward into the lamp's glow. Someone stole all the air from the room.

Shenandoah!

Laurel's gaze traveled to the tall loner's features. Her dry mouth fought for moisture. Creases beneath high cheekbones had deepened into valleys, underscoring the grim set of his mouth. And the dark hair sported a few gray streaks at the temples.

She sidled toward the obscurity of a group who jumped to their feet. Trouble had a way of making folks edgy. Some already headed for the door, their stomachs forgotten.

"I give you three seconds to apologize for that name-calling." The young bully shifted, a bit of his swagger fading.

"And I'll give you two to scrape that steak off the floor." Shenandoah rose lazily. "I believe it's mine and I haven't eaten in two days."

"What'll you do if'n I don't?"

"Choice is yours." The icy glare never faltered. "The easy way or the hard. Make it light on yourself, boy."

The Colt weighting Shenandoah's hip apparently gave Jeb plenty of concern. He flung an angry scowl about the room. If he'd been hoping for support, none came. Color drained from his face when he slapped holster leather and found empty air, realizing Ollie had confiscated his revolver at the door. Laurel wouldn't sympathize. Jeb had dealt plenty of misery.

"What's all the goldarned commotion?" Ollie propelled her petite frame between the towering men.

Shenandoah continued to hold Jeb with his stare. "This boy owes me a steak. Mine's on the floor. We're settling up."

Ollie lobbed a questioning glance her way. Laurel cringed but answered. "Jeb made me drop the plate."

The wiry woman swung back, directing a pointed stare at Shenandoah's hand resting on the butt of his gun. "Shootin' irons ain't allowed in here. No exceptions. Didn't you see the sign that said to leave 'em on the counter?"

"I saw it."

Though he spoke to Ollie, his granite gaze never wavered from Jeb. Laurel knew if the overgrown boy twitched he'd shake hands with St. Peter.

"Means what it says. That's my rule." Wiggling the pipe between her teeth, Ollie stood on tiptoe to get a better look. Furious puffing sent plumes of smoke toward the ceiling. "Don't I know you, mister?"

"Might."

"Ever been to Missouri?"

"Among a few hundred other places."

"I never forget a face." Ollie rubbed her chin. "Might you be the fellow they call Shenandoah?"

"According to who's asking."

Laurel's stomach churned. When she could take a breath, she wondered how Ollie knew him. Shenandoah had left years before the woman arrived at Taft's establishment.

Ollie swung back to Jeb. "You chuckle-headed shavetail. You don't have the sense God gave a piss ant. Here's a man you don't wanna mess with. You're mighty lucky he hasn't already filled you so full of holes your own mama would mistake you for a flour sifter."

Jeb bristled. "Gimme my forty-four an' we'll see who's able to see daylight through."

The pipe flew from her mouth as Ollie slapped Jeb's arm. If she thought to jar his feeble brain, she needn't have bothered.

"Pick up the man's lunch."

"I won't. He called me a mealy-mouthed swamp rat."

"I'd call that awfully kind. Now pick it up, I said." Few would've ordered such. The brash woman didn't frighten easy.

Red-faced, Jeb plucked the meat from shards of earthenware. He juggled the hot steak as though auditioning for a traveling circus act before shoving it at the newcomer. "Here."

Tense quiet stretched. Shenandoah didn't move. A tic in his jaw spoke of supreme effort to curb his anger.

Finally, Ollie snatched the slab of beef. "Never mind. You're buying another. Laurel girl, go throw one on."

A growl rumbled in Shenandoah's throat. "We're not finished. He owes the lady an apology."

"Boy, whatever you done, better own up to it before it gets you killed. And next time you come in here, bring some manners, dadgum it. Else you're not welcome."

While the majority of folk kowtowed, Olivia Applejack b'Dam didn't let her short stature, or her gender, tie her tongue in knots. Over the months, Laurel had witnessed that courage many times. Most learned too late the folly of going toe to toe with Ollie. Still, one day her friend's ornery nature could earn her a one-way ticket to the other side.

Jeb turned beet red. Shenandoah had dethroned him in front of fidgeting patrons he'd lorded over. The protective confines of the kitchen would take scant seconds to reach.

If not? She could despair of saving her new life.

Good fortune and hope deserted her. In the space of a

heartbeat, Shenandoah wrenched Jeb's arm behind his back. "Where I come from a man don't treat a lady like some common saloon girl. Show respect or I'll break it in half."

Unease pricked worse than a stiff horsehair petticoat. Reference to a lady of ill repute might've been pure chance had it come from another.

A diner named Mabel averted her gaze. No one ever told how the woman made a living. Her manner and eyes full of shame gave her away. Those things Laurel recognized.

Beads of sweat dotted Jeb's forehead. "Didn't mean no harm, Laurel."

"Miss Laurel. Call her Miss."

"M-m-miss Laurel." The face twisted into an ugly caricature.

Shenandoah dipped into Jeb's pocket. "For my steak."

Prater stumbled for the door, forgetting his confiscated revolver. Shenandoah straightened the leather vest.

Laurel whirled from the searching gaze that had the ability to heat every cold corner inside. But she couldn't outrun the pursuing hiss of snake rattles.

"The show's over. Go back to eatin'," Ollie shouted.

Memories of the pungent stench of sulfuric bathwater drenched the taste of her spit. Others equally tormenting rose.

How long before she could sleep without fear?

And how much time to erase the hurt of betrayal? She pushed through the door. Sagging, she buried her face in her hands.

What rotten luck! Tucked quietly on the banks of Big Cypress Bayou, she'd thought nothing would find her.

Ollie breezed in minutes later. "Someone die, girl?"

"Shenandoah . . . I know him."

"Every man, woman, and child west of Kentucky's heard of the legendary rebel spy."

"I enjoyed his company toward war's end." A brittle laugh broke free. "I learned the value of his word to return. He'll destroy everything."

"Maybe he didn't recognize you."

"And maybe I've grown horns from the top of my head."

"You worry too much. He's simply passing through."

"If not?" Her bones didn't lie. She couldn't stop the tremor in her heart, much less the quake in her voice.

Ollie patted her shoulder. "If he thinks to hurt my little girl, he'll have to step over my dead body first."

"That's cheery." Despite the image of Olivia lying cold and still, the loyalty touched a deep chord.

"Relax. Got you this far, haven't I?"

Tightness squeezed. The irascible lady had delivered her from wretched hands, taking risks no other dared. She could never repay that.

She kissed the weathered cheek. "You truly have."

"Now quit your brow-wrinkling and cook that steak. Hunger makes a man meaner than a lop-eared polecat in nothing flat. I'll serve the rest of those whey bellies."

Laurel eyed stacks of dirty plates lining the sideboard and ladled simmering soup into a bowl. "Most left. Take this to old Jonas and we can get Shenandoah out of here quicker."

"Ring the bell when that cow quits mooing. I'll fetch it."

Laurel's spirits rose just a bit. An unbreakable bond existed between them. Risking your life for someone tended to do that. Not that Ollie spoke of it. Laurel respected that, same as the gut feeling that Ollie ran from something, too.

With no destination in mind, the wind carried them to

Texas. Murky swamps and marshes righted an upside-down world.

Redemption was a place of being. What lurked in the bayou's water lilies and deep shadows had reborn her spirit. Majestic cypress knew her here and sympathized with the raw break she'd gotten. They forgave her sins.

She could become a whole person. Peace lay within her grasp.

Damn Shenandoah! Damn him for appearing from the blue and scaring her witless.

Chapter Two

Mystery surrounded the funds Ollie used to buy the cafe and small living quarters overhead. Seemed strange for a parlor house cook to fork over such a sum. Still, that was neither here nor there. She respected another's affairs. Besides, a desperate lady shouldn't look a gift horse in the mouth.

Everyone had secrets . . . some more than others.

She flipped the meat and stirred the hot coals.

Hungry flames licked the raw edges of the steak, consuming, scorching. The hiss and spit of juices dripping onto the fire mimicked her heart's loud protest.

A proper marriage to Murphy Yates could disappear into the thin air of a desert mirage. Instinct urged her to flee somewhere, anywhere safe from the familiar gray-eyed rebel.

Yet such a place didn't exist, not even in her dreams.

Through a haze she watched until an even dark color signaled the meat was done. She pulled it onto a plate and shook the cowbell.

The door swiveled on its hinges almost immediately.

From the corner of her eye, she watched Ollie plummet. The pipe flew from the woman's mouth, skidding across the floor. Laurel rushed to her side.

"What's wrong?"

Frightened eyes in the chalky face stared up. Ollie clutched her chest, gasping for air.

"Oh, God! What can I do?"

She stretched her on the floor, loosening the top of the threadbare bodice, then wet a cloth and placed it on the clammy brow.

If only the town had a doctor instead of a dentist. Jake Whitaker would have no inkling how to treat anything more than the usual chigger bites and earaches.

A lifetime passed before the pain eased. At last Ollie managed to speak. "Didn't mean to let you see this, girl."

"I'm going to get help. Even Jake—"

"Might as well dig a grave and throw me in."

At least the suggestion put a bit of color back in the wan cheeks. "He's better than nothing. At least give him—"

"Hmph! Reckon you don't recollect how that quack gave me pyrexia poisoning when he pulled my tooth."

Darn the ornery woman! She suffered too grievous a problem to split hairs. Besides, Ollie couldn't prove Jake made her puke up her toenails and put her abed with a fever. But the stubborn set of her lips left no room for mind-changing.

"We're closing the cafe. I'm taking you to Jefferson." She wouldn't let Ollie die and leave her all alone again. "I've heard they have fine doctors. The Lizzy Belle will come through tomorrow morning. We'll be on it."

With considerable effort, Ollie sat up. "A pure waste of time an' good money. Ain't nothing wrong with me. Besides, if I'm gonna die, I don't want the good Lord to find me with those carpetbagging leeches and riffraff."

14

"I beg to differ about the time-and-money part."

"Just my old ticker wearing out; something to look forward to when you get up in years," Ollie wheezed. "Nothing to fret about. Help me up so's I can get to business. Be a good girl and hand me my pipe, if you can see where the goldarned thing went."

"You're going upstairs and I won't hear a word about it."

The pain distorting Ollie's face matched the dull ache in her heart. Laurel lifted the frail form into a chair.

"Cain't abide a girl more contrary than me. Don't let Shenandoah get a good look, you hear? Give him his meal, then skedaddle back here." Ollie stopped for a breath.

Thankfully, it left a small crack to get a word in. "Yes, General Applejack b'Dam. I'll handle things."

Perhaps the root of their worry had left.

After Laurel located the errant pipe, she peeked through a crack in the door. Most of the patrons had vacated, leaving coins behind for their meal.

Yet there sat Shenandoah pretty as you please, with his back against the wall, Colt within easy reach. If trouble called, it'd not take him unaware. A glimpse of his hat again brought chills up her spine and a shiver through her bones.

He'd developed into a calloused, toughened hired gun. And she'd become a lot wiser. The question remained, how smart?

Nothing short of divine intervention would help in surviving this meeting. And Laurel had learned at fifteen that miracles didn't happen. Not for someone like her.

Whispering a desperate plea, she slid her arm under Ollie's shoulder and helped her stand.

Occupied with propelling Ollie up the narrow stairs, Laurel's heel caught on an uneven plank when she stepped onto the landing. Her shoulder jolted into the wall, causing her tongue to scrape the small chip in her front tooth. With a flash of anger, she remembered that long ago night as she slammed open Ollie's bedroom door. She'd never forget the sound of her own head hitting the floor. She clenched her fists.

Miracles? She'd gotten only one . . . getting away from Taft alive. And at the moment she questioned the blessing in that.

With Ollie tucked in bed, she braced for the chore at hand. Down in the kitchen she lifted the plate and took a deep breath.

One small hope stood between her and salvation.

Perhaps he truly hadn't recognized her. She'd worn her hair loose and flowing in those days, not pulled back in a severe knot on the back of her neck. She straightened her shoulders and strode into the dining room.

Walk briskly. Feel nothing.

Shenandoah's intense gaze burned, luring her concentration from the brisk, firm walk she'd planned. The faint smell of leather, bay rum, and cheroots jogged her senses.

Nights when her world seemed less hopeless.

Nights when she first dared thoughts of a new life.

Nights of passion. Her steps lagged.

The crooked half smile disturbed her far more than the shock of hair that dangled rakishly across his forehead. Rivulets of sweat trickled down her back. That devilish grin touched a longing deep inside her. A longing she knew she had to ignore.

Laurel willed herself forward, a desperate prayer sticking in her throat. She plunked the plate onto the table and turned on her heel.

Not quick enough.

He captured her hand.

"Much obliged. Sit with me a spell, Lil."

Cold fingers of doom clawed their way inside, wrapping around what remained of her soul.

Lavender Lil. No one had called her that since . . . She gave the other two patrons a skittish glance. Their forks never slowed from plate to mouth. They weren't listening.

"Sorry, cowboy." She meant to add the layer of flint. The bitter tinge surprised her. "You've got the wrong person."

Shenandoah pulled her into the chair beside him. Not a forceful tug, but one that offered no escape. The gentle touch spoke of remembrance and insatiable desire.

A crack in the floor came under intense scrutiny.

How could so much dirt get into such tiny places? It would take a good scrubbing to get it clean.

"Nice try. I'd recognize that silky black hair, those violet eyes . . . even if I wore a blindfold."

His husky drawl lodged somewhere in the vicinity of her fickle heart. *Dear God, for another lifetime, another chance!*

"You're mistaken."

"And certainly if you spoke." He brushed aside her denial. "I've never heard another with your throaty voice."

She swallowed the lump. "My name is Laurel James."

The release of his hold gave false hope, for he merely changed locations. She flinched when he cupped her jaw. Damning the touch that bound without rope or chains, she had no choice but to follow where he led. His rebel gaze reflected the futility of her lies. Her stomach twisted into a knot.

"Surprised to find you here. A bit far from St. Louis, aren't you, darlin'?"

"Please . . . don't—"

A loud yell from outside interrupted the desperate plea.

"Hey, you in there! I'm calling you out."

Jeb Prater. Shenandoah shifted in his seat. A glimmer of

disquiet crossed his features before it vanished, replaced by the cold, hard mask of a seasoned warrior.

"Face me now, meddler. I double-dog dare you. I'm gonna show a yellow-bellied, chicken-livered maggot we don't cotton to your kind here."

Shenandoah sighed and gave the succulent meat on the plate a longing glance before reaching for his hat. The rattles shook as he settled it on his head, filling the silent room with foreboding. Prater was the worst kind of fool, Laurel decided. *And I'm the second*.

"Keep this warm." He towered above her when he rose to his full height. "You and me have unfinished business."

Soft buckskin clung to lean thighs. His long stride and easy calm spoke of a man who had no need to prove anything to anyone. He knew who he was and didn't give a tinker's damn about the rest. Laurel drank in the sight.

Of all the ones they'd forced her to . . . entertain, he was the only one who gave of himself. He fit in a special class. She thought his caring genuine. In the long nights and wee hours of the morning, she fantasized that he'd come for her. What a foolish notion.

He never had.

Until today.

When she least needed rescuing.

Blue blazes! His appearance destroyed the belief he'd died a hero on some battlefield, a preference to the bald truth.

Still, despite the fear that he'd ruin her new life, she couldn't help wishing for something that could never be.

Though she abhorred the practice of gun play, she pressed her nose to the cafe window. Suppose Jeb got lucky. Suppose Shenandoah's pistol misfired. Her stomach landed in the middle of her throat.

A piece of lead would keep her secret intact. Her heart

hammered. Now that she knew he was alive, she couldn't bear the thought of him dying.

"You don't have to do this." Shenandoah's voice carried through the thick glass. "No way to settle a score."

The familiar hand hovered over the polished grip of the revolver. Solid and firm, he projected confidence in abilities that could prove most dangerous to a body's health.

"Scared, mister? Afraid now that I've strapped on a six-shooter?"

"It'd take more than a snot-nosed kid to scare me. Don't do anything stupid. Back away and we'll both win. You draw that iron and one of us will lose. Care to gamble it might be you, boy?"

He presented a powerful argument. For a moment, Jeb wavered, appearing to listen. Shenandoah must've shared her thoughts, for he turned slightly toward the cafe. The small motion set the rattles hissing in the quiet street.

"Watch out!" She clutched her apron, twisting it, afraid to look but finding it impossible to turn away.

Before Jeb's pistol cleared his holster, Shenandoah pulled and fired in a fluid movement. A thick puff of gray smoke enveloped the figure from her past. Prater lay moaning in the dirt, gripping his bloodstained leg, and cursing the men who came to carry him into the saloon.

War had ended and men continued to fight. They'd never learn that violence dug more graves. Sudden nausea had her running toward the back before she lost the contents of her stomach.

Gulps of air and a glass of water helped. Ten minutes later she eyed the kitchen mess, mindful of the ticking clock. Only a few hours before the supper crowd arrived. And she needed to check on Ollie.

Heavy-hearted, she climbed the stairs.

"What was all that ballyhooin' down there?"

"Stupidity." Laurel straightened the frayed patchwork quilt. "Jeb discovered his mistake in drawing down on Shenandoah. Probably walk with a permanent limp."

"A man goes spewing his mouth, he's liable to get it filled with something besides a chicken leg. Reckon he found lead a bit harder to swallow." Ollie cackled, puffing on her pipe. "Jeb never cast a shadow across anyone of this caliber."

She veered away from that subject. "How do you feel?"

"Fit as a four-legged mule." Ollie threw her legs over the side of the bed, dodging Laurel's attempt to feel her forehead. "Don't need any motherin' neither. Save it for your younguns."

"Don't have any." Nor did the prospect seem likely. Laurel lowered herself onto a chair beside the bed.

"Won't get any either, less'n you learn to stifle that godawful sassy tongue."

"No use trying to change my ways now."

"What happened to Shenandoah?"

"Eating, I suppose. Jeb interrupted his meal again."

"Fool boy. Just ain't right in the head." Ollie stared into her face. "Well?"

She knew what Ollie asked, but recognized what worry would add to a bad heart. "Well, what?"

"Did he remember you, that's what."

No use trying to plead ignorance. "He called me Lavender Lil. Spoke about unfinished business."

"Son of a blue jacket!"

"I tried to deny it, but he wouldn't listen. I don't know how to fix this mess." Her nerves were tightly stretched bowstrings. Each breath rasped over them in a quivering rush.

"Appeal to his better side. Did you ask for his silence?"

"Jeb stole that chance." Even had she found the words. Smoke curled about Ollie's head. "Gotta find out his

20

plans. Don't reckon he gave any hint of how long he's staying?"

"Not hardly."

"What's holding you back, girl? Get busy."

Heat scorched the back of her throat. It had taken too much strength. Too much time and planning. She wouldn't let one steely-eyed drifter snatch it away. If he thought her a daylily, she'd make him change that opinion quick. In twenty-one years she'd already lived several hundred. A person couldn't go through what she had without acquiring survival skills.

"I'm waiting for you not to die on me. Luckily, I see far too much mule blood in you to let that happen. Much as I loathe the thought, I intend to satisfy your curiosity and mine."

"I'm coming." Ollie's boots struck the floor.

"It's my past I have to face." Laurel stared horrified as the woman danced a jig around her. "What in heaven's name are you doing?"

"Proving I'm not ready for the undertaker yet."

Ollie wobbled when she stopped. Quick reflexes kept her from falling. Laurel held tight, glancing about in vain for a piece of strong rope. "I do this alone. By myself. That doesn't include you."

"Well, of all the ungrateful nerve." Ollie sniffed. "It's not as if I wouldn't let you do all the talking."

"Not even a case of lockjaw would keep you quiet. I'm ordering you back to bed. Don't make me lock you in."

"You're mighty bossy, you know that?"

"I had a good teacher." Laurel hugged her dear friend.

"I'll be more than happy to wring that fellow's neck."

What a picture—Ollie on tiptoe in front of Shenandoah, her bandy legs stretched, hands struggling to reach his throat.

Laurel kissed a thin, hollow cheek. "I love you. Don't know what I'd do if I lost you."

"Quit your dadblasted worrying. I ain't some favorite shoe that's likely to fall out the back of a wagon first time it hits a rock."

Foot apparel and people didn't bear much similarity, but both could fall from a wagon, and Ollie had run smack into a boulder once that day already. Laurel counted her blessings on the way downstairs. Minutes later, she cautiously pushed open the door to the dining room. Thank heavens: The steak and the man had both disappeared, leaving a shiny silver dollar behind.

This time the money paid for an honest living, not services of another nature. At least until they ran her out of town.

She dropped the coin into the pocket of her yellow dress and smoothed the white apron over it. Her clothing ranged in many shades . . . except one. She'd rot in hell before she wore purple again.

Shenandoah could already have spread his venom. Her quiet, respectable life might crash down around her. Dare she hope that he'd already had his fill of her little town?

The bell tied to the door tinkled merrily. Laurel braced herself and turned to face the door.

Shenandoah's mouth sat in a firm line as he watched the woman inside pocket the silver dollar he'd left.

His chest hurt from trying to fill his lungs with air.

Lil had tried to deny their acquaintance. She'd not shown a flicker of happiness at seeing him, nothing to indicate that she remembered the feel of his arms, the taste of his kisses. A corpse would've welcomed him with more warmth and feeling.

He'd thought he'd meant more than simply a body who

shared her bed. She'd turned into someone he never could've imagined.

The pain spread out in a searing arc.

What they once had should've been enough to at least warrant a "Hello, how are you?"

The rudeness rankled. In the old days she'd have rekindled the fire right there in front of God and everybody. Unless . . .

Sweet Georgia clay!

Maybe she'd married and left her heart in someone else's keeping. That would explain her attitude.

Quick jabbing pain almost doubled him. He didn't know if he could stomach her on another man's arm.

He had half a mind to march back in there and demand answers. She owed him that much. He tossed aside the matchstick he'd been gnawing and straightened. Before he could translate the thought into action, a figure strolled past.

His mouth went dry as the man pushed inside the cafe. The passing of eight long years didn't dull recognition.

Shenandoah untied Smokey. "Might as well get you bedded down, boy. No use waiting around for hell to freeze over."

One last backward glance assured him that the moisture on his face wasn't from melted ice. It was way too warm and he'd run out of wishes.

Chapter Three

Laurel pivoted, expecting to encounter roguish disdain. Relief bathed her at finding Murphy Yates instead.

"Is that any way to greet your betrothed? You'd have thought you'd seen a ghost." Long strides covered the short distance. He pulled her into his arms.

Little did he know how accurate his words were. She shuddered to think how quickly this man of the finest cloth would put her out of his life at the mere hint of scandal.

She forced cheery lightness. "Nothing more than a devil in disguise. That's certainly not you. I'm frazzled, that's all. Dueling in the streets tends to do that to me. Did you see or hear the shooting?"

"Bank business kept me busy. Sheriff Tucker gave me the gist of it. I'm surprised someone hasn't taken the wind from Prater's sails before this. I always suspected his bluster would get him in deep water sooner or later."

A gentle touch on her back strayed lower to pat her behind.

"My goodness, Murphy!" Laurel stepped back.

"I don't care who sees. We'd have tied the knot days ago if I had my way."

She turned from him, scooping up dirty dishes and hurrying toward the steaming washtub. Wedding Murphy would bring everything she coveted. Why then did she drag her feet, pushing the date further away?

The question barely formed before guilt arose. The gentle man had waited his whole life for the right woman to come along. He deserved the best. Lord knows she wasn't even in the running for that distinction. She owed him more than the high road to hell she'd attempted to saddle him with.

Sure, he'd probably try to whitewash over it at first, being the true gentleman he was, but regret would show with each passing day.

Murphy tagged behind with a load of plates. "Let's go to Jefferson right now. Within two hours you can be my wife."

How tempting to muzzle each rational thought and accept. Perhaps she could continue to successfully hide her past. Maybe he'd never realize he'd gotten a jaded lady instead of the noble wife he sought.

Respect and caring came near enough to love. Didn't it?

A close perusal revealed nothing displeasing. Never mind that everything wore a bit too perfectly and to crisp precision. Murphy's nicely trimmed hair brushed his collar in rich, sandy waves, each strand neatly in place. His bowtie and starched white shirt added a distinguished air. A gleam came from below.

Her reflection glimmered in the high gloss of his shoes.

. . . The face she couldn't bear to see in the mirror.

Laurel jerked away, setting the dishes in the bucket. "We've discussed this. We can't rush—"

His mouth smothered objections. The earnest kiss

25

caused no disruption in her heart's steady rhythm. She wiggled away, trying not to notice the hurt in his soulful gaze.

"I hope that settles any questions you have regarding my true feelings. You're the lady with whom to build my future."

"I believe you care for me. That's not at issue."

"Goes a hell of a lot deeper than that."

For now. Rueful whispers dodged her attempts to bottle them.

"What's wrong with wanting everything fitting and proper?"

"Enough fuss and bother. Seems an odd reason for concern."

Before a reply came to mind, Ollie ambled in from the alley door, blocking a furry blob with a quick foot. "Durn cats. They break their fool necks to get inside. At least something likes the taste of your cooking, Laurel girl."

The woman slapped her sides, enjoying the joke. Except for a slight pallor, she looked the picture of health.

Murphy covered his awkward position. "Afternoon, Ollie."

"You're just the one to put the bloom back in our girl's cheeks. Reckon you heard about the ruckus?"

"Yeah. Didn't get the particulars, though."

"Started right here over a man's lunch. Laurel got caught smack dab in the middle of the whole shootin' match."

"Sheriff mentioned the stranger stood up for her."

"Dadgum truth of it. And he did a fine job."

"Horsefeathers!" Laurel had to damper the steam before the train jumped the track. "You both know by now I'm fully capable of taking care of myself. Misplaced heroics caused two grown men to put pride before common sense."

Ollie turned a deaf ear and squinted at Murphy. "Do you know that fellow, Shenandoah?"

"Might say so. Puzzles me why he's come, though."

Laurel choked down a gasp and collapsed into a chair.

"You do? Who . . . how?" Ollie's words echoed her own.

Murphy pulled out a pocket watch and flipped the lid. "Certain matters demand my attention at the moment, I'm afraid. Our discussion isn't over. I'll be back soon, so be thinking about what I said."

The shock of his admission had scattered her thoughts. She'd taken all the jolts she could stand for one day. "But what about—?"

"Later, Miss Curiosity." Murphy tweaked her nose.

"Men! How infuriating to leave us in suspense."

"Ain't no changing 'em. That's the God's truth."

An hour later Murphy returned wearing a happy glow. "If you won't marry me today, will you accept a supper invitation?"

"I truly don't see how it's possible, Murphy."

"I have a surprise for you, my love." His eyes twinkled.

He'd snagged her interest. Besides, she needed to get some answers. "In that case, I can't very well refuse."

"How's six-thirty, after you serve the crowd?"

It wouldn't leave time to clean up the mess until after she returned. "Six-thirty it is."

He cast Ollie a cautious glance before giving Laurel a quick peck on the cheek.

When the tinkling bell announced his exit, Laurel exploded. "That low-down, four-flushing, two-bit gunfighter!"

"Simmer down. Murphy wouldn't give you a supper invite if he'd gotten a hint of your dealings with the man."

"One might if he were baiting a trap."

Ollie lit the pipe before she argued. "Oh, stop. If either of them believe for one measly second I'll stand by while they destroy you, they have another thing coming. Hell and be damned, I'll fight Satan himself—with his own pitchfork!"

A handful of regulars wandered in that Tuesday evening, along with a dozen passengers from a steamer bound for Shreveport. Laurel's shoulders ached by six o'clock. Only after she made sure Ollie could take care of a few stragglers did she dash upstairs to freshen up.

"I can beg off or make a tardy appearance," she'd offered.

"Go get gussied up now." The woman swatted her toward the overhead quarters. "I ain't gonna keel over."

But Laurel couldn't let go of that particular worry. Fear of being alone again haunted her every waking moment. Her tongue scraped the reminder of what she'd escaped. She shuddered.

Cold bumps on her flesh rose when she stripped off the yellow dress. St. Louis and death bore the same name. She clenched her fist. They best come armed and expecting a fight.

She stood still, trembling slightly, until the ticking clock finally penetrated the fear. Better hurry, or Murphy would wonder what happened. Her gaze strayed to the wardrobe. She opened the doors, fingering the green calico print. Too plain. The pale blue with a row of lace around the high collar? Too girlish.

It would have to be her most prized—a rose-colored silk Ollie bought to celebrate her freedom.

The crinoline rustled when she smoothed down the skirt. A quick brush of her hair, then she pulled back the sides and secured them with shell combs. The rest rippled down in a mass of loose curls. She gathered her shawl, not once glancing toward the mirror hidden behind a drape of heavy black cloth.

Out in the street a light fog rolled in from the bayou.

She picked up her steps and was soon at Murphy's door, lifting the heavy brass knocker. Deep in the house, the grandfather clock boomed the half hour. Murphy opened the wide portal.

"Sweetheart." He pecked her cheek and led her inside. "I see you've worn my favorite. What a happy occasion."

A tall man stood with his back to them, gazing into the courtyard in which Murphy took pride and joy. Had the fog not muted the colors, bright flowers would've splashed warmth into the room.

"I've waited a long time for this homecoming." Murphy beamed and tugged her forward. "Laurel, my prodigal brother."

The stranger turned, the soft hiss of rattles disturbing the tranquil mood.

"You!" The word exploded from Laurel's mouth.

Brother? Blood pounded in her temples.

Murphy's glance swung from one to the other while Shenandoah glared.

"You're going to leg shackle yourself to her?"

The barb pierced the small bubble of hope behind her sealed lips.

Suspicion etched Murphy's face. "You act as though you've met somewhere before."

"No . . . I mean yes . . . I mean . . ." She rushed to recover. "I've never laid eyes on your brother before." She'd admit nothing.

"Don't look at me." Shenandoah's dark glower promised no help. He'd given her enough rope to hang. The rat.

"Well, of course I met him a few hours ago, although I didn't know who he was. The shock of coming face to face with the object of the day's turn of events took me aback. I never expected to find such a man here. Then to discover he's your kin . . . Ollie called him Shenandoah."

"It seemed prudent to take that name during the war," the familiar voice answered for Murphy. "To protect us both."

"Yep, he's my brother, Brodie Yates." Pride lay in the tone. An affectionate grip rested on his brother's shoulder.

Brodie hadn't known of their betrothal plans. So he hadn't yet spread the news of her tarnished reputation. Before the evening expired she'd finagle a private word with Mr. Insolent. She'd protect her secret if she had to beg, cajole, or strike a match with Lucifer to do it.

Laurel forced a smile and stuck out her hand. "A pleasure to make your acquaintance. Murphy speaks highly of you."

More fibs added to the list. A magic lamp earned three wishes. What did three lies get you other than a splitting headache? She rubbed a throbbing temple with shaky fingertips.

Although Murphy had mentioned his brother once in passing, he hadn't provided a name. And she could classify seeing her old love again as pleasurable. At least the bumping of her heart against her ribs indicated proof of it.

Shenendoah hesitated for the barest of seconds. Her hand got lost in his large palm. Unexpected warmth sent delicious shivers up her arm to her fickle heart. Thank goodness he couldn't see the mess left in its wake.

"Which name do you prefer, Mr. . . . ?" Good heavens, was that squeaky voice hers?

"Brodie will do while I'm here."

"How long might that be?" She wished her words wouldn't burst in breathless rushes. "If you're at liberty to say."

The happiness of several lives depended on her keeping a clear head. She tugged her hand free of his hold, relieved when he didn't press the issue. She backed away.

"Until I wear out my welcome, I suppose." He smiled.

He'd worn that thin at the outset so he might as well move along. She rubbed dampness from her skin. Her annoyed gaze tangled with his. The sudden quirk of a brow relayed satisfaction in knowing the mayhem his touch caused. The room grew overheated.

You're going to leg shackle yourself to her?

A recollection of curt disdain aroused bristles anew. He was the pot calling the kettle black!

Murphy interrupted her thoughts. "Dearest, I know you'll come to love my brother once you get to know him. He's not always a prickly-tongued cactus. You'll soon find him family."

Laurel certainly doubted that.

"All horns and rattles, am I, little brother?"

"Only on occasion." Murphy wrapped an arm around her waist, drawing her against him. "This lady's the best thing that's ever happened to me. I'm forsaking bachelorhood for her."

Again an elevated eyebrow and a quiet reply. "Indeed."

That one word said enough. She prayed he'd not add more.

Murphy didn't give him a chance. "About time I tied the knot. You, too, Brodie. When are you going to settle down?"

"I've yet to meet the woman I wish to lend my name to." A dangerous glint sparkled in his eyes. "Laurel? Is that what you prefer . . . or is there another?"

Her ire grew. He toyed with her. Loss of control would simply egg him on. She breathed deep, swallowing the biting remark on the tip of her tongue.

"Laurel's the name I was born with." His cold stare raised her temperature another ten notches. "I've had no other."

"If you insist, *Miss Laurel James*. Tell me . . . is it true you're partial to lavender?"

Blood drained from her face, leaving behind limp remains of long-dead memories.

A feeble reply finally crept past the double-cross. "I can't imagine who would've spread such a preposterous tale."

"What brought this on?" Murphy blustered. "Makes no difference to you or anyone else what color my Laurel wears. If you have a burr under your saddle, just speak your piece."

Tucked within Murphy's arm, tension suspended her heartbeat, freezing the moment in a block of ice. Sure as the moon rose in the sky, Brodie intended to blurt out everything. She flinched, awaiting doom.

"Thought she resembled someone I once knew." He removed his hat. The lethal rattles commenced their clatter, sending a war party of chills through her. He laid the hat on a polished mahogany credenza. "Now that I've taken a second look, I can see I was mistaken. That woman wasn't the marrying kind."

Her knees buckled. With the night just beginning, she'd put nothing past this murdering desperado. More than likely, he wished her to sweat plenty before he denounced her.

Murphy apparently bought the half-truth. "That's better. Etta's outdone herself for this special night. You're home and beautiful Laurel is about to become my wife."

"When's the happy occasion, Murph?"

"Four weeks—unless my powers of persuasion kick in." Murphy's warm squeeze released crashing waves of guilt.

Laurel almost favored ending this charade now rather than continuing with the facade. Murphy would thank his lucky stars she'd refused a rush to the altar. The town would soon forget his disgrace. Memories faded. Sometimes.

"We didn't want to do anything rash. After all, we have the rest of our lives to spend together," she hurried to add.

The pressure at her waist brought mist to her eyes. No man more decent than Murphy Yates walked Redemption's streets. A landslide election had confirmed popular sentiment. Besides mayor, Murphy served as the town's only banker. He enjoyed the stellar reputation of a fair-minded businessman. More than one farmer would've lost his land if not for Murphy's genuine caring. She'd sensed his unique compassion the first moment they met.

Were her needs great enough to justify bringing him down? Naked truth plunged like a dagger. She hadn't willingly chosen to become what she had. It wasn't Murphy's, but her debt to pay.

Will Taft alone bore that responsibility, and she hoped he roasted in a fiery pit for it.

"Shall we?"

Murphy escorted her into the dining room. Showing manners and good breeding, he pulled out her chair. The scoundrel seated himself across the table without waiting. And yet he'd forced Jeb's apology for rudeness and made him call her "miss." A strange code he'd adopted.

Her mind wandered. Shenandoah once wouldn't have thought it tragic to tie her name to his.

She glanced up to find him staring as if he read her thoughts. Her mouth went dry. The tilted grin on his lips seemed more suited for foxes in hen houses than a civil dining room.

"Some yams, my sweet?" Murphy passed a dish.

Thankful Murphy had broken the spell, she scooped a small portion onto her plate.

"I must say, this is something." Brodie steepled his fingers over full, sensual lips.

She didn't care to explore his hidden meaning. The statement boded ill. She aimed for another path. "I get the

33

impression you've not visited in a while. Have you been away on . . . business?"

"At least the kind that keeps a Johnny Reb spy two steps ahead of a Union rope."

A hated spy. Yet he'd risked death to return. Why now? What made the gamble worthwhile?

"I assumed those who hunted Confederate soldiers long after the war's end bore more fiction than truth."

"Andrew Johnson's pardons were the fictitious part. I could tell stories that would curl your hair. I assure they're not mere babbling of toothless old men."

She crumpled the napkin in her lap. "Why did you take up arms in such a horrible war you had no hope of winning?"

"Anyone warn you what happens to little girls who ask too many questions?"

"But now you came back, knowing full well the thick army presence." Her tongue stumbled over the words.

"I did for a fact."

A mocking smile formed. She fought the urge to rush from the table when he tilted forward. The younger Yates brother, having turned his attention to the meal, seemed unbothered by a charge in the air.

"Brodie joined up with the South when the smoke cleared after the first Battle of Bull Run. Nothing I said kept him from going." Murphy gestured with his fork. "He sent several letters letting me know he'd escaped Yankee bullets and prison camps, but only one since Lee's surrender."

"It seemed better that way."

"That was four years ago," Murphy reminded him.

"Give or take a few lifetimes." Brodie's mood darkened.

The answer spoke of deep remorse, like hers, that ate from the inside until it destroyed everything, leaving only an empty shell. Regardless of the uproar his arrival brought, she sympathized with the man who'd evidently lost his way.

Laurel swallowed hard. Going home appeared next to impossible.

Chapter Four

The cork from the wine bottle exploded into the chandelier, setting the crystal prisms atwitter. Brodie filled the goblets while considering the value of a piece of Blue Belly hot metal. He preferred a quick end to this torment. Murphy's endearments, the tender touches, knowing Laurel would never be his Lil. It was too much to bear.

He should've stayed gone.

"I believe if a man drinks wine, he should offer a toast."

"That's a fine notion." Murphy rose. "A salute."

A frown marred Laurel's beauty. Tilting her stubborn chin, she extended her glass, meeting his antagonism.

Only a demented man would recall silky curves rippling beneath a light caress . . . and her unbridled response.

Memory overwhelmed him, haunted him with the faces of the lost and the damned. A mental shake returned him to the present. His glass clinked against theirs.

"May the South rise again! And to beautiful ladies who made the fight worthwhile."

"Long live the South."

Their subdued rejoinder paled beside his boisterous one.

"I've heard a louder show of patriotism from dying Rebs."

"What damn good did that war do except leave a bunch of families with holes in them? Children will grow up without fathers. Wives have no husbands. Is that victory? Hate between North and South runs deeper than ever. That's why we have to watch what we say and how loud we speak. Federal troops will lock you up for looking cross-eyed."

"I saw the heavy military occupation in Jefferson. Carpetbaggers, scalawags, and Union army overran the place." Brodie tossed the contents of the glass down his throat. "Hell and damnation!"

"They're trying to redeem us poor Southerners and save us from ruin."

"The situation should improve with the upcoming election," Laurel put in quietly.

"Readmitting Texas to the Union won't fix the sort of ills plaguing us." Murphy set down the wine and resumed his seat.

"But if we have a real governor, the military will pull out. We can make our own laws again. Isn't that the best thing for us and the state?"

Laurel always had a knack for getting to the bottom line.

He remembered wetness spilling down her cheeks. *I need you. We need each other because apart we're an unfinished painting, bodies lacking heads. Promise you'll return for me.*

That night was the last time he'd been a complete person.

"Edmund Davis will hardly bring us back to the Land of Milk and Honey!" Brodie let out a snort. "He's nothing but a Union puppet, and a bastard to boot."

"A free election would be a start," she argued. "Anything beats military appointees. Maybe A. J. Hamilton will beat him."

"Hamilton doesn't stand a prayer. Davis will get in if President Grant has to stuff the polls to do it." Murphy took a piece of bread and buttered it. "Politics gives me indigestion. Forget those fools and focus on this happy reunion."

Happy was not the word. "It's evident no amount of discussion amid china and cut crystal will change what's happened."

Or was about to.

The wayward brother tossed down the contents of another glass. Sheltered by lowered eyes, Laurel saw him refill it.

For a man who'd claimed a few hours ago to have gone without for two days, he ignored the succulent roast hen, creamed peas, and yams. What had happened to the steak—the one that almost caused a man's death? Had he eaten it or fed it to the strays?

A raised gaze floundered in the brooding stare across from her. A strange light turned the gray soot into sinful black.

Dangerous and defiant, the rogue lounged as if waiting in a parlor house for his favorite lady, intent on taking pleasure for the night.

She sucked air into her lungs, blocking hysteria. "This feast puts the cafe's to shame. Better try it."

"Later. The steak I had earlier filled the hollow spot." He leaned forward, propping his elbows on either side of the imported porcelain. "Don't sell yourself short. You're a mighty fine cook, Lil . . . Miss James."

A simple slip of the tongue, or was he persisting in some game? She feared what might emerge each time he opened his mouth.

"Nothing special. Just plain cooking."

"Skill in the kitchen first attracted me to her," Murphy

said. "But then, how could I overlook an angel when I saw one?"

"Indeed." Swirling red liquid in his goblet held her captive. Only when it sloshed over did he release her gaze. "She certainly appears the innocent."

"Pure as the driven snow. My Laurel's worth more than all the gold in California."

"Do tell."

Ice filled her veins. Brodie's smirk said he had nothing to lose. What gall to sit in judgment! He hadn't wanted her. And unless things took a drastic turn, neither would the younger Yates brother, once he discovered who she was.

"Spit and thunder! Stop talking about me as though I'm invisible." Her fork clattered against the plate when she dropped it. "And get one thing straight, Murphy Yates: Don't put me on a pedestal. I'm no saint. Don't try to make me into one. I've committed my share of mistakes and I'll make plenty more before they put me in the ground."

"I'd listen to her, Murph." Glints sparkled in Brodie's dark scowl. "The lady knows what she's talking about."

Heaven help the scoundrel. He'd need it if she could put to work the murderous plans spinning in her head.

"I believe I smell pie." She tried to steer the conversation from the storm-tossed waters of her character.

"Your favorite—pecan praline." Murphy's warm smile elicited undying gratitude. He rang the brass bell beside him, signaling Etta. "I do know the way to your heart, my love."

"Sweet Betsy! Had I only known, it might've made a difference in my marital status. Pecan praline pie. Smooth, sugary, sweet, and ahhhh so desirable." Brodie stretched, raking back an errant lock. The strand stayed put for an entire half second before it sprang back in a disreputable salute. The soft drawl didn't hide his smug confidence.

Laurel's stomach plummeted.

Etta took Laurel's plate and slid the first slice before her. The cook and housekeeper waited expectantly. "It's delicious. I have no secrets around you and Murphy."

Of all things to have said. She needed a good kicking to Main Street and back. Brodie grabbed the opening.

"Speaking of secrets and sugary sweet things . . . I remember a certain young lady in St. Louis. At the Black Garter to be exact. Ever been to St. Louis, Miss James?"

Her heart froze and she choked on a flaky morsel. She downed a full glass of water before dislodging the bite.

"You all right, sweetheart?" Murphy pressed her hand.

"I'm such a ninny. I apologize for making a scene."

Murphy lit into him. "What a dumb-fool question to ask. I doubt Laurel's been out of Texas, and I damn sure know she wouldn't go anywhere near a place called the Black Garter."

"Hold your horses, Murph. Can't fault a man for reminiscing. I met a woman there I could've shared more than a few nights with had Lady Luck smiled my way." The molten stare said he remembered every detail of their encounter.

And God forbid, so did she! With indelible clarity.

But he hadn't cared enough to find his way back.

How proper to adorn his hat with snake rattles. The man had two deadly skills—pistol and tongue.

Spit and thunder! She wondered how a girl trapped a sneaky diamondback. And more important, how could she escape its kiss of death in the attempt?

It never paid to let a scoundrel know he'd drawn blood, something she'd learned about survival.

She flashed her best smile. "I detect the makings of a pitiful tale. You'll never know whether it was a twist of fate or misfortune of your own choosing. Do you ever wonder what happened to her after you moved on?"

"Sometimes."

"For the record, I believe a woman of character would have landed on her feet."

A flash of surprise twisted into a half smile. "Touché."

Murphy glowered. "Are you right sure you've never met?"

Laurel doubled her efforts to keep conversation far removed from the state of Missouri and a certain gaming house. She gave Murphy her full attention. "Etta outdid herself tonight. Perhaps I could wheedle the recipe for the roasted hen. And the pie surely topped the meal. Ollie would dearly love a piece."

"Shoot, take the whole pie, sweetheart." He lifted the back of her hand to his lips. "Your very wish is my command."

Her throat tightened.

"Speaking of Ollie, I noticed she looked a bit puny today." Murphy smoothed the inside of her palm but didn't release it.

"She had a spell with her heart after the run-in with Jeb." Laurel shot Brodie a withering glare. The dear lady wouldn't have suffered it had he chosen another town to disgrace with his presence. Her voice broke. "I force myself not to think about losing her one day. She's like a mother to me."

". . . We had one of those. Didn't we, Murph?"

The bitter remark puzzled her. Her betrothed responded.

"Our mother died when we were youngsters. Without a father, that made us orphans. Aunt Lucy saw fit to step into Mother's shoes." Sadness seeped between Murphy's words like the cold wind of a blue norther. "She took us under her wing. In fact, we were all the family each other had."

Brodie suddenly straightened. "A true genteel lady if I ever saw one. I assume she's away right now."

"Died last winter. Pleurisy and pneumonia."

"You should've—"

"Found you? I tried. Knew you'd want to know." Murphy's hand shook in an effort to keep control. "That's what happens when you stay gone for a coon's age."

"Double damn!"

Torment deepened the crevices in Brodie's face. Laurel turned away, unable to bear the obvious pain. Losing family left a wound that never healed; she knew about that.

Replenishing his empty goblet, the man who lived by the quickness of his hand raised it high. "I salute you, Aunt Lucy, the finest woman God ever created. Rest in peace."

"Amen," Murphy added softly.

"Brother, you have anything stronger? This stuff makes lousy tonsil varnish. Not fit to drown a man's sorrows."

"I've a bottle of sipping whiskey in my study." Murphy flashed her a wry smile. "Purely for medicinal purposes."

"That'll do." Brodie rose, revealing himself as a man with an ache too large to carry and no way of ridding himself of it.

Laurel eyed the easy stride. She'd never been able to forget that loose walk. Long and lean, he moved with a purpose, but with all the time in the world to get there.

A heavy sigh left her lips. His exit meant prolonging the inevitable. Until she knew his intentions, as distasteful and ugly as they might be, time would stand still.

"Forgive my brother. He's not the man who left."

She found it difficult to devote herself to the man who'd asked for her hand and her heart. Her chair slid easily from the table. "It's getting late. I must go."

"Please, a brief moment in the garden, then I'll see you home. While Etta gets that pie for Ollie?" Murphy cajoled.

"I suppose it won't hurt." Laurel accepted his elbow.

The night air whispered when they stepped into the lush

paradise. Late-blooming chrysanthemums, asters, and brown-eyed Susans intoxicated her with fragrance.

Murphy pulled her against him. "The moonlight must be jealous of your beauty. I want you so badly."

Her thoughts scattered like naughty children. His breath ruffled the hair at her temples, adding to her confusion. Anyone with a shred of honor would tell him. His heart beating so strongly next to hers should seek out a more worthy mate.

He ran his fingers through the curls, tilting her head. His kiss sent pleasant warmth coursing through her.

Not earth-shattering.

Or passionate.

Just . . . pleasant.

A man's lips should make the woman he married feel hot and sultry as an August night. They should take the breath right out of her body and make her wonder if she truly needed air to begin with.

Laurel had that once. A long time ago.

Soft clapping jarred the stillness. They jerked apart, two lovers caught red-handed.

"Nice, little brother. Thought I might have to come out and give you some advice in the ways of women."

She whirled. A cigar's red glow outlined the shadowy form. He stepped toward them, a whiskey bottle dangling from his fingers. How long had he watched? No doubt he'd witnessed their embrace. She squirmed at the thought.

"Brodie, can't you see we're in the middle of . . ."

"Business? Yep, that's what it appears."

"Then you must know it doesn't require a third party."

Murphy's sharp tone took her aback. He'd revealed a side of himself she'd not seen before. A cool wind rustled the foliage. She shivered.

"Cold, my love?"

"I left my shawl inside. I'll get it."

"Let me. I'll only be gone a second."

He vanished into the house. But no article of clothing could give her the warmth she sought.

Without question, nothing other than the interloper's backside riding out of Redemption would put her world to rights. He unnerved her more than anything had since she'd become free. Several people's future happiness lay within his power. She'd not tuck tail and run as he'd done.

A slim-to-none chance was all she had. It'd have to do.

Her tongue found the edge of the sharp tooth. She moistened her dry lips and stuck out her jaw. "What low-down, spiteful game are you playing?"

The shadows darkened the day's beard growth. The devil-take-you saunter brought him within touching distance. He knew full well the irritation he caused.

"I could ask the same. Why do you pretend not to know me? I don't recall any reason to deny our association."

"Miserable rogue! What do you hope to prove?"

"Protecting my brother is all." He puffed on the cigar, paying no heed to the smoke drifting into her face.

"From me?"

"Farfetched, I know. I'm only looking out for him. He's the only salvageable part of Samuel and Elizabeth Yates."

"You've become a self-serving, pathetic rakehell."

"What assurance does anyone have you'll not move on to another once you tire of the thrill of conquest?"

"Your worry isn't for Murphy, it's about yourself. You don't want me, yet you'll stop anyone else from having me."

"Have you told him about your chosen profession? Does he know your penchant for good cigars and billiards?" Brodie took a long swig from the bottle and wiped his mouth with the back of his hand. "Does he know you've probably had more men in your bed than he or I both can count?"

The verbal blow sent her reeling. Pride kept her from crumpling to the ground. She'd die rather than let him see.

"So this is about revenge." She tried another tack. "If you truly care, as you claim, you'll recognize this folly before it destroys the very thing you wish to save. Whether you believe it or not, I've changed."

"From what? Way I see it, you're still trying to lure men into your bed. The method is the only difference I can tell. The institution of marriage may not be sacred to you—"

"You of all people dare to speak of sacred oaths and decency! At least I've not killed anyone."

Laurel strained to hear his soft reply.

"Not with a six gun. Your weapons are far more devious and devastating. You're not content unless you steal a man's soul."

A gush of breath left a sickly throbbing in her chest.

"Once you were warm and oh-so-willing, Lil."

He fingered wayward strands of hair that spilled over her shoulder. She winced at the touch that burned through clothing to the skin beneath. *Damn him. Damn them both.*

"I believe you stated earlier, that was two lifetimes ago."

"More or less. I reckon the faces blended together until they all looked the same. I understand that. Yep, mighty easy for someone who had eyes solely for the color of money."

He grabbed her wrist before she got it raised. The depth of her anger had taken her by storm. She'd not meant to strike him, only wipe the smirk from familiar features that despised her one minute and tried to rehash old memories the next.

"How dare you!"

Hard, glistening looks challenged in a battle of wills. Laurel finally lowered her gaze, unable to compete with the man who could look another in the eye and send him to his death.

"Dare?" Brodie let her arm drop. He tapped ashes from the cigar and stuck it in the corner of his mouth. His calm tone was deceptive. "I'll allow no one to trample Murph's tender feelings. Mark my words, I won't sit idly by."

Hostility thickened the damp air until it clung, depressing and heavy, to her skin. What had he endured during the years to make him so bitter? What could give cause to attack so cruelly?

There was no excuse.

Before tears could gather, she stiffened her backbone. He'd not humiliate her, revel in her shame. Not now, not ever.

"Telling him will do irreparable harm. He'll hate you, not me. I can't think you'd risk that."

"That's why I held back when the opportunity arose."

"I'm trying to start fresh, build a new life. Half a chance is all I ask."

Smoke swirled about her head, tickling her nose. Of the hardest cravings to stifle, cigars stood at the top. Proper ladies didn't indulge in that vice. Giving them up ranked high on her list of priorities.

"I'll see your bet and raise it. One week to break off the engagement. Speak the truth or tell a lie. Doesn't matter, long as you walk out of his life."

Thoughts of sinful cravings fled. "One week?"

"That's the deal." He widened the gap between them at the sound of footsteps on the stone path.

"Ahhhh, the two of you are getting acquainted." Murphy draped the shawl over Laurel's shoulders, then put an arm around her and Brodie and pulled them close. "My two favorite people. How lucky can a man get?"

Chapter Five

Brodie remained on the garden bench long after his brother walked Laurel home. Distant foghorns emerged from the thick soup, along with the sounds of chattering river otters and mockingbird chirps. Deep croaks of a froggie clan sang bass in the chorus.

Why did he have to run into her here?

Despite what time did to thicken a person's memory, he'd recognized Lil right off. Those eyes, that voice could do unforgettable things to a man. When he spied her in the cafe, he'd gotten the same tightness in his chest. It'd taken several seconds for his lungs to remind him that they had emptied.

Great Johnny Reb! He'd wanted to kill that fool boy for pawing her that way. No one treated his lady with disrespect.

Except you, a little voice whispered.

He wished he had some excuse for his crass behavior. Every wrong word had left his mouth, creating a disastrous evening.

Over the years he'd imagined crossing paths again with

the beauty who'd stolen a piece of his heart. He'd pictured the tender things he'd say, the taste of her lips.

He'd done none of those in spite of an urge so powerful it gnawed at him still. Instead, the shock of finding her engaged to his brother had plunged a dull blade into his heart.

Brodie sucked in a ragged breath that hurt all the way down to his toes. Present state of mind aside, he found peace here among the trimmed hedges and bordered flower beds.

Neatness and order. A far cry from the bloody killing fields that haunted his dreams.

Some called him a high plains drifter. Others called him worse. He'd given up on finding a place in which a man could hide.

His damnable reputation!

He'd tried to avoid the fight with Prater. It could've ended in his worst fear—that someday his luck would run out. But still instinct had kicked in. When the time came, he wanted to be able to feel it, to know he had more than the cold stone heart of a warrior.

From inside his shirt, he withdrew a soft deerskin pouch, sliding his thumb across the supple texture warmed by his skin.

A handmade memory bag protected items near and dear.

With care, he removed a scrap of lavender lace.

Thoughts whirled inside his head, a roulette wheel of sorts that stopped on the color black. St. Louis, the Black Garter, and a raven-haired beauty. He'd never met anyone before or since equal to Lil.

Had she missed the torn piece from one of her ruffles? Brodie raised the sacred reminder to his nose, imagining it still bore her scent. With her he escaped the horrors of war that raged with no end in sight.

Lil made him forget a lot of things when her body curled next to his. And spoiled all other women for him.

For a price.

Everything came with an almighty price.

Shrouded by darkness, he spoke of things he shouldn't. Then that blasted war ruined all hope. Paradise became pure hell, hurtling him headlong into its pit. Under General Price's orders, his regiment marched from St. Louis. At Pilot Knob he ran smack into a piece of shattering hot lead.

He always wondered what happened to her. Meant to find out one day . . .

After he got the hole in his heart mended first.

Well, now he'd found her. Funny, he still had that hole.

Why did she have to belong to Murphy?

Truth to tell, her sensual curves bewitched him even now.

Damn! She'd never believe the slurs he'd uttered sprang out of deep pain. No one would ever nominate him for sainthood. Not with his record.

The blood of too many men stained his name. Many only boys, their faces were etched into his rotten soul. They'd become as much a part of him as breathing. Even if he dared confess that he'd give anything to spend the rest of his life wrapped in her arms, what right did he have?

Men in his line of work couldn't entertain ideas of love, a home, children.

He'd not ask Lil or any other to share hidden danger.

The accusation about not wanting her hit a sore spot. He desired her in every way imaginable.

Nope, Brodie regretted a lot of things, but meeting her skipped the list of remorse.

Hell and be damned if he'd let her marry his brother!

49

"One week, Miss James." He folded the fragile lavender back inside the deerskin.

The memory bag held other treasures. The cold metal of his mother's simple gold ring brushed his fingers. A lock of Murphy's hair spoke of a brotherly bond. Aunt Lucy's faded note right after he'd joined up completed the collection.

A creak of the garden gate announced Murphy's return. Brodie secured the bag in its sacred place. Wouldn't do to let baby brother find him pining over a scrap of lavender.

"Nice night." Murphy settled beside him.

"Sight better than most I've spent. You get Miss James tucked in all nice and cozy?"

"I don't recognize the person you've become. Makes me wonder if I ever knew you at all."

Brodie held the cigar, watching the red glow. "War does things to a man's mind, changes priorities—rearranges his life. I apologize for tonight. Didn't mean to be a jackass."

"I suppose. Don't do it again. I mean it. Keep disrespecting her and you'll force me to turn you out."

All I'm asking for is a chance. Her plea brought unease.

"That's clear enough. I was sitting here thinking about leopards and their spots. Do you think he—or she—can change, Murph?"

"Anything acquired at birth they're probably stuck with. Like you and me."

"I'm relieved you think we're stuck with each other."

"But if the spots are painted on, I'd say they could. Where are you going with this anyway?"

"No place, little brother. No place at all."

The shake of Murphy's head suggested Brodie suffered from weakness north of his ears. Hell, he'd lost any sense a long time ago . . . to a silken-haired seductress.

"I've missed you. Never got accustomed to being alone. When we were boys, I tagged along not more than three steps from your shadow. I'd wake up shaking with fear that you'd die on some battlefield and I'd never know."

"Scared me, too, being by myself. For awhile I walked around thinking a mule stomped on me and left me for crow bait." He tilted the bottle and found a measure of comfort in the trail of fire to his belly. "Believe it or not, I still do."

Matter of fact, even more since arriving in Redemption.

"I own there's good reason to build a wall around yourself. Men who stare death in the face and have seen enough spilled blood would certainly be inclined to. You can tear it down, though. Unlike that leopard, your spots can come off. It's never too late."

Little brother should speak for himself.

"I'm tired of running, trying to do more than survive. You know how many times I've cheated the undertaker by being a split second faster?" He turned his face, finding his brother's advice an ill fit. Murphy should save it for someone more worthy.

"You're safe for a while. Rest while you can."

How could he, when she waited beneath his closed eyes? His thoughts, his blood, his very soul echoed her name. Brodie fought recollection of Laurel's exquisite features bathed in pale moonlight.

"Do you truly love her?"

"More than I ever thought possible."

An ache in his chest robbed him of air. How could he in good conscience steal their happiness? Dearly as he wished it, he suspected Lil's past had become as finely ingrained as his own sorry one. And maybe she truly did return Murphy's affection.

"Guess you do at that."

"I still gather you don't approve. Care to say why?"

"It's my job to make sure you don't get your heart broke."

"Quit upsetting her. You were way out of line tonight with that hogwash about St. Louis."

"Would another apology fix things?"

"Just watch it. I protect what's mine, even from you."

Brodie gave a low whistle. "So I see. You've grown up."

"About time you noticed." Murphy leaned forward, resting his arms on his legs. "I want to warn you about another matter. Despite enjoying your company, it's dangerous."

"I know." The measured words came low.

"I don't think you appreciate fully the hotbed we're in. Soldiers itch to capture the infamous Confederate Shenandoah. But frankly, I'm concerned about other things as well."

"I'm tired of the chase. I'll end my days here."

"Citizens have formed pockets of resistance, groups called—"

"Knights of the Rising Sun, Cullen Baker's Knights of the White Camelia, or any number of similar organizations?"

"You heard. Any plans on joining them?"

"Nope. Have they converted you, Murph?"

"I'm not their kind. I respect all people, no matter the color of their skin."

"I figured that, since you have Etta and her boy here."

"You and I never cottoned to slavery. She earns triple what anyone else would pay. She's part of this family."

"She should've gone north to safer climes after the war's end. The Freedman's Bureau gives precious little protection. Countless men and women wind up dead every day."

"Etta has nowhere else to go. I look out for her." Murphy stood and stretched. "Remember what I said: Be careful and watch your back. You coming to bed?"

"Believe I'll stay a bit longer."

The prospect of lying in bed across the hall from the

room in which Murphy and Laurel would soon make love held little appeal.

Brodie stopped his sibling. Thickness rose, making his voice hoarse. "I'm sorry I left you, Murph."

The kitchen sparkled by the time Laurel wearily climbed the stairs. No sign of Ollie, which answered a prayer. The catastrophe might go down better with bitter brew come morn.

She took off her shoes and padded silently down the hall. But, outside her door, guilt set in. Ollie could lie in the agonizing throes of another spell. Pausing to carefully listen, she smiled at the rumblings behind the door. The snoring recital stifled any worry.

Inside her room, she became all thumbs as she undressed and pulled on her nightgown. Shaking hands betrayed her turmoil.

Blue blazes!

Shenandoah . . . Brodie Yates seemed hell bent on yanking away everything and she hadn't the power to prevent it.

She ran through a quick list of options.

To call his bluff, if indeed it be that, held unknown risk. Pushing the scoundrel could lead to a quick, dire end.

No greater satisfaction came to mind than to beat Brodie at his own game. Telling Murphy herself would accomplish that. It might knock Murphy to his knees. Sure, he'd recover eventually, but, she knew from experience that secrets didn't stay that way long.

The gamble could cause her public disgrace.

Maybe she should quietly break off the engagement as Brodie advised. While that wouldn't spare Murphy hurt, it might cause less irreparable damage for them both.

A third solution chilled her bones . . . to leave Redemption in the dead of night, never to return.

And that meant forever giving up what she'd gained.

And Brodie would win a decisive victory.

Locked in a desperate tug-of-war, Laurel reached for a small music box. Through pleading, bargaining, and tears, she'd managed to hold on to the gift from her mother long ago. The feather mattress sank with her weight. She cradled the treasure. Fighting back a crush of images, she wound it.

The strains of an old childhood favorite fed a starved soul.

She imagined Mama's soothing touch and murmuring, "It'll be all right, my sweet darling. Everything will be right as rain."

Ollie knew of Mary and Ben James. Laurel had talked for hours about them and the piece of land between Marshall and Jefferson—the same farm from which Taft and his cohorts had abducted her. Strange how Ollie sensed her desire to be near them again, as if somehow their spirit would lend healing and strength. That is, if they still lived there.

She hadn't got enough nerve or spent enough time forgetting to find out.

Six years away from those she loved . . . an eternity.

They had seven hungry mouths to feed when she left, quite possibly more now. And suppose her father had perished in the war?

Her family presumed her dead and she'd leave it at that. Far too much pain and a mountain of shame to regain what Taft had stolen. Besides, it was the first place he'd look for her when he came. And she knew he'd come eventually.

No, it was better this way.

A soft rap made her jump. Never one to stand on ceremony, Ollie barged in.

"Dadburn it! Knew the minute I heard the tinkle of your music box trouble'd come a callin'."

Laurel brushed exhaustion from her eyes. Her friend's nightcap drooped over one ear, half on and half off, giving the fading, reddish tangle of her hair a life of its own.

"Sorry I woke you, although it seemed unlikely, judging from the snores raising the roof."

"Trying to get smart with me, aren't you? What's wrong?"

"Nothing. Merely that homesick feeling again. You know."

"Shore shootin' do. But this lump here says it's a bit more than that." Ollie plopped down and forced Laurel to meet her gaze. "My grandpappy, bless his poor soul, always warned, 'Girl, lying will only git you to hell on a fast horse. If you don't have good reason, it pays to speak the truth.'"

Did it count that Ollie suffered from a bad heart and required peace and quiet to live out her days? Or that their hard work had come for naught? Laurel bit a trembling lip.

"Go ahead, spit it out. I ain't leaving until you do."

"It'll keep. Go back to bed."

"This one's sturdy enough. Reckon it'll hold the both of us." Ollie patted the covers. "Appears comfortable, too."

"For pity's sake! Remember you insisted, so if you keel over, don't blame me. Shenandoah is Murphy's brother."

There, she'd said it . . . and hearing it on her own lips brought more misery than when it had sat quietly in her head.

"He's what!"

"Murphy's brother. His true name is Brodie Yates. Shenandoah is an alias he took up."

"Well, I'll be a suck egg mule!"

"Brodie gave me a week to break off the engagement."

"Or what?"

"He'll tell everyone and run me out of town."

"The dirty, low-down cheat. One week, huh?"

"That's the threat, and no doubt he'll do it."

"A real honorable man to give more than a few hours," Ollie dryly remarked. "Any stipulations on how you go about it?"

"He left that up to me." She fidgeted with the soft cotton threads. "I suppose I could claim second thoughts."

"Wouldn't work. Men pester the living daylights out of you unless you kick 'em right in the seat of their pants."

"That's awfully shabby treatment."

"No other way. Want your own heart, your dreams dragged through the mud?"

"They already have been. I thought this time I might succeed."

"Stop with that! Never thought I'd see the day you'd give up without a fight." Ollie squeezed her shoulders. "A body can have anything they desire if they have fire in their belly."

A sob lodged in Laurel's chest. She clenched a fist. "I want to outwit that rogue so badly I can taste it."

"From my dealings with men—actually quite a few— what sends them packing faster than anything is letting it slip you're sweet on someone else. They normally don't stick around long once another has stolen a woman's affections. Hard on their pride."

"And whom may I pretend to love?"

Except a rebel-eyed man with a searing touch? She couldn't pit brother against brother. The war had done that.

"Just tell Murphy you was set to marry some fellow years ago and he joined up to fight. You got word they buried him on the battlefield, but recently you learned he was still alive."

Lord knew how close Ollie came to the truth.

"I suppose it might work. I'm no good at fibbing, though. He'll see through me like daylight through a windowpane."

"All's you gotta do is dirty up the window a little."

"Easy for you to say."

"Never underestimate the value of tears and lacy hand-kerchiefs. Worked for me. We'll buy one of them fancy hats with dark net that hides your eyes. He'll never suspect."

A flicker of hope rose. The plan might save them.

Suddenly, snake rattles and the two-legged reptile who wore them flashed across her mind. How long would he keep silent?

"I just had an awful thought: Brodie might demand something else after we go through with this charade. Or he could have a slip of the tongue. The right word in the ear of a busybody like Florence Kempshaw and everyone in fourteen counties will have the news."

The petite woman whistled through her teeth. "I see what you mean. Some gents take pure delight in watching you squirm. Cain't trust Yates far as we can spit."

She'd once thought she'd found a true man of honor. What a farce.

"He taunted me the entire evening. This is a game with him. Each moment the words threatened to spill, he'd pull back. I can't see him relinquishing the upper hand."

Or herself letting go of memories steeped in passion and lustful cravings she couldn't deny.

God help her!

"In my world, that means he intends on testing your sanity and making your life worth nothing more than one of them goldarned Confederate notes."

Ever been to St. Louis, Miss James?

"I'm afraid so."

Ollie shot her a sharp glance. "You think it's time to whistle up the dogs and douse the fire?"

Chapter Six

"Leave. Give up?" Laurel couldn't believe her ears. The Ollie she knew would find the idea preposterous. "You made it clear from the start you had no sympathy for quitters."

"I wouldn't exactly use that strong a word." Ollie pulled the blasted pipe from within the folds of her nightgown. "*Son of a blue jacket!* Left my tobacco and matches across the hall. Don't suppose you'd be a good girl and traipse over there?"

"Smoking is bad for your health. Besides, it's late."

"If I wanted a sermon, I'd go to church." Ollie stuck the cold pipe between her teeth. "I ain't calling it quittin', mind you—merely moving on. A world of difference between the two."

"You're splitting hairs. It's the coward's way out, no matter how anyone slices it."

"Back in my days dabbling with betting and men who did, I learned a true gambler knows when to ride out a bluff and when to toss in the whole damn bunch of cards. This may be the time for foldin' and laying 'em down. I won't fault you for it."

"I can't expect to run from trouble all my life. Once a body starts, they have to keep on until there's no place left."

For her, Redemption represented the end of running.

"Girl, I've known you the better part of a year and you have no shortage of courage. One day you'll stand your ground and dare the world to knock you cross-eyed. No harm in waiting until you get more wind in your sails. Until a big gust comes along, there's merit in hightailing it while the getting's good."

Laurel rested her head wearily on Ollie's shoulder. A loving pat on her cheek chased away the chill. Damn the runty skinflint for sneaking under the barricades when she wasn't looking!

"My heart says stay—my head urges run and hide."

"You're the closest thing to a daughter I'll ever have. We're sailing this ship together. If you want to plant your feet here, I'll fight alongside you and dare anyone to come get us."

A curtain of tears blocked her vision. "You're quite loveable . . . for a crusty old coot."

"Now, don't get all-fired mushy on me. I love you, too, but you don't need to go around saying it." Ollie snatched the cap before it finished its slide. "I don't know why I wear this fool thing. No need for rash decisions. Sleep on it. Like my grandpappy always said, 'Never jump off a cliff less'n someone pushes you. A feller could find himself eyeball deep in dirt.'"

By daylight the next morning, Laurel's stomach churned deeper than the whirlpools on Big Cypress Bayou. A sleepless night had brought more questions than answers. Six days left.

When she went downstairs she found Ollie sipping a cup

of black dredge. The woman's idea of a drinkable pot of coffee resembled thick river bottom. Although Laurel tried her best, Ollie wasn't prone to taking suggestions about her cooking. At least not with any degree of patience.

Avoiding questions staring over the chipped cup, Laurel tied her apron around her waist and marched to the dwindling brine barrel.

Meat supplies had gotten awfully low. A promised shipment should've arrived by now. Odd that it hadn't. She fished out a piece, wishing it was the scoundrel's head she plopped into a large pot.

Spit and thunder, he could ruin a day!

A week.

A life.

The squeaky pump handle broke the silence as Ollie drew a pitcher of water and handed it to her. "Morning, girl."

"At least you didn't add *good* to it." Laurel emptied it into the pot, splashing water onto the stove's cast-iron plate.

"That can wait a minute. Have a cup of my coffee. I brewed it exactly the way I like it."

The statement dripped with attitude. Ollie delighted in jabbing her with a sharp stick merely to test her mettle. She raised her head from the vegetable bin only after filling the draped apron with onions, carrots, and potatoes.

"That stuff you drink might plug the hole in a dike, but it won't stop lunch from coming."

"Nothing sinful about asking for a measly bit of conversation."

Vegetables spilled onto the table. The smile gracing Ollie's face when she complied said who had won that round.

"We're family, and most ones I've known parlay over breakfast." Ollie shuffled to the stove to pour Laurel a cup. "Worry won't go away simply by pretending it ain't there."

Laurel pushed aside the thick liquid. "If we must talk, I'll have hot tea, thank you."

"Well, forevermore. You never let on you had something against my concoction. It'll learn you to stick your tongue to the roof of your mouth."

The laugh dispelled the gloom, at least temporarily. But by noon Laurel's nerves had knotted into one huge ball.

"You're jumpier than a horse thief in a noose," Ollie remarked. "Think I can't see how you watch the door?"

"Brodie will likely make an appearance if for nothing more than to keep me off-balance. He favors that tactic."

"This old gal might have a few tricks of her own to teach that gun-totin' blackmailer."

A record number of customers kept her hopping. When she watched the last of them depart without Shenandoah darkening the cafe door, she drew a sigh of relief.

Busy clearing away the remnants of chaos, she barely heard the late arrival. The sound drawing her attention came no louder than the whimper of a mouse caught in a trap.

She whirled, her heart sinking.

The deep, husky tone enveloped her in a heavy embrace. "Too late for a man to get a bite to eat?"

Laurel tried to disengage from the smoky warmth but found her focus riveted to the shadowed square jaw and mocking smile.

"Never too late . . . for feeding a rumbling belly." Ollie wandered out from the back. "What'll be your poison?"

"Another beefsteak, if you will, Miss James."

The petite war wagon swelled in height over the dismissal. Laurel worked to speak, but instead floundered in his stare.

Once more Ollie interjected. "Leave that hogleg of yours

on the counter and we might consider it. Don't allow shootin' irons in here. I done told you that."

The knot in her stomach grew. Laurel held her breath, unable to wrench herself from the bold scrutiny. The familiar hiss followed each twitch as he pulled out a chair and sat down.

"Go fetch the sheriff, girl."

Long seconds ticked by before Brodie finally unwound his tall frame from the seat. His hand slid to his muscular thigh. The thin leather strap keeping the holster secure on his leg fell away with a gentle tug. Inching back to his waist, he unbuckled the wide belt with one hand. Only after he handed it to Ollie did Laurel dare move . . . or swallow.

"That suit you?"

"See? It's painless. Now we'll rustle up some grub."

Laurel strode for the kitchen.

"Do you want to get yourself killed?" She pulled Ollie behind the door. "You succeeded in antagonizing him further. The rogue came to cause grief and you provided the match."

"Men like Shenandoah don't need reasons. They wake up with 'em every morning. Don't worry, I got him under control."

It sure looked like it. A gnat meeting Goliath!

"You have got to quit thinking yourself bigger. . . ." Laurel's sentence trailed off, cut short by a vanishing swish.

Ollie stood on the other side, full of purpose and righteous vigor. She squared her shoulders and marched straight for the threat, who'd propped his legs on a chair in front of him. The gun-toter's carefree pose didn't fool an old war horse like her.

"We need to come to an understandin'."

Brodie removed his feet and pushed the chair. "Whatever you have on your mind might best be said sitting, ma'am."

"Olivia. Olivia Applejack b'Dam." She perched on the edge. No need to get comfortable; this wouldn't take long. "My friends call me Ollie, only you don't qualify for that."

"Something eating you, Olivia Applejack b'Dam?"

Ollie narrowed her gaze. "Take that silly grin, and those nice manners, back where you came from. I'll thank you to leave Laurel alone."

"Lil, you mean?"

"I didn't stutter. Name's Laurel and don't ever forget it." She jabbed the table with a finger.

"No need to get hostile. What did she tell you?"

Heat rose like sweeping fire over dry prairie grass. "Enough to warn you to watch your tongue or someone might happen to put you to bed with a pick and shovel. I'd sure take it as an honor if it were me what did it. When you refer to Laurel, it'd pay to use a big helping of respect."

"Plain language for a short, scrappy pipe-smoker."

"Short or tall, don't need fancy words. My grandpappy, who was a mite taller'n a tadpole, bless his soul, said, 'Say it plain, girl, an' save some air for breathin'.'"

"Awful defensive, aren't you, to not be family?"

"I'm the nearest thing the poor darling's had in a while. I ain't gonna let you or anyone else sling mud across her good name." She met the scowl without flinching.

"This is between Laurel and me. It would behoove you to stay out of it."

"You've got a fight if that's what you want, sonny boy."

"Keep her away from my brother then."

"Son of a blue jacket! Give the lady some air. The doing will get done without hounding her."

"No law against averting a travesty. She's hoodwinked

him into believing her unsullied. She'll break Murphy's heart."

"Only mistake your brother made is having you as kith and kin. You're not fit to wipe his boots."

Brodie twitched, arching a brow. Ollie wished she could take back the words. It was never a good idea to mess with another man's pride or open old wounds.

Tension hung between them. Though Ollie shook inside, she flexed her hands and readied for a blood-letting.

His laughter caught her off guard. All of a sudden she felt thirsty. Her parched throat would welcome a tall drink. Preferably something stronger than a sarsaparilla.

"Probably right, Olivia b'Dam. Probably right."

Jovial chuckles greeted Laurel when she entered with his meal. What on earth? Peeking through the door at the dogged set to Ollie's chin, she imagined anything but relief.

"Girl, I remember I have business to tend across the way."

Laurel put down the plate, wondering what had thrown Ollie in such a tizzy. The door slammed behind the slight figure. Laurel turned, looking to retreat.

"Sit with me, Lil." The order didn't come with an alternative.

Bittersweet memories threatened to overwhelm her. She'd wished to hear those words about a thousand times. Deep in that locked vault, an ache throbbed.

"You paid for the steak, not idle conversation." The statement came hard and brittle as she faced him.

Brodie reached into his pocket and flipped a silver dollar onto the table. It spun for a second before clinking to rest with Lady Liberty staring up.

"I'm paying for the company."

Laurel's lips tightened. "Who do you think you are to barge into my life this way?

"A man no one wants to know. The devil with a six-shooter." His tone held quiet torture. "Someone who's been to heaven and hell and half the stops in between."

Doubting the wisdom, she dropped stiffly into the spot Ollie had vacated, hating the swish as the hem of her skirts floated lazily against his boots. "What does such a man talk about?"

Damn her voice for going soft on her. She blamed the glimmer in his eyes . . . and the smile that promised sin.

"Pain and regret. Happy times. Four days in St. Louis. Pecan praline pie that I have on good authority is the way to your heart. Should I continue?"

Foreboding swept her down a winding road. To follow would be inviting back the dark, unwelcome nightmares she strived daily to forget. The past lay buried beneath more grief and turmoil than any person should ever have to live with.

Brodie swallowed and laid down his fork when she didn't reply. He leaned forward, his intent clear. Laurel jerked her head aside and drew back. But such tactics didn't deter a man like him. With a firm grip of her chin, he forced her to meet the hunger in his smoky gaze.

"I recall a hot-blooded woman on a sultry summer night. The wet eagerness between—"

"Please . . ."

"That's what you said then, too. Begged for more. Pleaded with me to take you with me."

"Lil died. She doesn't exist anymore." A razor-sharp clarity brought her back to reality. He'd left her in that godforsaken place with never a backward glance.

"You're mistaken. Lil is very much alive." He tapped his leather-vested chest. "She's right here."

With the barest of fingertips he traced the line of her

parted mouth, leaving a scorched path. A fine sheen of perspiration pooled in the valley between her breasts.

"Kisses sweet as sun-ripened strawberries. Wonder if you taste the same as I remember."

"Stop!" Laurel twisted away and stood. "I can't."

Blue blazes! He touched her again—a caress more gentle than dewdrops on an early spring day. She shivered against the contact of his thumb as he caressed the hollow of her throat across a wildly beating pulse.

"What's a woman like you doing in Redemption? Surely not trying to find salvation."

"Is that so ridiculous a notion?"

"Think a leopard can change his spots?"

"I'm not the person you thought. Despite choosing to believe me unworthy, I had no control over my life back then. I do have that luxury now, however."

"So you say, Lil." Brodie's lazy drawl scraped across raw nerves, silk over sandpaper. "Time does tell all."

Memories tumbled end over end, colliding with a temptation she wasn't positive she had the strength to resist. Her head whirled in tune with a thundering heartbeat as she flew from the dining room. Splashing water from the porcelain bowl beneath the pump, she cooled her heated cheeks.

Please let me come with you. I promise I won't be any trouble.

Not now, darlin'. Can't, but I'll be back.

He'd heard nothing over the roar of his lust. He'd closed his eyes to her shame. In all fairness, he never knew they kept her prisoner. By the time she decided to trust him, he'd waltzed out the door. And left her behind.

The roughness of her tooth scraped her tongue.

Angry rattles coupled with easy footsteps aroused

alarm. A quick pivot found her staring at the man whom she wanted to forgive more than anything on earth.

He approached with slow, deliberate steps.

"Didn't get my dollar's worth of conversation."

"I didn't ask for or take your money. I owe you nothing." Laurel backed up until her shoulder blades flattened against the wall.

"You saying I can't pay for favors?" He took a step.

"Yes. I'm no longer the same. . . ." A roar began inside her head. She eyed the approaching storm, knowing it was too late for help.

"You saying you won't give that little moan like you used to if I touch you?" He progressed two steps this time.

She licked her parched lips. Didn't the man understand? Persisting in this folly would only awaken sleeping dogs that had no good reason to stir from their slumber.

"Dare I find out, will your lips remain cold and lifeless?" He inched closer, narrowing the space between them.

So close. A trickle of sweat slid down her back, soaking the tight waistband. The fragrance of leather and fresh-cut hay tickled her nose. Heaven help her! His mouth pressed to hers would rekindle everything she wished to bury. She wasn't made of stone . . . just flesh and blood and a hundred regrets.

The lazy half-smile indicated enjoyment. He knew his nearness suffocated her thoughts.

He meant to strip her of every shred of her newfound dignity.

He intended to kiss her.

And perhaps more? She gasped for air.

"Convince me. For old time's sake?" He reached for a dark curl. "Show me I'm no longer in your blood. I dare you."

A rabbit in a snare had a more reasonable chance. His

hand slipped beneath her head. Laurel sagged weakly against his chest, tired of fighting forbidden attraction. Beneath her ear, his heart raced, perhaps chased by memories of his own.

"I've dreamed of this for so long." His breath stirred the hair against her throbbing temple. "I've relived every detail of those nights in my mind. The faint scent of rose water behind your ears, the tiny pulse in the hollow of your throat. I remember every whispered endearment."

"Please . . . stop. I can't—"

His mouth smothered the plea. Her body betrayed, responding to desire born from hopeless fear long ago.

Laurel welcomed his thrusting tongue. When her breasts ached for his caress, he covered them with his palms, rolling the nipples to hard peaks. Delicious, shameful thrills played up her spine.

Soft mewling escaped from somewhere deep inside, a place where lies could not hide. A place she never thought to revisit.

The arousal pushing against supple buckskin spoke of equal need. Passion threatened to scorch everything in its path . . . including her lofty goals.

Low moans rumbled in his throat when she wound her fingers in the thickness of his hair.

What she wouldn't give to pretend he meant nothing. But the greater sin was denying he made her feel alive again.

Truth and lies, pleasure and pain. She'd pay any price to be wrong on all counts.

Abruptly, he pushed away. "Got my answer. The fire still burns. Cloak yourself in self-righteous claims that mean nothing. I daresay wet proof lies beneath your skirts."

Laurel recoiled, wishing him into the nearest grave.

"Go to Hell! I didn't come to you. It takes a big man to assault a helpless female."

Linda Broday

The imprint of his touch had left desire coursing through her, giving lie to her words even as she said them.

"Not force. Your body remembers a lover's touch. The supposed fresh start and tender feelings you claim for my brother? Fact remains, they're nothing but smoke and mirrors, darlin'."

Chapter Seven

Laurel steeled herself against the familiar pain of betrayal. She determined never to let him see those scars. Still, she craved to wipe off that bedeviled grin.

"It's in your blood, darlin'. I've no doubt should I want you in my bed, you'd come willingly . . . for a price."

"My, you flatter yourself, Shenandoah. Given a choice of jumping into a pool of quicksand or crawling up beside you on dry land, I'd not hesitate. Your bed? Not for any price!"

The lie left a foul tinge in her mouth. But she could never admit that his kiss, his touch, ignited embers of a long-cold fire. To keep a modicum of sanity meant denying her heart.

"Stay away from Murphy."

The warmth where he pressed against her belly still burned.

"And you?" The whisper gorged the space between them.

"I'm immune to your tricks, Lil." Brodie flashed a crooked smile. "But should you find yourself sinking in that quicksand, my door is always open."

The brimstone glare should've blistered the broad figure. But he merely left the same way he came.

Laurel collapsed into the nearest chair, emotionally drained. She wouldn't have known Ollie bustled in except for a scurrying movement too big for mice.

"I hope you enjoyed your little refreshment."

"Reckon you got a right to spit nails for deserting you."

Remorse nicked budding anger. Ollie needn't bear the brunt.

No one but her.

In all fairness, Brodie would've backed away had she positively insisted. He'd never exhibited cunning or evil.

But devilish, maddening, and charming?

Always.

Honest truth never hurt a body. She hadn't wanted to deny the pleasure that enveloped each tiny, sensual nerve ending, making it throb with life after a long sleep.

"I'm not mad at you." Laurel marched to the brine barrel and reached in.

"And that's why you're ready to throttle someone? Better tell me what that rascal did. I'll badger 'til you do." Smoke billowed from the overworked pipe. "You ain't crying?"

A sweep of her sleeve brushed away telltale signs. "This darn brine is strong. To which rascal do you refer?"

"Shenandoah or Yates, whichever name he's using today."

A band of soothsayers had to sit on a branch of Ollie's family tree. The way she braced an arm on her hip made Laurel curious. The pose appeared most natural for someone comfortable with strapping on a pistol. How odd to consider it.

"What makes you think he did anything?"

"I can see it on your face."

Laurel sighed, dropping the meat she'd plucked from the barrel onto the counter. "After you left, he waylaid me."

"The low-down, sneakin' skunk! He didn't pay no more attention to my warning than a flea. What else?"

"Nothing."

She couldn't speak of warm breath that nuzzled the corners of her mouth and weakened her knees.

"Spit it out."

"He talked about leopards and spots. He said I'd never wash mine off." That was close enough.

"Did you haul off and wallop him?"

Hiding her face, she lifted a long knife and set to work slicing the slab of pork. "It wouldn't have swayed him."

"Thought I taught you to have some gumption, girl."

"I'm facing facts. Despite how hard I try, I may not save the woman Will Taft turned me into."

Ollie closed her right eye and squinted with the left. "Unless you fight, you ain't fit for toad spit."

"Years of struggle don't buy back a stolen life."

Or crumbling dreams falling at her feet.

"Like Grandpappy said, 'There's a lot more to buildin' a fire than pickin' up a couple of sticks.' "

The knife slipped. "Darn it, you're distracting me."

"Then put that down for a minute. Changing things mean you gotta do more than just say it. A good fire takes finding the right kind of wood. Then you gotta get some leaves and such to stuff underneath it to catch the flame. And then picking the spot is most important of all. Cain't—"

"*Spit and thunder!* I don't need fire-building lessons."

From Ollie's openmouthed stare you'd have thought she'd sprouted horns and pointed ears.

"I ain't no big bag of wind." She took Laurel's hand, stroking the back. "Pick the place you want the change to begin. Start with the little things to get your flame to catch, then add big logs gradual-like. Gotta warn you, though, let that fire get outta control and it'll burn you alive."

Considering the inferno inside, it already had.

"Are you finished? I have work to do."

"One thing you gotta do before anything else and that's change your opinion of yourself." She released Laurel's hand and jabbed a finger into her chest. "Inside here."

"I'm making headway." Or at least she had been.

Ollie took her face in her hands. "Girl, I wish to high heaven I could turn back time to the day you got took. I'd do it in a heartbeat. Fact of the matter, I cain't."

"That's why I love you, despite how difficult you make it."

Had she only stayed with her brothers and not wandered off to pick blackberries alone. How quickly life can change.

"You're a fine one. Sometimes I think it'd be a sight easier living with a broken neck. I'm saying make do with what'cha got. To me you have a rare beauty both inside and out."

Suddenly she wasn't that scared little kid clutching a stranger's coattails anymore. She stuck out her jaw.

"I've made my decision, Ollie."

"How soon you want me to saddle the horses?"

"No one's going to threaten me into leaving. I'm about to prove to the world, including Brodie Yates, who Laurel Lillian James is, and what stern material she's made of."

Murphy strolled into the cafe that evening. Laurel turned a deaf ear to Florence Kempshaw's grumbles and met his wide grin. She dodged his reach, tucking her hands into the apron.

"What a pleasant surprise. Did Etta forget to cook?"

"I prefer your cooking, particularly when I might steal a kiss." Eager light flashed in his eyes. "Etta can't do that for me."

Florence lifted the fork, cocking an ear toward the

table Murphy took. Each nasty rumor in town originated from her.

"Shhhh!" She nodded toward the old spinster.

"Sweetheart, we don't have to hide. I'm going to marry you. Tonight, if I could." His hand joined hers inside the apron pocket. The glint said he wanted her more than ever.

Guilt settled faster than layers of silt in Big Cypress Bayou. How could she tell him? How could she not?

Cluttering his life with someone of her nature would not repay the kindness he'd showed her. But neither would she let his flinty-eyed brother dictate to her. She had rights.

"Murphy, I have to speak to you after everyone leaves."

"Sounds serious, my love."

Before she could go further, Florence began waving her arms furiously in the direction of the window, where two young boys flattened their noses against the pane. The silly woman resembled General Lee ordering a dozen regiments into battle.

"Shoo! Get away, you little heathens." Florence turned. "I'd like to finish my grits and fatback in peace, Miss James."

"I'll see what I can do. Most likely they're hungry."

Laurel expected them to scatter when they heard the doorknob rattle. Instead, two sets of sad brown eyes stared up. The oldest couldn't have yet seen an eighth birthday.

"Anything I help you boys with?"

The spokesman wiped his nose on the sleeve of a torn, dirty shirt that hung over thin bones. "We ain't hurting no one."

"I'm sure you wouldn't harm a soul. You look a little lost, though. Want to come inside?" She smiled warmly.

A sob broke the quiet, earning the smaller one a punch to the arm. The forlorn, wan eyes gave her heart a jolt.

"Where's your mother?" she asked gently.

Again the same boy replied. "Back at the wagon. Maw'd skin us for sure if she knew we was here."

"You must have an awfully good reason to disobey."

"We's hungry. Thought you might give us some scraps if you had a mind to feed the cats in the alley."

Her stomach lurched. She caressed the tops of the tow heads. "I just happen to have some stew that someone must eat tonight or it'll spoil. Think you might help me out?"

Exchanged glances flared in silent communication. The older boy said, "If'n it's no bother, ma'am."

Laurel's heart swelled at the natural fit of the small palms in hers. As she led the boys inside they pressed against her skirts when they neared Florence.

"Don't know what this world's coming to," Florence said an octave shy of a foghorn. "Can't eat without sniveling brats bursting in."

"I certainly believe feeding starved children will help make this a better place, Mrs. Kempshaw." She led her charges, marching past with her head high. "Murphy, we have guests."

"I see." He pulled out chairs. "Will you gentlemen honor me with your company?"

"You mean us? No one ever said that to us before."

"They are now." Murphy smiled brightly.

The smaller brother bit his lip to stop its tremble.

Florence huffed loudly. The woman might have developed a nosebleed, judging by how high her nose stuck in the air. Bumping her shin on a table leg, she hobbled from the cafe.

Smothering a laugh, Laurel turned back to the boys.

"I'm Miss Laurel. Do you have names?"

"Edgar Lee Cole," the more talkative boy said, "and he's Andy."

"Glad to meet you, Andy and Edgar Lee Cole." Murphy extended a hand. "Call me Murphy."

Swiping his hand on a pant leg, Edgar Lee accepted it. Andy mimicked his brother before sliding his palm forward.

"I'll get that stew we talked about. Don't go anywhere." Laurel flew to the kitchen and hurried back with steaming bowls and a loaf of bread. Andy rewarded her with the barest hint of a grin.

"Thank you, ma'am." Edgar Lee punched his brother, who shoveled a bite into his mouth. "What'dya say?"

The small forehead wrinkled. Andy stared, as though fearing she'd snatch the food from his mouth. "S-s-sorry. T-t-thanks, l-lady," he stuttered.

Edgar dipped his spoon into the stew. "We ain't got no money, but Maw says we're rich if we mind our manners."

Sudden mist clouded Laurel's vision. A loving mother had taught these children important things—lessons that would last them a lifetime.

"My goodness, I completely forgot your milk. And Murphy, you haven't ordered."

Brodie rested against the hitching post in front of Jake's Barbershop. The vantage point provided a clear view of the cafe. What he saw through the window softened a war-toughened hide.

Two hungry, ragged boys.

The warm kindness of a special woman.

And a man who'd give most anything for a wife and children of his own.

Forty lashes with a bullwhip would've stung far less than did his memories. He blinked hard and finally lit the smoke he'd toyed with for the last ten minutes.

The group inside could almost pose as a family of sorts.

He shifted the cheroot to the other side of his mouth.

Only two things wrong with the picture . . . the man was his brother and the charitable woman was spoken for.

All of a sudden he wanted to get closer, wanted to hear the conversation. . . .

Wanted to be included.

Solitude weighed heavy on a man sometimes. Telling himself for the hundredth time that an outsider could never belong didn't make the stars any brighter or the night less dark.

Brodie had vowed to stay clear of Laurel until the deadline.

Adjusting the angle of his hat, he sauntered toward the eating establishment. The hiss of rattles seemed in agreement with his decision. Smoke from the cheroot drifted in the breeze. He tossed the remains, grinding it with a boot heel.

To hell with noble intentions!

Making a fool of himself twice in one day had to break a personal record. Still, the small building drew him. He stepped inside. A quick hush enveloped him, reminding him that his place was with the creatures of the night. Not here.

Sudden panic clouded his gaze. He tried to ignore the twinges of guilt and blame he suddenly felt.

"Brodie, join us." Murphy gestured toward the empty chair.

Laurel's eyes called him a bastard of the most dastardly sort, assuming he came for no reason except to torment.

Little did the lady know such affliction belonged solely to him.

Agony knifed through him with the ease of a well-honed bayonet. A grievous error he'd made today. Strange to have forgotten how one drop of water to a dying man only called for more, until a thousand drinks couldn't quench the parched tongue.

"I'm not sure there's room. I didn't mean to intrude."

"You're not. I insist."

Only a coward would back out now. Besides, he wanted to be there more than any place on earth. He dropped into the seat. "Did you pick up a pair of strays?"

Both ragamuffins stopped chewing, a bite freezing midway down the small one's windpipe. He could tell they'd not eaten a decent meal in a month of Sundays.

"These are the Cole boys, Edgar Lee and Andy." Murphy's grin spread. "Don't let my grouch of a brother scare you. Brodie is truly harmless."

"You have a brother, too?"

Edgar Lee began the ritual, first brushing away the milk mustache on his sleeve, then wiping a hand on his pants before reaching out. Brodie's large grip might easily have crushed the small fingers. An aching hole in his chest made words impossible. The boys could have been him and Murphy. Edgar Lee nudged the other to shake hands, too, and the years turned yellowed, dust-covered pages.

"Where's your folks?" A gruff tone sneaked into his voice.

Tears swam in Edgar Lee's brown eyes. "Paw took real bad sick. Maw said the angels came an' flew him to heaven. We buried him under a pine tree. Reckon I'm head o' the family now. Leastways that's what Maw says."

"A bit young to be saddled with that, aren't you, son?"

Edgar Lee pulled up straight, sucking in his breath. "Almost eight. Plenty big to see about things."

"Where's your maw now?" It became imperative to know.

"We's camped down by the water. Ain't bothering no one."

Silent up to now, Andy found his voice. "W-w-wagon broke."

"Shhhh! Maw says we gotta be careful. Folks don't wanna hear about our troubles."

"That might apply to some, I suppose, but not us." Laurel's soft reply broke Brodie's concentration.

"What happened to your wagon?" Murphy asked.

"Busted wheel. Maw says the Lord'll provide, though."

With a little earthly help, Brodie decided.

"Did you come to eat, Mr. Yates?"

The throaty voice broke Brodie's train of thought all to hell. And worse, it fanned a tiny sputtering flame . . . one last flicker he had the devil of a time stomping out.

"I've already partaken, thanks anyway."

Riveting his attention on her midsection seemed safest when he fought overwhelming desire that left deep ruts all the way down to the holes in his socks.

"I swear, you come to a cafe and don't eat a blessed thing." She threw up her hands. "Think of our reputation."

Murphy looked sheepish. "I'll take some coffee and pie."

"A fine example you set for these children, asking for nothing more substantial than dessert."

"When Ollie spent a good hour this morning raving on your cherry cobbler? It'd make any grown man's mouth water."

His brother's tender gaze didn't escape Brodie.

She's just what he needs.

Remembrance of her lips, the pliable curves that perfectly fit, silenced his mind's wisdom.

"I could squeeze in some as well, if you don't mind," he said quietly after the noise in his head dulled.

Her quick annoyance didn't surprise him. Brodie rewarded the flash in her eyes with a ghost of a smile and the tilt of an eyebrow.

Georgia clay, she was a sight when riled!

Laurel returned with a round of cobbler for them all. He

could've imagined the little extra shove she gave his plate, but he didn't believe so. His coffee cup shielded a wayward grin.

She fluttered over the children like a mother hen with baby chicks. She had a certain knack, he had to admit. But before that, she'd have to become a wife.

Duty lay in making sure it wasn't to his brother.

"Ollie should be here." The brilliant beam caught his breath. "She has a soft spot for ones down on their luck."

"Where is the feisty watchdog?" Murphy sipped on the hot liquid. "I realized I missed something. Generally she hovers over you, growling whenever I come within a mile."

She whispered, "Over at the saloon."

"Never thought she'd wear out her heels on a brass rail."

"Although Ollie imbibes more than she wishes me to know, I'm quite positive her interest runs in a different direction."

"You don't say." Murphy's fork paused in midair. "Curley Madison, the owner?"

Brodie paid no heed to the conversation. Her vibrant beauty absorbed him completely.

"Curley, that old scamp!"

"Don't let her get wind I told you." Lilting humor colored the admonition.

Brodie thanked the good Lord he had sense enough to bust into the party. He soaked up her nearness. Laurel captured his attention so thoroughly, he almost missed Edgar Lee's furtive movement.

The small fingers slid a button through a hole to allow the barest of openings before pushing something inside.

Chapter Eight

Brodie clasped Edgar Lee's wrist. "Not trying to steal anything are you, boy?"

"N-no, sir." The child's Adam's apple bobbed. His big eyes resembled a snagged catfish. "It's only a little bit. Didn't think anyone would miss it."

Edgar Lee's clenched fist held a piece of bread.

"For Maw and Sissie. I'm the man o' the family now. That means I gotta feed 'em. I just gotta, mister."

Ice water doused Brodie. He and the boy were kindred spirits, each doing what they must to provide and protect the ones they loved. Before Aunt Lucy took them in, he'd done whatever it took to care for his abandoned mother and Murphy. Only it had never been enough. Not ever. His puny efforts hadn't stopped his mother from taking her life, and it darn sure hadn't protected his kid brother when he most needed it.

"You can have all you need," Laurel countered.

Murphy cleared his throat. "We'll see that your mother and anyone else back at the wagon doesn't starve. That's a fact."

"Maw says we cain't take no charity. Ain't right." The quivering chin dropped to his chest. Shame over stealing waged war against necessity. Brodie couldn't hold blame.

"Call it a gift—an early Christmas present." Laurel stroked the small back. "I'll dish up the rest of that stew and cobbler for you to take. And I've another loaf of bread that'll mold if someone doesn't take pity. It sure would do me a favor."

Her whispery breath mingled past and present, blurring the lines between. Everything Brodie had previously known had changed. This Lil was a stranger, and the prospect of discovery excited him. He'd savor every inch of the journey.

Even if it remained limited in duration.

Her dress swished around trim ankles. She moved as a quiet storm—no thunder or lightning, just efficient, steady strength toward the task. He rubbed his jaw. Her quiet calm deceived a man at first, leading some to take her for a weak, rainwater woman. Shoot, were they wrong! The depth of passion he'd sampled earlier had shaken him in ways he still tried to sort out. No storm gauge on earth could measure such wanton abandon or generosity.

The brothers' mouths flew open when she returned with food-filled arms. "For us?" Edgar Lee asked in amazement.

"I don't see any other little men in here."

"T-t-thanks, lady." Andy ducked his head.

Scooting from the chair, Edgar Lee hugged her waist. Laurel dabbed at the tears trickling down his face.

Her violet gaze swam in a rush of wetness. The woman who professed to turn over a new leaf couldn't fake genuine caring. He should give her the benefit of a doubt for old time's sake.

Except she was determined to marry the wrong man.

After the kiss that had seared his brain, he had to prevent a tragic mistake. The lady couldn't possibly love another.

He halted Murphy, who had pushed back his chair. "I'll take them back to camp. You stay."

"I appreciate it. Seems Laurel and I never get enough time alone. Besides, she has something of importance to discuss."

Laurel flashed Brodie a glittering stare that promised that tonight she'd do the deed and end the suspense.

And once she did?

A possibility chilled his bones. He could fail to convince her to spend the rest of her days with him.

Lord help him, he would never get her out of his blood!

Brodie intentionally brushed against her as he accepted the load of food, relishing the feel of satiny skin. The contact sent a charged pulse that left a lingering heat.

Spit and thunder!

Laurel jammed both fists into her apron, surprised they didn't poke out the bottom of the pockets.

Never had she known someone who so infuriated, bewildered, and enticed. She'd never been so relieved to see anyone go.

He'd be back, though, to give her another dose of Brodie charm.

Waves of weakness fluttered. Endurance had a limit.

Murphy enfolded her in the circle of his arms. She leaned into him, wishing it was someone else nibbling along her neck. She wearied of the battle for absolution dangling just beyond her reach.

Your body betrays you. It remembers a lover's touch.

The taunt clanged like a death knell in her head. Although despising herself for admitting the truth, she couldn't deny it.

Her fiancé brought pleasant, peaceful moments. Brodie

charged every fiber if her body with heightened awareness the instant he entered a room. And while Murphy was
a bite of fresh-baked bread, Brodie offered the entire
meal—plus dessert.

Marrying Murphy would be a disservice to them both.
Not because she wished to spare him ruin, or out of
shame for who she was, but because she must have all or
nothing. No half measures.

Not even to satisfy her craving for respect.

Laurel faced her future squarely. "You're going to hate
what I have to tell you. I can't—"

Halfway through the sentence, the door flew open with
a bang. "Girl, I brought someone to meet you. I see Murphy's here."

Ollie propelled a large man forward. The light of a
woman in love graced her face.

"Don't tell me: Curley Madison?"

A blush colored the man's face, and painted his bald
head as well. He took her hand.

"It's truly a pleasure, Miss Laurel."

"Yep, shore shootin' is. I told him all about you."

"You did?" She gulped in sudden panic.

"Don't worry, only the good parts. You already know our
fine mayor, who is set to wed Laurel."

"We've debated the finer points of the subject a time or
two," the saloon owner grinned.

"Indeed we have, Curley, my man." Murphy clapped his
back.

"Most likely sold you that panther piss he calls beer."

Laurel envied Ollie's twinkling, mischievous eyes.

"Panther piss, huh? Just wait until next time."

"Now, sugar, I wasn't aiming to rile you," Ollie wheedled.

"I took it the way you offered—straight up and down the

gullet." Curley's smile bypassed his lips to settle in his sparkling gaze. He turned to Laurel. "After finally meeting you, I'm certain I'm in the presence of an angel. Flip that coin over and my Ollie's more ornery than a buffalo gnat."

The petite woman threw back her head and cackled. "Orneriness is my calling, you big whiskey-pusher. Without some backbone, I'd be dead and buried." A sudden kiss planted on the man's cheek sent a new wave of redness upward.

"Why, darlin', if you don't say the prettiest things! Reminds me of a bald-faced heifer I once had on the farm."

Laurel felt a surge of affection for the rotund bald man. Whoever named him must've needed spectacles, because not one sprig of hair dotted the landscape. A fly would break his neck landing up there. But she'd learned not to judge a body by the meat on their bones or the amount of hair they did or didn't possess. Ollie deserved some happiness.

"Goldarned old coot. My grandpappy warned how a body gets plain mean when most of the sand in his hourglass settles to the afternoon side. And by daisy if he wasn't right."

"Bear that in mind when I turn you six ways to Sunday."

"Now, Curley, no call to get ugly. And just think, I was becoming real partial to you."

"If you lovebirds need some privacy, Murphy and I can scoot." Truth of the matter was, Laurel welcomed the interruption.

"We hate to interfere with your courting," Murphy seconded.

"Shoot, boy, just speak up if we're boring you. Thought you might take a gander at someone you'll see a lot of, Laurel girl. Besides, we're gonna help clean up the cafe."

"We have all night for the pleasurable stuff." Curley began gathering plates off a table. "I know how much elbow grease it takes to run a saloon. This takes twice that, ma'am."

"Ma'am belongs to a prim schoolmarm. I'm plain Laurel."

"Don't know about you, but she has more dignity and grace." Murphy draped an arm around her shoulders. "After the last hour I'll never look at you in quite the same way."

"What's this?" Ollie's ears perked up.

"Not much, really. Just a couple of starved boys."

While they cleaned and tidied the cafe, she told them about Edgar Lee and Andy Cole.

"You would've burst with pride. I glimpsed a side of Laurel I never knew." Wonder lightened Murphy's gaze.

"Our girl is quite a lady," Ollie agreed. "But I always saw her compassionate, loving side."

"She'll make a wonderful mother for our children."

"Spit and thunder, you're doing it again! Quit talking like I'm a million miles away. I didn't do a bit more than any other decent human being would've done."

Darn Murphy! She couldn't take much more of this adoration and talk of mothering his children. Not when she couldn't stop thinking about his damn brother.

Brodie approached the dying campfire with caution. A weary woman, probably far younger than her stooped shoulders suggested, stole from around a tilting wagon. She pointed an old musket.

"State your business, mister."

"I mean no harm."

The boys slid to the ground.

"Maw, wait'll you see what we brung." Edgar Lee's excitement drowned the whispering gentle breeze off the bayou.

Still leery, she propped the weapon against the shadowy side of a nearby tree.

"Child, I oughta switch you good for running off like that. You, too, Andy, for tagging after your brother. Where you been?"

"But Maw . . ."

Brodie threw his leg over Smokey's back and dismounted. "Sorry, ma'am. I appreciate how they must've worried you, but the boys did what they thought right. Don't punish them for needing to take care of you."

When their mother neared, moonlight etched deep ruts in her hollow cheeks. He'd seen the same hopelessness in countless others who suffered in the war. Long on problems, short on the means to solve them.

"I'm beholden to you for seeing to 'em. But they know better than to go agin me. These two require a tight rein."

"Begging your pardon, ma'am, they also need something to eat." His soft rebuke failed to dent her thick armor. Women sure did mystify him.

He unpacked the food from bulging saddlebags. The thin set of her mouth told of a prideful woman who even in desperate times wouldn't accept handouts. He had to convince her—if not for anyone but the starvelings. She spurned the grub he held.

"You got the boys back safe enough. Now hop back up on that horse and take your meddling intentions with you, mister."

"Name's Brodie Yates. It's not much, I assure you. I'll not ride back with it." He tacked on some force to the threat.

A baby's squalls drew the mother's attention, the noise breaking the standoff. "Edgar Lee, take care of your sister."

The youngster looked from the woman to Brodie, then

trudged toward the cries. Andy tripped over a log when he ran to catch up. He sniffled but shed no tears. The ache in Brodie doubled.

"Please, ma'am. Pride doesn't fill hungry bellies."

"Got a watered-down cup of coffee. All I can offer."

A glance around the neat camp located a blackened pot beside the fire. It sat alone. Although the family had nothing to spare, Mrs. Cole would take a refusal as unmannerly.

"That would be mighty good."

The baby's crying ceased abruptly. Brodie arranged the crocks and bread on an upended crate and squatted beside glowing embers. He accepted a tin cup.

"Much obliged, ma'am."

"I'm Betsy Cole." With a sigh, she dropped the stiff pretense. "Wheel broke. We're trying to get to my brother's place near Fort Richardson."

"How long since your husband passed?"

Shoulders that bore the weight of the world drooped lower. "A week yesterday. My Daniel had the fever. Me and the boys buried him after we crossed the Red River."

"No grief in the world worse than losing someone." Brodie sipped on the barely lukewarm brew and fished a small bag of Bull Durham and papers from his pocket. "You mind?"

"Haven't seen a man yet what didn't have the tobacco craving. Reckon I'm used to it."

After he rolled and lit it, he silently blew smoke into the night until she spoke again.

"Something says you fought for the Cause."

From the darkness cannons roared. Red flames shot from rifles. Men screamed in agony. He shivered. That special Hell remained as vivid as the moment he'd lived it. Images first born amid the chaos would never fade. Cause?

Nothing on earth lent credence to that carnage. Long minutes passed before he could answer, and when he did his voice cracked.

"For a fact, ma'am."

"Daniel, too. A shell of my husband came home. I suppose war does that to a man." She wiped a tear with the hem of her dress. "He was a hero at Chickamauga."

"We buried a bunch of heroes. Not many left anymore." Brodie tossed the cigarette into the smoldering ashes. It took barely a second to vanish—just like his life.

"You're a decent man. I reckon you can leave the food."

"A wise choice, ma'am."

"Don't want some stranger to sit here all night. That's the only reason. A woman likes her privacy."

He rose and dumped black sediment from the bottom of the metal cup before handing it back.

"I'll be back come daybreak to fix your wheel."

"Reckon you'd be welcome . . . long as you don't bring a passel of nosy do-gooders."

"You have some special boys. Remember that, Mrs. Cole." His hand brushed the memory bag before he stepped into the stirrups.

"What did you want to tell me, sweetheart? Bet you want to move up the wedding," Murphy teased.

Exactly how did one go about killing a man's future?

The wait, coupled with his tender regard, drove spikes in Laurel's composure. She took a deep breath and jumped.

"I'm not the person you think I am."

"I know all I need to for now. The rest I'll learn later, once we're married. Most married folk don't know everything right off. Shoot, we wouldn't have anything to talk about." He ran a palm up her arm and under her hair to caress her neck.

She gently pushed him away. This was hard enough without him making it any tougher. "Please, wait until I'm finished."

"My love, whatever it is, I frankly don't care." He nudged her chin upward. She stared miserably into the liquid brown gaze. "You mean more than anything else in this world. Accepting my proposal made me extremely happy. The only thing that can change that is to tell me you don't want to marry me."

Dry desert sand suddenly caked her mouth. How could she live with the consequences that came with clear obligation? Laurel licked her dry lips, trying desperately to moisten them.

"I have a past, Murphy."

Chapter Nine

There, she'd said it. The results she'd tack to Brodie's hide. Laurel peeked from beneath shadowed lids. Murphy had never mistreated or spoken ill of a living soul. He shouldn't have to bear the price of her dark history.

Murphy's wide-toothed smile didn't make sense.

Anyone in his right mind would be aghast at the bold disclosure. How could he be happy to discover the blight on his almost-wife's character?

"Of course you have a past, sweetheart. Everyone does. None of us arrived in the back of a turnip wagon."

Oh Lord, he mistook her words and the delicate situation.

"I'm trying to tell you—"

"You can say nothing that will destroy the love in my heart. Nothing."

Even if she'd done damnable things no decent woman would?

Even if he knew his brother heated her blood with a single look and she'd never get him out of her head?

Besides those facts, nothing stood to break Murphy's heart.

She didn't have the courage to poke holes in his bubble. Not tonight.

Perhaps in the light of day . . . perhaps tomorrow.

"Sweetheart, what dire secret lingers on the tip of your tongue that you can't find words to say?" His chuckle added to her unwillingness to hurt him.

The longer she stood silent, the grander his amusement.

"I—I don't have any parents," she blurted at last. "I just wanted you to know."

"So what? Neither do I. Makes for a smaller wedding."

"And I'm almost certain I snore in my sleep."

Laughter burst from Murphy's throat. "Love, you harbor the most farfetched notions. While we're engaged in soul-baring, I believe you should know that I don't have a nail on my big toe and I'm notorious for cracking my knuckles. In public no less."

No one could accuse her of not trying. She would have to carry the burden a day or two longer. Perhaps she'd find the right words when opportunity presented another chance.

After all, she still had five more days.

Laurel and Ollie rose early and stashed some staples into the rented buggy. A flick of the reins set them in motion. Locating the youngsters' encampment didn't seem too big an obstacle.

"Giddyup there, you lazy bag of bones." Satisfied, Ollie turned to her. "Did you remember some hen fruit and salt pork?"

"Of course. I packed the eggs carefully so not one shell would break, and I brought plenty of meat."

"Did you also get the sugar and flour I told you?"

Laurel sighed. General Sherman would have scribbled a much shorter list than Ollie's. The second she learned about the Coles' plight, Ollie became obsessed. Looking at her now, it appeared she hadn't caught a wink of sleep.

Neither a salty tongue nor unending questions could hide the dear woman's Texas-sized soft spot.

Circles rimming the woman's eyes might hint at lack of sleep upon first glance. Yet Laurel knew that Ollie wore weariness from declining health.

Her chest constricted. She couldn't lose the only family she had. Not yet. Fate wouldn't be that cruel.

"You gonna perch there and bore a hole clean through? If you're itching to say something, speak up, girl." Ollie puffed away on the pipe stuck in the corner of her mouth.

"I'm worried about you. Can't I persuade you to go to Jefferson and let a doc see what's wrong?"

"No sawbones can fix what's ailing me." Ollie covered the back of Laurel's hand. "Don't you lose any sleep over it. I got a whole lot of living yet to do before making the crossing."

She wanted to rattle the stubborn cuss's teeth. But that would merely set her mind in granite, the hardest stone in the state.

Laurel's blood froze.

They carved tombstones from granite.

She banished the thought. Someone else might hold more sway over Ollie. Curley Madison?

"I like your man friend. He obviously cares for you a great deal, although I can't for the life of me see why, what with your rough edges and all."

"That's the living part I just mentioned. That man makes my old bones think they're twenty again. He's taken a notion he can file those crusty patches smooth. Now quit your yappin.' Keep a look-out for those poor little younguns."

The dressing down warned Laurel in no uncertain terms to mind her own business. She buttoned her lip and drank in the beautiful scenery she'd missed for so long.

She'd almost forgotten the mysticism here on the bayou, home to long-legged cranes, loons, and bullfrogs. During summer months, lily pads and purple water hyacinth carpeted the water that gave sustenance to the bearded cypress. The trees had stood for decades, silent sentinels against encroachers. Could they sense dishonesty in those who passed by?

"Are you cold, girl?"

"A chill swept over me."

"I told you to bring a shawl, but you scoffed at me."

Tingling premonition crept from the dark shadows of her soul. Building a life on deceit had definite obstacles. A square peg would never fit into a round hole. Not ever.

Heavy gloom clutched her breast. One chance didn't seem too large a favor. "The day is warm enough."

"Whatever you say."

A clearing upstream revealed the camp and broken wagon. A tall figure was bent, hammering. He rose when the buggy coasted to a stop. The Navy Colt strapped to his leg caught the sun's rays.

Bare-chested, Brodie Yates's dismissive glance brushed her face before he resumed the task.

Her maddening pulse refused to slow in the humid air.

She adopted nonchalance, finding the buggy's metal step. Who could've predicted her heel would catch when she alighted? A hasty grip of the cracked leather seat stopped her from sprawling head-first. Call her grace and serenity; heat flooded her cheeks. The oaf probably enjoyed the spectacle. She riveted her attention on the two boys racing to meet them.

"Miss Laurel, Miss Laurel!" Edgar Lee and Andy skidded to a halt, spying Ollie.

"Someone wants to meet you. Ollie's the most special lady this side of heaven."

"You look like a couple of green-broke yearlings to me." Ollie winked and ruffled their hair. "Bet you're worth your salt though."

Each boy scuffed his toe in the dirt and pinkened.

"How about helping unload a few vittles?"

They nodded in unison, turning to the scowling woman who walked up behind them. "Can we, Maw?"

"We don't need whatever it is you come for."

The cold reception raised prickles on Laurel's neck. "I apologize for intruding. I fed Edgar Lee and Andy last evening. Fine lads they are. You've reason to be mighty proud of them."

"You're responsible for feeding them." Ice layered the reply.

"I take full blame. I'm Laurel James."

"Olivia Applejack b'Dam," Ollie offered stiffly.

"I don't cotton none to charity. We can take care of ourselves." The woman pushed back a strand of hair.

"I agree, ma'am." Ollie nodded. "But ain't no charity, just trading. The boys can wash dishes at the cafe until you get your wagon fixed. Sounds like good horse swapping to me."

"I suppose I can make an exception put that way. I'm Betsy Cole. I mind my own business and expect others to do the same."

The blunt statement explained the attitude. Pride was all that remained for the widow. And to keep that she'd hog-tie a cougar. Not much different from Laurel's own battle.

"We respect those wishes." Laurel spoke loud for a certain half-dressed rogue's benefit. The gaze flitting in his direction met a well-sculpted back.

A babe's lusty cry rent the fragrant breeze.

Mrs. Cole turned. "Guess I'd better go tend to her."

"Awful prideful, ain't she?" Ollie grumbled after the woman. "I'll get the younguns to unload the buggy. And Yates might need our services with that wheel. Come on, boys."

Laurel debated whether to follow Betsy Cole, the troop heading for the horse and buggy, or talk to Brodie, who after the unwelcome stare upon their arrival now completely ignored her. Betsy's frigid response seemed far wiser and a thousand times more safe.

"You've raised some wonderful children. I've met few whose manners come close."

"They're a handful at times." Betsy brushed eyes that told of too little sleep or were swollen from crying, or a combination of both. She reached into the wagon, lifting the baby. "Would you hold her while I get dry bundling?"

Small, tear-filled eyes stared in confusion at the transfer. Laurel couldn't help but feel her own panic rising.

Wiggling arms and legs hurtled her toward a place she resisted.

The girl twisted and reached for her nose with one hand while the other grabbed a fistful of hair.

Sweet baby's breath dredged up long forgotten portraits, the images chipped from chunks of ice around her heart. Curious, tiny fingers that clutched everything in sight . . . a mother's lullabies . . . the creak of the rocker . . . the baking bread that encompassed the house and clearing. . . .

Visions of home.

Reminders of family.

What she'd lost had opened wounds the size of Big Cypress Bayou.

"What a waste. Those arms weren't meant for babies, Lil."

The lazy drawl over her shoulder sent memories scurrying away.

Laurel wheeled around. The familiar hiss was missing from Brodie's approach. The hat likely kept the shirt company.

Her gaze tripped, falling headlong into a brown chest. Sparse, damp hairs narrowed into a line that ran down the center of his abdomen and disappeared into the waistband of his pants. A bouquet of shaving soap, tobacco, and perspiration aroused more fear than the Colt at his hip.

Blue blazes!

Brodie stood so near his breath caressed her neck. Corded muscles banding his arms prevented escape, although his presence alone sufficed to hold her captive.

"Don't call me that. It's Miss James to you."

The baby attempted to stick her fingers into Laurel's mouth, attracted to her teeth. She shifted her to one side and shot Brodie a withering glare.

"So you say. Your arms were made for other uses. I recall them holding me close, my face nuzzled to a soft breast."

The mocking smile dared a flare of anger. She searched for equal weapons.

"Mr. Yates, I would be hard pressed to remember one face among the thousand others. Yours I appear to have far more trouble sorting from the legions of admirers."

A glacial stare replaced the grin. She took great pleasure in the small victory, for admiration peeked beyond the frost.

"Touché. Your sparring skills compare to your talent in bed."

"Insufferable rogue. Don't you have someone to shoot?"

Not the most brilliant question, considering she stood in

the line of fire. She sucked in air when he brushed back the errant lock of hair curling onto his forehead.

"Not yet, but the day's young." He fingered the baby's curls. "After seeing you with the children, I almost buy that story about wanting to change. But I can't shake the picture of you anywhere except a house of ill repute. That throaty voice of yours, those half-closed eyes that would make a man sell his soul for one moment's ride into paradise. . . . It pitches motherhood clean out the window."

Laurel flinched but wouldn't show how much that stung.

"I can become anything I must to survive. Anything!"

"Even becoming wife to a man you don't love?"

The soft drawl flogged her conscience.

"I—I . . ."

Betsy Cole threw a leg over the back of the wagon. "Sorry it took so long. When Edgar Lee and Andy rise in the mornings, it looks like a hurricane passed through."

"I didn't mind."

The woman relieved Laurel of her load, frowning after Brodie as he sauntered back to work. When she spoke all traces of coldness fled. "He's a good man. The war left angry gashes inside men's spirits whether you see 'em or not."

"And every woman, don't forget." She could attest to that.

"True. A person bearing no scars never fought for anything she believed in."

A tender jab, without a doubt. Shame branded on her soul would not disappear until she battled hard enough. And even then, scars would remain. Those would never fade.

Ollie called, "Hate to break up the tea party, but we need extra hands."

"Mr. Brodie done fixed the wheel. We hafta put it back on," Edgar Lee piped up.

Betsy gave Andy the infant. "Watch Sissie."

"Aw, do I hafta?"

Ollie's ashen face and labored breathing caused concern. Lifting and straining would overtax a sickly heart.

"Why don't you hold the baby and let Andy help?"

"I'll do no such thing." Ollie jerked the pipe from her mouth. "I'll have you know I'm strong as an ox."

"You're not well."

"Squabbles can wait, ladies. This wheel won't." Brodie's dark scowl ended the argument. He motioned to Laurel. "Stand beside me. Mrs. Cole, you get on the other side. When we lift, Edgar Lee will take the barrel from under the axle. Ollie, do you think you can set the wheel on?"

"I dam . . . darn sure can," Ollie amended, flashing the children a guilty grin.

"I don't wanna do a girl's job." Edgar Lee's eyes brimmed. "I'm strong like my paw. See?" He flexed an arm.

Instead of losing patience, Brodie examined the small bulge. "That's quite a muscle there, son. Trade places with your mother. When I say, give it all you've got."

Against her better judgment, Laurel reluctantly took her place. A finger's breadth separated her from the man who sought to ruin her life. A current leaped across, sending gooseflesh up her arm. Heaven help her. If she made it through this day, she vowed to limit their contact to no less than a country mile. Chewing her lip, she avoided the intense gray scrutiny and braced her knees for leverage.

"Are you ready?" His breath teased a strand of hair curling beside her ear. "Everyone lift."

His heady nearness fueled a need to get it over with. The wood frame cut into her palms, yet she wouldn't yield. Peace would come only by completing the job. Brodie's guttural grunt stole intentions not to look. When she did, his rebel gaze held her prisoner even as sweat trickled down his face.

The wagon moved, but not high enough.

"I thought you had more in you than this," Brodie challenged, his half-smile mocking.

Laurel's blood became a molten river. An extra surge of power, and the wheel slid onto the greased axle, taking the weight off aching fingers. She relinquished her hold and hurried to escape. Before she realized where she headed, she sank to her ankles in the marshy bayou.

"This is just fine and dandy," she muttered into the air.

The harder she pulled, the more firmly imbedded her feet became in the muck.

"If you weren't too chicken to take my hand, I'd get you out," Brodie drawled from solid ground.

"Go away. My own doing got me in and I'll get myself out."

"There's something between us, Lil. I know it. You know it. You'll come around after you tire of fighting it."

"Get this straight: Were you the last man on the face of the earth, I'd happily die a spinster."

"The hell you say."

Laurel squirmed in the swamp's grip, wishing Brodie didn't ogle her like some expensive French pastry.

Suddenly she flailed, landing her behind in the squishy quagmire. His hearty laugh did things to a lady's pride. The miserable glare failed to squash his mirth.

"My offer stands. All you have to do is take hold." Brodie edged closer and reached.

Resigned, Laurel grasped his palm. The contact sizzled her flesh as though singed. A tightened grip and brisk tug did the trick. She flew from the dark prison into naked arms.

Indecent thoughts raced against the beating of his heart. Before she could react, his lips smothered her surprised yelp. Brodie boldly groped her backside, tugging her between virile thighs. His tongue explored her parted mouth. A strangled moan rose from a powerful need.

Behind lowered lids, Murphy's face floated between them. She instantly broke away.

"Damn you, Brodie Yates."

Damn them both. Part of her wanted to curl up and stay forever in the circle of his embrace. Painful remembrance had a way of bursting a rosy dream.

He'd left her behind.

Besides that, she was promised.

A sob clung as she pummeled the unyielding figure.

His arms trembled as he let her go. His ragged breath ruffled the top of her hair in a faint caress that did little to help her regain her sanity.

Laurel moved a few feet and worked to get the roar in her ears down to a low rumble.

"I'm beholden to you." The stiff murmur competed with a sudden gust of wind. She straightened the mud-soaked dress and fastened her gaze on the distant flight of a loon.

"Don't speak of it. Pleasure's all mine." He took several strides and turned. "You once welcomed my attention."

"I grew up and got a whole lot smarter."

And discovered that words of love flowed freely when men had no intention of ever returning. A body learned from dumb mistakes. Or at least it should.

A brittle snort conveyed his thoughts. "I assume you shared with Murph your sudden aversion to marriage?"

Fury ricocheted off every good intention known to man.

"*Spit and thunder!* Do us both a favor: Go ahead and tell him yourself—the sooner the better. I'm fed up to here with you and your threats."

Chapter Ten

Laurel's taunt stayed with Brodie through the night and into the next day. The lady had changed the rules in the middle of the skirmish.

She didn't fight the least fair. What to do now?

He wouldn't reveal her secret. That much he knew. And despite his stubborn denial of the attraction, she made him feel more alive than he had in a very long time.

Those lips, the taste of her . . . ahhhhh!

Beads of sweat dotted his forehead.

The fact that his brother had sampled her sweet delights gnawed at his very fiber.

Brodie contemplated the mess as he walked up the grassy knoll behind Murphy's house to the family plot. A white stone marked Elizabeth Yates's place beside her mother and father.

Heaviness draped his shoulders as he stooped to lay a bouquet of yellow and white blooms. The woman who'd brought him into the world had asked for pitiful little—a faithful husband and children to love. A lump blocked his windpipe. Pray to God she'd found the peace in death that had eluded her in life.

The deerskin bag caught on the leather of his vest. He blinked hard, removing the gold band that once graced her finger.

Memories washed through him. Elizabeth had gotten a rotten philanderer and a son who'd been better off to have died in the womb. Thickness coated his tongue.

Gossips had plenty of fodder after Samuel Yates abandoned them for a saloon girl. Elizabeth, Murphy, and he bore the brunt of that humiliating nightmare.

Even now Brodie's efforts to turn a blind eye to the pain were futile. No amount of wishing would banish the truth.

The sight of that early September morn remained clear.

A rope rubbing against the edge of the loft permanently creaked in his ears.

Her slight form swinging to and fro in the gentle breeze had made him retch, ashamed for not seeing the despair.

Barely ten, he learned to be a man. Rope shredded his tender flesh. After cutting her loose, he lowered her gently to the ground. Then he removed the traces of her suicide.

"Why?" Murphy asked. "Tell me why."

He had no answers then and none now.

Brodie kicked a clod of turf. They thrust a job on him he hadn't wanted. What did a kid know? He needed reassurance and guidance himself . . . things parents should provide.

Besides, a body couldn't teach values and self-worth when a mother and father didn't think enough to stick around.

Rotten substitute Brodie made.

Damn you, Samuel Yates!

To the day he died, he'd curse the man who passed his bad seed on to him. Surely sorry blood flowed in his veins.

Every good deed in the world would not atone for that. Fixing the wheel for the Cole family gave much satisfaction. Still, he'd canceled one right with a wrong by reminding Laurel of things she wished to forget.

But hell and damnation, he had to have her!

Movement below captured his attention. Etta's frantic charge up the incline sent chills down his spine. The ring fell from trembling fingers. He scooped it into the bag and met her halfway.

"Mr. Brodie, come quick. It's your brother!"

Laurel finished serving the last customer and tackled the cleanup. The morning's encounter with Brodie had twisted her inside out. The taste of his lips, his searing touch, branded themselves upon her skin.

Odd how fast she'd noted a distinction between Shenandoah and the scores of men who'd entered her life. A special, inner quiet set him apart. Among a hundred other things.

She plunged elbow deep into soapy water, surrendering to her mind's wandering.

The handsome stranger gave back more than the pleasure for which he bought. He let her glimpse inside a war-torn soul, and the pain there had equaled her own. She had been at rock bottom, despairing of ever escaping Taft. She'd believed she'd die alone, far from Texas.

Shenandoah provided hope. Hope that she would feel like a real woman—someone of worth rather than a mere commodity.

Nights of sharing precious tidbits of home renewed a desire for freedom she could taste. Curled in his arms, strength seeped into her bones. With bodies entangled in the bedding, she dreamed of pure passion and everlasting love. Grand ideas of children and a husband to cherish had taken her on a fanciful journey.

Laurel jerked loose from her meandering. Blind stupidity.

"Keep rubbing that plate and there won't be enough left to hold spit."

Uncanny the way Ollie read her moods. She tossed her a peeved glance. Lost in reverie, she'd forgotten that her friend stood with drying towel in hand.

"No harm in a person reflecting, is there?"

"Never said there was, girl. But your attention's a mite on the scattered side since running into Yates."

"Lack of dishes doesn't matter to hungry menfolk. We could serve them on a piece of tree bark for all they notice." She squirmed under Ollie's one-eyed squint.

"What happened at the Coles' campsite?"

"Nothing, absolutely nothing. You were there."

Silky caresses and kisses wouldn't happen again. She'd handle Brodie with a firm hand. He couldn't waltz into her life as though he'd never left. She'd show him.

Do us both a favor. Go ahead and tell him yourself.

What a dangerous, foolish dare.

"You might oughta consider a few fibbing lessons. I got eyes enough to see."

The porcelain snapped in her hands. Laurel muttered an oath, staring at the sudden cut in her palm. "I can't very well put that man from my mind when you're quite happy to remind me when he's not around."

Ollie huffed. "No call to get sideways. Grandpappy always said, 'Solving problems is like clearing pasture land. First, pull out the piddly little saplings, the ones that don't make a hill of beans, then set to work on the big ol' stumps. If'n you cain't pull 'em out whole, then chop 'em into small pieces and cart 'em off a chunk at a time.' "

"Spit and thunder! I'm sick of listening to your dear, departed grandfather. For once speak for yourself."

"Quit bellering. Brodie Yates ain't the log jam blocking your way. I'm saying get rid of the guilt and shame eating you alive." Ollie tapped her hand on the chest. "That's the stump you gotta work on. Everything else is pissy-ant little saplings."

Laurel wrapped the cut, muttering beneath her breath. How much patience would it take to wipe the layers of tarnish that had collected on her soul?

"I'm sorry I took my frustration out on you."

"Denying your feelings can cause nothing but grief and heartache. It's plain you're sweet on the man."

"Horsefeathers! Sweet on a lousy womanizer? He probably tallies women he's charmed the same way he carves notches in the handle of his Colt for each man he kills." And with as much conscience, she added quietly.

She cursed the fact that she had but to close her eyes to fetch from hiding every crease of his face.

In addition, lest she come close to forgetting those, rippling muscles encased in old leather refreshed her brain.

And the barest of contact melted firm resolve.

"A body never knows what lies around the next bend until he goes down that road. Ain't nothing good comes from denying the truth, Laurel girl."

A commotion beyond the cafe overshadowed the dire warning. Curiosity took them to the front with aprons flapping. Laurel reached the window, shaken by the clamor of hooves filling the street. Gunshots added to the melee.

"Stop them!" a man shouted, running past. Others followed, their boots pounding the wooden sidewalk.

More shots rang out, peppering the glass. Tiny fragments showered them.

"Git down!" Ollie shoved her to the floor amid the crunch of broken glass.

"What's happening?" Icy panic raced through her.

"Outlaws would be my guess." Ollie crawled behind the counter, where she stashed a revolver.

"What are you doing?"

"Ain't about to let no sidewinder take what's mine. You wait here and keep your head down."

"But you can't do a blooming thing. Let the men . . ." Her voice trailed off as she realized that Ollie was gone. Probably out the back door.

A rapid blast of shots, yells, and fleeing horses assaulted her ears. She crouched, waiting for it all to end . . . or the rest of the world to come crashing down. Who knew what had happened to Ollie out in the midst of that chaos. The woman never learned to leave well enough alone. She stood no chance against overwhelming odds but she'd never listen.

Long minutes passed. When blessed silence came Laurel almost failed to recognize it. She raised her head.

Ollie burst through the door a second later. "Come quick."

"What's wrong?"

"Murphy's in a bad way. They shot him."

"How? Why?" Trembling legs made her movements unsteady.

"Bank robbers. Someone said it was the Blanchard gang. Murphy tried to stop 'em. He wounded one before he stopped a bullet."

Laurel broke into a run. "The sheriff; why didn't he?"

"Murdering thieves killed Sheriff Tucker." Ollie panted,

trying to keep up. "Snatched little Darcy Hatcher and Willa Carver on the way out of town. Took the girls with 'em."

The news froze Laurel in her tracks. She gagged, tasting the dirty rag abductors had stuffed into her mouth so many years before. Sweat and cheap liquor blocked the sun's warmth. A shudder swept her into the swirling, black foreboding of a wild Texas wind. She breathed danger and despair.

"Dear God no! Someone has to go after them."

"They will. I understand how you feel, but—"

"No one knows unless they've lived the horror."

"Of course, girl. I only meant to point out that Murphy needs you right now. You gotta be strong for his sake."

A growing crowd jostled, returning her to her senses. Laurel and Ollie pushed through to the open bank door.

Nothing could have prepared her for the sight. Murphy's pale features contrasted with the blood puddling in a circle behind him. She swallowed a sob and knelt, paying no heed to the hem of her dress soaking up the sticky fluid.

"I'm here, Murphy." Shaking, she smoothed back the sandy hair. Eyes closed, he more resembled a corpse. A sudden gasp was the only indication he was still alive. "Please don't die."

The pressing sea of faces flushed when she looked up. Each flinched, avoiding eye contact.

All except one . . . Brodie Yates, who knelt opposite her.

"I'll take care of my brother. Nothing short of a miracle can help him." The accusing glare did a thorough job of riddling what calm she'd managed.

"A doctor? I assume you sent someone to Jefferson."

"The moment smoke cleared, for all the good it'll do. By the time one gets here . . ." The break in his voice revealed how deep his love for Murphy really ran.

A man squeezing past caught her attention. "Jake, can't you do something?"

The barber flushed. "Digging a grave comes to mind. Beyond that, nothing much left." He shoved through the gawkers.

"Laurel," Murphy muttered weakly, his eyes fluttering.

"I'm right here, dearest."

"Laurel, I . . . don't leave me." The lids drifted shut.

"Don't worry, I'm not going anywhere." She firmly held the limp hand, challenging Brodie to dispute the vow.

The rebel glared, speaking to no one in particular. "Some of you help carry him home."

The crowd clearly understood the difference between an order and a request. The teller produced a sturdy board and slid it under Murphy. Half a dozen men lifted him.

A tortured groan rolled from colorless lips, ripping at Laurel's heart. The squared set of Brodie's jaw told of a similar effect on him. She ran ahead to make arrangements, praying for a doctor even though Murphy's chances weren't enough to dare mention.

Etta wrung her hands, her eyes glistening with unshed tears. "Mr. Murphy? Is he passed?"

"He's hurt awful bad. Get water, clean towels, scissors, and"—her mind whirled, trying to think of what they'd need—"something to make bandages. A bunch of it."

"My feet's already movin'." Etta sped into the house, leaving Laurel holding the door for the men's precious cargo.

"Put him on the sofa in the sitting room." No need to worsen Murphy's suffering by going up the stairs.

They gently moved him onto soft leather.

"Hurry with those towels and water, Etta." Time had rendered his motionless body the color of chalk.

Brodie cut away a shirt no longer crisply white and starched.

"Is he . . . ?"

"Not enough so you can notice."

Her tender touch grazed Murphy's forehead. She felt a little sick when Brodie exposed the wound. A bullet had torn through the right side of his chest. Each heartbeat delivered a trickle of oozing stickiness. Relief swept over her when Etta arrived with a basin of water, a load of towels tucked under her arm. The woman's gasp reverberated.

· "Heaven help us! Mr. Murphy's not going to make it, is he?"

Engrossed in staunching the flow, no one answered.

"I'll fetch them scissors and bandages."

Brodie's presence bolstered Laurel to do what she must.

"Hold pressure on the wound. Press hard," he said.

Without question she followed his instruction but cringed at the faint pulse of his heart through the towel. Small signs of life should've brought hope but didn't. Lack of medical knowledge didn't prevent her realizing the obvious.

In tandem they worked, their hands touching frequently in a fight to save the man whose death would bring great loss.

Each fleeting brush prolonged the inevitable. Despite their bumbling efforts, he'd probably not survive.

"I . . . I can't do this. It's no use. I'm afraid."

"Remember your promise to stay with him?" Brodie's bloodstained hands clung to hers. His gaze recognized the coward in her and didn't seem to mind. "We're all he has. Don't buckle on him now."

The rogue's intense caring washed over Laurel. He did love his brother, no one could dispute that. The gentle admonition hinted that maybe he held a bit of regard for her as well. The brittle edge had vanished, the harsh lines softening around his mouth. Everything had changed with the day's events. They no longer played a game. Matching wits had no place here.

Laurel found new strength with her palm curled inside his. Brodie's touch conveyed hope and courage.

"I'm not going anywhere. Long as there's the barest prospect of change, I won't quit."

"That's my Lil."

An empty rush of cold air came when he reached for a clean cloth. The broken link left her again bereft and scared.

"Here, take this and give me the soaked one," he said.

The soft squish of it landing in his palm brought chills. She didn't recognize her own red-dyed fingers and hands.

Quite odd, the things noticed at inappropriate times—the way blood colored underneath and around, perfectly outlining her nails but leaving the center like unfinished porcelain to paint later.

Perhaps the unblemished portion represented a section of life she'd forgotten to live.

Or maybe it reminded her of parts so damaged they rejected color?

"Where is that doctor?"

"Raise him slightly." The order effectively ignored her question. "Help me get this binding around him."

"This god-awful waiting tries my patience to no end." Thankful for something to do besides reflect on stupid mistakes, she lifted Murphy, tilting him to get the binding situated.

Brodie pulled it tight across his brother's chest and went under again. His arm jostled her breast each time, spreading a heat throughout her body.

Laurel met his blank expression. He pretended well. Yet she knew the unintentional caresses had affected him. The clumsy tying of the cloth betrayed him.

Ollie spoke from the doorway. "Yates, can you spare a minute? Some folks would like a word."

"Not now." He waved her away. "Can't you see I'm busy?"

"Goldarned! It'll only take a minute. Wouldn't ask just to make conversation."

"Reckon we've finished for the moment." Brodie sighed and turned to the wash basin. "Make it quick."

Drying his hands, he followed Ollie down the hall.

Bellowing grumbles drifting from the study aroused Laurel's attention. Jake Whitaker and George Adams were hard to miss.

She edged closer.

"We've called a town meeting. The voting was unanimous."

"What the devil are you babbling about?"

"We've elected to pin Sheriff Tucker's tin star on you."

"You're not pinning anything on me, you crazy fools."

George became agitated. "Understand something, Yates: There's no one else. It's you or nothing."

"Then I suppose you won't have a lawman."

Brodie's eerie detachment puzzled her. Some stranger hadn't leaked red all over the leather sofa. Blood ran thicker than water. Didn't it? The dull answer made no sense.

But then, not much in this hellish day had.

"Furthermore, you're wasting my time."

"That money those thieving varmints took was all these folks had," Ollie spat back. "And there's the matter of those two little girls, don't forget."

"What in Sam hell are you talking about?"

"The hostages. They took Missus Hatcher and Miz Carver's daughters with 'em."

"And none of the rest of us would stand a snowball's chance in hell of going after them and coming back alive. My God, man." Jake's volume raised a notch. She envisioned his handlebar mustache twitching. "Bert Blanchard uses men for target practice and laughs about it."

"On top of that, Murphy managed to wound one of them before they drew a bead on him," came George Adams's nasal twang.

"Gentlemen, I'm sorry. I'd help if I could, but—"

"Son of a blue jacket, Yates!" Ollie exploded. "The savages shot your own brother and left him for dead. An' them poor innocent babes—you want to tell them no one gives a damn? What does it take to thaw your heart?"

Laurel held her breath. He couldn't turn them down. He represented Darcy and Willa's last hope. His deadly aim and nerves of steel made Brodie more than a match for Bert and his henchmen. He couldn't refuse.

"I'm no lawman—just a two-bit gunslinger."

She peeked through a crack in the door. His wide stance portrayed defiance. *Damn his rotten hide!*

Brodie continued, "Hell, I've skirted the law most my life, jumping over the line more often than not to suit my fancy."

"Our point exactly. You can get the job done."

"Get it through your thick skulls: no."

What was his reluctance about? Lack of courage or skill didn't hold him back, and he scoffed at fear. His refusal pelted harder than any hailstones she'd ever seen, making far greater dents.

What halted the air in her lungs didn't come from plunging ice but bitter truth.

He'd protect his brother from her but not seek retribution against the men who'd hurled Murphy to death's door and stolen two little girls.

Had the war changed him into someone she'd sooner not know?

Laurel sagged against the door frame. She doubted the lawless bunch would let the girls live. Her heart lurched when she touched the broken tooth. Might be a pure blessing should death take them quickly.

"Seems to me it didn't disturb you overmuch when you tried to fit Jeb Prater with a marble hat," Ollie reminded him.

"I answer to no one. This is your town, your money, your problem. Pardon a bit of frankness, but you men need to earn the right to grow hair on your chest."

"It's also your brother who lies still and white."

If Jake meant to prick him with the snide comment, he succeeded. From her listening post, Laurel felt the sting of Brodie's anger.

"That's right. And I'm trying to keep him alive. Getting your money back sure won't. Finding a doctor might."

She couldn't put her finger on the cause of Brodie's obstinacy. She'd witnessed his strong, capable hands at work. Mrs. Cole and her children provided ample proof of his compassion.

And when she'd found herself mired in the bayou's clutches? Even now she could taste the raw passion of his need.

She hadn't been kissed by a cold, heartless man. That much she knew.

115

Chapter Eleven

Brodie's mind staggered to areas too agonizing to linger in. He rubbed his eyes, but the images stayed, each one splintering off another piece of his soul. His chest ached from a cold that wouldn't leave him.

God have mercy.

Wanting to help wasn't the issue. He couldn't.

Not even for Murph. Some things came with a price beyond reach. That knowledge ripped the hole inside him even bigger.

"I think I get the jist. You're telling us we might as well toss our hard-earned money to the wind," the barber spat.

Brodie jammed both fists into his pockets to avert disarranging Whitaker's ugly features.

"I've had a gut full of killing."

That they thought him callous and hard rattled the pledge he'd made to himself. He didn't have the time to make this group understand his struggle. Besides, they'd mock a gunfighter's desire to call it quits, to make a stand once and for all here in Redemption, and to find out if his search for a bit of home had not been in vain.

116

REDEMPTION

The fight to stay breathing until he found a teaspoon of self-respect had taken more perseverance than anyone knew.

"I don't see that ridding the earth of one or two more bad seeds should make any difference to your sort." Jake twirled his mustache, shifting from one hip to the other.

"What the hell's that supposed to mean—my sort?"

"You know—someone who kills for the pleasure of it."

Brodie clenched his fists until the bones hurt. He'd never taken a life for sport. Nor would that day ever arrive.

"Find someone else, or do it yourself." Let them see how easily they could forget the gurgle of a final breath or the smell of blood after hot lead ripped flesh from bone.

"No one says you have to kill 'em, just bring back what they stole," George Adams muttered.

He glared, a derisive snort exploding. "You think to accomplish one without the other? I propose you try it."

Suddenly a heavyset woman entered the fray. "Mr. Yates, my husband, God rest his soul, gave his life for a cause he believed in. Most of you in this room lost loved ones. I'm tired of losing. How much do we have to sacrifice? My baby is out there with those murderin' robbers. If you have one shred of decency and goodness, I beg of you, please help."

"I respect your grief, Mrs. Hatcher—"

"Mr. Brodie, slavery is all my family has known for generations," a woman of color who he presumed to be Mrs. Carver spoke softly. "I thought my Willa would finally have a chance to grow up free and enjoy the kind of things denied black folk. I got nowhere else to turn except you, sir."

"Go tell that to your soldier friends over to Jefferson. They favor darkies. Don't give a damn about any white folk, though." Hate spat from George Adams's mouth.

"Yeah, scoot on over there, Miz Carver, and let us take

care of our white girls. Anyhow, they probably killed yours." A tobacco-chewing, surly man entered the debate.

The mother gasped and tried to muffle her sobs.

Brodie lunged at the man, pinning him against a wall. Beneath his forearm, the bastard's Adam's apple bobbled in a frantic attempt to stop the brown wad's migration, but the tobacco edged down the man's gullet.

"What the hell?" Jake's scrawny frame tried to intervene.

Maybe he'd been hasty in ruling out the *sort* he could be if provoked. He could certainly wring hate from this lick-spittle's neck without a bit of remorse.

"Any of you show disrespect for womenfolk of any kind again, I won't stop here." Brodie shoved the man into Jake.

"Hey, you got some nerve threatening Martin—and us," George whined.

"It's fair warning. I don't think you'd care to see my threats." He smoothed his vest and almost smiled at the sudden milky complexions sweeping the self-righteous bunch of bigots. Except for the two mothers and the b'Dam woman. Hell of a name.

"You addle-brained, limp-wristed ignorants, you'd best listen to him." The cafe owner shifted her pipe to the other corner of her mouth. "And fighting amongst ourselves won't solve our problem. Remember, you asked for his help. Ain't the lot of you with gumption enough to toss a stray cat out the back door."

"But—we aren't gonna stand for this," Jake spluttered.

Brodie's train of thought veered south as a slight figure pushed through the small gathering.

Damn, her!

Laurel had fire in her eyes and murder in her step.

"Yates, you're all air and bluff. It's all well and good to overpower a room of slackers." Shocked gasps didn't slow

118

her down. "At one time you might've had reason to call yourself a man. I can't say it holds true now."

"Tell him, girl," Ollie urged.

He caught the finger poking his chest. "Miss James, you're meddling in someone else's bubbling pot."

"Someone has to."

His narrowed gaze should've warned her that she'd overstepped her bounds. Yet she appeared unfazed by his stony scowl.

"Ollie, pass me your shooting iron."

"You sure of what you're doing, girl?"

"Never more. I think this overstuffed goose would fit nicely in a boiling pot once I make a hole to let out a bit of the quackery. Then we're going after those girls."

An icy glare accompanied the bold statement. She couldn't know every slur brought more pain than he could bear.

"And our money, don't forget," George Adams said.

"I could give a rat's hindquarter about that. Frankly, I shame you people for your narrow, selfish minds."

George huffed. "You forget your place, Miss James."

"It must throw you into shock to find a female who won't knuckle under to your stupid rules. Guess I've never been a bootlicker and won't start now. It sickens my gut that green is the only skin color you can see. Except . . . I wonder how quickly you'd have propped your gluttonous hide into a saddle had they stolen boys. If time permitted, I'd argue the point. Now step out of the way." She lurched for Ollie's pistol.

Brodie's quick reflexes stopped her. She cast a furious glance at the grip clamped around her wrist.

"Can't let you do that." He ignored her glare, renewing his hold when she yanked hard.

"Let me do what? Shoot you or go after those bandits?"

"Neither!"

Smoke curled about Ollie's head. The porky-spined woman must've tamped the tobacco down good, judging from the fog that screened those owl eyes.

"Looks like you'll have to dicker your way out of this one, Yates. She means business."

"What'll it be?" Laurel's breasts heaved much too near.

He uttered an oath beneath his breath before releasing her. "I'll go. Satisfied? But I absolutely refuse the sheriff job. And, by God, you're not coming with me. That's my terms."

He brushed aside her grim smile and stalked back to his brother's side. She hadn't won. No one had.

Truth of it, he could already feel the rip of another piece of him. He wouldn't lay odds on those two little girls making their next birthday. Maybe he wouldn't survive either.

Nor did Murphy have a fighting chance of seeing sunrise.

A short time later, Brodie sought the serenity of the garden. Fresh air not laden with the stench of blood filled his lungs, but it did nothing to help the churning in his belly.

Time was measured in the ticks of a feeble heartbeat while they waited for a doctor who had yet to show. Helplessness wasn't a role he knew well. Death lurked in the room with the only kin he had left in the world, and nothing he did could stave off the Grim Reaper.

Light footsteps on the rock path came from behind. Out of the corner of his eye he caught Laurel's approach.

"I've sent Etta for a healer who lives in the swamp off Caddo Lake. Nora Whitebird may be Murphy's last hope." The warmth of her shoulder settled next to his.

"For all the difference anything makes now."

"A horrid thing to say! What happened to your pretty speech about not giving up?"

"I've seen more death in the last five years than you'll see in a whole lifetime. No one can change its course. Same goes for altering the direction of anyone's path once it's set. Wise men call it destiny."

"Hogwash! Life isn't carved in a piece of stone. If you want something badly enough, you can have it. That's faith."

"Can't buy it at any price." Were that true, he'd gladly pay, even should it cost a king's ransom. Home and family fanned impossible dreams he couldn't attain.

"True, a person can't buy his way through trouble. But he can alter destiny with enough blood, sweat, and tears."

"The voice of authority." Sarcasm dripped from his voice.

Why did she have to be so beautiful? And why couldn't he stay away from her? Or she from him? For God's sake, she belonged to Murphy! That throaty voice, the vanilla and spice swirling around his head, would drive a sane man crazy. And Lord knew he'd gone there the second he stepped into that cafe.

She studied him for a long minute and shrugged. "Stick to your beliefs, such as they are, and quit belittling mine."

He'd earned a good and proper scolding, and so her mildness surprised him. Her intense scrutiny made up for it, though. He squirmed and tried to look away. A soft touch on his arm sent a sizzle clear to his toes.

"I appreciate the sacrifice you're making and I thank you for it. Had we anyone else, you'd get your rathers."

"Murphy's the last of the Yates. I wanted to be here in case he needed me, not off chasing more elusive shadows."

"Had fate reversed our roles, I'm not certain I could."

Brodie stared at her. "Still, you made saying no next to impossible. You, Lil, no one else."

Laurel hid her violet scrutiny beneath lowered lids. The wrinkle on her forehead deepened. The shade of pink flooding her cheeks only made her more desirable.

121

"There's nothing else you can do for Murphy except make the Blanchards pay for what they did."

"Peculiar thing about revenge—once it gets inside, it changes you into an outlander. I wanted to fit someplace."

"I'm so sorry." She reached for his hand. "That explains why you hesitated. I watched you defend Mrs. Carver. You have a noble heart that will never let you stand quietly."

"That's been my downfall. It baffles me why color should lower or raise a person's status. I'm curious where you fit."

"Alongside you. I'm surprised you had to ask."

"Making sure. You've given me a few starts of late."

Especially when she'd arm-wrestled him for the pistol.

"Aren't you wasting time? The trail only grows colder."

"Reckon they'll keep." He gauged the magnitude of shock by the jerk of her head.

"Of all the . . . ! You wouldn't drag your heels, unless—"

"I've seen their hideout. I'll saddle up come daybreak."

"You knew all along. You know the Blanchards!"

What he hadn't thought to hear hiding behind the accusation bore a strange resemblance to disappointment. That thorn pricked. Somehow the realization that she regarded him a darn sight better than he deserved increased his longing.

"I didn't want to get involved with them unless I had to."

"They shot Murphy!"

"Sweet Jezzie! Folks keep saying that as though it'd slipped my mind. Like I was some senile old man or a simpleton." He kicked a loose pebble into a clipped holly bush. Leaves scattered onto the walk. "You may as well hear this now—me and Luther Blanchard go back a ways. I owe an almighty debt."

Laurel sucked in her bottom lip. "Whatever it is, your brother and those poor little girls shouldn't have to pay."

Brodie nudged back his hat with a forefinger. The rattles added a buffer against the unceasing roar in his head. Without them, the pain and disillusion riddling every waking moment would hasten his demise. He pulled a cheroot from inside his vest, bit off the end, and lit it before answering.

"Luther saved my life in the Battle of Shiloh. I took a mini ball in the leg and lay bleeding. A Blue Belly drew his bayonet, taunting my screams. I clutched the spent rifle to my chest, unable to prevent him from adding me to the list of three thousand other casualties."

Smoke curled up into the breeze, the wisps vanishing.

He wondered at this ebony-haired lady who'd invaded his mind—and his heart. Would she fade into similar nothingness? He'd never spoken of these things to another living soul. The telling didn't come easy.

Strange how tobacco calmed twisted nerves. A filthy addiction. Nonetheless, smoking untangled some of the mess.

"Anyway, I waited . . . dreading, praying for the moment that would end the nightmare. Luther threw himself over me, taking the brunt of the bayonet. The blow shattered his left leg before he managed to shoot the damned Yank."

"That's how you knew. Someone mentioned one of them dragged his left leg." Laurel's whiskey voice became raspy.

"Luther and I recovered in a makeshift Confederate hospital. Had we wound up in Union hands they would've amputated his leg. As it turned out, the wound left him a cripple. And me? I'm a—"

"Man with grit and honor," she supplied. "The hellish things you suffered. Yet you survived. That's what counts."

"Tell that to Luther. He might beg to differ."

"I understand your predicament. Truly I do. But those men rode into this town, stole, and murdered. Don't you care about that? Surely they deserve what's coming to them."

Not at his expense. Somewhere deep inside him, a voice cried out to save what was left of his soul. Killing again would seal his fate.

"Just don't ask me to mete out the punishment."

But he would . . . for her. He'd do most anything for Lil. *Even if it damned him for eternity.*

Laurel stroked the length of his arm. She paused, her lingering fingertips exerting soft pressure, massaging the hurt.

"You're our last hope. Few stand a ghost of a chance. I still have to ask how you know where they'll holed up." Laden with disappointment, the strangle in her voice unnerved him.

A man couldn't talk about things he knew and profess an ambition more lofty than the callous gun hand she thought him.

A man didn't just blurt out that inside him beat the heart of a romantic. The situation made this neither the time nor place.

Besides, a man could expect complications in explaining exactly what put certain notions beyond reach. The lady had obligations elsewhere and seemed in no mood for "what ifs."

"I stumbled across it once. Luther asked me to join up."

"I'm glad you didn't take up that offer."

Silence stretched. He focused on the cigar's red glow. To hope for more than belief asked too much. His lungs expanded to accommodate the rush of air. Unfamiliar peace followed the brief glimpse he'd given her into his brand of hell, a place he'd never allowed anyone before.

No matter what he and Laurel had been or done, they shared kindred spirits.

Brodie's bold gaze slid her length and drank in the sight

of this exceptional woman. Wispy tendrils ruined the severity of the dark hair pulled back into a simple knot. They curled about her face with such alluring precision, he had trouble trying to concentrate. He should've stepped away from the fragrance that drenched his tongue. He couldn't.

Torturous, insatiable yearning nailed his boots to the ground.

For half a nickel he'd yank her to him, hold her tightly, and ignore the protest of decency his conscience would cry for.

Damn the fool inside!

His brother lay dying and all he could think about was the elegant column of her neck. His gaze dropped to the swell of her breasts, rising and falling rapidly with her breath.

Laurel fidgeted, twisting the folds of her skirt. He had experience with those slender hands. They possessed uncanny abilities.

Passion wound around his memory like vines encircling the cypress in the bayou, possessing, becoming as one.

Their sultry morning encounter lingered in the air. She could rebuke until she exhausted the vocabulary, but her body couldn't deny this thing between them. He cursed the weakness that left him equally weak.

"I've a story to tell you," she blurted.

He wrestled his thoughts and his gaze from lush, rounded contours. He'd seen many a condemned horse thief with less desperation than he found glistening in Laurel's eyes.

"That is, should you wish to hear," she hastened to add.

"Seems the day for getting things off our chests. Shoot."

Color drained from her face, leaving it two shades of pale. Maybe he should've left off the joking.

"It happened one day, six years, three months, and fourteen days ago."

Brodie had a feeling she knew the exact hour as well. He didn't ask. Only something real serious could make a person pinpoint with such accuracy.

"A young girl picked blackberries along the creek bank. Two brothers went with her, but their favorite fishing hole held more promise than berry picking. They left her all alone." Laurel stopped and moistened her lips.

Ashes fell from his cigar. He paid them no heed.

"A music box her parents had given her for her birthday tinkled merrily at her feet. She could almost smell the pie her mother would bake."

Again she paused, this time to wipe a hand across her eyes, as if erasing some horrible scene.

"You don't have to do this, Lil."

"Three men appeared from nowhere and grabbed her," Laurel continued, as if he'd not uttered a sound. "She fought, scratching and kicking as hard as she could. When she tried to scream to alert her brothers, they crammed a dirty cloth into her mouth. These stealers of children took her far away. They gave her a new name, made her do unspeakable things, and kept her under lock and key until they presumed she had no will left to escape."

The rasp dropped to a mere whisper. "I was that girl, barely fifteen."

The cheroot burned his fingers. He tossed it down, grinding it with a heel. Thickness grew in his throat.

Propriety be damned! He pulled her into his arms. She buried her face in his chest.

"I didn't know. I thought—"

"They forced me into what I became." The words tripped over a sob. "I prayed to die."

126

"I'm sorry, so sorry." He'd been so eager to prove her wrong. Self-loathing and regret burned deep inside him. He held her tight, caressing her back.

"I became a cheap piece of merchandise. I scrub daily, but even now filth imbeds my skin."

His gut twisted. He'd helped degrade her. Worse, he'd threatened to tell the entire town and heap further disgrace. "I didn't know."

"They laughed, proud they'd ruined me for any decent man."

"I'll kill every one of the bastards!"

She pushed back and leveled an accusing stare. "I kept hoping for a miracle. I thought . . . you . . . you promised."

Her hands curled into fists. He wished she'd lay into him. A good whaling might take the edge off the disgust and loathing.

"Laurel, I—"

"You made me believe you truly cared."

If she knew of the many nights he'd awakened bathed in a cold sweat. The days she'd filled his thoughts and given him reason to keep trying.

"Darlin', I did. I ran into another Yankee bullet on the return. Once I regained my health, I wasn't sure you'd like the man I became, not sure that what happened hadn't merely been a figment of my imagination." He coaxed her against him, resting his chin on the top of her head. "I drifted to California and back, dodging Blue Bellies and looking for something I'd lost."

"That's why Ollie and I settled here. Redemption fit."

Something about the word seemed to offer hope and belief that a man could save himself. It fit snug around him also.

"I take it Ollie helped you escape St. Louis."

"She worked in the kitchen of the Black Garter. We became close, and I finally confided in her. She got me out in the wee hours after everyone slept."

"Remind me to thank her. She's a good woman."

"We're family now. We adopted each other."

Laurel's lips enticed. He'd gladly risk life, limb, and certain death to sample them again.

The sun faded below the horizon. Dusk was made for lovers. Willowy curves snuggled into his arms. She belonged here. He slipped the pins from her hair, breathing into the silken waves. The moment spoke of everything—and nothing.

Her mouth met his in a blaze of sinful abandon. White dahlias and vanilla, the past and the present, dreams and reality merged in a single instant.

"You smell of moon mist and gentle rain." He breathed against her ear, reluctant to let her go.

"Moon mist? I'm not certain that's a good thing."

"My lady, lover's breath beneath the silvery rays creates moon mist. Some claim it carries the aroma of an aroused woman."

"But, we're not . . . and I'm not . . ." A becoming blush stained her cheeks.

The pulse in the hollow of her throat beat frantically, adding to her sensual charm. Everything added to her charm—the wisps of hair hugging her earlobes, the catch in her whiskey voice, the way she fussed over the Cole boys.

"You lie so well."

Laurel's mouth flew open. "I have to go."

"Wait."

She dodged the outstretched hand. "This isn't proper."

The lady spoke the truth. He owed his brother a sight more than stolen kisses with his woman. Although nothing that made Brodie feel he'd died and gone to heaven could be a sin.

Loving Laurel should never be wrong, he decided.

Ollie chose that moment to open the garden door. "Girl, the healer's come. Thought you'd want to know."

"Thanks, Ollie." She smoothed back her hair, scrambling for pins with which to secure it. She made do with only two.

The crusty woman's disapproving stare made him feel as if she'd caught him stealing from the cookie jar.

"I hope you're right about this Nora woman," he managed.

"One thing's for sure, it won't hurt. We're groping in the dark."

He clutched her hand when she started toward the open door and Ollie. He could've sworn she returned the light squeeze.

"One more thing and I'll let you be." He struggled to keep a betraying tremble from sneaking into his voice. "Since I won't be around . . . will you stay nearby . . . so Murphy won't be alone when he dies?"

"That goes without saying."

"And one more thing—should he by some miracle make it, I'll not stand in the way of your marrying him. I give you both my blessing."

Chapter Twelve

At daybreak Laurel stood on the verandah long after the gray-eyed rebel disappeared down the road. One last check on his brother had found him alive, but with no sign of improvement. Then Brodie silently gathered a few essentials, saddled up, and rode out.

Strangely enough, though she'd prayed for his leaving, she could scarcely breathe from the empty space he left behind.

Through her pounding pulse she heard the rattles dangling from his hat. Those didn't fade even after he'd passed from view.

Spit and thunder! Didn't Brodie know she'd risk almost anything to sleep in his arms again?

Dearly as she hoped Murphy would live, she couldn't marry him. Not now. Not even to obtain stature. Not for any reason.

The rumble of thunder interrupted her thoughts. Dark rain clouds that had escaped her notice in the wrenching of Brodie's departure appeared. She hoped the overstuffed saddlebags included an oilskin, although a serious drenching mattered least compared to other matters. She'd forced him into this dangerous mission. The outcome could end all wrong.

"Please keep my darling safe," she murmured into the wind. "Let him bring back those girls unharmed . . . and soon."

Among the lot of Redemption's citizens, only she held insight into the minds of Darcy and Willa. That brand of fear blocked her air passage, souring the contents of her stomach. Years had passed since her abduction, and yet this one incident had sent her hurtling back to the moment the nightmare began.

Hindsight let her see the bad mistake in speaking of it.

For pity's sake, Brodie had already accepted the task when she opened that door!

Clear as day he misunderstood why she had told her story. Giving his blessing to the betrothal confirmed the guilt he felt for not saving her. She'd have been wiser to leave it buried. Bringing those demons into the light of day smashed into a million pieces the odds of reclaiming lost love.

Damn, the familiar chord he struck in baring his own dark secrets!

Only yesterday she'd harbored the belief of betrayal, or at the very least that he'd misled her. But their moonlit confession, scented with hibiscus and lavender, vanquished those notions.

Yes, she must've taken leave of her senses.

And why had he shared his secret? For absolution? Acceptance? Or a cry to silence voices from the past? Each pain-filled word had sprung from his gut. Agony fracturing his deep baritone revealed how deeply rooted in honor they grew.

The door creaked. Nora Whitebird stood at the white

railing running the porch length. "Rain good. Wash away evil."

"I wish it could." She met the ageless woman's piercing gaze. Nora appeared to know things meant for sages. Smooth, tanned skin gave no hint of her age. "How is Murphy?"

"He sleeps. You go. Get rest."

Nora's stare dropped to the hem of her dress where blood had soaked, turning the yellow fabric a dull, rusty brown. Laurel realized she still wore the same clothes she'd donned yesterday.

"Perhaps I will."

"You do your man no good here."

She felt obliged to correct Nora and explain she'd merely followed the promise she made *her man,* but she didn't.

"I couldn't leave when he could die any second."

Last evening she'd shivered when Nora attached blood-sucking leeches. Though the woman explained their usefulness in keeping the wound clean, Laurel would not soon forget the horrifying sight of the burrowing parasites. She stifled a sob.

"Do you think . . . ?"

"Time tell if he stay or cross river into next life. We wait for Great Spirit."

She touched Nora's arm. "Thank you for coming."

"I am healer. Grandmother passed gift." Nora covered Laurel's hand with her own.

"You must be exhausted after spending most of the night mixing herbs and roots."

"I go long time no sleep."

Large raindrops pelted the ground just then. So much for praying Brodie would stay dry.

Ollie threw open the door. "Come quick, it's Murphy!"

* * *

Why did he persist in pushing away the one thing that would fulfill his every longing? He must be daft.

Brodie uttered a string of curses as big raindrops fell from the sky. It promised to be a miserable day. He adjusted the brim of the felt hat to better shield his face.

"For two cents I'd turn around and go back." He patted the Appaloosa's neck, knowing he couldn't.

He set his jaw and turned due north toward Stephenson's Ferry on the Sulphur River. He'd follow Trammel's Trace to Pecan Point, then head east to Fulton.

Worsening weather almost had him wishing for a yellow slicker, even though he didn't have much use for them. Bright colors made him more of a target. Killing Shenandoah would bring instant fame to some unlucky soul with a fast six-shooter. Such name-seekers dogged his shadow, sometimes so close their breath tickled his neck.

A passel of problems accompanied notoriety, the biggest of which was staying alive.

Brodie had learned long ago to appreciate every sunrise. The sudden urge to ride back overcame him again. He'd tempted fate too often.

"Damn, Smokey! I'll run out of poker chips one day."

Laurel's face swam before him in the cold, gray morn, and he remembered why he rode in a soaking rain. He was the only hope for those little girls. And it didn't matter the color of their skin.

The hate talk of George Adams suggesting he rescue the white one and leave the other made him bristle anew. North or South, black, white, or red, they'd all have to learn to live together. Had those Yanks let him be, he'd have gone back for Lil.

Bigotry, hate, and greed had ruined them.

"Georgia Clay! We've got our work cut out this time,

boy." The horse moved into a canter, perhaps sensing the urgency.

A cent for every mile Smokey had carried his hide would make him wealthy. Two years ago he plunked down twenty-five dollars and knew he found a bargain. The Appaloosa had already proved the strength of his heart and would again if Brodie asked.

"Yep, you're a jewel, all right."

Smokey snorted and nodded his head, as if to say he'd take the compliment and keep 'em coming.

"Don't go getting a swelled head. You have plenty of shortcomings to compensate. Maybe I should tell ya how close you came to finding yourself saddled with a new owner." A slow grin crossed his face. "I do believe Lil meant to shoot me. She lit into my hide something fearsome. Not much left of my hind-end after she got done chewing. Be glad you're a horse."

He didn't recall Lil wearing that mean-spirited streak. Of course, years had a way of dimming a man's memory. But he most certainly remembered she hadn't worn much of anything back then.

Good God a Friday! Such images would worsen his misery.

Not that Lil didn't have good grounds for being mad enough to stomp a wild hog barefoot. She had a whole bunch of 'em.

"I would've broken her out of that place, daring anyone to step in the way . . . if she'd just confided."

Long years of road behind him reeked with if-only excuses, the latest in a long string of regrets. Ignorance couldn't buy forgiveness. Some things were no use justifying.

Guilt-eaten thoughts turned to the parents and brothers of whom Laurel had spoken. Despite times passage they probably still fretted over what had happened to her. He'd make a few inquiries once this distasteful business ended—should he continue to suck air, that is. The James's would likely welcome news of their long-lost daughter.

Thunder rumbled, quaking through his bones. Rain peppered his face as he urged Smokey into a gallop.

It was a far piece to Arkansas.

Laurel's heart hammered. Brodie trusted her. He'd never understand if Murphy died alone. She raced past Ollie, almost knocking the woman down. Why hadn't she kept vigilance beside the bed instead of thinking of her own wants?

Murphy's body shook violently with chills when she reached him. Perspiration poured off his forehead, mixing with bloody fluids coming from his mouth.

"Dear God!"

Nora quickly rolled him on his side to prevent choking. Laurel wet cloths to bathe his face.

"Ollie, get more blankets."

"Here you are, girl. There's more if you need 'em."

They managed to prop him into a half-sitting position and wrap him snugly.

"Don't you die on me, Murphy! I'm not going to let you get out of marrying me this easy." Tears blurred the figure until he blended into the patchwork color of blankets and guilt.

Her arms ached from clutching them so tightly to her chest. Through the wet haze she saw Nora put her cheek to his mouth.

"Is he . . . ?"

"He have breath."

"Thank God."

"Laurel girl, you gotta let him go. He's in the Almighty's hands now. Nothing more a soul can do."

"I can't do that." She collapsed against Ollie's shoulder. "Not yet. I need to tell him something first."

"Goldarn it! Murphy's got more luck than a cat in a roomful of rockers. Were I of a betting nature, which I'm not, I'd place my money on him."

She kissed the face that resembled a weathered old boot. The dark circles under Ollie's eyes worried her. "Do me a favor."

"Anything for my girl."

"Get some men to board up the busted window, stick a notice on the cafe that we won't open today, then go upstairs and sleep."

"Good idea about the sign."

"And the crawling into bed part?"

"I get all the dadgum rest I need." Ollie shifted the pipe that had long grown cold and gave her a one-eyed squint. "My grandpappy, God rest his soul, was fond of saying that a body born on a Wednesday and lookin' six ways to Sunday is nothing but a no-account. Worse than a mangy mongrel."

A wan smile formed. Her friend would always have the last word. Still, Ollie did hitch up her skirt and make for the door.

Relieved, Laurel stooped to mop blood from the floor.

"I'll do that." Etta took the damp towels from her hand. "You shouldn't worry your pretty head about such. I took hot biscuits from the oven to go with my Creole omelet and grits. Get along there now and eat."

"I surely applaud Murphy's choice of kitchen help." She wished Etta hadn't gone to the trouble. Now she'd have to force down a bite or two or deal with hurt feelings.

A horse out front set frazzled nerves on edge. The haste

with which Etta hurried to beat the caller to the door indicated that Laurel wasn't the only one affected. Even Murphy moaned. He calmed down when Laurel touched his pale face and smoothed back his hair.

Etta returned. "Miss James, you better come."

Dear heaven, what more could happen? Wrestling with dread, she whirled. "What is it now?"

"Out on the front porch . . . maybe the doctor."

"What are you waiting for? Show him inside."

Etta wrung her hands. Dismay lined her features. "I can't. Oh, my!"

Laurel sighed, wondering what demanded her personal attention. She spied trouble immediately from the porch. A man sprawled on the ground beside a horse. Pouring rain had plastered his clothes to his skin. He clutched a familiar black bag in one hand. Besides the satchel, nothing else suggested this must be the physician. Laurel flew down the steps.

"Mister, did you fall? Are you hurt?"

Snores erupted from his mouth. She immediately recognized the stench of liquor.

A quick gaze located the housekeeper, who remained beneath the sheltering verandah.

"Etta, come help get him inside."

The portly man had to weigh a ton. They tugged and struggled, managing to drag him out of the cloudburst. With not a dry stitch on them, they collapsed to catch a breath.

"We ain't gonna take him inside, is we?"

"I believe he can recover quite well out here." Disgust rippled over her. "After the buffoon sufficiently recovers, I'll send him packing. Now be a dear and have Jacob take the horse to the barn. We can't begrudge the poor animal hay and shelter."

"This man can't do Mr. Murphy any good."

"Nora has excellent skills, and at least she's sober."

Etta bustled off to the stables while Laurel traipsed into the deluge to retrieve the precious medical bag and quiet the animal, which became walleyed at a tremendous clap of thunder. The housekeeper's son wasted no time.

"I got him, Miz Laurel." The boy took the reins from her.

She lifted her limp skirts and followed in case Jacob had his hands full with the agitated mare. No telling how long the poor excuse for a doctor had left the mare exposed to the elements. Thank goodness the leather satchel protected its contents. Perhaps it held something useful.

Inside a dry stall, Jacob draped a blanket over the frightened horse and spread fresh hay on the ground.

"There now, isn't that nice and warm," she murmured softly.

"What happened to the man laid out on the porch?"

"Liquored up. He'll be fine in a while."

"My mama said she'll knock me in the head and throw me to the 'gators if she catches me drinking rotgut."

"A pretty smart woman."

"I figure long as she don't catch me, I'll be all right." Jacob patted the mare's jaw. "You don't hafta stay out here. Mr. Murphy pays me to handle things. He's a good man. I shore hope he keeps outrunning the angel of death. My mama and me—we got nowhere else to go. Taking care of Mr. Murphy is our life. Wouldn't know how to do anything else, I don't expect."

Laurel pondered the boy's worries on the way to the house. She'd never considered the devastating effects of Murphy's death to people like Etta and her son. The whole town depended on him. It appeared quite a few had a stake in him surviving. The lump lodged in her chest shifted. Her steps quickened.

Hours later, Etta yelled that the doctor was trying to sit up. Laurel took him a cup of Ollie's too strong coffee.

"Mister, take it, for this is all you'll get here."

Bleary eyes stared up. "What's 'at you say, dearie?"

"I'm not your dearie, you old goat. It'll help ward off the chill to keep you from taking up permanent residence on this verandah—coffee, very hot and very stout."

The man shook so badly she helped him get the cup to his lips for a careful sip. He wrinkled his face.

"Ooooooh, that's awful. Need a little sump'in in it. I generally mix it with spirits."

"You won't get any of that here."

"Got a spoon then? It'll help me get it down."

She and the caller shared that opinion. She hid a smile and helped him drink more. "Mind if I ask who you are?"

"Nope, if you'll tell me where in hell I'm at. Doc Gates, in case it matters."

"From Jefferson?"

"Gotta gunshot to treat." Unsteady movement sloshed coffee onto his shirt, though it was a pure mystery how the thick stuff managed to escape.

Laurel hastily grabbed the cup when Gates tried to stand. He teetered on the edge of the top step, threatening to topple backward into the mud. She looked for a place to unload the coffee, wishing problems arrived by telegraph so a body could have a right to refuse to take them.

"Whoa there, sawbones." Ollie arrived out of breath from the direction of the cafe. "Them legs are trying to ride a mighty rough sea. Might oughta sit a spell first."

Gates gave up the folly of balancing and dropped back onto the porch's wooden slabs. "I'm sorry, Mildred."

Ollie gave her a bemused glance and circled an ear with her finger to indicate that the man had fallen out of his rocker and left it still rocking. "Mildred must be your wife. I'm Olivia Applejack b'Dam."

"Well, I'll be damned, too! You sure favor my Mildred."

"I never found occasion to seek a husband." Ollie sniffed.

"Me neither. It's the wives I can't outrun or convince marriage isn't an occasion, but an occupation—a most hazardous one at that."

Laurel wearily tucked a strand of hair behind her ear. She had a hundred more pressing things to deal with, each one requiring more courage and stamina than she possibly possessed.

"Excuse me. Mister, I leave you in capable hands."

Doc appeared bewildered. "But I have a patient. . . ."

"Not anymore." She made no attempt to hide her anger or brittle tone. "No one here requires your services."

"A banker fellow, something Yates, got hisself shot."

"You're too late. He died."

Chapter Thirteen

A friend named Hawkshaw once advised Brodie, "When danger comes calling, don't hem-haw around. Do what you hafta, boy. A half-second often separates driving a hearse to riding in one."

The dead mountain lion at Brodie's feet confirmed that he'd been a watch tick away from becoming worm food.

Wafting smoke from the Sharps rifle barrel tinged the scene a familiar shade of lead gray—cannons, Johnny Rebs, storms, and the iron weight of a heart. He shook away fuzzy cobwebs to nudge the big cat with a toe.

It seemed irrelevant that Hawkshaw's tutelage pertained to the finer points of killing men instead of animals. But then, making the impossible distinction between them kept him awake many a night. He brushed rain from weary eyes and holstered the Sharps in a leather sling hanging from his saddle. Tendons quivered beneath Smokey's drenched hide.

"Appreciate the warning, boy," he murmured into the horse's neck. "I could've had a lot bigger problem."

Brodie led the Appaloosa toward woodland cover.

Squatting, he rolled up his sleeve, where the cat had ripped a jagged gash. He'd bled worse on occasion. The knot in a faded red bandanna took the devil of a time to loosen one-handed. He pressed it tightly to the wound. An experienced eye said dark would fall quickly.

"We'll pass the night here, Smokey. Good a place as any."

His companion had horse sense. Soft nickering followed by three nods of his head confirmed that. Smokey earned the name from the smattering of white that spotted charcoal flanks, giving his coat a hazy appearance. A trail rider could ask for no finer piece of horseflesh. He wound the neckerchief tight around his arm, cinching it with his teeth and fingers before giving the horse a final pat.

At least the rain showed slight promise of letting up. He gathered drier firewood and buried leaves that would catch. With the warmth of a fire going, he addressed a rumbling belly.

"Those steaks Lil cooks would beat coffee and beans all to hell." The horse feasted on a patch of lush rye grass, ignoring the chatter. "Appears you've already found your supper."

The cold biscuits Etta pushed on him and a heated can of beans silenced his growls. He leaned back on the bedroll with a steaming cup of brew. Though September and October days in east Texas heated up, a man had to cozy up to a fire come sundown.

This night's moist air carried an extra chill.

His arm's sting dredged up thoughts to sort out. The mountain lion went in the dull gray category—blood, pain, and raw fear. He considered Lady Luck and felt grateful for the sparing.

That road led back to Hawkshaw, who he'd put in the one-of-a-rare-breed pleasurable department.

Hawkshaw. Brodie never knew whether the name was

given, surname, actual, or made up. Not that it made a smidgen of difference. The friend took that ride in the hearse shortly after meeting up with the widow, Mrs. Sugarbaker. He sure missed Hawkshaw. Now that surely went in the gray section, too.

Brodie next mulled over the Blanchards. The downpour had erased any sign, but he knew they'd come this way and he hated all the reasons for knowing why.

Lust for money numbered Ike and Bert's worst sin. Even so, Brodie couldn't overlook the debt he owed to Luther.

But the other two gang members froze his blood.

Reno Darnell and Nat Jude were natural born killers. Both cut their teeth on the infamous Quantrill terrorizing rampage through Missouri and Kansas years earlier, the experience sharply honing their thrill for torture and murder.

His jaw tightened. They shouldn't have taken those little girls. And if they hadn't treated them kindly? He jabbed a long twig into the fire and stared into the flame.

One thing for certain, he'd not return empty-handed.

Laurel's revelations had walloped his sense of honor sideways and crooked. She'd placed a powerful burden on him. In his travels he'd learned of twisted men and their perversions, yet the depth sometimes jarred him. He ground his jaw.

Smokey whinnied softly, the soulful eyes meeting his. The animal pawed at the ground, perhaps conveying similar thoughts, yet Brodie hadn't uttered a word.

"You reading minds now?" The Appaloosa nodded three times. He set down his cup and rose to stroke Smokey's powerful neck.

"We'll get 'em back. Might strew a few dead carcasses over Arkansas. Way I see it, they deserve everything coming to them. The weather taking a turn for the better will make it easier."

With a grim stare into the heavens, he rolled a smoke and lit it. The smoldering tobacco took the edge off most things.

Except his dying brother.

He wondered bleakly if Murphy had made the crossing. He'd not seen many survive a hole that large. And yet? With a final puff he flicked short remains into the embers. Dropping to the bedroll, he lay back, forming a pillow with his hands.

Why in the name of Jericho had he told Laurel he'd not stop her from marrying? Maybe he'd gotten hold of some baneberry. Only that tended to kill a man. On second thought—the sharp spasms piercing his heart suggested the possibility.

"You're mine, Laurel James." He muttered it into the breeze, wishing to climb the highest mountain and shout it for all to hear. "Whoever lays claim to you can't change that."

Conviction had glistened in Laurel's violet gaze when she spoke of changing her life. Though it seemed far-fetched, maybe one *could* go from scarlet lady to house-wife and mother. That she believed it so sincerely held sway over him.

She'd make a fine wife.

Jagged pain enveloped him with that parcel of reality.

Should he return to find Murphy mending, he'd stay not a day longer than necessary. He'd pack up and take himself far from the misery of watching her with someone else—for he'd not go back on his word.

Even if it ripped his heart from its mooring.

But should things swing the opposite?

The half-formed thought settled in ice. He refused to dwell on barren ground. While his brother might present the toughest obstacle, it wasn't the only one standing in the way.

Laurel crimped the edges of the soft dough topping the apple pie. Her mind wandered back to Jefferson's sorry excuse for a doctor. Thank goodness the growing populace had many others from which to choose or they'd get her condolences.

Yesterday's horrible lie to Doc Gates—telling him Murphy had died—brought no remorse. In her estimation he'd left her no choice. Gates's shaking hands could barely help him climb into the saddle, much less aid in the treatment of a critically wounded patient.

She did color a mite at the memory of lifting a few items from the doctor's bag. But necessity justified her crime.

The back door opened and Ollie blew in, blustering like a north wind. "I dropped in on Murphy, and Nora says his color's a tad improved today."

"What wonderful news!" She slipped the pie into the oven. "I questioned whether we were opening the cafe prematurely, but we . . . I need . . . to get a normal routine going again."

"My grandpappy, God bless him, always said, 'Cowards never start and the weak ones die on the way.'" Ollie took an apron from a nail and slipped it on. "Murphy will be fit in no time. He's got the constitution of a mule. It's prudent to get on with the business of living."

Bedecked in a filly apron, the bandy woman appeared like a hurdy-gurdy dancer. Laurel suppressed a giggle.

"What do you think you're doing?"

"If it's any of your never-mind, I'm gonna help get ready for the Sunday noon crowd. The *Nancy Belle* will dock in roughly two hours, and we'd best have enough for Sherman's army."

"I have a large pot of mulligan stew on, pies baking, and fresh bread cooling. Green beans and potatoes simmer on the back and I've cut up six chickens for frying." Laurel untied the apron and lifted the frills over Ollie's head. "There's nothing left to do. I want you to rest."

"Goldarned upstart! You must've kissed the Blarney stone. Since I'm not wanted or appreciated, you'll find me over at the saloon—visiting someone who values my company," she huffed.

"Ha! Wait until Curley knows you better."

The door slammed back, interrupting the exchange. Edgar Lee and Andy Cole ran inside as if a pack of wolves were chasing them.

"Miss Laurel, guess what? Maw says we git to wash your dishes!" The boys hopped around in circles. "Oh, boy!"

"Whoa." Ollie caught each by an arm. "Were you born in a hurricane?"

"Nope. What's that?"

Mrs. Cole followed quite breathless, shifting the baby on her hip. "I apologize. They're excited to help in the cafe."

"No reason in the world for children to be otherwise, Mrs. Cole." Laurel wiped flour off her hands.

"Betsy, please."

"Agreed, if you'll call me Laurel."

"Well, if this don't beat all I'll kiss your foot. Reckon you shore don't need an old woman now."

"Tell Curley I send my regards." Laurel shooed the skinflint toward the sidewalk.

"Where you going, Miz Ollie?" Edgar Lee swiped his face on a sleeve.

"Business, boy." Ollie turned three shades of red. Laurel

wondered how she'd squirm out of explaining the saloon's star attraction. "Uh, I've got some dadgum business to attend too."

"Can we come, too?"

Ollie jerked out her pipe only to stick it back in.

"Edgar Lee, we're here to work, not play." Betsy scowled. "We have a debt to pay off."

Short, bandy legs could move awfully swift when they had reason. She pulled a chair from the work table and tweaked Sissie's fat cheek. The baby giggled.

"Sit down. I'll get the boys started and we'll chat."

"Didn't come to socialize. Where's your broom?"

The thin line of Betsy's mouth promised serious head-butting. Laurel pointed toward the corner. "This isn't necessary."

"Let me be the judge." She sat Sissie on the floor and handed her a rag doll and a string of crude wooden beads. "I heard about the trouble and Mr. Brodie's brother. It's a pure shame."

"Murphy is in a bad way."

Lost in their own world, Edgar Lee and Andy indulged in a playful scuffle.

"Stop it, boys. Remember where you're at." Betsy snatched the broom. "If the young Mr. Yates is anything like Mr. Brodie, he's some kind of man. And I keep thinking of those poor little girls. Those mothers must be sick to death with worry."

"Mrs. Carver and Mrs. Hatcher do indeed have heartbreak. But it'll turn out right as rain in the end, I do believe."

Bitter thoughts turned down a different path. Mary James would not share such a sentiment. That mother still waited for a whisper of news. There had been no Brodie Yates back then to track Will Taft. Sissie's toothy, silly grin got lost in the misty blur.

"Laurel, if someone took my children I'd follow them to kingdom come and make them sorry they ever did."

The threat didn't seem idle or strange. It came from a woman who'd buried a husband beside a river and had the will to press on by herself. Laurel knew Brodie would catch up with the Blanchards, but what then? The odds were stacked against him. Her hand flew to her mouth. She should've insisted on going along. An extra pistol would help. He needed someone.

The Cole brothers continued their roughhousing, but Betsy's stern eye quickly brought them in line.

"Mr. Brodie will make them rue the day, never fear," she said, patting her shoulder. "That man's got plenty of guts."

Manhandling the broom, Betsy stalked into the dining room. Laurel stared, the truth echoing in her mind until it finally stuck.

No one but a fool would accuse Brodie Yates of tucking tail and running, or describe his nature as normal. Bold facts spoke of a man special in every way. Grit and determination wouldn't let him quit. The set of his jaw and the steel in his eyes made him continue when everyone else gave up. *Because he couldn't.* Overwhelming numbers meant the job would take a little longer, that's all. Despite great personal risk he'd find a way to win. That was what separated the rebel from the rest.

"Miss Laurel?" Edgar Lee tugged on her elbow.

Impatience lined the boy's face. She put aside her mulling. "Oh, yes, the dishes. First, though, I want you to roll up your sleeves."

Andy struggled until she took pity and helped. Scrawny arms contrasted with tough, stubborn pride to carry his weight.

Shyness wouldn't let him glance up, although he pressed close enough to crumple the lace on her apron. The warm glow that had swept her the night she met them settled inside. She cherished it. She had a lot of ground to make up.

"You're a baby. I can do mine by myself," Edgar Lee goaded.

"No, I'm not."

"I hate to burst your bubble, Edgar Lee, but you didn't do any better." Laurel wouldn't tolerate hateful snubs in her kitchen. "We all do the best we can and don't have to apologize for anything less than what we're capable of."

"I'm sorry, Andy."

"That's more like it."

She adjusted his handiwork and grabbed a block of lye soap. Hot water from the stove mixed with cold from the pump to ensure that sensitive skin could tolerate it. Then she pulled a bench up to the counter for the helpers. Both wasted no time diving in elbow deep.

Laurel found keeping an eye on Sissie exhausting work. The child not only located every vegetable peel, dirty knothole, and tiniest insect imaginable, but tasted each treat.

"I think Mr. Brodie must be awful brave." Edgar Lee's startling statement came from out of the blue.

Determined to dislodge a small pebble from Sissie's mouth, Laurel glanced up at the freckled face. Edgar Lee toted far too much concern for a mere lad. She regretted him overhearing the conversation. The little one already took on more than any child should.

Teeth suddenly clamped onto her finger added thoughts of an agonizing variety.

"Mr. Brodie is indeed very courageous, Edgar Lee." Laurel grimaced as she extracted the throbbing digit, leaving the pebble inside. Babies' teeth were razor sharp.

"Those mean ol' bandits might kill him, though."

The simple fear made her quake. Chills scurried through, seeking a hiding place.

"He would never allow that. Let's find something a bit more cheery to discuss."

"M-M-Mr. Brodie'll shoot 'em d-d-dead," Andy stammered, his cheeks turning an angry, ruddy hue. "H-he's f-f-fast."

"When I get big I'm gonna be jus' like Mr. Brodie. I'm gonna own me a shooting iron and get rid of all the bad people." The older brother stuck out a finger covered with soap suds and formed the barrel of a weapon. "Pow, pow, pow!"

Betsy stepped through the door. "Stop that this instant, you hear? Your paw gave his life so you kids could grow up in a better world than he did. Over my dead body will I see you turn into a no-account, good-for-nothing gun hand."

"Sorry, Maw." Edgar Lee ducked his head.

"Heed what I said. I don't want to hear that kind of foolishness." She lifted Sissie from the floor.

To Laurel's amazement, Betsy stuck a finger into the child's mouth and plucked out the pebble. The motion was quick, smooth, and accomplished with no effort. Laurel had so much to learn.

"You boys get busy with those dishes, and while you're at it, scrub your minds of shootin' and killin' outlaws and such."

"Yes, Maw."

Downcast eyes stifled Laurel's spirit. She hated to see children who had no time for playing or believing.

"They meant no harm, Betsy," she murmured, hoping curious ears wouldn't hear her. "It appears Brodie Yates found a couple of young champions."

"Those two worship the ground that man walks on. I try to explain he's only human." Betsy sighed, pushing back a strand of streaked hair. "But they won't hear of it."

"Children need a hero, plain and simple. Adults, too. It's nothing to shame out of them."

"But Mr. Brodie won't fly up to heaven like Paw did, will he?" Edgar Lee's voice held thick tears. "He won't, will he, Miss Laurel?"

She fought back wetness. How could one expert marksman survive the barrage of gunfire of five desperate bushwhackers?

"No, dear. Of course not. He'll be back with nary a scratch. We must hold that dearly in our hearts."

The murdering Blanchards wouldn't dare snuff out the vitality that colored her world. Besides . . . Brodie hadn't survived these last years without learning a trick or two. Hopefully, this bunch would prove no match.

The scoundrel who made her pulse pound with excitement most definitely loomed larger than life.

Even if he didn't want to fight for her.

Even if he gave her up to his brother.

And even if he never again enclosed her in the circle of his arms and whispered fanciful words of moon mist and passion.

A part of him would always and forever remain hers.

Chapter Fourteen

"Are your staples running short, Betsy?" Laurel wiped her hands on the apron and stepped quickly to the pie safe.

Pausing in the doorway with her brood, Mrs. Cole's stark features stiffened. Her head snapped around. "We got plenty."

The brusque tone stung. And yet she admired the woman's desperation to owe no one anything.

Tired lines etched fear too deeply imbedded to disguise—something put there by hard times, uncertainty, and doubts that one more trial or setback would do her in. Betsy couldn't see that Laurel shared the same worries.

Some things a body would never admit to a living soul.

Today, Betsy had scrubbed the entire place from stem to stern. In addition, she made Edgar Lee and Andy wash every dish in sight and inspected them afterward.

"Words of gratitude come cheap for the hours of toil. You must at least accept a custard pie for your services."

The boys' eyes lit up. "Can we, Maw? Please?"

"No, and that's final. We'll return tomorrow to complete

our bargain, then me and the children head for Fort Richardson."

Edgar Lee and Andy's crestfallen glances spread bleakness.

The loss of the steely-spined woman and her loving children would leave Laurel bereft. The distraction eased the rigors of waiting for Murphy to gain consciousness and Brodie's return.

Each brother hugged her in turn.

"See ya tomorrow. Don't wash any dishes 'til we get here, 'cause that's our job, ain't it, Andy?"

The smaller version nodded. "I-i-it's fun. W-we like it."

"But I 'spect we won't be mad if you wash just a few."

Laurel smiled. Despite pretending to be men, they couldn't hide the children inside. She shut the door behind them.

"We're gonna miss them younguns." Ollie was seated at the table sharpening kitchen knives on a long razor strop. "Though they can ask more questions than anyone has answers for."

"Made you hobble-tongued, did they?" Laurel hung her apron on the nail, thankful lunchtime had come and gone. She dropped into a chair, propping up her feet. A record number of customers had passed through the cafe's doors that day. Their reputation grew by leaps and bounds. Thank heavens Betsy had pitched in.

"I reckon that about says it." Ollie filled the bowl of the pipe, tamped it down, and lit it. "Didn't exactly know how to explain the business a lady has with a gentleman."

"Guess you could've called it monkey business."

Ollie grumbled in her throat. "Making light of an old woman's pleasures, are you?"

A giggle slipped out.

"Does my heart good to hear you laugh. You faced mighty hard times of late, what with Yates threatening to spill the beans and Murphy getting shot. It's enough to drive you daffy."

"I haven't been altogether truthful about something."

The knife Ollie honed to a sharp blade halted in midair. "Spit it out. Let the hide go with the tallow."

"Remember when you found Brodie and me in the garden?"

"I wanted to smash his face for making you cry." Ollie's gaze narrowed. "I also recall how your hair was all undone."

She'd wondered when Ollie would mention that. She passed over the remark, struggling to keep a tremble from spilling into the words. The ache made it nigh impossible.

"Brodie no longer fights Murphy and my wedding plans." Taking deep breaths, she added, "He even gave his blessing."

Ollie resumed the slapping motion of the knife on the strop. "Why the long face, pray tell?"

Had she not blinked several times, hovering tears would've spilled. "I can't marry Murphy. I don't love him—not proper, the way a wife should a husband."

"I wouldn't have much call to know about them things, me being a spinster and all, but I reckon tender feelings grow on a body if you give 'em half a chance."

A lump that refused to budge reduced Laurel's declaration to a raspy whisper. "And should I love someone else?"

"Son of a blue jacket, I figured something like that! You gotta get up mighty early in the morn to fool one of us b'Dams."

"Horsefeathers. You made up that name after a half-deaf Missourian mistook Burrdan as b'Dam."

"Shore, but who's to dispute it ain't real?" Ollie gave her

a one-eyed squint. "So, does Brodie's change of heart mean he's not reading from the same hymn book you are?"

The harsh reality hit her. He had offered her to another after kissing her silly!

"Moon mist my eye!"

"What in God's name is that crazy babbling?"

The flowery words and phrases meant nothing to the rogue. They'd only suited a purpose that she had yet to determine.

"Nothing. Getting back to the change of heart: It merely confirms the gentleman harbors no sentiment for me. And I've been studious in keeping any hint of my affections from him."

She crossed her fingers and hoped so. That finely cocked eyebrow was something she cared not to see.

"Son of a blue jacket! Everyone'd be better off if I blast that man with my forty-four the minute he steps back into town."

Except her . . . and the rebel gentleman, of course.

Not one to waste words in idle chatter, Nora's quiet presence comforted. The questions cluttering Laurel's head required concentration. Yet, somehow logic skittered worse than rambunctious children.

This yanking back and forth kept her reeling. She was much too old for such games.

Stellar didn't begin to describe Brodie's record. Lord knew she'd invested a lifetime of emotion since they met. The latest round only heaped fresh pain atop the old. Although to his credit, he had gone after those little girls. No matter what else, she had reason to owe him for that.

When he returned she'd badger him regarding his intentions.

Or none? That last left a bitter taste on her tongue.

A stone Nora used to crush dried plants scraped against a hollowed out piece of granite. The woman ground them into fine powder exactly the way her forebearers had.

Laurel recognized jimsonweed, sagebrush, wild ginger, and sassafras leaves. The roots and bark neatly piled to the side escaped her, yet she knew Nora could tell each and their usage.

Seated beside Murphy's bed, Laurel met mysterious dark eyes, wondering what thoughts filled Nora's head. Did she share her tepee with a man? Or have babies?

Murphy's hand twitched inside hers. A slight pressure assured the unconscious man of her presence.

Strange how, now that she knew which path not to take, she had to sit silently and wait for the man to wake up. His reaction crossed her mind. For certain he'd be disappointed and perhaps angry. But crushed? She prayed not.

"Nora, how long do you think he'll slumber like this?"

"Only the Great One knows. Many moons perhaps." Nora shrugged. "I do not guess. Why ask a foolish thing?"

"I have something of great importance to tell him."

Irritation crossed high cheekbones. "This thing—is it important to the man or to you?"

Laurel's face grew hot. Poor Murphy fought for every breath, yet her need to correct a bad mistake became selfishly paramount. She'd jilt a gentle, kind man to justify ill-fated love for a rebel who seemed more inclined to think her a bothersome fly and would move on when the urge struck.

"It's vital only to me." Shame kept her reply low. "I've deeply wronged Murphy and desire to fix it."

"Then find forgiveness in your heart, not in the eyes of a sick man. It will wait. All things come in time."

Truth of the ages. And even should he regain his senses

this second, she'd have to continue with a pretense. No telling when he'd grow strong enough to hear what she had to say.

She was stuck in a lie.

Brodie slid from horseback to view a bloodstained boulder where someone had rested. Once bright red, the tacky secretion had begun to brown. With the rain stopping, the trail yielded other drops and smudges, none more fresh than this.

Pray to God it hadn't come from one of those girls.

"The bleeding's worsening, Smokey." Whomever it belonged to could die soon.

The Appaloosa snorted and pawed the ground.

"I swear, if I didn't have so much time and effort invested, I'd turn you out to pasture for being smart-assed." He kept his voice low, grabbed the saddle horn, and swung up.

"Take that strawberry roan I had. Pearly Gates was one hell of a horse. Unlike you, he knew his place." Smokey bent his neck to shoot him a baleful look. "Asked or otherwise, Pearly Gates never voiced an opinion.

"That roan did have one fault, I reckon. He fancied himself a lady-killer. Tried to mount every mare he came near."

The Appaloosa broke into a canter.

"No need to go getting jealous. Pearly Gates met his end when a posse ran us into the Black Hills of Dakota territory."

Brodie draped the reins over an arm while he rolled a smoke. He recalled a day he'd never forget and the horse that had never known his limits. Pearly Gates thought he could do anything, even jump that canyon to escape Blue Bellies. They didn't make it. Gravity carried them into the river below. The force broke the animal's legs and he had to shoot the roan that'd seen him through the war. The memory sliced through his chest as if it'd happened days ago. How fortunate to own two horses whose hearts were bigger than the universe.

He smoothed Smokey's withers. "I've been mighty blessed and that's a fact. Couldn't ask for more."

Except for Lil's love.

And Murphy had that. She'd never be his.

Brodie wondered if his brother drew breath. The bond tying them couldn't be severed, not by Laurel, not by anything. He wouldn't fight his brother. He brought Smokey to a standstill and looked up through the pine trees into a patch of blue sky.

"It's been a long while," he began reverently, "and you may have your ears closed to the likes of my kind, but I'm asking a favor. That is, if you've a mind to listen."

He took a deep breath. "I'm willing to strike a bargain. You let my brother live . . . and I'll forget Laurel."

Something rustled the scrub brush. He jerked around, his palm automatically sliding to the revolver.

"Morning, Ollie." Jake finished winding the barber pole in front of the shop. "Care to come sit a spell?"

Ollie skirted mud puddles left by a morning shower and took one of several chairs where she could take in the goings on. Despite loathing the barber, she took advantage of every opportunity to needle him. It provided untold entertainment.

"Jake, how's the world treatin' you?"

"Can't complain."

Thumbs stuck inside his galluses, Jake leaned back. From all appearances, his hair, slicked and parted down the middle, might've gotten a dousing in the lard bucket. The mustache hadn't escaped a dipping either. Something had stiffened it into a bow. The twirled-up ends resembled hairy buggy springs. Ollie disguised laughter behind a cough.

"I've got some tonic sure to cure that," he offered.

"Stuff your remedies into your mustache, you old coot, 'cause I ain't taking your god-awful skunk tonic."

"Just being helpful. Why do you insist on smoking that nasty pipe anyway? It's likely what's making you cough."

She sucked in smoke and blew into his face. "I could ask why you hafta use lard for pomade, but I reckon you're an expert on those things, you being in the barbering profession and all."

"Do you figure Yates caught up with the Blanchard gang?"

"Can't speculate. But those murdering bushwhackers will wish to God he hadn't when he gets done with 'em." She spied Jeb Prater hobbling from the stage depot on crutches. "Bet Jeb's regretting his smart mouth."

"Wonder if the boy's leaving soon. You know, I still can't figure why Yates gets so riled. Take Martin: Black is black and white is white. No changing it."

"I ain't gonna waste breath explaining to an ignoramus who's too goldarned stupid. Girls are girls and boys are boys—different but the same. That's all I'm saying on the subject."

Ollie grinned when Florence Kempshaw strolled hell bent for them. Everyone in town knew the vinegary-tongued busybody had set her cap for Jake, although personally she had no idea what Florence would want with the greasy-haired bag of bones.

"Thank goodness she left me alone." Jake relaxed his grip on the chair when Florence veered into the office of Thomas Hutson, attorney at law. He swatted a fly from his mustache. "Appears the old biddy found someone else to gripe at."

Linda Broday

"I swear, you're as charitable as a preacher in a hurdy-gurdy house. If you'd loosen up a mite and sweet-talk her, she might not be so plumb soured on life."

"No one has that many words in their vocabulary. Besides, I'd rather spend 'em on you, Ollie b'Dam."

She wished to tell Jake he could kiss her rear end if he washed his face first. Instead she planted a seed to watch what grew. "Reckon you haven't heard: I'm spoken for."

"You don't say. And who would that be?"

"Curley Madison."

"Of the Dry Gulch Saloon?"

She nodded with delight. "The one and only."

"What would a prosperous gent want with an old sourdough biscuit-eater?"

"Why, you!" Ollie kicked the nearest shin bone.

"Ow! I won't be able to stand up to cut hair."

"I hope you cain't. Teach you to mend your nasty ways."

"Don't know why you get the cream of the crop and I'm left with old biddies."

"I rest my case. With your whiny jabber, you're lucky to attract curdled milk."

Ollie spied Betsy Cole and her tow-heads heading up the street. The woman carried the baby on one hip, struggling to keep up with the boys, who raced in front.

"Howdy, Miss Ollie," Edgar Lee hollered.

"Morning, boys."

"What're ya doing, Miss Ollie?"

"Mildew-ing." She cackled when Edgar Lee's hold slipped on the toad he held and it leaped onto Jake's lap.

"Good God, what the hell!" The barber jumped to his feet. "Don't you know those things cause warts?"

"N-n-not if you don't kiss 'em," Andy said.

"You ain't a gonna do that, are you, Jake? Come to think on it, might be more exciting than Florence."

"Are you the town hair-cutter? Why is your hair so wet?"

"I happen to be the barber, young man. And dentist. Have any teeth that needs pulling?"

Edgar Lee and Andy began backing up, their eyes big as dollars.

"Boys, he's harmless. Jake, meet the best question-asking, ring-tailed tooters in the whole dadgum state."

Betsy arrived, completely winded.

"Mrs. Cole, have a sit down. You don't look so good."

"No time to waste." Betsy brushed back a lock of hair from her eyes. "We got work to do. Come along, boys."

"Aw, Maw, cain't we stay a while?"

"We didn't come to jaw. We came to work."

Edgar Lee's shoulders hunched with dejection. A twinge of sadness swept Ollie. The tykes hungered for little boy things. They were too young to be saddled with such adult burdens.

"You mind your maw and I'll tell you a secret place to catch crawdads."

Their faces lit up before they trudged after their mother.

A dark horse and rider emerged from the woods just then, capturing Ollie's attention. The saunter down the street made her heart shift into a frantic beat.

"Who in thunder do you suppose that is, Jake?"

"Sure hope he's not looking for a shave."

She shuddered, as if someone stomped across her grave. The stranger sat cocky, dressed head to toe in black, whispering a warning too loud to ignore.

Eighteen hands tall if the gelding stood an inch, he high-stepped past lumbering wagons and the bustle of mid-morning business. The shiny coat glistened, matching the funerary black the man wore. They halted across the street. She didn't notice the gray beast, a mix of wolf and dog, until horse and rider came to a standstill. The lean animal bared its fangs at Ollie and Jake, a growl rumbling in its throat.

Ollie gripped her hands tightly, giving silent thanks for the closed sign swinging on the cafe. Coupled with the boarded window the Blanchard gang had shot out, maybe he'd think it vacant. She could hope to God he moved on before he found out different.

The stranger's profile was all she'd seen until then. When he favored her with a frontal stare, Ollie couldn't move past the coldness freezing her breath in its tracks.

A scar, more terrifying than any she'd ever seen, ran diagonally from his jaw line across one eye, vanishing under the brim of his hat. Her mouth went slack. The pipe clattered unheeded onto the sidewalk.

"Dog . . . stay." The order sprang from a guttural voice.

Though he was a stranger, he brought the familiarity of his kind. Frost coated Ollie's breath.

Son of a blue devil!

Whatever name the stranger bore, it would start with a capital *D* for deadly.

Chapter Fifteen

Laurel peeked from a crack in the door for a glimpse of the death angel, as Ollie called him, who'd instilled such terror. The runty benefactress provided explicit detail of the newcomer, who now sat in the cafe dining room with the wolf-dog at his feet.

Spit and thunder! She saw nothing except his backside.

"What're ya looking at, Miz Laurel?"

She jumped a foot at Edgar Lee's twang beside her. The door banged into her forehead with its quick release.

"A man—nothing but a man." Thank goodness for roomy pockets to hide trembling hands.

"Are you skeered of him?"

"For pity's sake, I would hope not." *Liar, liar, pants on fire.* Grim Reaper fit the creepy man in dismal trappings, even down to the black hat. And according to Ollie, he rode a horse darker than midnight.

"If he hurts you, I'll get Paw's musket and kill him. I'd be real mad if anyone made you dead."

Another David to meet Goliath. Meager kindness had earned such devotion. Laurel's chest tightened. Just when speech appeared possible, Andy rushed to throw his arms around her waist. Tears sparkled on the shy brother's cheeks.

"You know what? You're brave little soldiers to take up for me. I think I'd be really angry if someone hurt you, too. That man is harmless. Don't worry your heads. And remember how your maw feels about shooting." She ruffled the towheads, grateful Betsy had found a spot on the upstairs banister to wipe.

Edgar Lee solemnly nodded. "But I'm a man now, and men hafta stand up for their fam'ly no matter how skeered they are."

To think of her as kin opened raw sores. She'd not seen her family in ages, nor had much chance of it.

"There's no need to take on so. It'll be right as rain."

Laurel hated the hollow sound in her voice. Ollie had suffered another spell after her encounter with the death angel and had to lie down. It took a lot of persuading to get the woman to take a buggy ride with Curley for a leisurely afternoon. Laurel merely wished waiting on the stranger befell someone else's lot.

"I had best go see what he wants, I suppose."

The sturdy kid leather shoes seemed fashioned of lead as she wound toward her unlucky lot. The dog rumbled low, the back of its neck bristling. She drew back in alarm.

"Dog! Quiet or I'll carve out your gullet."

Laurel put the table between herself and the beast. The man's glance froze her blood. Ollie hadn't embellished the menacing appearance or disposition. It took effort to unglue her tongue.

"I'll kindly ask you to leave your animal outside or vacate the premises."

"He stays."

Not a soul to help besides the boys. She stood her ground and met his stare, determined not to shrink into the woodwork.

"I truly can't allow . . ."

The bell over the door jangled, to her relief. Lars Frederiksen, the burly steamboat captain of the *Mystic Queen*, entered with four of his crewmen. Bolstered, she eyed the disrupter's long Colt Dragoon.

"So be it for now, but I won't have that dog running off business. Furthermore, we uphold a policy of no firearms. I insist you respect the sign and leave it on the front counter."

"Who's going to make ol' Zeke Vallens if he don't? You oughta grow some before you go ordering folks around."

Captain Frederiksen flexed beefy fists and paused before taking a seat. "The gentleman causing trouble, Miss Laurel?"

Vallens glared but handed over the weapon.

"Thank you, Captain, but everything is under control."

She placed the Colt in the box up front and returned.

"Monday's special is pot roast."

"That all you got?"

"We also offer mulligan stew and beef steak."

Pray to heaven he didn't want overmuch of any. Their meat stock had dwindled to nothing since the expected shipment was five days late. Perhaps Lars had brought it on the *Queen*.

"Two of those steaks, and don't take all day."

"Do you wish those raw or cooked, sir?"

Nothing surprised her. The question seemed legitimate.

The wolf dog sprang to all fours. Laurel gave a horrified shriek, and the riverboat crew got to their feet.

"Damn you, I said shut up. You gonna mind me, dog?

You can't tear into girlie here before she feeds us. Now lay the hell down." He grabbed a handful of the bristling neck and forced the dog to the floor. That it didn't sink powerful jaws around the arm surprised Laurel. "Cooked will suit us."

Thankful that the man called Vallens had a bit of control over the animal, she hastened to the others.

"Say the word and me and the boys will roust them out. It would be pure pleasure." Lars flashed daggers at the newcomer.

"I appreciate that." To get sideways with the man would only bring more grief to heap on top of what she already had.

"You change your mind, just nod." Lars winked.

"Hopefully your cargo consists of meat for the cafe?"

"Nope. Sorry."

Laurel took their request and barely reached the swinging portal to the kitchen when more customers strolled in. Surely Vallens would behave in a packed house.

Smokey's ears perked up at the soft moan. Brodie slowly lifted the hat and hung it on the saddle horn. It wouldn't do for the noisy rattles to announce him. He slid the forty-four from the holster, easing to the ground.

The moan came from his right. A cautious turn around a stand of cedars gave a glimpse of two men. One lay next to a trickling creek. The other knelt beside him.

"Get your hands up slow and easy."

Brodie found instant recognition in the face when he turned. "What are you doing, Ike?"

"My brother's hurt real bad."

His insides tightened into a hard ball. "Which one?"

"It's Luther." Ike's voice trembled.

Damn the luck!

"Toss your pistol into the creek and don't try anything."

"Ain't got no bullets in it, Shenandoah."

"Throw it in anyway—along with Luther's." The weapons splashed and sank to the bottom. Brodie moved closer.

"He's dying. Some fool man in Redemption gut-shot him."

"That fool was *my* brother."

"If we'd knowed that was your town, we'd never have gone anywhere near it. We respect another man's territory."

"It doesn't belong to me." Except for his name and the clothes on his back, Brodie owned nothing. He hated the brittle, dry feel to his insides. Everything he desired had shriveled. "My brother's dying, too, compliments of your gang. I'd call that brother for brother."

Keeping his six iron on Ike, Brodie knelt by Luther. Blood soaked the clothing until it bore no sign of the original color.

"Luther, it's me . . . Shenandoah."

The old friend tried to moisten his dry lips. "Them's angels singing. Sweetest music I ever heard. You hear it?"

Smokey nickering softly was all Brodie could distinguish.

"Ike, get the canteen from my saddlebag." He holstered the Colt, lifting Luther's head. Ike uncorked the tin vessel and passed it. Brodie trickled some onto the man's tongue.

"Paw, is that you?" A thin stream of red oozed from the sides of his mouth. Luther's eyes stared unseeingly. "Paw, I done some terrible bad things."

Brodie's gut clenched fighter.

"He's out of his head," Ike whispered.

No harm in granting a dying man's wish that he saw. "It's all right, son. You can make amends."

"No time, Paw." Sobs racked the body. "I didn't mean to do 'em, honest. I tried to be good like you and Maw taught me."

"You did your best and that's what counts. Your maw and me are proud of our boy."

"I didn't let you down? You're not ashamed?"

Wetness blurred the familiar face until Brodie no longer made it out.

"Close your eyes now and rest. Let the angels carry you home."

Luther's lids drifted peacefully shut. A shudder, a whoosh of air, and the body sagged limp in his arms. The ache created a hole unlike any Brodie had known since the war. He well imagined the scene repeated when he returned to Redemption.

Damn destiny, damn fate, and damn his sorry timing!

"Reckon I'll carry him on back to Missouri." Ike wiped his nose on a shirtsleeve. "Bury him next to Maw and Paw."

"He'd appreciate that, I imagine."

Together they tied Luther across Ike's horse. Brodie didn't speak until they finished.

"The girls . . . what happened to those little girls, Ike?"

"Reno and Nat have 'em." The middle Blanchard brother brushed a hand across his eyes. "Bert tried to talk some sense into 'em, but they wouldn't listen. They said they're keeping 'em in case of a posse showing up."

Two murdering desperadoes with nothing to lose. His jaw clenched. "They'll have hell to pay if they harm either."

Ike jerked back. "You're a man of your word, Shenandoah. Thank God it's them and not me who'll be on the receiving end of your justice."

"Are you saying they've already hurt them?"

"Well, I ain't exactly saying that in particular, but they ain't been none too gentle either. They're alive, though, or leastways they were when they dumped Luther." A hard glitter shone in Ike's eyes. "Put a bullet for me and my brother, will you?"

Brodie snatched his hat from the horn and jammed it on his head. The rattles' vibration added deadly assurance. Nat and Reno's next stop was the hereafter—and he'd be sure to drag out their departure. First, they'd pay.

"Where are they going?" Hard flint layered the question.

"Arkansas. Said they'd lay low for a while."

Smokey stood motionless while Brodie put a foot in the stirrup and pulled himself up. He spared no parting word or backward glance at the friend to whom he owed his life.

Laurel's stomach knotted as she seared the steaks brown. Dishing up plates of roast and bowls of stew kept her from stealing the nearest horse and running.

Called himself Zeke Vallens, did he?

Keeping busy didn't prevent questions from circling like vultures. Vallens could work for Will Taft. The flesh-den owner might have hired the man to track her and Ollie. If so, he'd come a long way for nothing. Her lips tightened.

"What's wrong, Laurel?" Betsy touched her shoulder.

"I'm fine." *Except that I'm lousy, I've got rotten luck, and I wish Brodie was back.*

Brodie would protect her if for no other reason than, heaven forbid, to make sure she married his brother.

"Beggin' your pardon, a white face disputes that. Got anything to do with the man in the other room? I almost choked when he gave a plateful of meat to that mean ol' dog."

"I appreciate you taking that to him, Betsy. I have a premonition he's bent on making our lives miserable."

"Ain't asking, mind you, but I wondered if you knew him."

"I can happily state I've never had the misfortune."

"A body would be well off to avoid him." Betsy gazed sadly out the back door, where the children waited. "I hate to run off with him sittin' there. Don't see I have much choice in the matter. We roll at dawn. Fort Richardson is a long ways."

Tears lurked behind Laurel's eyelids. "I'll miss you."

"Reckon you've been as good a friend as I've ever had. But it's time to get on with things." Betsy swung open the door.

"Will you stop by to let me say good-bye?"

Betsy gave her a long stare. "I'd like that."

After she left, Laurel glanced around the spotless kitchen. A lick and a promise was all she'd ever had a second to spare. She glowered at the dining room entrance. She'd rather rake embers in hell and feed the furnace than face Vallens again.

But she'd delayed it long enough. No one else occupied the tables. Vallens sat with both feet propped on a chair like the king of his castle. The wolf dog warily eyed the dining room, without uttering a sound.

"Empty plates generally indicate a good sign." She prayed he'd not tarry.

"Is that pie I smell?"

"Rhubarb." Her heart sank.

"I'll take some. Got a hankering for something sweet."

Shivers chased up her spine when his gaze swept her body from head to toe. She almost lost her grip on the plate. The statement pertained to more than pie, and she'd seen that leer in men's eyes far too often to play innocent. His eyes followed each twitch, the rise and fall of her steps on her return. Vallens removed his feet from the chair. The beast bared its teeth.

"Oblige me with your company, girlie."

The sharp order split the air like a thin piece of rawhide. Laurel edged her hand beneath the apron into a pocket to grip the knife she'd hidden. Whether this black-clothed man bore deadly intent or not, she'd prove a worthy adversary. A clenched jaw and jutting chin should relay that.

"Who do you think you are? You can't come in here and treat people as though we're slaves to your bidding. We have laws here. Change your tune or I'll get the sheriff."

"Be sorta hard, seeing as how he's stiff as a two-by-four and six feet under."

Laurel's heart pounded. The strange man knew too much.

Vallens took a bite and chewed. "You make this?"

She nodded.

"Didn't hear you, girl. Cat got your tongue?"

"I made it." The words came through stiff lips.

"Pretty good, if I do say so. You're too comely to waste those talents on cooking. You appear more suited to parlor houses and such. You have a man?"

Vallens stared through the scarred eye. She'd not run and give him pleasure. It took great effort to stand her ground.

"It's none of your affair. I have a kitchen to ready before the supper hour." She pivoted, dismissing him.

The dog uncoiled with killer instincts. She became a statue with labored breath.

"Quiet, dog. Lay!" The animal stretched beside his master's boots. Every muscle remained tense. "The lady ain't going nowhere less'n I say," Vallens added softly.

"State what you came for, because I have things to do." She eased the knife from her pocket, hiding it beneath the apron.

"All in good time, dearie. Ol' Zeke ain't in any hurry." Vallens finished the last bite. He laid down his fork, wiping his mouth on the back of his hand. "Mighty good. What pleasures can a traveler find around these parts?"

Laurel wanted to reveal their favorite pastime was feeding sinister men like him to the 'gators. But she doubted even those creatures, who fed off the most unsavory, would find Vallens a tasty morsel.

"The business of eking out a daily living keeps us far too busy for other forms of entertainment."

"Pray tell, to what business do you refer?"

Vallens' coarse voice sliced into her chest and plucked her heart from its hiding place. He hinted at lurid things.

Ollie's sudden entrance saved her a reply. "There you are, Laurel. I see . . ."

The woman pulled up short, swallowing hard. Clearly, this man disturbed Ollie more than anyone. When Laurel's gaze drifted from the dear face, she spied a holster slung around the petite hips and the butt of a forty-four. The sight shook her.

"I didn't think to have customers so long past the lunch hour." Ollie's short steps suggested someone who dodged a field littered with dynamite and blasting powder.

"The gentleman is about to leave."

"You're interrupting a nice chat. Not wise for a body to do that. Could prove unhealthy."

"Anything pertaining to Laurel pertains to me as well."

"You're a little on the squatty side to speak so bold."

All four feet nine inches of the woman drew up. "I might be the one to teach an ugly swamp rat some manners." Ollie glared. "Or I might be the man on the moon. And I damn sure might be the one to answer to next time you disrespect my girl."

Vallens seemed taken aback. "You her maw?"

172

"You could goldarned sure say that."

"Then I reckon we got things straight, old woman." Vallens thrust two fingers into a vest pocket. Ollie deftly caught the silver dollar he pitched in midair. "For the meal. We'll cross paths again."

Low rumbling came from the dog when his master stood.

"You'd best count on it."

Vallens's fleeting grin exposed an evil heart. "For less'n a spit in the eye I'd sic Dog on you. Teach you to leave a man be when he has dealings with a lady."

Ollie whipped out the revolver, brandishing it. "Get out or I'll see what improvement a bullet between your eyes makes."

Vallens held up both hands. "Just leaving."

"Good choice."

The vermin paused to throw Laurel a cracked stare. "A pleasure, ma'am. Let me know when you get tired of wearing your fingers to the bone here. There's easier ways . . . but then, I suspect you already know that."

Chapter Sixteen

"I oughta pepper that smug rear end for such a remark!"

Despite the sort of dark gloom that had visited frequently back in St. Louis, Laurel couldn't help noticing how Ollie waited until Vallens collected his pistol and left before voicing her latest threat. Although she had said plenty to his face.

"Taft sent him. Otherwise, why say what he did?"

The gleam in Vallens's eye left no room for coincidence.

"Aw, the walleyed polecat was just trying to rattle you. Honey, he'd have snatched you in a second and been halfway back to Missouri if Will Taft employed him."

"The man may work for the highest bidder and wants to see if we'll up the ante."

"Don't go borrowing trouble. Girl, let's go see Murphy before the supper hour. Nora might appreciate company."

Afternoon sun filtered through the mossy cypress, creating lacy shadows that swayed in the breeze. Welcome warmth dispelled the chills the disfigured visitor had left. The stroll to the trim clapboard house at the end of State Street provided for a bit of teasing.

"Per chance could I blame Curley for your rosy glow? You came back bursting with happiness until Vallens ruined it."

"Don't have any idea what you're gabbing about."

"Stop playing coy. Finding the man of your dreams is nothing to be ashamed of."

Except if you were bound to the man's brother. Guilt twisted Laurel's stomach. Sometimes the more she tried to forget things, the more vivid they grew.

That low, lazy drawl.

The unpretentious scuffle of his boots on the floor.

The hiss of snake rattles on a well-worn felt hat.

Most of all, though, she remembered the storm of flutters he unleashed from the barest touch of his breath mingling with hers or the quirk of his mouth in a crooked smile.

"Ain't ashamed of a blooming thing. I just ain't one to kiss and tell."

"Ollie, how long do you suppose before Brodie returns?"

The petite woman came to a standstill, staring long and hard. "You're pining for him, ain't you?"

Laurel developed a sudden fixation on the condition of her broken nails. "No crime in wondering."

A sidelong glance said she didn't fool Ollie, who divined each thought that popped into her head before she even had it.

They climbed the steps and crossed the verandah.

"I reckon Yates should be back in four, maybe five days with luck," Ollie said.

A lifetime when the death angel had taken up squatter's rights in the hotel. Laurel quaked, lifting the brass knocker.

"My land, don't stand there like common folk. Come on in." Etta greeted them, taking Laurel's shawl.

"How's Murphy today?"

"Doin' right smart. That Nora's of a mind he'll come around soon. Ain't that something?"

"I'll be my mama's stepchild! See? I told you, girl."

"It's a miracle." She kissed Etta's cheek.

"Mr. Brodie's gonna be tickled to death when he gets back, all right. That's a fact, sure 'nuff."

A much lighter step carried Laurel to the bedroom. Though Murphy lay unmoving, a more natural color had replaced his skin's ghastly pallor.

Nora met her questioning gaze. "It is good."

"I'm here, Murphy. Do you hear me?" She squeezed his hand gently. "I'm waiting for you. I've much to say."

Amazement almost knocked her over when he moved his fingers. "Did you see that?"

"He come from the land of sleep. Talk to him. Your voice help guide him through the fog."

"We've been so worried. You have no idea how sick you've been. Brodie went after the gang who shot you." Laurel touched the angled jaw sporting beard growth.

Murphy's eyes fluttered, struggling, as if weighted down. Seconds stretched. Her breath held suspended. Finally they lifted and he stared into her face. The wan smile was beautiful to behold. She leaned to press her lips to a cool forehead.

"I knew you could do it," she whispered. "You've come back to us. You're going to make it. Thank God."

The effort was too much. After a brief instant, he drifted back to the dreamland from whence he had come. He'd passed through the shadow of death and returned.

With luck, Brodie might not have a burial to cope with.

. . . Unless the black-clothed stranger and his wolf went to work.

Weary clear to his soul, Brodie reined Smokey to a halt. They'd ridden for hours after Ike told of Darcy and Willa's harsh treatment. Rosy dawn broke overhead when he slid the Winchester from its sling and dropped to the ground. Inching through a tangle of wood fern, Virginia creeper, and red foliage of yaupon, he pushed aside thick clumps of switch cane. A shanty stood in a clearing amid the Arkansas woods.

Memory hadn't failed. He'd come to the right place.

A crow's shrill caw-caw broke the early morning slumber. A wisp of thin smoke from a flue on the roof gave the sole indication that anyone occupied the shack. A child's muffled sobs reached his ears and closed a fist around his heart.

He studied the layout carefully as the door opened. Bert Blanchard emerged with a bucket.

The man's grumbles carried in the stillness. "Don't know why I hafta draw the water. Hell, I gotta do everything, even to leaving poor Luther behind."

Brodie didn't hesitate. He crept behind, and before the robber-turned-kidnapper got wind, cracked the thick skull with the butt of his Colt. Bert slumped to the ground in a heap. Emptying the man's holster of its hardware, he tossed it down the well. When Bert came to, he'd not pose a threat. Brodie tried to drag the man from view.

"Don't take all day with that water," Nat called. "We need coffee. You know how quarrelsome Reno gets without it."

Bert would have to lie in the open. Brodie raced for cover, beating Nat Jude as he came out to investigate. The speed with which the man reached inside for a rifle said he spied the body beside the well. Quickly, Brodie squeezed off a shot, slid another cartridge in and sent it behind the first. Both caught the ruthless child-stealer and murderer in the shoulder.

Nat fell back inside, slamming the bolt on the door.

Dammit to Hell! He'd just put the odds in their favor.

"Who's out yonder?" Nat called.

"Shenandoah."

"Hell, you should've said something," Reno broke in. "We took you for a lawman. Why'd you hafta go and shoot Nat for?"

"It's no social call. I came for the children you took."

"You been smoking dandelion weeds? Ain't no little girls."

Nat added, "That's right. It's just me and Reno."

"You'll go to Hell for lying." And for lots more . . .

"Reckon I've been thinking we might already be edging on down there." Reno spoke again. "You bring a posse?"

"Naw. I figure I can handle you boys by myself."

"We're not going peaceful-like," Nat snarled.

"I didn't expect it, you sorry piece of dirt," he muttered into the wind. A faint shape crossed the dingy, broken window. They were trying to rig up a plan, in addition to drawing a bead on his position. Brodie shifted further into the undergrowth.

"Who sent you, Shenandoah?"

Tall, dry grass swayed around the shack. Laurel's gaze, awash with unshed tears, flashed from between each dead clump. Impassioned pleas of a pretty lady, nothing more. Failing to find the abductees dumped along the trail, he now shared Laurel's fear. Those girls might end up ruined for life.

He should've torn himself away sooner.

Jude and Darnell had no idea of the justice he'd inflict. Brodie tightened his grip on the Winchester. They'd earned a free trip to Glory Land this fine September morn.

"It purely seems to me you should worry about the why, instead of the who part. Get the wax out of your ears and the lead out of your britches. Send the captives out and we'll call this a day free of bloodletting."

"Don't know why you're raising all this fuss over a darkie and her carpet-bagging playmate." Hate spat from Nat Jude.

Anger ricocheted, but Brodie didn't rise to the bait.

A rifle poked through the window. Three flashes burst from the barrel. Brodie leaned back. No use burning powder until he had a target. Reno, the hothead, would be his guess.

"We ain't giving back the money. You can forget that."

The high-pitched scream of a youngster suddenly pricked the morning chill. Gooseflesh rose on the back of his neck. His hardened stare never left the tumble-down hideout.

"Boys, you better hope a panther made that cry. Otherwise, you'll be real sorry."

"We ain't scared of you," Nat Jude answered. "Men say you're not so fearsome anymore. You're getting old. Do what you gotta do or shut the hell up and leave us be. I don't think you've got the guts to take what you want."

A slight adjustment of the accurate weapon and a keen sense of where Jude stood would deliver the answer. Brodie aimed just a hair or two right of the window. An orange ball, a puff of smoke sent the bullet on a mission. The wood splintered when it hit. Groans and cussing punctured the tranquil Arkansas hills.

He figured Nat's opinion of age and guts might differ now.

"Damn you, Shenandoah! Now you've gone and made us mad." For the first time, Reno's bravado cracked. "Hold on to your rattlers. We're coming out."

Precious minutes came and went with no movement. Brodie dare not sit idle while they plotted. Reno and Nat could simply wait him out or hope he made a mistake.

Besides, his birth certificate made no mention of patience.

And he didn't make too many mistakes.

Except where Laurel was concerned.

The dry grass danced. One spark would create an inferno. A family of squirrels cavorted along the limbs of a mighty oak towering above the hideout. They scampered down an overhang and dropped easily to the flat tin roof, giving him a better notion.

Dense foliage concealed Brodie's wide circle. Blocked from the window's limited view, he reached the structure's rear.

Rough tree bark scraped his palms. Crawling out on a limb, he swung silently to the roof. The stained bandanna stuffed into the flue wouldn't take long for the ol' smoke-'em-out strategy.

He shimmied down and positioned the shack firmly in the middle of his sights in time to see a figure run from the shack.

A child strained against the man's grip as he dragged her along by an arm.

Brodie aimed for the bulky upper body and made his peace. Then he introduced Reno Darnell to a chunk of hot Winchester lead. The girl screamed while her captor sprawled facedown.

Inside the cabin, the other child coughed and sobbed, but no one poked out a head.

That could only mean one thing. . . .

Five o'clock sneaked into Laurel's bedroom. She squinted at the unwelcome thief, her thoughts on Murphy's miraculous awakening. Though thrilled he would live, she still had to consider when to break her news. She couldn't risk telling him for days, or perhaps weeks.

And the matter of Vallens entered into the equation. The man might steal the luxury of waiting.

Fear shook the length of her. She jerked the bed sheet over her head and burrowed further.

The death angel had not sought their town for his health. A specific goal lurked inside that black heart. Something deadly frightening, known only to her sixth sense.

Lord help her if they didn't get rid of him soon.

The hinges on the door squeaked.

"Why in tarnation are you lazing around in bed at this hour?" Ollie shook her. "And what are you doing under there?"

Laurel lifted her head, glaring through a curtain of hair. "For your information, I'm hiding."

"It ain't working too well."

"Everyone doesn't have your sharp wit, General b'Dam."

"Maybe you should stick with cooking and such. You have more skill at that." Ollie peeled back the sheet. "Remember the Cole family? They'll be here shortly."

She groaned. "I completely forgot."

Another reason for the ache sitting on her chest. She would dearly love to pile in and go with them. Escape Vallens and that evil dog of his.

But then . . . it might be worth hanging around to give Brodie an earful that she'd not be doled out to anyone.

She alone would decide who to marry . . . and love.

Although the rebel didn't appear to give that much thought.

"Ollie, why does fate always have to switch things back and forth and upside down the moment you get comfortable?"

"Girl, don't do a damn bit of good to rant and rave and blame fate. Change is a fact of life. Without a shake up occasionally things'd get about as dull as a bunch of widow women knitting long johns."

"Fine thing for you to say. I prefer boring."

"Accept what is, dearie, and go on. Asking all these goldarned questions won't bring any peace I know of."

"Do you know how long it's been since I had reason to be carefree? I miss that and lots more."

Ollie patted Laurel's cheek. "Happiness is nothing but a state of mind. Joy comes from tiny details, not how perfect life is. Girl, you gotta keep your eyes peeled or it'll slide on past you." She swatted her leg. "Get dressed, lazy bones. I'll make some of my special coffee. It's purely a waste of energy fuming and fussing over stuff you got no control over."

"Don't make that horrible brew of yours on my account," Laurel yelled at the closing door.

Ten minutes later, the stench of the vile coffee swam up her nose halfway down the stairs. She knew Ollie would have a cup waiting and persist in feigned innocence.

"About time. Thought you'd sleep the whole day."

Laurel spied a steaming cup at her usual place. She slid into the chair, wrinkling her nose at the cup's dark contents.

"An extra ten minutes doesn't quite equal twelve hours."

"Might as well." The corncob pipe between Ollie's lips jiggled up and down with the statement. "Drink up, girl. It'll pop those eyelids open good and proper."

That wasn't all it'd pop.

"You know I can't stomach it."

"How do you know if you don't try?" Daring sparkled in her eyes.

"You're not about to shush until I do." Laurel glared, lifting the cup. Funny, it didn't smell all that bad. And this liquid actually moved. A cautious sip slid onto her taste buds. "This is tea. You should be ashamed."

GET UP TO 5 FREE BOOKS!

Sign up for one of our book clubs today, and we'll send you
FREE* BOOKS
just for trying it out...**with no obligation to buy, ever!**

HISTORICAL ROMANCE BOOK CLUB

Travel from the Scottish Highlands to the American West, the decadent ballrooms of Regency England to Viking ships. Your shipments will include authors such as CONNIE MASON, CASSIE EDWARDS, LYNSAY SANDS, LEIGH GREENWOOD, and many, many more.

LOVE SPELL BOOK CLUB

Bring a little magic into your life with the romances of Love Spell—fun contemporaries, paranormals, time-travels, futuristics, and more. Your shipments will include authors such as KATIE MACALISTER, SUSAN GRANT, NINA BANGS, SANDRA HILL, and more.

As a book club member you also receive the following special benefits:

- **30% OFF all orders through our website & telecenter!**
  (Plus, you still get 1 book FREE for every 5 books you buy!)
- **Exclusive access to special discounts!**
- **Convenient home delivery and 10 days to return any books you don't want to keep.**

There is **no minimum number of books to buy**, and you may cancel membership at any time. See back to sign up!

*Please include $2.00 for shipping and handling.

YES! ☐

Sign me up for the **Historical Romance Book Club** and send my THREE FREE BOOKS! If I choose to stay in the club, I will pay only $13.50* each month, a savings of $6.47!

YES! ☐

Sign me up for the **Love Spell Book Club** and send my TWO FREE BOOKS! If I choose to stay in the club, I will pay only $8.50* each month, a savings of $5.48!

NAME: _____

ADDRESS: _____

_____

TELEPHONE: _____

E-MAIL: _____

☐ **I WANT TO PAY BY CREDIT CARD.**

☐ VISA   ☐ MasterCard   ☐ DISCOVER

ACCOUNT #: _____

EXPIRATION DATE: _____

SIGNATURE: _____

Send this card along with $2.00 shipping & handling for each club you wish to join, to:

Romance Book Clubs
20 Academy Street
Norwalk, CT 06850-4032

Or fax (must include credit card information!) to: 610.995.9274. You can also sign up online at www.dorchesterpub.com.

*Plus $2.00 for shipping. Offer open to residents of the U.S. and Canada only. Canadian residents please call 1.800.481.9191 for pricing information.
If under 18, a parent or guardian must sign. Terms, prices and conditions subject to change. Subscription subject to acceptance. Dorchester Publishing reserves the right to reject any order or cancel any subscription.

JOIN NOW!

"Well, I ain't. Now, about that hiding nonsense . . . I reckon the death angel put your head under the bedcovers."

"He makes my flesh crawl. I can't help it."

"I'd lie if I said he didn't make me shake in my boots. We can't let him know it, though. Think what he'd do to cowards."

"I realized that while I was dressing. I'm not admitting he came to take me back or anything, but he'd better know right now that I'm not a little girl anymore. I can fight a whole lot harder this time."

She kept a knife under the pillow and one in her pocket.

"That's the spirit." Ollie cocked her head. "Unless I miss my guess, that's Mrs. Cole and those younguns."

Laurel grabbed the basket of food she'd packed last evening, trying to quiet the uproar inside her that railed against the lousy ungraciousness of life, love, and losing.

Ollie beat her to the door. The woman would deny how attached she'd grown to the pitiful family, but Laurel saw it.

"'Morning, Miss Laurel and Miz Ollie!" Edgar Lee hopped down, almost upending Ollie, who wasn't much taller than he.

"Well, I'll be slickered, if it ain't two tadpoles."

Betsy climbed from the high seat and reached inside the wagon for the baby. "Kept my word like I promised."

"W-w-we wanna stay here." Andy fought back tears.

"But we cain't." Edgar Lee kicked a clump of dirt. "Maw says we gotta live with Uncle John."

"U-U-Uncle J-John has a r-r-r-ranch."

"That'll be exciting. You'll have great adventures and learn how to brand cattle."

"I reckon. Only I bet we don't have more fun than here."

She offered Betsy the basket of goodies.

"Ollie and I packed a few things to help get you there."

"You have no call to think I changed my mind about accepting handouts and such."

"It won't do a dam . . . darn bit of good to refuse. I'm sticking it in when you roll outta here."

Laurel jolted when Andy threw his small arms around her waist.

"I-I-I love you."

Laurel kissed the top of his head, wiping the tears that trickled down Andy's cheek. A big lump choked her.

"I love you and Edgar Lee, too. I'm already missing you."

"Shore shooting right! Don't rightly know who's gonna wash them dishes now." The blustering voice cracked. Ollie turned to address Edgar Lee. "Boy, you're might near a grown man. Watch after your maw and brother and Sissie, you hear?"

"I will," the little man sniffled.

Laurel breathed a sigh of relief when Betsy took the basket. It would be downright shameful for Ollie to engage in fisticuffs with the woman.

"I don't know what I'd have done without your help—and kindness. It truly saved us."

How strange to hear something other than hard flint in Betsy's tone. Perhaps their acquaintance had benefited everyone.

"If we managed to ease the weight of your burden a mite, then we done what we should've." Ollie rested a hand on Betsy's shoulder.

Baby Sissie reached for Laurel, cooing happily when she took her. The child snuggled against her breast. Laurel blinked hard and buried her face in the soft curls.

"I'll never forget you." Betsy collected her daughter. "Back in the wagon, boys."

"You're always welcome should you ever need a place." Laurel's arms, and heart, were suddenly empty.

"I appreciate that." Betsy handed up the baby to Edgar Lee. Before she climbed to the seat, she hugged Laurel tight. "You're real lucky to find a man like Mr. Brodie. He loves you, you know. Be patient. War's a terrible affliction."

Wetness blurred her last glimpse of the family. Though Ollie shuffled back inside, Laurel waved until the loblolly pines and river birch swallowed them up.

The demonic laughter of loons from the bayou mocked her loneliness. Hundreds of long-tailed grackle settled in the treetops, adding their lusty calls.

She didn't hear the footsteps until they crunched directly behind her. She dabbed her eyes before turning.

"Never took you for a sappy, weak-willy sister." Zeke Vallens and his wild animal gave her a start.

"What I am is of no consequence to you."

"I been checking around. Asked some questions. Folks say you're about to marry the town mayor. That is, if the poor devil lives. That true?" The man's gaze absorbed the sunlight, yet gave back none of the warmth.

"You're the one with the information. Now, excuse me, please. I won't feed your curiosity."

"Cain't imagine you wasting all that softness on one man. Nope, just can't figure it."

Laurel clenched her fists. The smirk on the fearsome face both angered and terrified her. The wolf dog's sharp eyes glittered, his long tongue hanging out of one side to expose razor-sharp teeth.

Dear God, Ollie should've let her stay under the sheet!

"Good day, Mr. Vallens." She turned slowly, measuring the distance inside.

"It's my duty to remind you of your place, little missy. You don't belong in a two-bit town feeding hungry bellies. Bet you don't make enough to buy a dead man's supper. Ain't that right? Just saying there's easier ways."

Chapter Seventeen

Laurel whirled on her heel, forgetting the folly of that. The animal made a sudden lunge. Had Vallens not snatched a handful of gray neck, the wolf would've torn her to shreds. Her pounding heart told her how close it'd come.

Sometimes being that frightened helped unleash old-fashioned fury. If it was a fight he wanted, then a fight he'd get.

"What do you want? How much will it take for you to leave and forget you ever stumbled upon this town?"

"Ain't your money I'm wanting, little missy. Got more than enough from selling wanted men's sorry hides."

"You're a bounty hunter?"

"By trade. I'm not above dabbling in other persuasions should the job require."

Blood drained from her face, leaving her stone cold and faint.

"In case you think that pertains to anyone here, there's not a soul who'd pay one shiny copper for Ollie or me."

But what about Brodie? The army would pay dearly for him.

186

Spit and thunder! The thought slid down sideways. Her prayers doubled for Vallens to ride on before Brodie returned.

The wolf dog's powerful legs strained to leap.

"Now, that depends. You might fetch a handsome price."

The pitiful attempt to approach him with logic withered.

"Over my dead body, that's the only way."

"That's purely a crying shame, girlie. A crying shame."

Laurel's stand took every ounce of strength. She flew inside the cafe door, slamming and locking it behind her. Only then did she sink to the floor, shaking.

Ollie glanced up from peeling onions. She threw down the knife and knelt beside her. "Who's chasing you?"

"That . . . that horrible man."

She let Ollie help her to a chair.

"Who? The alley was deserted when I came inside."

"Your grim reaper."

The woman's lips narrowed in a thin line. She whipped the pistol from the table, then fumbled with the door latch. When it finally opened, sheer force sent it thundering against the wall. Ollie glanced up and down.

"Dadburn it! The devil's gone." She shut the door.

"Thank God." Badgering Vallens would cause more danger and possibly trigger events no one wished.

"What did he say?"

"He's a bounty hunter. Leastways that's his claim."

"Any idea who in hell he's sniffing after?"

"Maybe me." Or Ollie. Or Brodie. Or all three. Who knew? Taft had taught her to distrust the obvious. The walls seemed to close in as Laurel repeated the conversation.

"Son of a blue jacket! He'd better not try it or he'll find himself on the hurting end of this six iron trying to plug a few leaks. I ain't about to let him get you."

"You'll do your level best." The assurance didn't comfort her.

"I need to come clean about something, girl."

Laurel's heart sank at the solemn statement. She knew it would bring a change that would serve no practical purpose.

"We should get lunch cooking."

Ollie continued, unfazed. "That night we sneaked out of the Black Garter . . . I struck Will Taft, rendering him almost dead. Then I stole the money he was counting."

"You didn't!" She covered her mouth.

"I ain't sorry. I'd do it again for his devil ways. That's what brought us to Texas and how we purchased this cafe. Vallens is here because of me."

"It could be any number of reasons."

"Stop humoring a sick old woman. You know I'm right."

The revelation made sense. Ollie had unwittingly put them both at great risk. By finding one, Taft would find the other.

"We'll think of something."

"I'll go to Vallens and fix it. Don't worry about them taking you again. I'll protect you."

All the heart and will of a crusty lady wouldn't be enough for this fight. Only one man had the ability to boot Vallens out of their lives. Heaven only knew where he was.

"Help! Help me!"

Brodie pried Darcy's arms from his neck and gripped the Colt. "Wait here. I'll be back."

Shielding his mouth with a shirtsleeve, he ran into the billowing gray plumes.

Suffocating haze robbed his sight. Panic rose. A man could get turned around real fast when blinded. For a second he gave thanks he hadn't set the grass afire. Smoke filled his lungs, but at least he didn't have a blaze to fight.

He nearly tripped on a form on the floor. Kneeling, he saw Nat Jude. Dead or wounded didn't matter. At the moment he had greater concerns. He slid the Colt into the holster.

Smothered coughs and a whimper penetrated the dense cloud. Plunging ahead, Brodie groped soft flesh that shrank back.

"Don't be afraid. I'm here to help you."

Something held her fast when he tried to lift her.

The bastards had bound her.

His lungs ached with the urge to fill them. Unable to see, he fumbled for the dagger he carried in his boot. With a finger between the ropes and tender skin, he freed the girl.

Slinging her over a shoulder, he raced for sunlight and fresh air.

Darcy met them, latching onto his waist. "Watch out!"

A deep voice buried into his brain. "Hold it, Shenandoah!"

Damnation!

The guttural warning contrasted with the musical kerloo calls of migrating whooping cranes.

Brodie's eyes watered too badly to focus, but memory served to assign the voice to the eldest Blanchard. Through the blur he couldn't tell if Bert pointed a weapon or not.

It had been a crucial error, not ridding Reno's carcass of the sidearm.

"I should've finished you off when I had the opportunity."

"Reckon that was your last mistake, Shenandoah."

One he'd gladly rectify had he eyesight and no child on his shoulder. He'd have to depend on his wits to get them out of there alive.

"You've got me dead to rights." He inched toward the vague figure, trying to block the choking noises his cargo made.

"Damn right I do. About time you noticed."

"Let me put this little lady down and make sure they're both all right. Then you and me can unravel this mess."

"Good try. You think I'm stupid?"

"I don't have to tell you where two dead girls will lead. Folks might be lenient for the kidnapping, especially when I tell how you helped keep them from harm. But murder has the makings of a lynch mob." He took a few more cautious steps.

"Won't make a hill of beans. My best shot is killing all of you and running."

"You're not a murderer, Bert. No need to start now."

"An eye for an eye. For Reno and Nat."

"They drew their fate after what they put these innocent children through." Brodie uttered a low oath when stinging sweat trickled into his eyes. "Besides, remember how Reno and Nat left your poor shot-up brother behind with no more regard than a slab of spoiled meat."

"Take out that iron and throw it over here."

"Now how do you think I can manage that—with my teeth? You'll have to come get it."

"My mama didn't raise no fool. Do as I say."

"Don't get nervous, now. I'm going to put the girl down."

When he bent to do so, his vision cleared just enough to spy a horse moseying behind Blanchard.

Smokey? It had to be his old friend.

Brodie gently lowered Willa and let out a quick whistle. The horse reared, his forefeet knocking Bert to the hard clay.

If he didn't act now, Lady Luck might turn her back.

Brodie leaped toward the figure, swinging a hard left

and crossing with a right. Bert's harsh grunts silenced a family of squawking blue jays in the treetops. Quickly locating Reno's pistol, Brodie stuck it in his waist before hauling Blanchard to his feet. A length of rope looped over the saddle horn on Smokey provided ample binding for the outlaw's hands and feet. Only then did he turn to the one that'd saved his butt.

"Good work, boy." He patted the smooth neck.

Smokey snorted and nibbled on his shirt.

Children's coughs mingled with sobs brought back his attention. He drew a pail of water from the well and knelt in the Arkansas wild rye to wash tear-stained cheeks.

"It's all right. You're safe, darlin'."

Willa's big eyes stared into his. The child shook when he put his arms around her.

"I'm skeered."

"I know, but I would never hurt you."

"Who you be?"

"A friend. Your mamas sent me to bring you ladies home."

Darcy sniffled and sat up. "Are you sure? Those men said they'd sell us and we'd never see the bayou again."

"Yep, I'm certain. They won't ever threaten you again."

"I want my mama. I need my mama."

Brodie didn't know whether to blame the moisture in his eyes on smoke or on Darcy's pleading gaze. It held the same lost fear Laurel's had. His gut wrenched as he cleared his throat.

"I'll have you back in Redemption before you know it."

"You promise?" Willa asked. "You won't leave me here 'cause I'm black? Mama says most folk hate people of color and don't trust 'em."

"Not all do. I'm not one of those. I promise."

* * *

Purpose. That's what Ollie harped on and that's the way Laurel marched down the street—a woman with a purpose who wouldn't let a pitted, washed-out road waylay her. She'd geared herself up for battle and chosen her weapon.

The clerk at the desk glanced up at the sound of the hotel door. "May I help you?"

"Zeke Vallens?"

"Let's see. That's number six at the top."

Her best shoes drummed the beat of a platoon's drill as she mounted the stairs. Pausing at the door, she first straightened the lace-trimmed bonnet and adjusted the skirt to hide the bulge within the folds. Long white gloves somewhat disguised the trembles. Fighting rising panic, she sharply rapped twice.

"To what do I owe the pleasure?" Vallens showed surprise. "If you'd let me know in advance of your visit, I would've taken a bath. Or at least washed my feet."

Her cheeks burned.

"You devil, it's not that kind of call."

Horror swept over her when he tried to pull her into the room. She'd not be alone with Vallens. Not willingly.

The metal shaft in her skirt helped bring calm. Her grip tightened, ready to plunge it into his rotten chest.

Ollie had been determined to pay Vallens a visit. Had she not snuck out on the dear lady, it would've meant the grave for sure.

And still might. For someone.

No one had to tell Laurel the Grim Reaper never lost.

She'd given that terrifying thought great consideration.

Anything to repay Ollie's kindness.

"You want others to overhear and know what sort you are?" Vallens touched her face, running a finger across her cheek.

The contact repulsed her. "I'm who I am and that's enough."

"Cain't rightly think of any other reason you'd stroll over to see ol' Zeke. Figured you to hunger for a man's body."

Darkness surrounding her soul turned to pitch under the cynical stare.

"I haven't the time or inclination to debate ill-gotten assumptions. I wish to strike a bargain." Releasing the knife, she moved to the small canvas bag it rested on. Adopting brazen courage she didn't feel, she jerked it out.

"What kind of deal are you proposing, little missy?"

"This two hundred dollars is free and clear money. I believe you'll find it adequate, considering no one will pay you a cent for anyone in Redemption."

"You're sure hell bent on convincing me of that. Causes a man to wonder."

"Take it and leave. It's as fair a bargain as you'll get."

"Ain't in no hurry. I haven't completed my stay."

"You might reconsider. There'll be no more payments. The milk cow has dried up."

A quick pitch found the bull's-eye on his chest. He made no move to catch it. The blackmail money fell to the floor, scattering like dry leaves on a blustery fall afternoon.

"I'm betting different," Vallens snarled after her.

Three days passed after the unsuccessful venture. Despite Laurel's efforts, Vallens remained a fixture in town. The man's ominous presence cast a shadow over all of Redemption. No one knew why he'd appeared or why he stayed. Speculation that he stalked someone ran rampant. But who? Each person whispered a different name.

"If the Blanchards hadn't laid Sheriff Tucker to rest, he'd find out what the devil keeps Vallens here," George Adams had grumbled at a secret town meeting.

Laurel hadn't pointed out the obvious. Had the sheriff escaped the bullet, he still couldn't help because it would be his job to face the child thieves instead of Brodie's.

And her heart wouldn't ache with uncertainty that perhaps the love of her life would never find his way back.

"How will we run the likes of Vallens out of town when he keeps us shaking in our beds? That dog of his snarls and we break our fool necks running backward. Someone should stand up to him." Jake had twirled the ends of his mustache.

"Like you, Jake? I could put a drop or two of strychnine in his whiskey," Curley suggested in a low tone.

"Son of a blue jacket! Your whiskey is poison enough. Don't rightly understand how that sidewinder keeps standing with the bottles he's poured down his gullet already." Ollie took out her pipe and tapped it against the floor.

"What does that leave? Talk him to death?" John Miller, the blacksmith, quietly rose in the back of the room.

"Jeb Prater could've helped if he hadn't tried to bully Yates. Prater's not afraid of much, 'cause he don't have a lick of sense." Jake leaned his matchstick frame against a wall.

The meeting had adjourned shortly thereafter with simply a hearty wish for Brodie Yates's reappearance. Everyone knew he could end the visit from the unwelcome angel of death.

Laurel swept the sidewalk in front of the cafe the following morning when a subtle change rustled the air.

Half expecting to find Vallens nearby, she turned abruptly, staring in surprise at the Appaloosa trotting down the street. The sight of the lanky figure riding tall in the saddle sent her pulse racing.

Thank God!

The girls? She clutched the broom tightly. From this distance she couldn't tell who rode the two horses following Brodie's. Shielding her eyes against the sunlight, she spotted two small heads bobbing on a dappled mare. Brodie held the reins of the third animal. A man whose hands were bound sat astride it.

The broom went flying in one direction, her feet in the other.

"Ollie, come quick!"

When the woman poked out her head, Laurel swung her around.

"Tarnation, girl! You got buffalo fever or something?"

"Brodie's here with little Darcy and Willa."

"Well, I'll be the son of a bug-eater!"

The group halted at the hitching rail. Laurel tried to wipe away a smile, but it pulled rank and did as it pleased.

"You're back," she breathed, reaching up for Willa and swinging her down. She spoke to Ollie before helping Darcy. "Mrs. Hatcher just went into the mercantile, and I think I saw Mrs. Carver head toward the livery."

"I want my mama," Darcy sniffled.

"Hold on there, sweetie. I'll get her here before you can say Singapore Jack." Ollie's skirts became a swirling wind.

"You brave darling." Laurel smoothed Willa's tangled hair, picking out a piece of straw. "We'll fix you up in no time."

Both girls' dresses hung in tatters from thin shoulders. Would their redemption be like hers—nothing but a dream?

Darcy's blue gaze gripped Laurel. "I'm scared."

"Not a soul will hurt you here. We won't let them."

The gray-eyed rebel's warmth trapped her in his snare. He threw a leg over Smokey's back and slid down, the motion setting off the snake rattles.

Lord, how she'd missed that sound.

Her chest ached as though she'd run the length of the bayou.

A weary scowl deepened the lines around his mouth. It told how difficult the task had been. Dust flew when he brushed at his clothes. Beneath the layers of trail grit, she noticed scratches on his arm. And dark bloodstains.

"You're injured!"

Looping three sets of reins over the railing, he grinned. "A scratch. Nothing to get upset about."

"I can see perfectly well that it's more than that."

He stepped from reach, stiffening. "How's Murphy?"

"Doing quite nicely, thanks to Nora. You'll be surprised."

Until then, she hadn't taken account of the man on the other horse. He wore a sullen sneer. "What'cha staring at, Miz Uppity? I ain't no sideshow."

Repulsed, Laurel turned away.

"My baby!" Mrs. Hatcher hugged her daughter as the curious half of town gathered.

"Good work, son." Ollie had to tiptoe to slap Brodie on the back. "I knowed you was made of fine-grained leather."

Since when? Come to think of it, Laurel supposed the change of opinion drifted to the more favorable side when Vallens moved in.

Mrs. Carver arrived out of breath, her arms outstretched. "Willa, come to your poor mama."

"What about the bank's money?" George Adams huffed from scurrying to get in on the commotion.

Brodie opened a saddlebag, pulled out a scorched canvas sack, and lobbed it.

Adams dumped out a handful of charred bank notes. "What happened to all the rest?"

"You accusing me of stealing?"

"I'd check his pockets there if'n I was you folk," Blanchard warned. "Can't trust these hired guns, you know."

"I'm saying it's mighty suspicious with your reputation and all." George Adams shuffled his feet when Brodie advanced. "But then, I'm sure we have no reason to doubt your word."

"How did it get burned, Yates?" Jake demanded.

Thank goodness Jake wasn't a piece of raw meat, or Brodie's glare would've seared him. A shake of disgust set the rattles in motion. He jerked the reins from the rail and led the horse carrying the robber toward the empty jail.

Ollie whacked Jake's arm. "You crazy fool. Let the man be. Cain't you see he's worn plumb to the soles of his boots?"

Darcy and Willa ran after the man who'd rescued them. "Mr. Brodie! Wait."

He stopped in his tracks. When he turned, both threw their arms around him. Laurel watched through a misty gaze as the tough gunslinger scooped up the girls. Brodie truly cared. It hadn't been merely a job she'd asked him to do.

"I don't know how to thank you proper, Mr. Yates," Darcy's mother said. "I don't have much money, but you're welcome at our door anytime day or night."

"Ours, too," Mrs. Carver added. "You're a special man."

Chapter Eighteen

Once Brodie made Blanchard nice and cozy behind a locked cell door, he hurried to the frame house on State Street. The color in Murphy's face reinforced Laurel's claims of progress.

After keeping vigil for half an hour with no sign of his brother awakening, Brodie turned to needs of a more liberal sort.

The saloon had a fair amount of business for an early Saturday morning. He hooked his heels on the metal rail and gulped a lukewarm mug of beer. The liquid wet down the first two coatings of dust inside his mouth but little else.

"Let me buy you one." Ollie brushed his elbow.

Georgia clay! The jackanapes was harder to get rid of than stink on fresh cow patty. He wasn't in the mood for company. Leastways not of the ill-tempered sort.

Let him quench his thirst, soak in a tub for about a week, and he might possibly feel human again . . . or enough to venture over to the cafe for an extra helping of pecan praline pie before all hell broke loose when the Yanks came for him.

Had he more than a speck of sense he'd ride on before then.

"Reckon the town owes you, Yates." Jake pushed Ollie aside.

Brodie stared at the sloshed beer dripping from his hand. The thought of leaving became more attractive by the minute. Deep irritation grew at the circus that followed him in.

"You should've recovered more of our hard-earned money," George whined in a nasal twang.

"Son of a blue jacket! He done more than any of you sniveling two-bit chorus girls, including you, Adams." Ollie refilled her pipe from a pouch Brodie figured she slept with.

"Yates, would you be of a mind to reconsider the previous offer? We need a sheriff in a real hurtful kind of way."

"Goldarned it, Jake! You can't pour piss out of a boot. Don't you see the man's tuckered out? Let him get some shut-eye and put food in his belly before pestering him."

"Ollie Applejack d'Dam, don't you tell me what to do!"

"Watch it there, Jake." The saloon owner entered the fracas. "Don't use that tone with the lady. You can take your flea-bitten hide outta here if you can't button your trap."

The gilt-edged mirror above the bar reflected a man in black who rose from a corner table. Patrons hastily parted, clearing a path through the hubbub. Brodie reached for the smooth walnut of the Colt without thought.

He swung from the long mahogany bar to face the stranger before he glanced downward. Beside the man stood a dog with its lips curled back. Snarls swept the area clear.

The man's low hat shaded his eyes. Yet some keen sense

told Brodie of a dangerous glint. Although the demeanor jabbed needles into each nerve ending, it was the jagged, diagonal scar that left bitterness in his mouth.

He'd crossed shadows with such a disfigured man before.

"Something's got the good folk of Redemption mighty stirred up. Quite a celebration, I'd say," the stranger sneered.

"What do you want, Vallens?" Brodie cut to the chase.

"Ahhh, Shenandoah. Wondered if you might remember me. I recollect it's been a while."

"Not a face I ever wished to see again. Now, what're you here for? I had no price on my head last time I checked."

"Hey, mister," Jake yelled a safe distance from the far end of the bar, "better watch it. He just went up single-handed against the Blanchard gang. I warn you not to get him riled."

Vallens's sunken cheeks twitched. The funerary attire suggested an undertaker come to claim the next victim with a devil dog by his side.

"Or what? No lawman around to stop me from doing whatever I please. Town don't have no sheriff."

The guttural dare gave the wolf dog courage. A growl rumbled. The animal leaned on his haunches, ready to spring.

"Better think again, Vallens. It does now." Brodie's clipped answer left his rival at a loss for words.

"I see someone managed to lasso you." Murphy smiled weakly the next day, pointing to the silver star on Brodie's shirt.

"Sorta looks that way." He touched the shiny badge that burdened with its weight. "I swore and be damned I'd go to my grave before I'd be a tin star."

"You could do worse, big brother."

Brodie placed his hat at the foot of the bed and rubbed the weariness from eyes that hadn't seen decent sleep in a week. "Thing is—I'm not cut out for upholding law and order."

He knew the Ten Commandments by heart simply because he'd broken every one.

"Beats me why you took it on."

"Zeke Vallens and his damn defiance. I had to put him in his place. Claiming the job just slipped out. I only meant to wipe the sneer off the smug piece of slime."

"He's here to cause trouble, isn't he?"

"I feel it in my bones."

Vallens had expertise at creating mystery. He took extra pleasure in making folks jumpy, unable to predict his next move.

Murphy's struggle to sit up ended in total failure. An ache swept Brodie as he gathered the narrow shoulders and raised him. He propped a mountain of pillows, hoping to hide concern that must show despite the mask he tried to wear.

"Appreciate it. Ollie says I'm so weak I can't even lick my upper lip. And I hate to admit she doesn't lie."

"It'll pass. When I left here I wouldn't have given a plugged nickel for your chances of making it." He wouldn't tell him how dearly it had cost him to ride out. Some feelings a man didn't wish to discuss.

"Getting back to Vallens . . . are his sights on you?"

"Aside from the army, I have no price on my head."

Although he did once, after a scrape out Tucson way when warring ranchers attempted to pin the murder of a prominent land owner on him. It'd taken might near a year to track down the culprit and clear up the mistake.

"I'd say having the army's target on your back would give Vallens reason enough." Murphy groaned from sudden movement but waved Brodie away. "The scuttlebutt I hear says the man doesn't require much excuse to start trouble."

Brodie extracted tobacco and papers from a vest pocket and rolled a smoke. "Want one?"

"Does a garden need water? These darn womenfolk coddle me worse than a newborn."

The complaint filled Brodie with dread. Younger brother wouldn't be laid up too long. Brodie licked the edge of the paper and twisted one end. He no more had it lit and stuck in Murphy's mouth when Nora came through the door.

"Mr. Murphy! I tell you, no smoke. Bad. Very bad."

"Get away, woman." He shooed her. "It's my house, by God, and I'll smoke if I darn well please. Don't you have some nasty-tasting potions to grind up or something?"

The pretty Indian sighed with irritation, her dark glare slinging arrows in all directions. Brodie ducked before one landed his way. One thing he'd learned—don't go up against anyone on the warpath, particularly one who wore skirts.

"Maybe half-breed needs to go back to swamp. Maybe sick man not need Nora now." She crossed her arms and glared. "Maybe Nora let leeches suck you dry."

"Now, Nora darlin', I didn't mean it that way."

Sugar dripping from Murphy's plea snapped Brodie's concentration.

"Hmph!"

"You know I'm not well enough for you to leave." Sensing Brodie's curious regard, Murphy's tone became abrupt. "And don't let me hear that half-breed remark again. The color of a person's skin only proves our Creator liked variety. How bored we'd be if we all looked the same. You're a fine, intelligent woman—albeit far more handsome than most."

"And you are stubborn yellow-eyes."

The cigarette fell from Murphy's grasp onto the sheet. "Hellfire and damnation!"

Quickly plucking up the danger, Nora's hand collided with the patient's. For a brief moment a spark sizzled, held captive by the shimmer in their gaze.

Surely Brodie hadn't imagined it. The possibility intrigued him, so much so that he trembled when he held a match to the cigarette. He couldn't stop hope tingling up his spine.

The supple doeskin garment Nora wore made no sound as she smoothed the sheet, tucking it around Murphy. Each gentle movement revealed expert care.

Nora turned to address Brodie. "I offer prayer for safe return. Great Mighty One answered. My heart smiles."

Brodie met the brown warmth of her features.

"Your heart isn't the only one smiling, Miss Whitebird."

"The little ones?"

"A few days and they'll be fine." He emptied his lungs, aiming the smoke toward a cracked window in case her anger flared. "They suffered no worse than a bad case of fright."

Mere minutes had stood between the girls and . . . distaste lingered in his mouth. He'd rather not consider the what ifs.

"They have a lot to thank you for." Murphy eyed the cigarette with longing.

"You bring one bad man. The others? You take many scalps, Mr. Brodie?"

"They caught some luck. I let them keep their hair." His dry statements held a handful of remorse as he thought of Luther.

Ashes dangled from the tip of the cigarette. He looked about for a proper place to flick them. Giving up, he tapped them into the palm of his left hand.

"Good." Nora paused at the door and pointed a finger at Murphy. "No more smoke. You eat or Nora go home."

Murphy's grin stretched. "You'd best unpack then. Suddenly I'm hungry enough to eat the blades off a windmill."

A man would be deaf, dumb . . . and unconscious to miss the crackle in the air.

"I swear I just witnessed something," he dropped casually when the door shut. "What's with you and Nora?"

"Don't know what you're talking about."

"And I'm a three-legged, blind donkey."

"I hoped you wouldn't notice." Murphy sighed. "When she touches me, it's as if a branding iron sears my insides. I've never felt this way before that I recall."

"Not even with Laurel?" His breath became glacial and harsh.

"Laurel's different. She's the one I'm marrying."

Brodie wiped off a sick smile before it finished forming.

"Whatever you say, Mr. Expert Lady Killer." He took his palm full of ashes and raised the window high enough to dust them onto the lawn.

"Let's get back to your problems and leave my affairs of the heart alone." A coughing spasm gripped Murphy and several minutes elapsed before he could continue. "Damn, I hate this!"

"Have patience. Being blasted by an elephant cannon tends to hobble a man. You're lucky to do the slow-poke shuffle."

"I can't abide much more of this." Murphy wiped his mouth.

Conversation drifted up the stairs. No mistaking the throaty caller.

"Laws a mercy. Shore is fine to see you, Miss James."

"Likewise, Etta. Is Murphy awake?"

"For a fact. Get your sweet self right on up there."

Laurel's delicate features brought a heart full of misery and a kick smack in the middle of Brodie's gut.

"Come here, Laurel my love. I need a kiss from my girl."

She hesitated, meeting Brodie's quizzical gaze. He turned quickly away, unable to bear the sight of their lips touching.

"You seem quite . . . spirited today," she remarked.

"Don't know how you get that idea. Frankly, I'm upset. I dreamt you called off the wedding. Said you had no wish to marry me." Murphy closed his eyes for a moment. "Tell me it's nothing more than nonsense concocted by a figment of the mind. I don't think I could bear it should—"

"Don't get yourself in a dither over a dream, Murphy."

"Thank God! We do have to settle the details, however."

"What is that?" Laurel's dress rustled in a hasty retreat to the window, where she gazed out, keeping her back to the two.

Brodie wondered what had unnerved her. Surely not his presence. She knew he'd visit Murph at the first opportunity. And he harbored no illusion that the upcoming nuptials would not take place, given his blessing pretty much sealed it. Still, her behavior reflected guilt of some sort.

"How could you forget our wedding date barely a week off? Do we proceed with me laid up, or postpone until full recovery?"

A wild, cornered expression shone on her face when she slowly turned.

Brodie favored putting it off—forever. Murphy's directness flustered her even more, evident in the way she smoothed the quilt backward and forward.

"I believe we should discuss this in private."

"My brother doesn't mind. We're family."

"Just pretend I'm not here," he piped up dryly, receiving a glare for his efforts. "Murph, I dare say Laurel will agree it depends on whether you prefer tying the knot lying or standing."

"Exactly my point. Only a healthy man can do the marriage bed justice," Murphy replied.

"That settles it. See how simple that was? Whatever would you do without big brother around?" A bit of hope rose. A marriage put on hold could turn into one that never occurred.

Laurel's mood lightened to match his. "No need to rush. We have the rest of our lives; what's a few more months?"

"Not a chance, my love. I won't wait that long and give you a chance to back out. No siree, two weeks from today and that's final, one way or another."

Georgia clay! The smattering of hope crashed around him.

"Oh, dear, look at the time." Laurel raced for the door. "Folks will kick down the door to get to the feeding trough. Ollie must wonder what on earth is keeping me."

Footsteps padded on the stairs before Murphy spoke. "Where were we? Oh, yes. What are you going to do with Blanchard?"

"A mighty good question. I'll have to think on it."

"I'll wager you've a trick or two up your sleeve yet."

He scooped his hat off the end of the bed, pondering the statement. Magical feats hadn't run in the family, unless a boy counted the swift departure of a father who left in the dead of night with a painted lady.

. . . The same misbegotten ways Brodie shared with Samuel Yates, it would appear.

Suddenly he had one more thing to cross off the list before bedding down for the night over at the jail.

The comforting hiss of rattlers ignited purpose inside him. "One thing I know: I'll make Vallens rue the day he rode into this damn town. If he's come to find trouble, I won't be shy about obliging him."

Chapter Nineteen

The jingle announcing a customer drew an exasperated *"Spit and thunder"* from under Laurel's breath. With Murphy pressuring her about wedding plans the long day had stolen her spirit.

"Sorry, we're closed." She swiped crumbs from the table into her hand before glancing up.

"I'm not here for that."

The deep baritone unleashed a storm of flutters. Tiny droplets began to dampen the crevice between her breasts.

She might've laid blame on the warmth of his stare.

Assuredly, the lopsided grin.

And most definitely the lock of hair drooping onto his forehead bore responsibility for her heart's flip flop.

The quiet, gray-eyed rebel was sleeping danger at best.

And at worst? Heaven help her.

"Ah, the new sheriff. I suspect you pay no social call."

"Only came to . . ." He suddenly yanked the hat from his head. Dancing rattles fussed with the fury of a whole den

208

of deadly vipers. ". . . to check on things before I bed down. Noticed the lanterns still burning."

"I have a cup of coffee left. Not exactly fresh, though."

"A fair enough offer."

She led the way to the kitchen and thanked providence she'd brewed the last pot. Serving Ollie's thick mud might get her shot for the trouble. Sitting opposite him, she wished the butterflies in her stomach would light somewhere.

He was a rogue, she reminded herself, clasping her hands tightly. He'd offered her to his brother free and clear.

"Would you care for something . . . else?" What a stupid thing to ask. Having him mistake it for a proposition of some kind, especially the sordid variety, was hardly what she needed.

"Lil, I wish I was at liberty . . ."

Use of that name increased her vulnerability threefold.

Awkward silence stretched, yet he added nothing more.

"I meant pie, of course. I'm glad you're back," she finally ventured. "Although you letting them rope you into the sheriff job surprised me. You were dead set against it."

Brodie's stare wrestled with hers. "A man can change his mind. I had reasons."

Blue blazes, it was as if he spoke in a foreign tongue! Nothing made any sense, and with each word she grew more confused. What had happened to his direct, to-the-point manner?

"I expect Murphy's rapid improvement brought relief."

"Nora has exceptional abilities. My brother is quite taken with her—powers—for bringing him back from the brink of death."

The lifted cup and lowered gaze effectively hid the expression she sought to read. She couldn't recall him this guarded or mysterious before.

Only irresistible.

Laurel rose to bank the fire in the wood stove, determined to keep from doing something she'd regret.

"We found a godsend. By the time the good doctor finally arrived, the loop-legged man was in no shape to treat a sick cat, much less a human. I sent him packing."

"You make it most difficult for a man. I thought—"

"Hard for you? You waltz in and tempt me to forget . . . make my dreams disappear fast as mist in moonlight."

"How've you been, Lil?"

The brittle tone took her aback. She didn't reply until she emptied the ash chute into the galvanized pail.

"Who exactly wants to know, the sheriff or you?"

"Let me have that." He brushed her aside and took the pail before she realized he'd gotten up from his chair. "I'll set it outside. Ollie says Zeke Vallens threatened you."

He closed the back door and returned.

"The dear woman has many admirable qualities, but having a closed mouth isn't one of them." The table hid Laurel's trembles, yet she met his rebel grays unflinchingly. "Should I admit the truth, he scares the devil out of me. His evil eye gives me the shakes. And refusing to say why he's here keeps my nerves jumping. I'm almost positive he works for Will Taft."

Laurel kept Ollie's confession to herself. She had to respect the secret. She would go to her grave before she told.

"Has Vallens hinted that?"

"In a sense, but nothing concrete. I resorted to desperate measures, thinking two hundred dollars would provide incentive for him to leave. Hindsight shows a clear mistake on my part."

Brodie's fingertips traced the curve of her quivering lips ever so softly. She rested her face against his palm, wanting more than a touch, but somehow knowing it wouldn't come. He'd never act on the unbridled desire that made her pulse race, for he'd blessed her upcoming nuptials with Murphy. "What are we going to do?" The whisper bubbled from a well deep within.

"About what?"

"Vallens . . . Bert Blanchard . . . the Union army . . . ," and, she added before losing courage, ". . . and us."

"I've wanted you since the first time I laid eyes on that vision in lavender and lace. I won't deny it."

"So much that you gave me to your brother? Strange way of showing it."

Disappointment swept through her. He didn't refute her words.

"Things change; notions and feelings a man most desires to hold on to fade over time."

This confirmed that she'd become nothing but a memory.

"The night in Murphy's garden before you left—was it lust that made you hold me in your arms? Was it pure notion that kissed me breathless?"

"Just let it be! Why do females have to examine and pick apart every little thing?"

"I believe you answered my question. Now, if you don't mind, Sheriff, it's late." Her knees wobbled when she pushed to her feet.

The muscles in Brodie's jaw twitched. "Vallens lays one hand on you, he'll be a dead man. Put that in your bonnet."

Ollie crept in quietly from the alley as the clock struck midnight. Laurel still sat at the kitchen table. The barely touched cup of tea in her hands had long grown cold. She cradled the cup as if she could magically change the past hour. The noise of the latch unglazed her eyes.

"Out sparking with Curley tonight?"

"Son of a blue belly, I swear you have divining powers."

"It doesn't take a fortune-teller to know when a woman is happy. No one but Curley can do that."

"That man can sure start a fire in me, yes indeed."

"Guess that's fine and dandy long as the gentleman stays around to put it out once he lights it."

"What's taken the starch from your sails, girl? You were in fine enough spirits when I left."

Frustration disturbed the night's quiet. "Brodie came by."

"No need to say more. Nothing quite worse'n to leave a lady with a heap of embers sizzling and nary an attempt to cool 'em with so much as a drop of water."

Truth burrowed past Laurel's irritation and brought a flush to her checks. The warmth of his fingertips stayed on her lips.

"I hate to disappoint you, Miss Know-it-all b'Dam, but I have no embers—sizzling or otherwise." Denial came easier than admitting Brodie had trampled tender feelings. His rejection embarrassed and hurt her. She raised her chin a bit higher. "Not that it's any of your affair. Furthermore, it appears a certain meddlesome woman, whom I won't name, told Brodie about Vallens and his threats."

At least Ollie had the courtesy to appear sheepish.

"My grandpappy, bless his soul, always said that if a problem's got its teeth in your privates and you ain't big enough to shake it loose, find someone to help pry that mouth apart before it has you singing in the Jesus choir." Ollie squinted through one eye while rummaging in her pocket, probably for that blasted pipe. "Figured it wouldn't hurt to give our new sheriff a full tally of the situation."

"I would appreciate being consulted before you run to him with our problems."

"You ain't got me hoodwinked for a minute. That's not the reason you got your tail feathers bunched up tight, is it?"

"*Spit and thunder!* He should either lay out where we stand or get the hell from my life. He gave me some song and dance about regret and notions and feelings changing."

Ollie finally located the pipe. She pinched some tobacco between finger and thumb, sticking it in the corncob bowl.

"Girl, I can see you're on the warpath. Lord knows you have just cause. The man plain don't know his own mind. One minute he's hot, the next he's cold. Something you gotta understand: He's scared of horning in on his brother's territory. I've seen it a thousand times."

"I'm stuck in a lie in the middle of a no man's land I can't cross. But why does Brodie keep coming around—to jab me with a sharp stick? If he carried an ounce of regard you'd think he'd stay far away."

Unless he took pleasure in watching her bleed.

"Because he cain't help it, and don't do a lick of good to piss and moan about it."

"Heaven forbid, is it too much to know why he's bound and determined to relinquish everything to Murphy? And don't I have a right to ask why?"

"Long as you don't expect no answer. Men like Brodie develop lockjaw when it comes to discussing such."

"No other has ever made my toes curl, my skin tingle, or given me reason to feel safe in my own bed."

"Snatch that shootin' star before it vanishes into the sunset. Look at this old fool standing before you. I could've had it, only I let it get away. Wished I hadn't."

Laurel wanted the courage to throw convention to the wind. How blessed to lie in the arms of the man she loved without dishonor or regret and not have him push her away.

And yet, would she grab hold if given a chance?

The journey had taken so long. She'd never gotten this close to redeeming her tattered soul.

To sacrifice it now?

Shameless desire scampered with naughty abandon.

Dear God, she prayed the source of temptation would stay beyond reach!

"Sheriff Yates, yeah, right." Brodie punched the pillow. On his back in the darkness, he stared at the red glow of the cigarette and listened to Blanchard's snores.

What in almighty had he gotten himself into? He glanced at the piece of metal he'd unpinned and laid beside him. Wayward moonbeams bounced off it.

He didn't need the sparkle to remind him that he'd messed up.

Men of his sort? They had no need for anything other than a fast hand and a moving target.

No emotional ties.

No ladies who waited through long, dreary nights.

No Lil.

Maybe Murphy would develop a softness for Nora. Maybe not. He dare not bank on it. However it played, Lil deserved more. Of all the ones he'd come across, she alone held power to blot out the nameless faces of all the men he'd sent to eternity.

The ropes beneath the feather mattress creaked when he shifted to finger the shiny badge.

Its raised lettering spoke of ties and a purpose for staying. Roots could grow if given half a shot and a speck of rain. But that was the danger. The little piece of tin stole his freedom to leave when he chose.

Even as the wish formed, he knew he couldn't consider more until he rid the town of Vallens. Keeping safe those he loved took priority no matter his own fate. He'd not returned to Redemption blindfolded.

Risk came with his decision—risk he accepted in exchange for seeing Murphy and laying flowers on his mother's grave.

But now that he'd done that?

This is what you've searched for over the whole country and half of Georgia. It's the one place you can call home and know the full meaning of the word.

Damn the truth!

Smoke from the dangling cigarette was probably to blame for the sudden watering in his eyes.

Curse those roots that already burrowed tender shoots.

When he ripped them from the fertile soil, it would make the god-awful pain gripping him now feel like a tiny pinprick.

Stay and fight or . . . fight to stay?

Either way he'd lose something—his life, redemption, or his sanity.

Damn Vallens's sorry hide to hell and back!

Without that man taking up residence, Brodie could've delivered the little ladies and handed Blanchard over to the town's bravest—should he find any. He would've told his brother good-bye and ridden on.

The bayou held a million areas far better suited for hiding. Few white men had seen some of the backwater places he knew existed.

Meanwhile, the bargain he'd made with himself, not to mention the man upstairs, to spare Murphy's life hung by a thread.

It was too much, fighting the urge to take Laurel in his arms and kiss her until he stripped the ache from his soul. It had sapped every ounce of fortitude and then some.

Pure weakness almost destroyed them both.

"Sweet Georgia clay! Why did I have to give her the go

ahead to marry Murph? I pushed her straight into his arms." Brodie's noisy grumbling disturbed the prisoner. Bert grunted and rolled over before he resumed snoring.

This silver star trapped him. Circumstances forced him to see her each day and not touch her. The odds worked against him. Resistance to the current would wear down to nothing.

Certain reality about tempting fate . . . something would break sooner or later.

He mulled over the likelihood of being worthy of Laurel's love and trust. Heat rushed to his middle. A Utopian wish. And yet one that bore little hope of fruition.

A familiar need tightened and rose, drawing taut the buckskin trousers.

Damn her throaty voice and big violet eyes!

For argument's sake he let his imagination run wild.

Chapter Twenty

"Heard that goldarned music box." Ollie shoved a cup in her hand when she came downstairs. "Slept nary a wink."

Laurel sniffed the liquid before she took a sip.

"I tried to keep quiet. Sorry."

"Truth of the matter, it weren't that. Couldn't shake Vallens's ugly leer over at the saloon. The cunning devil's so mean he'd suck eggs from a widow woman's basket. Bet he'd even hide the shells on a neighbor's porch."

"Stay away from him. Far away."

"Cain't very well do that when he slinks around, popping up here and there when a body least expects."

"Maybe you should tell Curley. He could help."

"Not ready to do that right yet. Don't want to see the disappointment in his eyes when he finds out I'm a thief. I ain't had a man treat me as some sort of prize before. It's sorta nice, and I don't want to hurry the ruination of it."

"Do you think hearing it from Vallens will make it less hurtful?"

Ollie twisted the dishcloth. "Maybe just a mite longer."

How disconcerting—this sadness and agony in a voice

that had always spat out exactly what was on her mind, paying no heed to whether a body wished to hear it or not. Laurel didn't exactly take comfort, either, in the drawn whiteness around Ollie's lips.

"I have an idea. We're down to bare cupboards and it appears our long overdue shipment of meat went by way of China."

"And overland by camel through Egypt," Ollie added dryly.

"Let's catch the steamer to Jefferson. The *Lazy Jane* docks in a couple of hours. A peaceful ride up Big Cypress Bayou and back might soothe our jangled nerves. We'll forget the Grim Reaper for a day. The sound of water swishing over paddlewheels, staring up at big, fluffy clouds, it might be nice."

"You've lost your mind. Folks'll expect open doors."

"With low stores, we can't offer much anyway."

"Nope. I ain't going anywhere near that carpetbagging, rabble-rousing mess. No, siree. You go, and I'll take care of these wheybellies. I can whip up a mean batch of corn pones and boil a big pot of beans. I reckon that'll suffice. And if it don't, they can go jump in the swamp."

"You're the most stubborn, cantankerous woman I've ever met or I'll eat your hat."

"You saying I cain't serve up a few vittles?" Smoke curled, blocking the one-eyed glare. "You saying I'm old and not up to such a measly task? I was cooking long before you ever seen a pot."

"Spit and thunder! You've got your back bowed. That you can do whatever you set a mind to isn't the issue."

The state of a frail heart didn't make it past her lips.

Or leaving her with God knows what up Vallens's sleeve.

"I have no earthly desire to go mixing with blue bellies

so thick you can't put one foot in front of the other without kicking one in the shins. No thank ye. Ain't anything I'd take joy in—except maybe the kicking part."

"What about your angel of death and when he'll pounce?"

"Curley's here. That swill-pusher's been dying to sling out something more'n whiskey. I'll do just fine, thank you."

Ollie raised her skirt, tugged a crisp roll of bills from beneath a garter, and pressed them into Laurel's palm. "Might as well use some of these new gen-u-wine railroad notes. I hear they're liable to spend better than the rest. Leastwise folks tend to think they do."

She felt weak . . . and suspicious.

"Don't tell me you've gone into counterfeiting?"

"A fool thing to say." Ollie dipped down into her bosom and fished out a gold double eagle. "Buy a new dress or a hat, one of them frilly kind with flowers on it. Turning a man's head could loosen up his tongue. Might make him reveal his intentions. Even Yates."

Laurel's watery smile doubted. That she'd have to see.

"Son of a blue jacket! Unless you go, we might as well board up the joint. You've earned a break for working your fingers plumb to the bone. I only ask one favor."

"That depends." Some things a girl couldn't promise.

"I want you to get shed of that store-bought smile. Come home wearing a real one that grows from deep inside, the kind that lights up your face."

Laurel's throat caught at the mention of home. Truly Ollie was her family, and the cafe more than just a place to sleep.

"And another thing—steer clear of them damn, boot-licking soldiers and that stockade, you hear?"

* * *

The jailhouse door shielded Brodie from view. It wasn't that he ogled Laurel as she walked up the *Lazy Jane*'s gang plank. He simply preferred to admire . . . from a distance.

A soft bayou breeze ruffled the mass of raven ringlets piled atop her head, seeming to taunt his cowardice. She blew a kiss to Ollie and waved good-bye as the boat slowly gathered steam.

The razor-tongued, monkey woman had paid him an early visit, informing him of Laurel's outing.

"Just in case you're interested." She'd winked.

He wished in vain for the ability to turn a blind eye. Fact remained that everything the lady did caught his full attention.

With vanilla and pecan praline pie filling his head, he barely noticed the stage halting in front of the hotel. Jeb Prater hobbled on a cane toward the conveyance. With every step, the boy's eyes flicked in constant motion. Word had it Jeb had decided the climate had grown a mite on the warmish side.

Then movement at Gordon's Livery drew his attention. How the town bustled on this Monday.

Vallens's horse reared coming from the stables, its forelegs flailing. Brodie winced when the man dealt angry blows from a short crop. Apparently finding defiance futile, the horse let Vallens mount and they trotted west.

"Now where is he going?" Brodie didn't enjoy the sensation of something walking over his grave.

The wolf dog sprang from the shadows, loping beside his master down the road that would take them to Jefferson.

In an instant, the solution to the problem with Blanchard whipped into Brodie's mind. He yanked off the sheriff badge, tossing it, and snatched keys from a desk drawer.

"Get a move on, Bert. I'm taking you for a ride."

The prisoner sat up. "Ain't going to no hanging without a trial first. I have rights, you know."

A stroll along the promenade deck melted Laurel's tension. The fresh breeze hinted at nothing more than rain and the coming of autumn.

No sign here of threats . . . or broken hearts.

A flock of hungry egrets eager for scraps of bread must've taken joy in pelting the boat with droppings to mar the tranquil day. She hastened from the line of fire to an overhang.

Preoccupied, Laurel almost dove over the railing when the steam engine flushed out in a loud blow-down. It shouldn't have lifted her two feet in the air, considering how many times a day the sound echoed up and down the bayou. But it had been an unfortunate decision to stand directly above the outlet, for she'd received the full blast. She suddenly felt unnerved.

She closed her eyes and tried to recall every wrinkle in Ollie's features, the sound of the little bell over the cafe door, and Murphy's happy glow when she vowed to marry him.

Instead, a deeply lined face sculpted by the wind of a thousand battles flashed before her eyes.

And a sweat-stained hat that rattled.

By the time the gangplank was lowered in Jefferson, her jitters vanished . . . until a sweeping glance lit upon the huge Sandtown stockade looming above the bayou at Texas and Common streets. She'd take pains to stay away from that.

Considerable change had occurred since she last viewed the town through the eyes of an innocent young girl.

However, some sights remained true to recollection. Bales of cotton lined the wharf. Dock workers formed a steady stream, unloading crates and boxes that bore the King of Spades playing card. With few able to read, she recalled her father telling her how each city's assigned card eliminated costly errors.

Pieces of her former self fell into place with the haunting "Coonjines" the deckhands sang while they worked.

She hurried down Walnut to Polk Street, taking care of business first and foremost. Thank her lucky stars for the office in town; otherwise she'd have to traipse all the way out to the smelly packing plant two miles south. This saved hiring a hack and paying the toll to cross the bridge.

A gentleman who might've passed for Jake's twin twirled a mustache when she entered the J. P. Dunn Meat Cannery.

"Yes, madam?"

"I'm inquiring about an order for Ollie's Cafe bound for Redemption three weeks ago. It never arrived."

"Let me check our records." The man opened a thick book and ran a bony finger down a list. "Hmmmmm. It appears someone scratched through the name, thus we never shipped."

The odd and costly misunderstanding raised her ire.

"Why would one do such a thing? I can assure you, good man, no one canceled the shipment."

"I wouldn't know of matters that go on in the female mind."

"Meaning?" She stiffened, glaring at the pompous oaf.

"To state it delicately, women have a somewhat, shall we say, notorious peculiarity for changing their minds on a whim. Give them this and they want that."

"Well, I never!"

A graying man walked out from behind a curtain. "Pennybacker, what the devil are you doing? Customers keep our doors open and pay your wage, by the way, which could be terminated very quickly."

"Indeed. I beg your pardon." Pennybacker's face reddened. "I deeply regret the error and my statement, madam."

"As do I," she mumbled.

"If I were you, I'd get moving to the rear door. A farmer brought a load of hogs to take to the packing plant for slaughter. While you're at it, stay there until I decide you're fit to be around something other than dead carcasses."

"Yes, sir, Mr. Dunn. I'm already on my way, sir."

Mr. Dunn swiveled back to her. "Now, tell me what I can do to fix the problem, young lady."

Laurel emerged with a promise that the beef and pork would be on the *Lazy Jane*'s return trip.

Sedberry's Apothecary on Dallas came next for a certain elixir touted for amazing cures. Perhaps it would fix Ollie's heart. That would, indeed, be miraculous.

Newly cut lumber prevailed over burned hulks of businesses left gutted by a huge fire the previous year. Carpenters worked in a frenzy—some hammering while others carried long boards up ladders. Laurel swiveled this way and that to dodge a collision. The hubbub grated. Redemption's quiet had advantages. Eager to prevent a trampling and bypass an ogling group of soldiers, she crossed to the other side of the street and didn't slow for several blocks.

A cameo necklace in the window of Ney and Brothers drew her attention. The white silhouette overlaid on onyx spoke of purity that a respected, fashionable lady might wear. Mindful to turn away from her reflection, she fancied tying the black velvet ribbon and letting the cameo rest in the hollow of her throat.

The daydream burst.

Ladies of questionable virtue would never own such beauty.

Meanwhile, Sedberry's beckoned.

"Would you have some tincture of hawthorne berries?" she inquired of the gentleman inside.

"Yes, indeed. However, I fervently hope someone other than yourself has need of it. What a shame to lose a pretty one in the flower of her youth."

"It's for another. How much do I owe?"

The man accepted the gold double eagle and bit down. "Can't be too careful these days. Some feller's coating silver coins and passing them." A warning came along with the appropriate change, "Follow the directions carefully."

Laurel slipped the precious bottle into her handbag. She closed the door behind her, praying she'd bought Ollie a few extra days.

Jars of candy and dry goods in J. M. Murphy and Company waylaid her. Redemption's small mercantile devoted its limited space to things less frivolous. Busy tallying a woman's bill, the clerk gave her a fleeting glance.

"Make yourself at home. Someone will be with you shortly."

She spied the ready-made dresses hanging from hooks on the wall, more rare in the bayou than candy. She moved toward the stylish cut of a pretty blue, fingering the taffeta and silk.

"You have the figure for that, if I do say so."

Laurel turned. A few gray streaks added matronly flair to the dark-haired woman. Twinkling eyes added humor.

"Oh, I can't buy it. I'm only browsing."

"Passionflower . . . that's what they call the color. Isn't that the most romantic name you ever heard tell of?"

The woman's bold examination gave Laurel warning pricks.

"You're not from here. I know every dog, coon, and hen house. I'm Mrs. Georgia Rutabaga of the Tyler Rutabagas. But say, you do resemble the James clan over at Turkey Creek."

Her heart skipped a beat. "I just arrived on the *Lazy Jane*. I wouldn't know them."

Mrs. Rutabaga whipped out a shimmering lavender dress hidden behind the others. "This was made for you. With those violet eyes, I guarantee it'd catch a young gentleman's attention."

The pulse roared in Laurel's ears. She struggled to breathe, but the air hung in the rawness of her throat.

"No!" The word burst harsh and brittle.

Alarm crossed the woman's face. "Oh, dear. I wouldn't have upset you for the world and everything in it."

Laurel fought nausea and spun for the door, leaving poor Mrs. Rutabaga, of the Tyler Rutabagas, mouth gaping.

Barbershop, millinery, and stables passed in a blur. When Laurel regained her senses, she stood in front of a sign identifying the Excelsior Hotel. Years ago it'd carried the Irvine House name. She dropped to a bench amid the jangle of the departing stage.

Contact with the lavender shook her to the core. Time should've lessened that pain. Ollie had assured her it would. The agony shouldn't persist afresh as the night she escaped.

Maybe she and normalcy had forever parted company.

Streams of people entered and exited the hotel, each sending curious stares her way. Afraid they might approach, she moved on. Sidestepping blue bellies set her on an aimless path that led back to Dallas Street in front of the telegraph office.

A chance glance through the open door froze the blood in her veins. A black-clad figure stood inside. The dog poised beside the man confirmed it.

That Vallens might have followed made her head whirl. Had he telegraphed Will Taft?

Laurel ducked into the nearest shop when he exited. Through the window she stared in horror as he gripped a young girl's arm. There was something familiar in the sweet dimples.

Shock rippled. The features of a forgotten vision took shape.

Her resemblance to her sister was more than wishful fancy.

In the back of her mind she had wondered if she would run into some of her family. They lived so near, but it hadn't seemed anything beyond a lost daydream. Until this moment.

The shiny, cinnamon-colored hair, pert nose, and sparkling hazel eyes were no mistake. Hannah had grown into a striking beauty. Quick calculation made Hannah, who'd been nine the last time she'd seen her, fifteen . . . Laurel's age when the world had turned upside down.

Vallens dragged Hannah down an alley while the wolf dog chased an apple wagon, much to his master's ire. Hatred overwhelmed her.

She wouldn't let him steal her sister.

Keeping out of sight, she followed them. Luckily, barrels littered the alley. She ducked behind one, wondering why the girl didn't scream. Then she noticed the hand over her mouth. A discarded piece of two-by-four fit Laurel's palm perfectly. Silently, she crept. Intent on subduing the struggling form, Vallens didn't hear her approach.

Cracking his head with a mighty blow, Laurel grabbed

the girl and sprinted toward the bustle. The instant they gained the street, an arm reached out and pulled them around the corner.

The hiss of snake rattles seemed part of some illusion, but the voice lent credence.

"Get behind me, Lil. I'll take care of this."

Brodie blocked Vallens, who'd come after his prize.

"Touch them again and you die."

Laurel couldn't take her eyes from Vallens. Surprise, then anger, switched places when they collided at the jagged scar. Brodie's frigid advice suspended the bounty hunter's hand in mid-reach.

How or from where Brodie had come didn't matter. Relief that he had quelled Laurel's shaking knees.

"Shenandoah . . . or should I say Sheriff?"

Vallens's foolhardy attempt to provoke a fight would buy trouble he likely hadn't considered.

"I don't give a flying squirrel which you use, though if you bothered to notice, I'm not wearing a badge. Although I feel obliged to inform you that molesting young women happens to still be a crime in Texas." The Navy Colt hung low on his hip.

Brodie's hands flexed, the cold rebel in him once again finding a home on familiar ground.

Others less accustomed to the subtle tic of his jaw, the steel gray in his eye, or the defiant crooked smile might've missed the signs. But their souls had interlaced in those long, steamy nights, weaving a sturdy cloth no weapon could penetrate.

Only two things could unravel the threads . . .

Treachery and mistrust.

Heaven help her! The rent began when he broke his word.

A mass exodus of onlookers who suspected abruptly flying lead brought her back to the present.

"Don't want any trouble. Just having a polite conversation with the little miss." A sneer curled the man's upper lip. "No law agin that, is there?"

Hannah shivered, huddling closer.

"Leave them be unless you desire the services of an undertaker." Brodie never blinked, his gaze focused.

"You're mighty self-righteous for one who could end up in the stockade. A word in the right ear will take care of you."

The air Laurel sucked in struggled to fill the ache in her chest. Why had Brodie walked into a place fraught with danger when he knew the possible result?

Surely he couldn't think himself invincible.

. . . . Or think her worthy of such a great risk.

Even while Laurel denied that speculation, chills raced through her. No one would spin a weighted roulette wheel against the house and think to win.

Not on her account.

Dear God! It forever landed on black, the color of sin.

And the number thirteen.

"One thing I learned well during the war—men with holes can't make any noise. Just give me half a reason."

Arrogance twisted the scarred face into a hundred different roads, all of them leading to places he shouldn't go.

"This ain't your town. You got no rights here."

"Why do men suddenly think they can *own* towns? Me and Persuader might dispute that logic. It's a damn good day to lose a bet."

Finally, Vallens raised his hands and stood back.

Brodie flashed a grim stare. "Laurel, take your friend and wait at the sheriff's."

Perhaps she'd wronged him.

Perhaps the cloth hadn't unraveled, merely snagged, needing repair.

And perhaps he did think her someone of worth.

Vallens spoke softly, words meant for her alone. "I'm thinking. Taft might consider a younger surrogate fair trade."

The threat reached further than Vallens intended. Brodie grabbed his throat, pinning him against the rough stone wall.

"Should either lady get so much as a hair out of place, I'll come for you. No rock'll be big enough for your mangy hide to crawl under."

Chapter Twenty-one

Brodie Yates found satisfaction when color drained from the man's face, leaving the scar a ghostly trail to a past that persisted in haunting. His grip tightened. How easy to give in and snap Vallens's neck!

One thing kept him from murder—the lady who held his heart.

Each time he gazed into her eyes, he saw the person he could become.

The one she believed he could be.

His hold slackened, releasing the rotten piece of humanity. Vallens straightened the drab frock coat. Brodie carefully observed each subtle movement through narrowed slits.

He'd lived with hatred of one kind or another for most of his life. Though he'd sent more men to glory than any judge or jury, each death had occurred only when things reached the kill-or-be-killed stage. Never had he stolen a man's life's blood in anger.

The depth of rage scared the living daylights out of him.

The cold, lethal steel at his side called to him.

Scum such as Vallens had cost Laurel six years. By God almighty, she'd have an opportunity to reclaim her soul even if Brodie had to help it along. He shot the man in black an icy glare, but Vallens avoided eye contact, preferring to edge toward his six-shooter instead.

"Go ahead. I'd love to itch this trigger finger."

"Ain't over yet." Vallens's arm dropped limply. "There's a time and place coming."

"Name it. Me and Persuader will be there."

Once Vallens backed away Brodie started toward the sheriff's office.

The two girls paced in front of the stone building where he'd told them to wait. The bright glimmer swimming in Laurel's stare released a rush of emotion so intense he choked.

He longed to take her in his arms, comfort her, and kiss away each sorrow. But he didn't. Instead, he let her fresh scent pillage the best part remaining of a lost love that used to be . . . and prayed for strength to pull himself from the whirlpool trying to suck him under.

"Don't worry. The man's not too bright, but I don't think he'll bother you." At least not until he got reinforcements. But he didn't share that tidbit with her. He couldn't.

"What happens when you're not around? What will Vallens do then?" The sob strangling her voice tightened his jaw.

Great Johnny Reb!

He'd rearrange each star in the sky and move Texas to the other side of the world if he held that in his power. Only it wouldn't fix anyone's problems.

Not hers, not his, and neither would it heal the ache in his chest.

"That man; what did he want?" Except for the hair and hazel eyes, the young woman could pass for Laurel.

"Zeke Vallens has a death wish and is looking for easy money. Selling human flesh wouldn't make him a bit squeamish."

"Sell me? To whom?" The fear in her pale face deepened.

"It doesn't matter. We're not about to let him, so put that from your mind." Laurel placed protective arms about the girl's shoulders. "This is Brodie Yates. He's a friend."

"I apologize for scaring you, miss. Just be aware of the man's capabilities." He opened the door for them. "We don't warn lightly. I'll bend Sheriff Roberts's ear about the particulars so he'll know."

"I haven't thanked you for coming to my aid," Hannah said.

"Honey, there's no need. You'd have done the same."

"I should've paid more attention. Mama says I'm too trusting for my own good." Soft laughter stole from the girl's lips. "I'm Hannah James."

Brodie jerked about. No wonder she resembled Laurel. The warning shake of Laurel's head told him to keep quiet. She hadn't told the girl who she was. He wondered why.

Hannah suddenly hugged Laurel. "Take pity and tell me again who you are so I won't feel like an imbecile."

Laurel's soft tug was a bolt of lightning. "Brodie, go on inside. Hannah and I want to gab a bit out here. Lady talk."

"I suppose, but don't wander off."

Laurel pretended to adjust the laces of her high-topped shoe. Excitement at seeing the girl had swept aside caution. A fake name? A harmless thing, really. Others likely did it on a regular basis. No one would know.

Except her.

And living with lies grew old. Adding more could further hinder reaching the pinnacle she most coveted.

"It's Laurel."

"That's pretty. I once had a sister by that name."

Pain spiraled, gouging a deep path inside before it lodged in her chest. How foolish to risk discovery. Still, she couldn't stifle a thirst for tidbits about her loved ones.

A million questions poised on the tip of her tongue.

"I gather from your tone that you've suffered tragedy."

"It's dreadful." Tears welled in Hannah's eyes.

Laurel shifted her gaze to a distant spot, wishing she'd stuck to polite topics, like the prospect of a cold winter or how many drops of water it took to fill Big Cypress.

"Then you shan't speak of it. Let's enjoy the sunshine."

"How silly of me. Mama says we must go on. Some days it's very hard. I miss my Laurel as much now as the day she vanished. Do you have any brothers or sisters?"

She swallowed a startled gasp. "I regret I don't."

"That's a pity. I can't imagine life without family."

Excruciating torture came from being unable to forget that very closeness. She'd not shared that with anyone but Ollie.

"Your mother . . . does she live near by?" Laurel's voice dropped to a raspy whisper. "And what of your father?"

"We have a place on Turkey Creek. They continue to farm the same parcel of land they've owned thirty-odd years. Of course, they couldn't now without my brothers' help."

The news made her breath quicken. Less than a half hour away by buggy. So near . . .

Hannah's tentative smile raised haunting memories. "Where's your home, Laurel?"

"Miles down the bayou."

"Papa and my brothers keep a tight rein. I've not traveled more than ten miles from the farm. I guess I can't hold that against them, considering what happened."

Will Taft's ugly face loomed. Hannah didn't realize what evil awaited those who strayed unprotected from home.

"Advice from someone who knows—you haven't missed out."

"You've probably been just about everywhere. I think someday I'd like to visit St. Louis."

"No!" It resounded like a rifle shot. Hannah jumped. "I only wish to stress that you're better off. The most precious things in life are here. Don't throw away what you have believing life is more grand and interesting elsewhere. Believe me, it isn't."

Her family had celebrated birthdays, Christmases, and baptisms. Each holiday and joyous time missed.

She wondered about Jeremiah and his pet raccoon. About Millie, who no longer had need of the baby blanket Laurel had sewn with uneven stitches.

And about the fading of her mother's hair.

Spit and thunder!

To discover more carried too steep a price, with no guarantee that they'd accept a tainted daughter.

"Thank you again, Laurel. I almost felt my sister had returned. My brothers Quaid and Rafe must worry what happened."

"They're here?" More ripples went through her.

"Most likely at the saloon. The bottle eases powerful guilt over letting Laurel disappear. Papa'll have their hides, though, if they've gotten lickered up again."

Her heart lurched. Other casualties lay in the wake of the crime. How ironic to have thought herself the only victim.

Less than an hour later, Laurel straddled the big Appaloosa in front of Brodie. She was a tangled mass of nerves. Her sister had walked out of her life again, ripping open unhealed scars. Heaven only knew when she'd get that close to family again.

Between thought of Zeke Vallens, the parting with Hannah, and half expecting a contingent of soldiers to surround the hated rebel spy any second, her head was pounding something fierce.

"Smokey, take us home, boy." Brodie gave a gentle nudge.

In horse-talk, the snort and toss of his head might've said the animal thought it high time to get out of hostile territory.

"I should've gone back on the steamer."

Male heat where her bottom rested snugly against Brodie's lap aroused a yearning she'd worked night, day, and years to forget. Such ridiculous ideas came half past late.

Notions and feelings change, he'd said.

"Not a chance. I'm not letting you out of my sight."

"You expect Vallens to make good on his threats?"

"I may have given him second thoughts when I told him what to expect with his persistence. But time will tell."

The clipped statement left no doubt what had transpired. Brodie must've laid down some strong advice, although it brought meager comfort. Icy fear held her in a glacial clutch.

"I'll stretch anyone on a marble slab who tries to harm Hannah. What those monsters did to me they will never do to another member of my family; not while I live."

"So Hannah James is truly your kin?"

"My younger sister. Our meeting almost seemed fated." She wished she could say likewise for the arms brushing against each of her hips.

His light touch seemed most protective. . . .

Most safe and valued . . .

And most wishful of her not to accept that the bridge had already washed out. Hope of crossing back over it had long passed.

"I fail to understand why you didn't tell her who you are."

"Discovering certain facts would add grief, not ease it." She gripped the saddle horn tighter. "What can she remember, anyway?"

"Plenty. Why in God's name don't you go home?"

"I can't." A lump of hard clay sat in her stomach much easier than bitter truth. "I won't."

"You can live with them fearing what happened yet never knowing?" His voice held deceptive softness. "That's not the lady I knew."

"They believe I'm dead. That's the way it'll stay. That's my final word on the subject. It's much better for everyone." Laurel despised the brittle edge sneaking into her tone. She could no more help it than stop loving the wrong man.

"For everyone except you."

The answer came like a soft, whispering wind. His breath ruffled the top of her hair, sending shivers down her spine. Dare he know what he did, the fire their closeness ignited, he'd hustle her back to the *Lazy Jane* faster than lightning could split the heavens.

"Things change. I can do just fine."

Smokey meandered through tall pines toward home. Moss-bearded water tupelo in the bayou reflected her spirit, for they also appeared old and weary from keeping constant vigil. Autumn's approach also brought yellow color to the river birch and the black gum's slow turn to scarlet. A pair of loons played catch-me-if-you-can across the placid swamp.

"Have you ever seen such a beautiful place?" he whispered in her ear, his arms stealing around her waist.

Sick of fighting, Laurel relaxed. To rest against him for the barest moment was a mistake. Beneath flesh and muscle beat a steady rhythm she'd have to be dead to ignore—along with the pressure of the rigid bulge against her skirts.

A bittersweet smile crossed her lips. What she'd give to be free. Respectability, honor, presented more of a challenge than she'd dreamed.

"The sunlight on your hair would turn a raven green with jealousy—so dark it's almost blue."

Laurel kept silent, torn between stopping what they both couldn't live without and fear that he would. Lord knew she'd love nothing more than to have the gray-eyed rebel touch her bare skin. Tingles fluttered up and down her body, inside and out.

Before she could nip passion in the bud, Brodie nuzzled her neck. The same gentle caress from long ago; his lips traced a path up to her jaw.

"Pure silk. You carry the scent of fresh rainwater. You've driven me out of my mind since I saw you in the cafe."

The hoarse lament was wrenched from his throat, sending tremors of gladness. More proof he'd lied last night: He wanted her.

And yet despite everything she couldn't let him have her. It was painfully wrong. Regardless if the sensation of his tender embrace, regardless of the dewy flush his kisses brought to her skin, and regardless of how very much she wanted to welcome glorious abandon, she must honor one simple promise.

"We can't do this. I won't wrong Murphy."

"Then why does it feel so damn right?"

"I spent too many years in that hellhole to throw away what I've gained." Laurel twisted to face him. "Do you know what it's like to see your reflection without turning away in disgust? I don't want to ruin my chances of finding out. One day I'll remove the black cloth and actually like the woman staring back. I have a chance to hold my head up, look honest folks in the eye and not feel shame for a single, blessed thing."

"We both have a lot of black water swamp to tread before we reach that point, don't we?"

"Then understand that pushing away what you're offering is the hardest thing I've ever done."

"The thought of you married to Murph . . . I can't let it happen. You ask too much." Pure torture thickened Brodie's voice.

She traced the crevices around his mouth and fingered the rebellious lock of hour that fell across his forehead.

"Murphy found something decent in me. I won't dishonor him. Let me break the engagement first." She couldn't help rubbing a little salt. "Besides, you gave your blessing, don't forget."

"You're devilish, you know? Just had to bring that up, didn't you? Get one thing clear, little Miss Tease. I won't let you marry my brother! You're mine."

Though a crooked grin accompanied the statement, it brought out her Irish blood. "You won't *let* me?"

"You can wipe that warpaint off your face. You know what I mean. You belong to me. Always have. Always will."

Smokey came to a standstill and swung his head around, as if sensing a good argument and wanting to catch every word.

"Is that a fact? I think the excitement in town must've addled your brain. Should I wish to marry your brother, that's what I'll do. I'm no child to order about."

Why had she said that? She didn't want to wed Murphy.

"Of a certainty, I've never found anything but full-grown woman." Snake rattles on the hat warned of danger. "Would you ruin three lives simply to prove a point?"

"If you think that, you don't know me at all."

"Then why in sweet Jezzie did you cause such a ruckus?"

"I didn't care for your lordly attitude."

He noticed at last that they weren't moving and touched the animal's flanks. "Smokey, you flea-bitten snot bag, what'd you stop for? It's impolite to eavesdrop on a conversation."

"You're doing it again."

His deep sigh fluttered the top of her hair. "What?"

"Now you're bossing around your poor horse."

"He's used to it. Besides, he has no choice."

A great blue heron passed over them and landed in the boggy marsh, a low-pitched croak breaking the silence.

"Arguing is the last thing I want," he went on. "In my feeble bumbling I merely tried to clarify my stance on the subject."

"I accept your apology."

One bit of good came from it all—the sparring had doused a heated passion that had come came close to scorching them both.

"I'll thank you to keep your hands—and your kisses—to yourself for now. Never tempt me into sullying my honor again."

"Yes, ma'am. When I see how far you've come, I can almost buy an acre or two of your dream. Maybe putting down roots can give a man a purpose other than staying alive."

"Like Ollie's grandpappy told her, 'If'n you don't take that first step, you ain't ever going nowhere.'" Laurel suddenly laughed, realizing what she'd said. "Blue blazes! That old skin-flinty woman's got me quoting chapter and verse now."

"That salty tongue does tend to grow on you, doesn't it?"

She touched the saddlebag to make sure the elixir rode easy and said a silent prayer that it would work.

"If you're so all-fired het up on becoming a respectable lady, then quit rubbing the match against the flint." A groan followed the order. "Remember, you still belong to me."

Laurel squirmed, trying to move from the snug pocket the juncture of his legs created.

"You keep doing that and I'm likely to forget about our agreement and your purpose. I'll sling that made-for-loving body of yours off this horse onto a patch of sweet grass so quick it'll make you dizzy."

Heat flooded her face. "I'm only trying to keep from—"

"Hellfire and damnation! Be still."

She sniffed, and kept her back ramrod straight and her hands glued to the saddle horn. He had a lot of nerve blaming her, seeing how he insisted she ride with him instead of taking the steamer.

Men!

"You never explained why you pranced into the devil's den, of all places. You're a fine one to speak of death wishes. Please say you didn't do such a dim-witted thing for my benefit."

"And if I did? What'd be wrong with that?"

The afternoon sun blazed.

"Plenty, Mr. Rebel. You could've hired a street crier to advertise your presence and gotten less notice. Now the Billy Yanks definitely know your whereabouts. A man would have to perceive himself invincible to waltz in there."

Guilt would make living with that burden impossible.

"I had a job to do and I did it."

"For me."

"Whom I happen to care about. Besides, keeping you safe only played a part in my . . . how did you put it? Dim-witted plan? I needed to get rid of Blanchard. I told Sheriff Roberts how Redemption lacked a lawman: my solution to a problem."

"You already quit the job?"

Her heart sank. Breaking ties to the town seemed a sure sign he intended to head for high ground again.

Did he simply seek another source of amusement?

Or torture?

Old doubts taunted her. Had he truly moved that far from tricks and deceit?

Yet he'd ridden into the midst of enemy territory to assure no harm came to her. Hadn't he?

Chapter Twenty-two

Laurel should've blessed the sight of Redemption. Instead regret and forlorn sadness weighed heavily on her by the time she slid from Brodie's lap to solid ground.

Ollie scrambled through the cafe door, her bandy legs reminding Laurel of the pump handle on a water spout.

"Goldarned it! What happened? I put you aboard the steamer and you come back riding on horseback."

"Vallens followed me. I'll give you the full gist." She turned and got stuck in the anguished stare of a thousand disappointments. "I don't express gratitude well. They didn't exactly teach that in charm school . . . take care, Brodie."

He handed her the precious package from Sedberry's.

"Likewise. Promise to keep up your guard."

Against Vallens or himself? He failed to say. Perhaps both. He'd not offered to expand further on why he'd given up the sheriff job. It didn't bode well.

Before he coaxed Smokey toward the stables, he leaned over with a quiet warning. "Remember who you belong to, lady."

The horse pranced down the street with its tall rider. The

fragrance of shaving soap and leather—and the soft hiss of familiar rattles—wafted on the bayou breeze.

"You gonna fiddle-faddle there all day? The *Lazy Jane* brought a whole passel of meat to do something with."

"Thank goodness. The trip accomplished something, at least."

Other than twisting her emotions six ways to Sunday.

"Give me the lowdown. I'm about to bust a gut here."

"Which version do you want, plain or fancy?"

"Pretty sassy, aren't you?" Ollie perched on the edge of a chair, puffing away on her pipe. "Fancy'll do."

The account evoked a longer string of *dadblasted*s and *son of a blue jacket*s than Laurel could ever remember in one sitting. Of course, she never breathed a word of the ride, lodged firmly in a position in which she had no right being. That would've brought out the *damn scoundrel*s and *scalawag*s list.

"I'll blame myself and rightly so if harm befalls Hannah."

"Cain't help what a mealy-mouthed swamp rat does. You didn't tell your sister who you are, did you?"

"I couldn't."

"You should've. The girl deserves the truth."

"Peace serves my family better than shame and disgrace." Both had become regular visitors and neither made the pillow softer at night.

"You have pretty odd thoughts for a smart gal." Ollie put the teakettle on to boil. "You think they rest easy? Your sister's so brokenhearted she cain't bear to speak of you, your brothers have taken to drowning their guilt in a bottle, and your poor mama and daddy—Lord only knows what they lug around day in and day out. Don't sound like any peace I ever knew."

Laurel evaded the look that said she'd been nesting with a gaggle of loons all afternoon.

"This continues to be a bone of contention. After what happened today, it's simply not safe for Hannah or them."

"A limp, sorry answer. Ever heard of secret visiting? There's ways, should you want to. Not knowing whether you're dead or alive will eat a hole clean through. Give 'em an end to the grieving. Let 'em bury the past, dang it."

"I can't. I don't know how or where to start."

Callused palms rubbed hers; tears filled her eyes.

"That's what I'm here for."

When did the rightness of it become lost in what she'd have to sacrifice? Loathing in her parent's eyes would destroy what remained of the spirit Will Taft had left her.

"I think of them each morning and their faces are the last things I see at night. I die a little more inside every day."

"Then do it. Go see them. Set the past straight."

"And should they spit disgust and turn from me? What then?"

"Being scared is as natural as breathing. The longer you hold off, the harder it is to suck in air. Take it from an old sourdough, find a speck of happiness. Give 'em a chance, girl."

Doubts churned some of that Georgia clay into hard cement. How great were the odds that they'd forgive and forget?

"I promise to give it some thought."

"Now, what's in the package you brought from Jefferson? Too small for a dress or hat." Ollie rubbed her hands together. "Let me see."

"It's something for you—tincture of hawthorne berries."

"Well, you can guzzle it, 'cause I ain't putting a drop of that stuff in my mouth. Nope. One of those carpetbagging leeches talked you into parting with good money, did he?"

Laurel sighed. This might be harder than she thought.

* * *

Waking before the sun rose the next morning, she decided Murphy would hear the truth—the whole, sordid, unvarnished truth.

He'd thank her for releasing him from scandal.

In a few hours, she'd breathe freely without laboring under the heavy weight of lies. She hopped from bed.

Ollie's open door and absence from the kitchen raised a few concerns, which Laurel reasoned away. She'd probably spent the night with Curley, doing what lovers did. Color rose in her cheeks. She didn't care for such thoughts. Not that Ollie didn't deserve the full measure of life and all it entailed. Laurel merely preferred to not think of a parent engaged in a sexual act.

Like it or not, the woman had assumed a motherly role.

Still, Ollie hadn't appeared at a den of sin like the Black Garter looking for salvation. And she had spent a goodly amount of time in cardsharp Frenchie Devereaux's company.

A hot cup of tea during the wait for appropriate calling hours helped clear unsettling thoughts.

It would take every ounce of courage to say what she had put off too long. Ollie had yet to make an appearance when the clock landed on eight. She grabbed her shawl.

"My lands, child. Come on in." Etta wiped the flour off her hands with her apron and took Laurel's wrap.

"Perhaps I've arrived too early."

"Not in this house. Mr. Murphy is raring to go. Now Mr. Brodie, he's another story. That one hasn't bothered to rouse for breakfast."

Even better. After narrowly averting disaster yesterday, she'd prefer to skip another meeting with him at the moment.

The intimate scene inside Murphy's room stopped her

short. Nora bent over the patient, giving him a shave. The Indian woman's long braids snaked down her breasts and rested on Murphy's bare chest. Several seconds elapsed, during which Laurel debated leaving. But when she backed out, he saw her.

"Don't go," he called. "You're in time to watch Nora shear the sheep. I had hoped to surprise you."

Laurel took the empty chair and clasped her hands to stop their nervous twitter. "I'll enjoy your helplessness," she said, her eyes on the sharp straight razor Nora held.

"No mercy. A man in his sick bed can't get any respect from you females."

"Pay price for pretty smile and winsome ways." Nora scraped rough whiskers from a section of jaw.

Murphy winked. "Got Nora fooled. And here she thought I had the charm of a potato digger."

"Better watch it. Remember who's holding the razor."

"Lady right." Nora's mischievous eyes glistened. "Ever hear them say the only good Injun is a dead one?"

Abruptly, Murphy's face darkened. "I warned you, never say that again. Doesn't matter what your origin—not to me. There are more important things in life."

Would he think differently when Laurel told him of her scarlet past? He appeared willing to overlook other things.

Nora shrugged. "I hear worse. Not deaf."

Uncomfortable silence lay in the wake of that exchange, but at last Murphy's mood lightened. "Besides, Nora's worked too hard snatching me from the jaws of death. She'll not ruin her handiwork by slitting my throat now."

"Keep talking, yellow eyes, and we see."

Nora finished the task without further banter, gathered the utensils, and left the room.

"Come here, love. See how a clean-shaven face kisses."

Kissing wouldn't make the truth-telling come easier. He noticed her hesitation and patted the bed.

Laurel's knees trembled when she stood. "We must talk."

"After you come and perform your pre-wifely duty."

So much for doing the right thing.

He pulled her into his arms once she sank onto the mattress. Hope for averting close contact fled.

Desperate though she was to get things out in the open, she had no heart for kicking a man flat on his back.

"Now, what pressing business do you have today?"

Strands of guilt twisted around her soul like ivy encircling a tree trunk—poison ivy. If only he knew she'd already changed her mind and given her heart to another. What would it do to him? How would he feel when he discovered his own brother occupied the place he should hold?

Dear God, what a mess she'd made of things!

Brodie wiped away the shaving residue and listened to voices from the next room. It was an early hour for Laurel to visit. He dressed quickly and opened the door.

"I want out of this bed and I won't argue about it!" Murphy's thunder echoed in the hall.

"Nora thinks it's too soon and I happen to agree."

The throaty voice made Brodie reconsider. He could do without another dose the of misery their encounters left. The last one lingered in his mind.

Before he could move swiftly past, Laurel sped from the room and into his chest.

He lunged to break her fall, the contact jarring the breath from him in more ways than one. Warning bells clanged when he found himself floating in smoky lavender pools.

The pink, open mouth drew him and every rational

thought vanished at their kiss. Brodie savored the taste of her on his tongue very gently and with extreme laziness. Her stiff body relaxed under his caress as if it, too, had grown weary of fighting the forbidden. She melted into his embrace, leaving him one wish . . . to hold her until each tomorrow faded.

The sound of someone clearing her throat startled him back to awareness. Nora stood with arms folded. Laurel pushed away from him.

Sweet Bessie! The woman had bad timing.

"Mr. Brodie, what beautiful day."

"Yes, isn't it?" He caught a twinkle in the dark gaze.

"I come look for you. Please to help Mr. Murphy from bed. If crazy man insists on pulling wound open, we help him."

He shot Laurel a contrite glance, which she ignored, choosing instead to turn away and smooth back the sides of her hair. Never would he deliberately embarrass her.

Lodestone to iron didn't pull with a greater force than their bodies. The emotions she raised were by no means her fault but his own. He had to show restraint.

Lord knew he'd failed in that each time they came within a mile of each other.

Brodie lifted a rueful brow and strolled into the room. "Murph, I hear you're giving these ladies grief."

"Don't go starting on me, too. Dammit, I want up, and now!"

"Where do you insist on going, pray tell?"

"Out of these four walls. I want sunshine and fresh air."

"I suppose that would be the garden. Then take hold of my neck and I'll fix you right up."

"I have my own two feet, thank you very much." Murphy's stew indicated no sign of changing to a more pleasant disposition.

"Whatever suits you beats the hell out of me."

Murphy took a couple of shuffling steps before collapsing. Brodie easily lifted and carried him to a seat outdoors. Laurel and Nora followed with blankets they tucked around him.

"Quit your hovering. You'll turn a man into a milksop before he can spit." The bluster had lost its fire. A pale face and a trembling hand bespoke sapped strength.

"I get you coffee and plenty food," Nora said.

"Stop rushing it, will you?" Brodie pulled tobacco makings from a pocket.

"That's the problem." Murphy took Laurel's hand. "We've postponed the wedding long enough. I want to make her my wife . . . in every way."

Despite the logic of waiting for Murphy to recover, despite the fact that they had more at stake than destroying three lives by haste, and despite the love that anchored him to his brother, Brodie couldn't help resisting. Plain and simple, Laurel fettered him with her insistence on respectability, which he admitted everyone could use a lot more of—even him. Yet, the encumbrance of it chafed worse than the silver star had.

He wanted her. Seeing no way out of the quagmire grated on his raw nerves.

Rolling a good smoke—now that was something he could do well. Tapping the right amount of Bull Durham evenly in a row and rolling it between finger and thumb not too tight and not too loose. He'd call himself an expert. He lit up and passed it to Murphy.

"Thanks. Only a man can appreciate the value of tobacco."

Laurel's guilty stare warned Brodie not to make a peep, for he alone knew her weakness for fine cigars. The tip of her tongue slowly wet passion-swollen lips, sending a shiver through him. He could kiss her for the next hundred years and never lose the craving for that wild honey taste.

The warmth of their morning encounter had left its brand. He'd soaked up her touch in the way a parched desert soaked up spring rains.

Odd how nothing ever quenched this thirst.

"Coffee, Mr. Brodie?" Etta brought a tray.

It would do, he supposed. Anything to moisten his mouth until he figured out a way to get spring rains in his direction.

"Don't mind if I do. Thanks, Etta." He accepted a cup.

All of a sudden a parade of citizens marched single file through the gate, past the sleeping crepe myrtle and into the garden. A trombone and drum would've completed the spectacle.

"Sheriff, we have news of a disturbing nature to report," Jake hollered, leading the pack.

"Whatever it is, you're in the wrong place. I'm not sheriff anymore."

"Since when? No one bothered to inform us."

"Since I don't want the job, that's when."

Laurel tripped when she heard his statement and nearly spilled the cup of tea Etta brought her. Hearing it blurted that way made her ill.

"You can't just up and quit. We have to call a town meeting in which we require you to appear and submit a valid reason." George's whine, coupled with the barber's sanctimonious quirks, irritated Brodie worse than a dull blade on a whetstone.

"Did you get that, Thomas? You're an attorney. Don't we have procedures to go through?" Jake twirled his mustache.

"What explanation can you offer for barging onto my property without an invite, ladies and gentlemen?" Murphy glowered at the crowd that continued to gather in the yard.

"Accept our apologies, Murphy. Didn't see that we had a choice." At least a contrite John Miller shuffled his feet, staring at the ground.

"We've come to report a murder," Florence Kempshaw blurted out.

"What the devil are you babbling about?" Brodie's patience wore thin. "If this is a trick to get me to bend to your will, it won't work."

"At least we *think* he's met a foul end," lawyer-trained Thomas Hutson attempted to accurately state.

"Think? Don't you know?" Murphy's bluster returned, along with a bit of ire. "You interrupted a fine day with mere supposition?"

"Who in the name of God do you *think* met a foul end?" Brodie's cup rattled on the small table Etta had brought out.

"Zeke Vallens, that's who."

Chapter Twenty-three

"You caused this unholy stink over a man you despise and wished dead to begin with? Since when exactly did this worriment kick in? Besides, I ran into the man in Jefferson yesterday, and I assure you, for a dead man he appeared awfully spry. Probably still there, or else he rode on to spread good cheer elsewhere." The red flush rising from Brodie's neck signaled his boiling point. He looked like he wanted to throttle them all.

"We have reason to suspect different," Florence put in.

Laurel bit her lip. She didn't know which caused more concern . . . that Vallens perhaps still stalked Hannah, that he had carried out his threat to inform the military where they could find Shenandoah . . . or that Brodie had quit the sheriff job.

Ollie's unslept bed also troubled her.

Where was the woman, and why didn't she number in this parade? She was not one to miss a confrontation.

Laurel craned her neck and located Curley, who stood alone at the back of the group.

"What do you base your suspicion on?" Laurel held her breath.

"Two gunshots around midnight," Jake explained. "One broke the alley window of the barber shop."

"Did you happen to look out?" Murphy asked.

"I dove under the bed. I'm not crazy, you know."

The crowd tittered.

"I heard 'em, too," John Miller added quietly.

"Did you get enough gumption to check for a body this morning, Jake?" Laurel couldn't shake her unease.

The barber thrust out his chest. "Sure did. Not hide nor hair of anything dead—just some drops of blood."

"There you have it." Brodie stretched out his feet.

"Not so fast; there's more." George Adams put up his hand. "Vallens's horse is in the stables and his clothes are in the hotel. Haven't seen that mangy dog of his yet, though."

"It doesn't prove murder." Laurel sorted the chilling facts in her head-gunshots, blood, and a certain missing lady.

She prayed Ollie hadn't taken matters into her own hands.

A new thought was worse. Perhaps Vallens had disposed of Ollie.

"It's your worry, not mine. Vallens can sleep in Hell for all I care." Brodie wouldn't budge on the subject.

"You're sheriff until we decide you ain't," Jake huffed. "You cain't jump up and change your mind. Like I said—"

"You have procedure. Yeah, I heard, and you can take your town meetings and stuff 'em up you-know-where."

"Well, I never!" Florence fanned her face furiously.

"What did you do with Blanchard is what we'd like to know," Martin said, then ducked behind George. He'd already received a dose of Brodie. "If it ain't too much bother."

"Yeah, did you take him out and lynch him?" This time George did the asking. "I wouldn't put it past your sort."

Laurel wouldn't have them think for one minute that Brodie would stoop so low. By the set of his jaw she saw he wouldn't dignify his comment with an answer. "Bert is enjoying Jefferson jail hospitality."

Brodie shot a warning look for her trouble.

"That means every one of you who witnessed the robbery and abduction will have to traipse over there to testify when his trial comes up." The gray-eyed rebel grinned at the ruckus that prospect raised.

"I'm not going anywhere near that place until the army pulls out," George stated.

"Me either." A mumble of voices agreed.

Curley spoke up from the back. "Who's going to volunteer to be sheriff now? I nominate Jake, since he has the loudest voice. Everyone in favor say aye."

A chorus of ayes bounced off the clusters of asters, chrysanthemums, and tall, noble oaks.

"Hey, wait a minute. This ain't legal, Curley Madison."

"Anyone opposed except Jake?"

Not a soul spoke.

"Folks, you have a new sheriff," Brodie drawled.

"You can't do this. I'm refusing."

But the rank and file had already turned and headed back where they'd come from, leaving Jake scratching his head.

"Looks like you're stuck with it, Whitaker. Better pray Vallens met a foul end or you may have to earn your keep." Brodie propped a matchstick in the corner of his mouth.

Laurel would've taken delight in the color draining from around the handlebar mustache, but she hurried to try to catch Curley. Wedged in the crowd, she found he'd disappeared from view. Hope sank. She'd not visit the saloon. She couldn't.

"Ollie, where in thunder have you been? I had no idea what to think or—"

The sight of Ollie washing what looked to be blood off her hands at the kitchen pump stopped Laurel in midsentence. A haggard face turned to face her. Bloodshot eyes suggested a lack of sleep.

"Son of a blue jacket! Cain't a grown woman spend the night how she sees fit without a body making a fuss about it?"

"With your failing heart, you can't blame me for worrying. I thought you might be lying dead somewhere."

"My ticker's fine. I went out, and that's all I'm saying."

That Ollie wasn't forthcoming added a chill to her bones.

"You probably haven't heard the latest circulating the rumor mill—someone might have murdered Vallens." She couldn't control the quiver in her voice. "And then I see you washing something red off your hands. . . ."

"And you thought I might have done the deed," Ollie cackled.

"You threatened to often enough. I didn't have to stretch my imagination too far. You had more than good reason."

"We both did, you forgettin' that?"

"Should you say it was you, no one ever need know."

Ollie swiped her hands on a towel and patted Laurel's shoulder. "Give me a bed and a couple of hours and we'll discuss it. I'm a little tired right now."

"That's all you're going to say?"

With a heavy heart, Laurel's gaze followed Ollie up the stairs. The woman might as well have confessed.

She'd never noticed before how closely the chimes of

the clock resembled a death knell. They struck ten and gave her a jolt. Two hours before lunch and she'd barely begun preparation. Leaving suspicion and innuendo in bigger hands, she flew about. No time to make stew. She stoked the fire, remembering the smoked venison Mr. Dunn included yesterday to make amends for Pennybacker's slight. Smoked through and through, it only required heating. A quick trip to the cellar and she had it in a roasting pan along with potatoes, carrots, and onions. If she whipped up a cake and baked the bread she set to rise that morning, customers would have a feast.

Jake was the only interruption she hadn't counted on.

He opened the back door and made himself at home. The badge on his shirt accounted for the new swagger in his walk.

"Need to ask you a few questions."

"I'm quite busy right now. Come back a little later."

"Cain't. I have a job to do in regards to Vallens' death."

"You mean disappearance—unless you've found a body?"

"Not yet, but I'm keeping on my toes."

"That might pay off in case the man shows up alive."

Jake ignored that. Propping himself in a chair, he leaned back. "How much do you know about Miss b'Dam?"

"You mean Ollie?"

"One and the same. How long have you known her?"

"A while," she evaded. "I've lost track, it's been so long. Are you thinking she waved a magic wand and Vallens went up in a puff of smoke?"

"I'm supposed to ask the questions." Jake shined the tin star with his shirtsleeve. "Where did you come from?"

Laurel actually might've had fun without a lunch crowd breathing down her neck. Yet a sneaking fear said he might accidentally get a little closer to the truth than she cared.

"Back east. Neither of us had ties, so we decided Texas might give us a new place to start."

"Start what, may I ask?"

"This cafe, what else?"

"Just where did you get the money to purchase said cafe?"

The bell over the front door put an end to the interview.

"You know, Jake, I fail to understand what this curiosity has to do with Vallens. I suggest you wait. I'm sure Miss b'Dam would love to chew the fat regarding anything your official duties require."

"That's Sheriff Whitaker, not Jake."

"I hate to be rude, but I'm busy. If you want to hang around, though, I have an apron that would definitely bring out the best in you. And I dearly need the help."

He rose in a flash. "I just recalled a few other . . . suspects I should pay a visit to."

She breathed a sigh of relief that the man possessed only a pebble-sized brain—or else he'd be dangerous.

Murphy heard Brodie's footsteps in the hallway. His brother had returned from his haunts earlier than usual. The grandfather clock downstairs clanged the hour. He counted nine.

"Nora, don't you ever get lonely down in the swamp, away from everyone?" He winced as she peeled back the bandage.

"The swamp hold many mysteries—secrets long forgotten. I am one with nature there. Loneliness finds no place in me."

The beautiful Caddo woman examined the leeches and

their work in keeping the wound clean and free of the yellowish green ooze that could kill. Her gaze met his, and he lost his bearings in the dark pools.

Her gentle caring made him feel extremely virile and shamefully aroused.

The woman's quiet wisdom embraced his spirit. He only now realized the daily contact with her had extended beyond healer and patient. That worried him.

How could he promise to love and cherish Laurel, seeing how important Nora had become to him?

But he couldn't stop the persistent current dragging him toward an unknown destination.

"Do you want for male companionship in your world?" The question came in a husky whisper.

The wrong answer would pain him greatly.

Nora's curved lips came within inches of his as she leaned to work. The tip of a long braid fell over her shoulder, tantalizing his naked chest when it swished across an exposed nipple. Tiny shivers coursed through him.

She appeared to weigh her reply with much caution. "Often in the midnight hours I would have such a want."

Her candor surprised him. He expected some degree of evasion. The air crackled in the space between them. It pulled him deeper into uncharted, unexplored swamp water.

The dark braids skimming his sensitive skin inflamed his yearning. An enticing pull crushed lush breasts to him. No protest came as she allowed her body to follow the length of his.

Murphy traced the curves her deerskin dress accentuated.

He sensed a need in her, sensed her responding to his own desire. Their lips met on sacred ground in a kiss full of tenderness. Not until Murphy released her did the complete reality of what he'd done enter his mind.

Remorse should've washed over any sane, engaged man. None came. Nor did regret for his actions.

In fact, he'd never before heard this song of love in his heart. He reveled in the newfound joy.

Her midnight gaze held questions, yet she said nothing, settling in the crook of his arm. Murphy drew the blanket over them.

"It's all right, Nora. Lie here. For now I want nothing more than your sweet breath whispering on my skin." As he said the words he tried to silence his body's desires. He'd not ask of her more than she wished to give.

"Your heart cannot see sleeping danger?" She spoke softly.

"I know only the beauty and total serenity of this moment. You, my pretty maiden, healed my spirit even while tending to my wound."

"And in daylight?"

What then? his conscience asked. What of his commitment to Laurel?

"Tomorrow's soon enough to sort out propriety. Rest for now, my sweet Nora." He kissed the top of her head, tightening the embrace. "Let me absorb your wisdom and strength."

Brodie sat on the side of the bed, pondering the sorry state of affairs.

Too early to go to bed.

Besides, he had yet to remove his clothing and boots. And he might not. He reckoned he'd slept fully dressed more than once—particularly after a snoot-full of Mexican tequila.

Damn, he should've brought up some of Murph's private whiskey stash. For a moment he considered slipping back out.

He propped himself up against the sturdy oak bedstead that had belonged to dozens of Yateses before him. He bit the end off one of the three precious cheroots he had left. The smooth, mellow tobacco beat his hand-rolled Bull Durhams, but he couldn't justify the extra expense too often. Only on special occasions when he most needed comfort did he indulge.

He considered tonight one of those occasions.

Striking a match, he stared at the toes of his worn boots. They'd traveled many a mile, a lot of that through hostile territory.

He'd spent the better part of the evening across the street from Ollie's Cafe, and he wasn't certain if that classified as hostile. Then again, the atmosphere hadn't been all that welcoming, either. Laurel's strange mood had spooked him.

His feet had numbed up on him as he watched for hours through the window, groaning aloud with each bend, twist, and sway of those alluring hips.

Herman Green and his wife, Mabel, had passed by with their wagonload of thirteen kids. From their bold stare, he guessed they must've heard the rumble in his throat. He returned the look, but as they passed by his thoughts quickly returned to Laurel and her intriguing hourglass figure.

How snug her rounded bottom had fit into his lap yesterday. The friction had tested his control severely. He never again wished to come that close to letting go.

Not unless he was deep inside her.

Georgia clay! He'd break the news to Murph himself if it'd get her into his bed faster.

Brodie adjusted his pants, hoping to relieve a bit of the pressure on the bulge that suddenly made them too tight.

Removing them would solve the problem. After all, he had privacy. Yet, in some strange way, he welcomed the uncomfortable sensation.

One of these days, he promised.

He punched a pillow and stuffed it behind his head. His hand brushed the memory bag hidden beneath the dark shirt.

Three women whose lives intertwined with his . . . three women who had never received true justice; not Elizabeth Yates nor Aunt Lucy, and certainly not Laurel.

The men who kidnapped and forced her into that lurid world walked free and unencumbered, while Laurel remained locked in a prison, perhaps unable to ever regain what she'd lost. He'd seen proof of that in her dealings with Hannah. Her family lived only miles away, yet she couldn't bring herself to seek the solace they could give.

Justice? Hardly.

Losing one's family could yank a person's soul right from its moorings. He knew from experience how bad it hurt.

It scared the piss out of him to think what it might do to a sensitive lady like Laurel.

"Zeke Vallens, you'd better hope to God you're dead, because you and Will Taft have a bunch of answering to do."

Chapter Twenty-four

"Git upstairs and grab your bonnet, girl. We're taking a buggy ride," Ollie announced a full five days after tense questions and speculation had first arisen around Vallens's vanishing act.

"A buggy ride? Wherever to?"

"Never you mind." The woman hustled Laurel toward the narrow stairs. "Do as you're told and you'll be a lot better off. Cain't go nowhere if you stand there dragging your rear."

"And what about the cafe that everyone expects open on a Sunday? Last week the mere mention of closing for a boat trip to Jefferson curled your hair. Not that it couldn't stand a curl or two. Beats me what Curley sees in those spikes. But then, I'm no expert on affairs of the heart."

"Exactly. And my hair is my business." Ollie twisted a wiry lock around her finger to make it reach for the ceiling.

"You didn't answer about the cafe."

"Folks ain't supposed to work on Sunday. It's the Lord's day. Reason why we have until now was because we had to. Now we don't, so we ain't."

Laurel shook her head. The woman would have the last word or die. Somehow, she had trouble believing Olivia Applejack d'Dam had suddenly gotten filled with the spirit.

A half hour later they loaded a wicker picnic basket into a rented rig.

"You could've said we're having a picnic."

"Could've but didn't. Wanted to surprise you."

"You invited Curley to join us, I suppose?"

"Nope."

Ollie jiggled the reins, urging the horse into a canter.

"Am I allowed to ask where we're going in such a rush?"

"Dadblasted! I'm done answering questions. Sit back and put your mind on pleasant things."

Judging the attempt useless, Laurel moved slightly to keep the torn leather from poking her. Escape would be nice after the grinding their nerves had taken.

But one gratifying thing . . . she had gotten a little of the elixir down Ollie, which she considered a pure miracle.

The chestnut mare wound through cottonwood and pine trees. Clusters of white Indian tobacco blossoms blended with pink smartweed, painting a wondrous mural of the bayou. Big Cypress existed nowhere else on earth. No wonder Nora's Caddo people called this home. How sad only a handful remained of the once huge tribe.

"Ollie, what do you suppose happened to the Indians who lived here in the swamp?"

"Heard tell most of 'em died, and them what didn't got run off by money-hungry land-grubbers."

"That's a god-awful shame."

Potter's Point loomed ahead, a place of mystery. She prayed they'd steer clear of Rob Potter's grave. The sight made her skin crawl.

"Shame belongs to men like Potter, who lied, cheated,

and stole whenever he took a notion." Ollie squinted at her through one eye. "You remind me of his poor wife, Harriet, in a kindly sort of way. Felt sorry for her. Potter put her through a living hell. The strength of that lady is still legendary."

"I grew up hearing the stories, but I'd not dare utter her name and mine in the same breath."

"Don't be so quick. Harriet had more reason than most to quit living. Instead, she fought with everything she had and over came the odds. I'd say you might share part of that."

Love and happiness for her? Both seemed as far removed as the stars in the sky. She'd only glimpsed Brodie from a distance since the day in Murphy's garden. Still, she counted a glimpse now and then a blessing, half expecting him to move on since quitting the sheriff's job. It simply hurt to know he'd give someone with the plague less snubbing than he did her and the cafe. She cleared the lump blocking her windpipe.

"*Horsefeathers!* I'm an outcast. Six months hasn't changed anyone's opinion." Least of all those who mattered most.

Ollie pulled back on the reins to stop the rig and turned to face her. "Reminds me of something my grandpappy said a long time ago, God rest his poor old soul. He said, 'If'n you go around calling a gold nugget a rock, ain't never gonna be nothing but a measly rock. But you shine it up and call it what it is and you'll have a regular stampede on your hands.'"

"Your grandsire talked in riddles—probably just to flap his tired old gums."

"I call 'em pearls of wisdom." The woman shook her head.

"Well, I'm no gold nugget. You can spit and shine until there's no tomorrow, be my guest."

"Son of a blue jacket! Call yourself a rock and that's all folks'll see." Ollie clicked her tongue to move the horse onward. "There's a whole mess of jewels buried inside you—diamonds and rubies and those green sparkly ones."

"Emeralds," Laurel provided.

"Yep, and them, too. Mostly you have a heart of pure gold, the finest grade a man ever did find."

The mare turned south, away from the river, and Ollie stopped beneath a loblolly pine.

"I reckon this'll do for a picnic. About halfway there."

"Tell me where we're going, you crabby kidnapper."

"Nope."

The wind gusted abruptly. She shivered, but not from cold.

"Is it someplace I wish to go?"

"Yep, you do. Now shush and help me."

Laurel spread out the blanket, trying to ignore the quiet voice that warned her that the woman had some dirty trick up her sleeve. They dined on cold fried chicken, a loaf of Laurel's homemade bread, and fresh pickles.

When they resumed their mysterious journey, the landscape became painfully familiar. She'd romped here as a child.

She clutched Ollie's arm. "Turn around right now."

"Sorry, girl. We've come too far."

"I can't. I truly can't." Icy cold crept over her.

"I'm taking you home. Goldarned it, its time to face your demons!"

"Not today." A harsh roar in her head made her voice unrecognizable. Ollie, of all people, would force this on her?

"Nothing wrong with now. You can let go my arm any time. That is, if you can pry your fingernails loose from the skin."

"I never thought you'd misuse my trust."

"Hide and watch from the trees is all I ask. I ain't gonna make you go up to the house. You have to decide that yourself."

A dried soup bone gnawed on by a pack of wolves would've had more moisture than Laurel's mouth. Before reaching the James's farmhouse, Ollie found a thicket to pull the rig into.

"Skirt though the woods over there." The woman's face turned ashen. She clutched her chest. "I'm a bit poorly."

"How gullible do you take me? This ruse is an all-time low, even for you."

A gasping moan and wide-eyed stare was her only response.

Laurel fumbled to loosen the high-necked collar.

"Up and die on me and I'll never forgive you."

"Ain't planning to . . . unless the good Lord . . . says otherwise."

The lid flew off the picnic basket. Laurel grabbed the crock of water, holding it to the pale lips. Ollie took several sips and didn't protest when Laurel laid her back in the seat.

"Give me a minute. My old ticker's getting awfully tired."

"I think I should light a fire under this mare and get to Jefferson." Laurel smoothed Ollie's forehead. She'd have to prop her head in her lap to sit, but at least they'd reach help. She slid onto the seat and reached for the reins.

"Maybe I should tell you something."

"Not now, Ollie. It'll wait."

"I think I killed Vallens."

Laurel froze. "You think?"

"Yep. I'm pretty sure, all right."

Oh, Lord, the woman had not only thieved but murdered! That tied her hands. She couldn't take Ollie to Jefferson and risk having the soldiers arrest her. Better she die peacefully in the woods than strung up for murder. Or pass over while in the midst of those scalawags and carpetbaggers—Ollie's worst nightmare.

Color eked back into the white face and Ollie breathed without grimacing.

"You killed the angel of death? You went out and shot him, just like that?"

"I know my time grows short. Someone had to protect you."

"Now's a fine time to confess, I must say."

"Better now than carry the baggage across."

"What am I supposed to do? I can't get you to a doctor, have you blab the news, and wind up in the stockade."

"I expect you to follow my wishes, and your heart. Go see your poor old mama and papa. I brung you this far, girl. From here it's up to you. You don't need me holding your hand."

"And leave you alone in the middle of the woods?"

"I'll be fine and dandy resting here. And after you get done with what you need to do, we'll go home. Now, quit dilly-dallying. Move them legs of yours and get, dad-blasted!"

The steel in Ollie's bark made her wonder anew. Ollie had never recovered this fast before. Heaven help the trickster.

Still, one peek wouldn't hurt. They'd never know of her visit.

Strange excitement stirred when she found a path toward the wooden farmhouse. Her heart pounded faster with each step. The trees and overgrowth gave her confidence. Each bird, each blade of grass, the very wind seemed to whisper a welcome home. The hushed, silent land held arms open wide.

At last the house glimmered through silvery branches. Jagged pieces of her soul inched closer together.

From the screen of the hiding place, Laurel watched. The familiar creak of the rocking chair on the wide porch encouraged a better look. The skirted figure leaned to pluck a kitten rubbing against her legs. Laurel crept closer.

White streaked her mother's dark hair. Common sense had prepared her for that. It was the heavy wrinkles that brought shock and dismay.

"Millie, come and get Boots," Mary James called. "Give the little thing a dish of milk."

"All right, Mama." A girl ran from the side of the house.

Millie? Laurel never imagined the baby who hadn't even reached the walking stage had grown into a six-year-old.

An elderly man stepped through the open door. Laurel's breath caught. She pushed the brush aside for a clear view.

"The darn kitten's supposed to catch mice. You keep feeding it milk and it won't have an appetite for the pests."

"Oh, Papa, it's a baby. When she gets big, it'll catch your smelly old mice. Besides, Mama agrees."

"Jeremiah and Virgil's idea of drowning the litter in the bayou might have merit," Ben James teased.

"They better not!" Millie snatched the kitten and ran as her father bent his lanky form to sit on the top step.

Misty-eyed, Laurel watched him take an object from his bibbed overalls. Blurred vision didn't prevent her from making out the Jew's harp he'd carried since before her birth.

"Nice time of day, ain't it?" He cupped the harp in his palms and blew lightly across the reeds.

"Same as any other—sitting here and waiting for the miracle I won't ever live to see."

"Don't get maudlin. Can't dwell on the past. Not good."

Crouched low, Laurel heard the catch in her mother's wishful thinking. Gut-wrenching pain wracked her.

"I know, Ben. But a mother still can't just let go."

"I curse that war! Me and the boys would've found Laurel if not for the Cause sending the country into uproar and chaos. I know that in my bones."

Despair flew straight across the clearing and punctured her heart. She shouldn't have come. What did she think to gain?

"Not your fault, Ben. You did all that was humanly possible."

Her father lifted the harp to his lips again. The first strains of *Home, Sweet Home* drifted in the air. Laurel shut her eyes, blocking the tears. Allowing herself to feel, to savor the taste of home, was her biggest mistake. Want and need suffocated her.

A barking dog drowned out the music. Panic forced open her eyes. Ol' Blue Boy bounded straight for the lush, green shield.

"Wonder what he treed?" her father remarked.

"Probably a coon. Play some more, Ben, it soothes frazzled nerves."

Laurel scurried, but not quickly enough. The bloodhound crashed through, knocking her over. Blue Boy had smelled her scent. The hound joyfully licked every exposed bit of skin. She buried her face in his fur.

"I've missed you. Oh God, I've missed you so much."

The dog couldn't contain his exuberance. He jumped on top, his floppy ears slapping her cheecks.

She jerked at a sudden, shrill whistle.

"Here, Blue. Where'd you go, you flea-bitten hound?" The yell came from a much younger male.

Heavy feet crunched the tangle of brush and fallen limbs.

"Hannah, are you up here? Here, Blue. I mean it now."

Seconds separated her brother, Quaid, and her. She had

to go. But part of her wanted Quaid to find her. It would end the agonizing years of longing for her family.

They'd ask questions . . . lots of them.

Condemnation and judgment would follow. They'd find out.

"I can't," she whispered into the beloved fur.

Sad, brown eyes stared back in confusion.

"Go Blue Boy, go home." She swallowed the rising sob.

The dog's low whimper seemed to say he didn't want her to leave again. She blocked the noise, lifting her skirts for flight. After a few leaps, she turned for one last look at the home she'd learn to forget, the animal who remembered and loved her no matter what she'd done, and then at Quaid as he scrambled up the small incline.

In the moment's hesitation, she found herself overcome by the glistening trickle running down Blue's face. Dogs didn't cry. Did they?

Blue Boy tilted his head to the sky and released a mournful howl, raising gooseflesh on her arms.

"Hey, who goes there?" Quaid had caught sight of her through the saplings. "Stop!"

Two days later, Blue Boy's grief-stricken howls remained burrowed deep in Laurel's memory. The teary-eyed hound blocked her vision each second.

And then, there was Ollie's confession of killing Vallens. Laurel hadn't pried out much more on the subject. Ollie only claimed she left him lying in the alley, and it mystified her what had happened to the body.

To escape, she set a relentless pace from sunup to sundown.

"*Son of a blue belly*, you're gonna drive yourself into an early grave."

"Work never killed anyone."

"Might not, but it dadblamed sure makes it hard on a pitiful old woman." Ollie glared. "And I cain't find a blessed thing either. What did you do with my sparking dress?"

Guilt swallowed her. Until now, Laurel never considered the clothing's importance. She had added the threadbare dress to her rag drawer.

"It practically fell apart in my hands. It doesn't even make a good rag."

"You have some gall. That dress brought me good luck. Now what'll I wear next time Curley asks me over to his place, nothing but my holey stockings and knit cap?"

Laurel tried to dodge the piercing stare.

"Some folks might object to seeing that much of you."

"You been acting strange since that visit to your home place. Wish you'd found it in you to talk to your family."

"We've been over this a dozen times."

"Stop livin' in the dark. Spooks 'n such only prey in the dead of night. If you face that fear and stare it in the eye, daylight'll come. That's what grandpappy always said."

"I promise I will." Laurel kissed a wrinkled cheek. "A baby takes small, teetering steps before it learns to walk."

"Leastways you ain't crawling anymore. Reckon I can be grateful for that. Cain't believe you threw away my dress."

"I'll buy you a new one."

"Don't want a stiff, store-bought dress. Cain't get in the mood for loving when I'm all bound up."

Laurel's thoughts turned in another direction, toward things that bound. She whipped off her apron and grabbed a shawl.

"I have an errand to attend to. I'll be right back."

Chapter Twenty-five

"To what do I owe this surprise?" Murphy's wide smile crinkled the corners of his eyes.

Laurel fidgeted under the warm welcome. It made her job no less difficult. Nothing would deter her this time, not even if Hell froze over, which it might before she finished.

"You have healthy color in your face at last." Indeed, he added a certain bloom to the fading plants around him. "I take it you walked to the garden on your own steam?"

"Yep, and it didn't tire me a bit. Come, sit next to me."

"Don't tell me you fired Nora. I didn't see her when Annie let me in." Or Brodie, whom she prayed had business elsewhere. She perched on the stone bench Murphy dusted with a pristine white handkerchief.

"Nora had neglected her mother and herb garden long enough, so I sent her home. However, she comes to check on me every day."

A deep breath bolstered courage for what she must do.

"I should've spoken of this matter sooner and intended to the day of the shooting. You've been so ill . . . I couldn't bring myself to mention it until you recovered."

"Sounds all-fired important."

Laurel clenched her hands tightly in her lap.

"Please don't hate me. You must believe I never meant to hurt you in any way."

"I could never hate you." Murphy's questioning glance didn't ease the waves of remorse. She easily imagined how rapidly anger and betrayal could swap ends with the curious stare.

"Reserve that until you know." Laurel wet her dry lips. "I can't marry you, not now, not tomorrow, not ever. I care so for you, but I don't love you."

She focused on the cracks in the walk. A few weeds sprouted between the mortar of the bricks—weeds that would take over unless a body kept them pulled. Once they got hold, getting them out required a lot of back-breaking work.

"You're breaking our engagement?"

"I should've told you sooner. I'm extremely sorry." She dared not glance up from the weeds. "I don't expect you—"

"Whew! That's a relief."

Shock sped through her blood. She whirled to face him and ran smack into a most whimsical gleam.

"You're not angry? Not disappointed, or humiliated?"

"Nope. I didn't know how to go about telling you that I've fallen in love with Nora. This saves more loss of sleep."

"You and Nora?"

Could she have misunderstood? Ollie always accused her of choosing to hear only what she wanted to.

"I didn't realize how deep my love was. It just sneaked up on me over time and in the course of daily contact. I woke up one morning and knew Nora and I were meant to be."

Laurel didn't know what to say. "I'm elated for you both." Yet, this twinge of desolation confused her.

"I haven't asked Nora to marry me. I first had to set things straight with you. No hard feelings, I hope."

"She's truly a lucky woman and had better appreciate what she has." Laurel realized the other burrs and thistles would remain unless she told him everything. "I have more, Murphy, some of which may alter your opinion of me drastically."

"Nothing can change what I've already come to know."

"We'll see." Another cleansing gulp of air helped. "I lived on a farm not far from here until a fateful day right after I turned fifteen."

For the next half hour, she bared her soul, telling of her life in St. Louis and what Taft had forced on her.

"One night your brother came to the Black Garter."

"Brodie? So my mind didn't play tricks on me after all."

Now came the judging part she'd most dreaded. She didn't think she heard reproach behind the question. It hadn't arrived unexpectedly. Surely any warm-blooded man would experience a sense of betrayal that she'd kept horrible secrets.

"I knew him as Shenandoah, and yes, he paid for the privilege of my services."

"You must've had a good laugh at my expense."

"On the contrary, we had no wish to keep you in the dark. I never had anything other than the utmost respect and admiration for you."

"I hope those aren't simply words to mollify."

"They're not. And another thing—Brodie loves you. He'd cut off his right arm to prevent causing you a minute's anguish."

"I knew something ate at him. Couldn't guess why."

"The secret tore him apart." She slid off the bench and took his hand. "You gave me hope that I might one day live a normal life. Deceit goes against my nature, but the belief that I'd do more harm by confiding in you convinced me to keep quiet."

"That's enough. What purpose can dredging this up serve?"

"Telling you the whole sordid mess is the only way for me to absolve myself. I'm tired of living lies. You want the ugly truth? I tried to use you. In the struggle to redeem myself, I willingly did whatever I had to—even accepting a proposal from someone I didn't love. I had no right to do that."

"Sit back down. I'll not have you belittling yourself." Murphy pulled her back on the seat. "How did you escape from that hellish place? Did Brodie help?"

"He never kept his promise to return. Ollie got me out. We came to Redemption for a fresh start and opened up the cafe."

"My brother showing up must've soured things."

"He threatened to tell my secret. I begged him not to and bought a week's time so I could break the engagement in my own way."

"The bank robbery took care of that."

"So I waited for the day when you grew strong enough." She cast him a wry smile. "And to gain courage for the task."

"You could've left and I would never have been the wiser."

"I've gotten weary of running from problems."

"My dear Laurel. You have innate goodness and honor that nothing and no one will ever destroy."

Murphy's declaration summoned the gold nugget story Ollie had tried to sell her. Perhaps the lump of coal she saw herself as had developed a bit of a shine. But she had one more truth to tell.

"I've saved this last part on purpose. I never meant this

to happen, but it has, and no amount of wishing can change it."

"I already know of your love for Brodie."

Spit and thunder! Did the man read tea leaves?

"I fell head over heels in love the first time I laid eyes on him in St. Louis. But when he never returned for me, I didn't expect to see him again. I figured he'd lost his life in the war or else lost his affection for me. Truth be told, Brodie Yates stirs a longing in my blood unlike any man." Her voice dropped to a whisper. "I love him with all my heart and soul."

"A bullet might've laid me low, but it didn't take away my sense. I'll have to admit you hid your truths far better than did my dear brother. I notice how he follows your every move. He has a bad case of smitten-itis."

"About whom would you swap tales?" Brodie's deep baritone made them both jump.

Laurel blushed that he'd caught them. Still, she had to admire the tall figure striding silently across the grass.

Brodie lounged inside the empty cafe after the last diner left for the evening. He preferred watching Laurel work from here much more than hiding in the shadows across the street. A need to have her naked beneath him swelled a vital part of him until the seams of his britches threatened to split.

"Can I get you anything else?"

Coffee sloshed from his cup onto the table. He'd be remiss in thinking he affected her that much. Yet he didn't fool himself. He noticed the tired lines in her face.

"Darlin', looking at you is feast enough. You wouldn't understand a man's appreciation for the provocative sway of hips in the quiet glow of lantern light . . . what it does to me."

"What on earth gives you the right to suddenly spout such things after pretending I ceased to exist? Best take your endearments and suggestive talk to another who might appreciate it."

Spots colored her cheeks bright pink. Flashing violet sparks declared battle and he had no dueling pistols.

Or a wall to hide behind. Nothing but a white flag.

"I had no idea you missed me that much." A lopsided grin drifted into place. "I thought you wanted time to yourself."

She wouldn't know how often he'd turned toward the cafe.

Only to stop.

"That's the thing, Brodie; your blessed desires are more important, without a care about when or what a lady might wish."

He probably deserved a tongue-lashing for a lot of reasons, but not for loving her.

Seemed odd that she continued to stand there tapping her foot instead of turning her back on him. The harmless compliment sure had made her mad enough to melt lead and make bullets.

"After you left the other day Murphy told me about your conversation."

"And you presume that changes everything and I'll fall in a puddle at your feet."

"If memory serves, dear lady, you set the boundaries. Do you recall your order to stop tempting you? I suppose I could've fabricated that conversation—along with the pull of our bodies when we're near." Then he added softly, "Like now, when I want you so badly and I know you have the same yearning. Dare you deny that?"

Laurel did more crack-counting of the floor before she answered. "I can't. Dear God, I wish it weren't so."

A gentle squeeze of her hand, a tug into the chair he

pulled out, and she was at eye level. He cupped her face and tucked a strand of hair behind a delicate ear.

"Will you resist should I beg to have you in my bed?"

Her head dropped wearily to his shoulder. He drew her into the shelter of his arms.

"I'm afraid."

"Of me? I left the chains and whip in my saddlebags."

"Of myself. I trusted you once and lived to regret it. What happens this time when you satisfy your needs? Will you ride on to other conquests? I've known men who want only that which is unattainable. Once they have it, the luster fades."

"Close your eyes and make a wish. I'll wave a magic wand."

"You can't turn wishful thought into reality when you don't know the nature of it."

"Oh, but I do. Therefore, I have the power."

Laurel leaned back. A teardrop poised on the tip of one sooty lash. More wetness glistened in her gaze as she slowly opened her eyes.

For the first time he saw how deeply he'd hurt her. Anger, bitterness, and distance kept the depth of that pain hidden. Making up for misdeeds presented a mountainous task, but he hadn't shown the reserve card up his sleeve yet.

Brodie lightly traced the curve of her jaw. "Do as I ask. Pretend we're at a masquerade. Be whoever or whatever you choose—bejeweled queen or beauteous Gypsy maiden."

Laurel bit her bottom lip, but lowered her lids. "And you shall wear no disguise, Sir Rogue?"

"No need when I'm probably the most charming, debonair sort of chap you'll ever meet. I could be a ruthless buccaneer. I've always yearned to sail the seven seas on a frigate."

At least the frown vanished. When she opened her eyes he'd moved to the floor on one knee.

"I want you more than anything in this world. I assure you, my interest lies not in conquest, and I've never had the slightest desire for the unattainable. Will you share my bed, beautiful masked lady, before I perish on the spot?"

"No . . . I wouldn't feel right making love in Murphy's house." A smile flirted with the edges of her mouth. "Mine is private and much closer."

He fumbled, extinguishing the lanterns, before following her up the creaking stairs. In case Ollie occupied the room across, he closed the door with care.

She came into his arms, and the heat of their kiss dispelled any lingering qualms either might have had.

"My pirate scoundrel, are you sure you won't have second thoughts?" Laurel asked, her voice husky with desire when he freed her mouth. "You know, the men in my bed too numerous to count? Worried the color of your coin makes recalling your face impossible come light of day?"

"Darlin', your mask is slipping. Remember, you can be anyone you desire."

A silver shaft of moonlight through the window bathed her slim form in unearthly beauty. The die was cast and the bullet mold safely put away. Brodie could no more turn back now than cease drawing air.

"This game . . . does it call for capture and plunder?"

"Only the most painless kind. Worried?"

"I believe in our love and that destiny meant us to be together."

"You've been a fire in my blood ever since before I arrived at this party, and more so after spying you across the room. You drive me utterly, totally, indescribably insane."

"Don't throw yourself on your sword this soon, my pirate."

The easing of a few buttons gave access to her elegant

neck. Trailing a path, he tongue-danced down the curve, exploring the rapid pulse at her throat before lace and fabric prevented further progress.

Quick work on the remaining buttons and her bodice slid to the floor in a rippling heap.

The thin chemise created a flimsy shield at best. He cupped a breast and expertly rolled a nipple to a hard nub. Laurel jerked his own shirt over his head, apparently finding the fastenings too slow, before starting on his britches.

Other hindrances were torn off in a fevered rush. He buried his face in the fragrant softness of her breasts. The beat of her racing heart mesmerized him. He didn't know what the future held. He didn't give a damn. He wanted only to freeze this moment and preserve it until time and eternity merged into one.

"When you didn't come back, I thought you didn't want me."

"Foolish lady. Don't you know I always will?"

His mouth met hers again. Her lips parted, allowing his tongue freedom.

Tasting . . .

Thrusting . . .

Each time Brodie gently touched her bare skin, she felt herself tremble with desire. A slight lift curled her leg around his. Exploration led him across her navel to the downy juncture of her thighs.

Laurel's fingertips grazed his chest hair and each brown nipple. And when she dropped to grasp his stiff arousal, he shuddered and clenched his jaw to keep from giving in to pleasure so close he feared to draw another breath.

As if reading his mind, she stopped and became very still.

Between them no space existed. Brodie could no

longer tell where soft curves began and hard muscle ended.

Vague thoughts intruded on passion-dulled senses—faint remembrances of a line in the sand he'd drawn and now had crossed. He could never return there, for Laurel stole his good sense, his very thoughts. She gave him a reason for seeking to become a better man.

Pins from her hair dropped quietly to the floor, letting the raven strands cascade around him.

Laurel's silky caresses wandered lazily up his back.

Muscles long bereft of female attention quivered when she loitered to etch her name over each.

Her nimble touch flitted, inflicting torture of the most maddening kind.

And yet he fought to hold himself in check.

A need to prolong the moment dominated his crazed thoughts, for he wanted to bring her equal satisfaction.

She held his entire being in her hands, and whether she believed it or not, she was all lady—a most honorable one.

The agonizing dawdle ended with the tangling of her fingers in his hair. Laurel grabbed a handful and pressed him still closer while the palm of her other hand dipped lower, further fueling the roaring blaze. A sensuous burn inched upward, through the maze of muscle and sinew, knotting each in the passing.

Brodie realized he'd become more than flesh and bone. He belonged to her . . . they belonged to each other.

The humid swampland of Big Cypress Bayou on the hottest summer's day couldn't compare to the sultry film coating her skin. The rise and fall of her lush breasts revealed a desire that the come-hither smile only hinted at.

He'd never known such a bottomless, drowning hunger. The lazy storm that began at the onset developed into a huge cyclone that swept away everything in its path.

The small bed yielded to their fall.

"I want you, Laurel Lillian James. I need you."

"Groveling at my feet at last, are you?"

"I'm not greedy . . . all right, maybe a bit." He nibbled her earlobe. "I'll take whatever I can beg, plead, or bargain for. Is the plundering option still on the table?"

"You indeed have the heart of a dangerous brigand."

"Can't argue with that. At least I'm a happy one."

"Hush. Talking wastes too much energy, Sir Buccaneer."

"That so?"

Their breath mingled in a searing kiss. Brodie fondled the weight of her breasts, and a moan tumbled from her throat when he rolled a puckered nipple between thumb and forefinger.

A powerful onslaught of tenderness battered down the last bit of restraint. He crushed her to him, shamefully reveling in all that he knew and more he hoped to learn.

The ropes on which the feather mattress rested creaked in protest. Other than a soft gasp, that was the only noise when he filled her, fully and deeply.

Strange how he'd been here before, yet this seemed the first time in which their bodies had joined.

In a sense, he reckoned it was.

They weren't the same two people. They'd grown and changed in the passing years. Laurel had learned to take what she wanted and speak her mind.

And him?

He'd never be the same.

He found himself grateful for her experience.

Not only did she graciously accept all he gave, but returned pure, shimmering gold to his paltry silver.

Her grip held him fast as she shuddered. Warm contractions pulsated around him, unleashing tremors that traveled the length of his body.

Long weeks of torment and waiting came to an end in a surging release that shook him to his core.

The sheer curtains floated in a breeze through the open window. Brodie locked the memory away for safekeeping. He'd remember always this moonlit night, her dew-kissed softness when their hearts joined.

Even until the day they laid him six feet under.

Then, if God willed, in the hereafter.

Chapter Twenty-six

Laurel nestled in the only arms she'd ever desired. Brodie's quiet breaths at her temple fluttered wisps of hair. She brushed back the rebellious lock from his forehead.

"I'm curious."

"Does it pertain to scuttling ships or plundering? Because if it does, I'll lay it to my seafaring great-grandfather, Bartholomew Yates. I understand he did a fair amount of it."

"No, silly." Memory traced each line and crevice in his face. "I wondered why you adorn your hat with snake rattles, of all things. They make such ungodly noise."

"They remind me how precious staying alive is."

The strength of symbols came in various forms. A broken tooth had become such for her.

"I cut those off the biggest, meanest snake I ever killed. Had it not shaken 'em, I'd be dead. Figured the noise would warn others not to shy away, and what would come if they didn't."

"A lot are too dumb. Look at Jeb Prater."

"When God handed out brains He certainly missed a

few souls." He nipped at her finger with his teeth. "But I have another reason, if you promise not to laugh."

"I swear not to crack a smile."

Anyone who let the harmless color of lavender frighten the wits out of them dare not sit in judgment of others.

"The hiss of those rattles sort of comforts. Reminds me I fear no man . . . only fate."

Or destiny. Laurel's thoughts turned to Ollie and her confession. She'd do anything to keep the dear woman free—anything.

"Have you ever been in prison for killing anyone?"

"I've gotten on the personal side of more calabooses than I care to recall but missed progressing beyond that. Why?"

"I can't tell."

"Does this pertain to Vallens? You saying you shot him?"

Laurel pushed away from him and fumbled to raise the lamp wick, calling herself nine kinds of crazy.

"You should leave now."

Lowering defenses proved definite impairment in sound judgment. She should've known better. The soldier she fell in love with wouldn't find her capable of murder. A sudden mist blurred the heap of garments littering the floor. Snatching them, a calculated throw landed the britches in his face, covering narrowed rebel grays that set her pulse in overtime.

An object—a drawstring pouch—brushed a foot when she stood. Buttery leather molded to the shape of her palm.

"What's this?"

"Nothing of much value, I fear."

Brodie lifted the bag without sparing a glance and drew on his pants. Anger lay heavy in the air, an ugly closure to the contentment their lovemaking had brought.

She'd mistaken him for a granter of wishes.

A lump in her chest hindered in matching holes to corresponding bodice buttons.

"For God's sake!" He spun her around and one by one put each button in place. "What did I say?"

"Vallens doesn't belong in our bed."

"I'll remember that." Brodie kissed the tip of her nose. "We're survivors. We know what it takes to make it to the next sunrise because we've seen our share of pitch-dark nights."

He sauntered to the door. "You know where to find me." Laurel swallowed hard as he stepped into the hall.

"Brodie?"

"Yes, darlin'?"

"Thank you for tonight."

"For the record, which lady lurked behind the mask in our game of pretense?"

"Myself. I'm sick of trying to be something I'm not."

Brodie failed to stop by the following day. Evening drew to a close without the familiar noise of his snake rattles gracing the cafe.

Just as Laurel was finishing the dishes Ollie burst into the kitchen with Curley in tow. "Girl, Curley wants to ask a favor." Ollie tugged at his arm. "Go on ahead."

The ring on the plump man's finger sparkled as he twisted his hands. Laurel cast a suspicious glance.

"I'm at my wit's end. Ollie said maybe you could help."

"I'll surely do what I can."

"First off, Ollie sort of spilled the beans about your previous . . . line of work."

"You didn't!" Laurel sent the woman an angry glare.

"Hold on to your blooming mule train." Ollie wore a sheepish squint. "It merely slipped out during a—"

"Lull in the conversation? How could you?"

"Your secret's safe with Curley."

"What about those *you* guard so carefully? I don't suppose they happened to *slip out* while you shot the breeze."

"Now that I think on it . . ."

"Exactly what I thought."

"Ladies, blood sure would mess up this clean kitchen." Curley turned to Laurel. "Here's the problem: A pitiful little creature named Adeline arrived today wanting to work in the saloon. I can't turn her out with no place to go."

"Ain't no bigger than a corn nubbin'," Ollie stepped in. "Needs a chance to grow up afore she sets out to ruin herself."

"How exactly will serving liquor ruin her life?"

Curley squirmed. "Not what she has in mind. She's determined to invite paying customers upstairs for a tumble."

Her tongue scrapped the rough edge of her tooth.

"No, I won't go there! Not under any circumstances."

"Laurel girl, I understand your vow to steer clear of those places, but Adeline will only go on to Jefferson. Think about them murdering scalawags and riffraff."

"A person that stubborn won't listen to me."

Curley scratched his head. "You've been down that road. It might make her think."

No less than ten minutes later, Curley let Laurel in through the back door of the saloon and pointed out Adeline's room.

Whiskey and stale air mingled, taunting her.

Harsh laughter surged from below. A piano tinkled, no one minding it being a little off key. Chills enveloped Laurel. A male voice escaped under a closed door opposite the narrow hall.

"I've paid good money, dearie. Get undressed or else."

The salty taste of sweat drenched raw memories. Hurt and despair stung behind tightly closed lids. Her mouth dry, she leaned against the wall, too queasy to stand. A foolhardy move, stepping inside the one place she'd sworn never to darken again.

Ollie's plea stopped a lurch toward fresh air. Laurel had asked herself many times how long she had to wear the mark of shame.

The answer kept her steadfast: "Until it doesn't fit anymore." Lately, she'd begun to fashion a new, roomy garment.

A young girl answered the light tap. Curley might've bought the stated age of fifteen, but twelve or thirteen seemed more accurate.

"Adeline?"

"Who's asking?"

"A friend—Laurel James."

The innocence in Adeline's sky blue gaze twisted the knot in Laurel's stomach. The girl flicked her head in defiance, setting blond hair swaying.

"Don't need friends. None ever did me a lick of good."

"May I come inside?"

"I'm busy. Got paying customers waiting. Before the night's over I'm gonna have money in my pocket. Reckon it cain't be worse than doing other things."

A shiver swept through Laurel.

"Please, I promise I won't take long."

"Better not. I can spare only a minute."

The sparce furnishings repulsed her. But it was the rag doll's button eyes staring from the pillows that broke her heart. Loving hands had fashioned hair of yellow yarn and stitched a smile. Funny how each girl brought along something to cling to.

For Laurel it was the music box.

Careful scrutiny found etchings above the door—crude efforts to preserve true names. She blinked hard. Her name was still etched inside the third room to the right at the Black Garter.

A flush deepened Adeline's cheeks, and she quickly stuffed the doll beneath the mattress.

"Well?" The girl tapped her foot nervously. "This ain't no place for social calling."

Laurel perched on the edge of the bed, careful not to squish the little doll. "I see that. Where's your home?"

"Came upriver from New Orleans." Adeline shivered, as if bad memories walked across her mind. Her shoulders sagged when she sat beside Laurel. "Not home now. Ain't ever going back."

A shared misery. "I understand what you mean."

"How can someone like you know?"

"Because I've walked in your shoes. There are better ways to survive."

"Words come cheap, don't they?"

"Not if they offer a way out."

A ragged sigh disturbed the stale air. "Fever took my ma last year. After she passed, my pa . . . he made me . . ."

Laurel imagined the rest. A lot had the same story.

Adeline's defiance returned. "Like I said—my pa—he took me to his bed . . . forced me to do things. He told me I had to pay for Ma up and dying on him. I'm a disgrace."

Bile clogged Laurel's throat. She swallowed bitterness.

"The sin belongs to your father, not you." She folded her arms around the sobbing child, adding a few tears of her own. "Hush now, it'll be all right. Your pa won't ever hurt you again. I promise."

"You don't know him."

"We'll keep you safe."

"Hardest part is not having a home, no family to call your own. You probably can't understand that."

"Let me tell you a little story, Adeline."

After Laurel finished she crossed to the small window. "We are who we are. Hold your head high." She turned. "I want to hire you. Show up tomorrow morning at Ollie's Cafe. Don't pay a whole lot and it's hard work. But it's respectable."

Marching to the bed, she lifted the mattress and freed the rag doll.

"Don't ever let your treasures embarrass you. They're part of us in the way filling our lungs with air keeps us alive."

Chapter Twenty-seven

Laurel felt emotionally drained by the time she headed for the cafe. She hoped she'd started the child down a road that didn't lead to deadends like hers always seemed to.

Preoccupied, she never saw the shadow leap forward until too late. Suddenly she stared face-to-face with the wild-eyed glitter of the wolf dog.

The hated, fearsome beast froze her in her tracks.

She scoured the building for signs of life. It appeared locked tight for the night. Failing to see a safe place to run, she searched for a rock or a piece of wood. None came to light.

What she wouldn't give to have the knife back in her pocket. She'd ceased carrying it when Vallens disappeared.

She half expected to discover the man leering at her. That he didn't come forth brought an eerie shiver. Ollie must truly have killed him.

Yet the dog showing up meant something.

She'd heard that a soothing, calm voice could prevent a dog's attack.

"Hey, boy, where did you come from? I'll bet you're starving. Let me pass and I'll feed you a big steak."

The animal whined low and pitiful, a stark change from the guttural growl. Then she noticed a dark splotch near its rib cage. The short fur had matted.

"You must've gotten in a fight. I'm going to move now. Nice and easy. I just want to look."

Laurel prayed her shaky legs wouldn't give way. She inched forward, trying to push aside the image of him lunging and tearing her limb from limb with razor-sharp fangs. In daylight the animal's eyes had a grayish-green cast, yet the moonlight turned them an odd yellow.

"I won't hurt you. So don't bite. Agreed?"

Shock swept over her when she drew closer. The wolf dropped to the ground in submission, watching each movement warily.

Common sense said she should run.

Before she could, treasured Blue Boy flashed across her mind's eye. Animals depended on people for help. She couldn't leave anything hurt. Even wolves deserved a bit of kindness.

Besides, maybe saving the dog could clear Ollie. Although at the moment she didn't know how, there might be a connection.

"I'm going to reach out to touch you very slowly. I want to see what's wrong, that's all. Then we can both go on our way. I'll be gentle." The animal smelled her outstretched hand and whimpered once more. Thankfully, those fearful teeth stayed hidden inside a closed mouth, which gave her a bit more confidence. Laurel bent to touch the stiff, dried fur.

A gentle probe pushed aside the hair to reveal a hole where something had pierced the skin.

"*Spit and thunder!* Someone shot you."

Ollie's threat to do so rumbled in the stillness.

A chill pricked her flesh.

The woman had many secrets—and a loaded pistol.

The wolf dog licked her arm. His baleful yellow gaze melted her remaining fear, for it said he thought her friend, not foe.

"Come on, then. Let's get you home."

Laurel started for the cafe. Surprisingly, he followed.

"*Son of a blue jacket!* Have you lost your dadblasted mind?" Ollie turned pasty white and caught the pipe from her gaping mouth before it tumbled to the floor.

"He's been injured, maybe shot. I couldn't leave him."

"You should've. We don't owe the beast anything. Likely he'll pounce on our throats in our sleep."

"Don't you see? Vallens may not have met his Maker. You're clear. Perhaps you only shot the dog instead."

"Well, Miss Smartypants, where is the angel of death?"

The wolf dog crawled on a burlap bag she spread in the corner but curled a lip at Ollie.

"Shhhh, you're frightening him. And if I knew where Vallens went, I'd tell you."

"I don't feel so good." Ollie put a hand on her stomach.

Laurel bustled to the pump with a bucket and filled it.

"Why don't you fetch Jake while I wash the wound? I'm sure he'll find this interesting."

"Ain't exactly the word I'd use." Ollie cackled and slapped a knee. "Jake's gonna piss all over hisself."

While the woman hurried to spread good cheer and tidings, Laurel cleaned off the blood. She spied a piece of lead embedded in the muscle. It would have to come out. She poured a generous amount of whiskey over two chunks of meat and fed the dog. Then she ran upstairs for the tweezers before Ollie returned. Jake, eyes bulging, peeked around the door.

"Good God! I ain't wearing this badge. Vallens'll be spitting nails at someone shooting his dog."

"Jake, you have experience in removing bullets."

The man crumpled to the floor, half in and half out.

"He fainted," Ollie announced, lifting one of his limp arms.

"Should've known he'd do this."

"Reckon I should drag him in or push him out?"

"Whichever is easiest. I need you here."

Ollie pulled him in far enough to close the door. They removed the fragment from the doped-up dog and applied a bandage. Through it all, the wolf dog remained amazingly calm. Laurel stroked the dozing animal's slender neck.

"No telling where he's been. I wonder why he came to me of all people. It's odd how pure hatred can turn peaceable."

Ollie squatted on her heels. "Boggles the mind. How did things go with the young girl over at the Dry Gulch?"

"I hope we can afford another hand."

"Praise be, you hired her."

"It doesn't take much to make you happy."

"While you were upstairs, guess who I ran into at the bar?"

Tired eyes and pea soup for brains soured Laurel's mood. "Who?"

"Yates. Trying to climb head first into a whiskey bottle."

Nothing except regret would make a man drown his sorrows. Or did Brodie wrestle with the idea of running out on her again?

The idea kicked her in the teeth and poured Ollie's tincture of Hawthorne down a raw throat. Laurel closed her eyes to hide the vivid memory of their lovemaking. Walking a tightrope made one old and weary.

" 'Course, I tried to show him the error of his ways, but

294

he'd slipped too far over the edge to pay me any never mind."

Her eyes flew open with a jerk of her head.

"Please tell me you didn't meddle."

She didn't welcome Ollie's brand of help. Generally speaking, the dear woman botched everything.

Wide-eyed innocence didn't fool her for a minute. "Who, me? You know I'd never breathe a word to anyone."

Chapter Twenty-eight

Jake had vanished by breakfast. The wolf rose from his burlap pallet to sniff Laurel's hand. She could imagine how fast the honorable sheriff ran when he came to and saw the animal. And the door wasn't even in splinters. Amazing.

"Bet you're wanting to eat, aren't you, boy?"

She rubbed his ears and upturned throat. Even the worst of God's creatures responded to kindness. With a master like Vallens, no wonder he'd tried to eat everyone alive.

"You're not so mean."

Ollie caught her hand feeding meat and stale gingerbread to the dog. "Stop that! Next thing I know, you'll have him in an apron, waiting tables. On second thought, the idea—"

A knock on the back door interrupted Ollie.

"Unless I'm mistaken, that's Adeline." Laurel let the girl in, pleased she'd accepted her offer.

"Git yourself on in here, little lady, and make yourself at home before Laurel has you doing tricks and begging. I'm

Olivia Applejack b'Dam, by the way. But you can call me Ollie."

Adeline's blues sparkled with wetness. Laurel marveled at Ollie's ability to make even the loneliest feel loved and wanted.

"It seems as if I've come home, thanks to you both."

Laurel took the ragged valise from the girl. "I hope you won't mind sharing my bed?"

"Anywhere beats the saloon. With the drunken sots raising a ruckus, I never got a wink of sleep."

"A few nights of Ollie's snoring may change that opinion."

"I swear to my time, insult a woman in her own house, why don't you? You should make a body welcome, not run 'em off."

"What a beautiful animal." Adeline knelt to put her arms around the wolf's neck, showing no fear. "What's his name?"

"Reckon he don't have none other than wolf dog, leastways not that we ever heard." Ollie lit the pipe that had gone cold. "Don't belong to us, only keeping him . . . uh, for someone. He's sure taken a shine to you, young lady."

Inspiration hit Laurel.

"He needs a proper name. Something more than wolf dog. Every living thing deserves self-respect. Adeline, any ideas?"

"I'm sorta partial to my mother's maiden name of Hannibal."

"Perfect. Hannibal it is."

Laurel led the way to the living quarters and watched the girl unpack her meager belongings. The rag doll propped up by the pillows added a fitting touch to the faded old quilt.

"Why is that covered?" Adeline pointed to the mirror.

She'd forgotten how strange another might take her phobia.

"Quite an oddity, I suppose, not bearing to see my own reflection." Or the color purple, though she didn't add that. The girl thought her an escapee from the madhouse already. "I can't seem to fix the problem. Not yet, at any rate."

"After Paw stole what belonged to me, all I see is a dirty, rotten tramp. He turned a twelve-year-old into thirty. Seeing that puts us both in the same boat."

"Shhhh, don't think about it. When Ollie spouts her golden rule enough, you'll soon learn that no one can roll back months or years, and it don't do an ounce of good trying." She drew Adeline close and smoothed back her blond hair. "From here we keep our eyes on the future and focus on making ourselves better than we were before. Ollie says hopeless are those who refuse to step out of a quagmire once someone hands them a strong branch."

Unbidden, pictures of the James family gathered on the porch popped into Laurel's mind. She could take her own advice.

And she would.

One of these fine days at the appropriate time.

"I'll wager you're a flapjack eater."

"Oh, shoot, I can eat a whole plateful."

Brodie knew his luck had run out when he heard the thunder of hooves halting in front of the Yates residence early Thursday morn, interrupting breakfast. Blood roaring in his ears almost drowned the fists pounding on the polished cypress. Through the curtained window, birds in the garden appeared unaffected by the commotion. The nearby back door urged him to flee. A sane man would.

That is, if said man hadn't grown tired of the chase.

If he hadn't let roots burrow so deep in Texas swampland he couldn't chop them loose with the sharpest hoe.

. . . And if he hadn't found Lil.

He forced down the bite of ham and calmly reached for another biscuit, spooning jam onto one half.

Murphy jumped to his feet when soldiers in blue barged into the dining room followed by Etta. They yanked Brodie from the chair, toppling it over.

"What the . . . ?" Murphy glared, his voice thick.

"Shenandoah, by the authority of the president of these United States and governor of the rebellious Texas territory, I hereby place you under arrest." Two bars on the man's shoulders ranked the speaker as a captain.

"This is my brother, Brodie Yates. I fear you've made a grievous error. I intend to register a complaint immediately."

"Won't do a cent's worth of good. It doesn't make any difference what name he chooses to call himself. He's a treasonous Confederate spy."

"May I remind you gentlemen the war ended over three years ago and Andrew Johnson issued amnesty for Johnny Rebs?" Brodie spoke in a quiet tone, willing himself to avoid his brother's gaze. They both had known the danger that dogged his return.

"We haven't forgotten the scores of men who died at Shenandoah's hand. No amnesty erases that."

Had they not bound him, Brodie would have smashed the nose jutting a finger's width from his. Even so, he strained to free himself, if only for a moment. The damn war would never be over as long as hate and revenge ran rampant.

"We can take you back in pieces if you prefer, you misbegotten scum." The captain shoved him.

"Yeah, General Buell didn't say it had to be pretty." The second voice spoke near his left ear—a lowly private, no doubt, who found bravery after they had Brodie securely tied.

"Murphy, will you take care of Laurel?"

"No need to ask. You know me. We'll get this straightened out and soon have you back."

The group hustled Brodie toward the front, the captain pausing only long enough to deliver a parting insult.

"Far as me and the rest of the Union army are concerned, his neck needs to be straightened. A rope will see to that very quickly."

"My brother deserves a fair trial before execution."

"Before or after, it's all the same. Sit down, sir, or we'll take you, too."

"Murph, please. You'll only make matters worse."

The glare of the morning rays usually required a hat. In the last twenty years Brodie could count on his fingers the days he'd stepped out bare-headed. Captain Blue Belly scoffed at the simple request, heaving him onto a horse.

People stared at the procession. Jake came from the barber shop, and Brodie realized the tin star was missing from the weasel's chest.

A glance swung to the cafe. Laurel stopped cleaning the brand-new window, the rag slipping unheeded from her hand.

The shocked lavender gaze shattered his heart.

Not ever holding her again, her heart beating next to his.

. . . . And not voicing the words of love he carried silently inside for so long.

His luck had run out.

The reality that he loved her, without reservation and forevermore, came too late.

Moss-draped cypress standing proud and tall shed tears he dare not allow. The giant trees told a truth few men wished to hear—that Redemption came free of charge for those seeking it.

Ahhhhh, but he'd found true pleasure for a little while anyway. That consolation would have to do.

Brodie tried to drag his gaze from hers, but it held fast. That was when a lean animal leaped around Laurel's skirts.

The wolf dog!

Did that mean Vallens hadn't died? A sick whirl whipped his breakfast into a froth. Jake's shirt minus the badge made sense all of a sudden. Yet nothing explained why Laurel patted the beast's head without it ripping off a hand.

"How-do, ma'am." The captain halted the line of men and tipped his head. "Fine day, isn't it?"

"They shore grow 'em handsome here in Texas, eh, Cap'n?" a soldier hollered.

No doubt a bold leer accompanied the yell, accounting for Laurel's flush. Brodie strained to break the bonds, for he'd take joy in putting a fist in the face of the coarse-mouthed Yank.

Before the captain issued the command to continue, Brodie watched her embarrassment fade. Helpless fear swept aside all other emotions. The beautiful features couldn't hide raw terror.

Had he one favor to ask, he'd use it to assure Laurel he'd gladly follow her to Hell and beyond in order to keep her free of men like of Vallens and Taft . . . despite it meaning a walk right up the steps to the gallows.

Regret? You could say he had plenty to keep him company.

But never in protecting the love of his life.

The square-jawed captain seemed in no mood to grant favors, not even small ones to ease a tormented soul. Brodie had trusted too little and so quickly thrown away what he'd battled great odds to find.

He glanced back when the column moved.

Sweet Jezzie!

Laurel stumbled, wetness creating rivers down pale

cheeks until she fell to her knees in the middle of the street.

"I'll love you always, my darlin'." His whispered breath couldn't rise past the hole in his chest. "For all eternity."

The ride gave him time to mask the misery that his face surely reflected, for he'd not give the enemy more reason to taunt. Arriving at the Jefferson stockade, Brodie noted its similarity to the shameless conditions at Andersonville and Camp Douglas. It was nothing more than a dungeon beneath the stars. Its sole saving grace, if a man called it that, was that there was no roof to trap the stench.

Sand Town. An accurate name for the place where men died in numbers, their bones returning to the dust from whence they came.

His gut sank when the immense fifteen-foot-high timbers of the prison's gate slammed behind him.

Men in rags shuffled around the compound. Glaze-covered eyes stared, welcoming him to a deplorable existence. Blankets spread on the ground indicated the sleeping quarters. The second thing to catch his eye was a gallows at the far end.

"There's no place like home, eh, Shenandoah?" The captain yanked him from the horse by the chains binding his wrists. "Don't get too accustomed to it, though. You won't be here long."

"About what I'd expect from yellow-hearted Billy Yanks."

"Tsk, tsk. Mr. Shenandoah needs a few lessons in manners. Don't he, boys?"

Fists pummeled muscle and flesh, reminding Brodie of the value of keeping opinions to himself. Pain in his midsection and kidneys doubled him over. He slumped to the ground and prayed they'd tire.

Laurel's face flashed across his memory. The night they made love her sooty gaze had held anger.

He'd disappointed her once again. How many times did that make? Must surely set a record. And how many chances did a man get to right wrongs? No more, it seemed.

Useless to think about it now, for he'd not leave this stockade except in a pine box. That much remained clear.

Yep, he bore much regret.

Then a well-placed boot to the skull delivered Brodie into the black pit that he'd dreaded.

Now he would never know when the last breath came.

Laurel set about business in a fog. Had Ollie not vetoed the notion, she'd have closed the cafe and curled up under the covers.

"I think we've fed every mouth, belly, and hollow spot in the vicinity." Adeline sank into the nearest chair.

"Young lady, it's hard but honest work. You'll get the hang of it. Gotta get your feet wet before you learn to dog-paddle." Ollie patted Laurel. "Girl, go talk to Murphy and get his two cents on springing Brodie from that Blue Belly hell. You ain't gonna do much good here anyhow. Go put your heads together while I teach Adeline the finer points of dishwashing."

Within minutes, Laurel lifted the brass knocker at the house on State Street. Etta opened the door with the shiny ornament still in midair.

"I'm glad you came. Mr. Murphy's been in a tizzy since the soldiers invaded the privacy of his home. Them men snatched Mr. Brodie straight out of his chair before we knowed the reason why. Plumb disgraceful treatment of God-fearing folk."

Hannibal posted himself outside the entryway. His devotion touched her deeply. She'd spent a good part of the day wondering whom the animal would choose should

Vallens reappear, for deep in her gut she knew the man would show up sooner or later.

Laurel barely glimpsed her former betrothed's colorless face before she threw herself into his arms.

"What are we going to do? It's all my fault."

"Come into the parlor. We'll figure out something."

"They're going to kill him. Probably without benefit of a trial. They may have already."

"Not with the stink Mr. Loughery keeps raising with editorials in Marshall's *Texas Republican* newspaper. He keeps an eagle eye on that bunch, particularly since most of the injustices occur against Jefferson's most influential." Murphy smoothed her hand to reassure her, but the worry lining his features said his reasoning didn't necessarily hold water. "Did you know that Mr. Loughery even wrote the President of the United States, detailing a list of basic rights they've denied prisoners?"

"Letters! They're a waste of time and postage."

"Don't discount the power of words, my dear. Since he did, General Buell and his underlings have gotten more careful. I hear government spies watch and report back to Washington."

Laurel jumped up to pace the length of the room.

"Brodie isn't influential or anyone of consequence. The soldiers can simply claim they shot him trying to escape."

The thought filled her with bitter rage.

"Sit down. I can't think if you insist on pacing."

She returned to perch stiffly beside him. "Spit and thunder! He had to have lost his mind to come back with Texas under military occupation. And why did he have to follow Vallens and try to save me? He flaunted himself in Jefferson."

"He did. And he would gladly do it again."

"Why, for heaven's sake? Does he place so little value on his own life?"

"You don't understand my brother very well. He does whatever it takes to ensure the welfare of those he loves, even should he find death in the process. The answer to your question . . . he cares for you with body and soul, so much he'd risk anything on this earth for your safety."

Brodie's mocking smile haunted her.

At least I'm not the one claiming something they're not, Lil. I hold no misconception of the sort I am.

Strange how it took losing the man she loved to discover a truth Ollie had tried to pound into her. . . .

Wearing a mask and pretending to be someone else wouldn't earn her a place of respect.

She'd had it all this time and couldn't see it.

He couldn't die because of her foolish notions.

But he would. He'd chosen that.

For her.

Laurel gripped the tufted arm of the settee.

Chapter Twenty-nine

Laurel fought sickening nausea.

"I have an idea worth trying." Murphy steepled his hands, thumbs against his mouth. "It requires a trip into Jefferson, which I'm not up to—and a lie. It's a lot to ask."

"I'll say anything. Go anywhere."

"It may not work, but I believe it's all we have." Murphy quickly outlined the scheme.

Two hours later, Laurel walked down the gangplank and went straight to the office of Epperson & Maxey, Attorneys at Law.

Laurel groaned when Georgia Rutabaga of the Tyler Rutabagas just happened to emerge from the hatmaker nearby.

"Miss James, how delightful." The clerk of the mercantile pursed her lips. "I've spent sleepless nights worrying about whatever I said or did to upset you."

"You needn't give it a second thought. I'm fine—truly."

Georgia Rutabaga peered over Laurel's shoulder. "Business with Mr. Epperson?"

"Forgive me, but I can't bear to discuss an extremely sensitive matter." She sniffled and dabbed her eyes. "I pray you understand."

"I must get home to Mr. Rutabaga anyway. How time flies."

After the woman rounded a corner, Laurel patted herself on the back for a stroke of brilliance, then calmed shaking hands and turned the doorknob.

"Benjamin Epperson at your service, miss." A dapper man closed a large volume on his desk. Gray sprinkles shot through once-dark hair.

"I have it on good authority you can assist me with a grievous problem." He raised a quizzical brow and she went on. "I travel seeking the head of Citizens for Peace."

Mr. Epperson hustled her into an inner room.

"Merely speaking the name in broad daylight gets innocent men killed. However, I have no knowledge any such organization exists and advise against pursuing this. Whoever claims otherwise committed a falsehood. I practice law."

"Murphy Yates of Redemption gave me your name. Perhaps he erred. I apologize." She turned quickly, swirling her skirts about, but despair clouded the doorway. Laurel stumbled, slamming her shoulder into a paneled wall.

"Wait, miss. You said Murphy Yates?"

"He's a friend. A contingent of soldiers took his brother to the stockade. A bullet wound during a bank robbery prevented Mr. Yates from coming himself."

"The devils finally caught Brodie. I understand he gave them quite a slippery chase."

One that ended largely because of her.

"Then you grasp the importance of my need. Could you direct me to anyone who has affiliations with Citizens for Peace?"

"Please follow me, Miss . . . ?"

"James. Laurel James."

A small group of men jumped to their feet when she entered a secret room after Mr. Epperson tapped a code of sorts on what appeared to be an ordinary wall inside a coat closet.

"No cause for alarm, gentlemen. This pretty lady asks for our help. Mr. Crump, we should consider obliging."

In less than half an hour she tucked a hastily designed document into a satchel and headed for the tall gates that imprisoned her love. She held hope of fixing the mess she'd had a hand in creating.

She only prayed the plan worked

Brodie had no strength to resist when he was pulled roughly from an airless sweat coffin designed to break a man's will.

"Commander wants to see ya," the voice yelled in his good ear—the one they'd overlooked in teaching him a the "lesson."

Getting a clear view of the figure with swollen eyes took some doing. And when a shove sent him sprawling at the feet of a woman who bore a great similarity to Laurel, he decided the confinement and beatings had left him delusional.

They must've bashed out his brains to think she'd take tea with his tormenter.

"Shenandoah, good of you to place yourself at my beck and call." General Buell smiled and leaned forward. "Your lovely wife has brought a document to my attention. It states your name as Brodie Yates. If that's true, you can't possibly be the infamous spy. You were too busy marrying and taking care of your wife."

A wife?

The brutes had indeed ruined his hearing, along with

breaking two fingers and half his ribs, for he could've sworn the man called Laurel his wife.

"What have you done to my husband?"

A hundred needles pierced his body in his struggle to stand. Although lying on the floor was tempting, he wished to meet the Yankee's smirk from an upright position. He didn't push aside the firm grip around his waist or the gentle brush of her lips to his cheek as she helped him into a chair.

Thumbscrews brought less misery than seeing her again.

He was facing the only woman he'd ever loved. He wanted to measure each word with the greatest care.

Making amends called for softer surroundings far away from curious ears. Preferably in a downy featherbed. Now he found himself speechless.

"I must compliment your excellent taste in women. Not that I buy this charade for an instant." Buell bit off the end of a fat cigar and struck a match to it. "No, it's going to take a lot more than paper. It looks phoney to me."

Brodie felt Laurel stiffen and clutch a handkerchief.

"I have no reason to lie. Besides, I have eight children I can march in here to prove he preferred bedding me over fighting a silly war. And you still haven't answered my question. How did my husband receive this mauling?"

A marriage *and* children—eight of them to be exact. One thing for sure, had he partaken of such pleasure, it would never slip his mind.

"Madam, I don't care if you parade half the children in the state of Texas through this room. It won't prove he's not Shenandoah."

"Perhaps the word of a learned physician would carry more weight." Laurel puffed up like a toad. "Dr. Whitaker will explain why Brodie couldn't join the Cause on account of he took sick with cholera." The raven-haired beauty sobbed quietly into a lace-edged cloth. "But for the pure grace of God, I would've lost him. Once he recovered, a horse threw him and broke a leg—my husband's, not the horse's."

"I do declare, Mrs. Yates, that tragic concoction seems too good to waste. Unfortunately for you, I don't believe a word."

"Disputing my wife's integrity, General?" Brodie snapped.

"Sure am, even if a Dr. Whitaker does exist beyond her own imagination."

"Well, I never!" She placed a hand on her hip. "For the last time, I beg you for an answer to my question concerning Brodie's condition."

"He fell! Does that suit you?"

"Spit and thunder, it does not! I intend to pay a visit to Mr. Loughrey. One would think with the trouble he's stirred up recounting the atrocious prisoner maltreatment in the newspaper you'd take more care not to get on his front page again."

"Loughrey's nothing but a rabble-rouser. Before this is over, he may find himself in my stockade if he doesn't watch out."

"May I appeal to your sense of fairness and beg a private word with my husband?" Laurel leaned forward to touch General Buell's arm. "Please."

Brodie knew the effect of that contact; still it amazed him how quickly it shredded the hardened man's resistance.

"I'm no ogre, my dear lady. Ten minutes, no more."

The door latch slid into place before either of them spoke. Brodie broke the silence first. "Why didn't you stay away?"

How could he explain that her presence poured salt in wounds that'd already festered?

"I couldn't. Darn it, I can't find a spot that's not bruised or bloody. They've reduced you to a shambles." She examined each stinging laceration.

"It's nothing I didn't expect. Comes with the territory."

"They didn't need to beat the living daylights out of you."

"Appears I made 'em mad. They have a name for the thrashing."

Brodie winced when she gently brushed the lock of hair from his forehead. Everything about him hurt . . . mostly his heart. He jerked away. Give him back the thumbscrews any day.

"Go home. Surely I don't have to lay out the risks to an intelligent lady."

"I'm well aware of what's at stake. But I had to come when you're here on my account. I can't leave you to the mercy of these Yankees without trying to repay a debt."

"Darlin', I'm reduced to nothing but a debt? Maybe it was a merchant's mask you wore that night."

"Murphy has devised a plan. I contacted some men here."

"Dare I point out, General Buell saw through that, dear wife? By the way, remind me again when we said our vows. Was that before or after we made love?"

"Believe in me. You did once. For God's sake, I love you. I wouldn't do anything to ruin that. In your own way, when you give yourself a chance, I think you love me back."

Love? It was too late for that . . . too late for wishing for something he couldn't have. He was as good as dead.

"The only way I'm leaving is in a box, understand?"

"Quitting at the first skirmish? Strange, I never thought they'd break the legendary Reb so quickly."

"Stop it. Forget me. Get on with your life."

"So we simply have dead dreams left? I mean nothing?"

The whisper came from hurt and misery that cut to the quick. He'd lost the one woman who could've brought him peace.

"Don't look so sad, love. It's reality. We aren't starry-eyed schoolchildren." Brodie lifted her palm to his face. The smooth skin cooled a fevered cheek. "For what it's worth, I wish things were different. Only they aren't. There's a price for dancing to the music. You gotta pay that old fiddler for the privilege at some point."

"Don't say that! We deserve happiness and a chance."

"It won't happen. You can't rub the spots off a leopard."

He traced the moist line of her lips with a finger. When the tip of her tongue came in contact with his skin, he shivered with longing. She moved into the circle of his arm and burrowed her face into his chest. He closed his eyes tight to block the assault of her fragrance, soft curves that molded to him, and desire to have one more second with her.

"It doesn't matter. We can go forward from here and sort it out later," Laurel murmured.

Couldn't she see that they didn't have a forward? Movement in any direction would get him a walk up the gallows.

"I dearly wish I could meet these eight kids of ours before that hearse rolls up to cart me away." He kissed the upturned mouth very gently, surprised he could still pucker.

The squeak of the door silenced a reply. "Time's over. General said . . . uh, you hafta leave now . . . uh, madam."

Brodie quirked an eyebrow at the brawny soldier's sudden shyness. The man certainly hadn't displayed a speck of it when he drove those boots into his ribs.

"I'll be back tomorrow." Laurel's lips brushed a battered cheek. "That's a promise."

Pushing her away didn't make sense. A beggarly man would snatch up every morsel of food that fell his way. Yet he did. The pain in her gaze spoke of deep wounds he could do little to heal. Misery born long ago wouldn't let her understand. She wouldn't see that he had to keep her from hands that would snuff out her breath in an instant.

"Let it go, I said! You can't save me—not now, not ever. Mind your knitting and quit trying to mend things that are better off thrown into a trash heap. I'm not redeemable."

"I'd ask the general's permission first, ma'am." Then the soldier blushed. "I mean . . . he generally allows visitors only once a week. But, he, uh . . . might make an exception."

"Heed me: Don't visit again." Brodie stared into the cloudless day, his voice brittle and hard. For her safety and his sanity, he could show no weakness. Or his breaking heart.

Laurel stumbled through the gates, mud splattering her as she walked.

She could wash it off.

Her quivering chin rose. A granite stare replaced tears. Some she'd already scrubbed.

"Fancy meeting the beautiful Miss James in Sand Town."

In her grief, she'd failed to notice the man in the shadows.

"Vallens! You're alive and well in spite of the rumors. Folks in Redemption figured you were dead." The good news was, they couldn't arrest Ollie for a murder she hadn't committed. "Did you miss your hound?"

"Not particularly. Dog's a scrapper."

"You put Brodie here."

Vallens rubbed the jagged scar on his face as though it ached down to his rotten soul.

"A word to the right source can cure problems . . . and lure a woman from secure surroundings."

Suddenly everything began to add up.

"The mystery with the meat shipment has your name all over it. Correct?"

"Except Taft failed to show, forcing a change in tactics."

"I should've known it'd take more than a bullet to send you to Hell."

"Reckon that's 'cause I'm already there." He moved aside to reveal a second figure.

"I do declare. You're looking splendid, Lil."

Laurel didn't need to feel the rough edge of her broken tooth to recall the face that brought nightmares to life. Icicles formed in the darkest corners of her being.

Will Taft's mouth settled in a grim line.

"I'm a bit tired of trifling with you. That woman who stole you away from the Black Garter cost me dear. I want recompense—the money and you."

The hoarse voice filled her with terror, but she'd not let him see that. It would please him too much.

"Grab a shovel because I'm dead to you. You'll never get Ollie or me. The money's gone, too."

"Reckon your hide will do just fine. I've never skinned a woman before. I anticipate the pleasure." The mouth barely visible in Taft's whiskered face turned up in a smile. "And you have two younger sisters."

Chapter Thirty

Laurel gasped. No one could help her.

"Touch them and rue the day you were born. I've come a long way from the child you stole. I fight much better now."

A persistent bell rang somewhere in the middle of the afternoon. The clanging penetrated dull senses that reeled from one surprise to the next. How very strange indeed. Perhaps a fire? But no one had shouted orders to form a bucket brigade.

"There you are, Miss James." Georgia Rutabaga appeared at her side, taking an arm. "Did you forget?"

"Forget?"

"The Garden Club tea I invited you to earlier. Come along or we'll be late. The ladies get impatient waiting for stragglers. Mrs. Crump grows most fretful when it comes to eyeing teacakes and mouth-watering scones." The woman moved her from Vallens and Taft's reach with the expertise of a soldier.

"I suppose." Although Laurel had no clue what was going on she was extremely grateful for Mrs. Rutabaga's intervention.

"Keep walking and don't look back," the woman murmured.

The bell continued to clang as they traveled the streets. At last her rescuer unlatched the gate of a picket fence surrounding a dilapidated house. If the Garden Club met here, they were in dire straits.

Inside, Laurel found the lavish furnishings quite a shock.

"No one followed, did they?"

The question came from a gentleman who took her hand. She recognized him from the secret room at the law office.

"I took every precaution." Georgia removed hat pins, lifted the feathered finery, and laid it on the marble table.

"I don't understand. . . ." Laurel stared at the two.

"Alfred, please explain to the poor dear that we're not kidnapping her before she faints dead away."

"I'm a bit confused, I must admit."

Holding her head, she sank into the silk upholstered chair Mr. Rutabaga shoved under wobbly legs.

"We followed you to the stockade and saw the two men accost you. Vallens and Taft's shenanigans have given them an unsavory reputation, to say the least. I alerted fellow Citizens for Peace with the bell and sent my wife to the rescue."

"I can never thank you enough. They've cost me and my family untold grief." Tears rose again at her close call.

"We always assumed you'd been abducted all those years ago," Alfred said.

Georgia Rutabaga patted her arm. "You're safe here."

Within minutes the parlor filled with a group of men. Each wore grim features from fighting a cause none expected to win. They'd try with every ounce of strength in their bodies anyway.

"General Buell didn't accept the document." Laurel met Benjamin Epperson's concern head on.

"I gathered as much. Never fear, we aren't giving up."

"That's right," Phillip Crump added. "We're not licked yet. I have a brilliant plan. Excuse us while we confer, Miss James." A wall panel opened to reveal another secret room.

"You haven't let your family know you're alive and well?"

"I can't. I care too much." Her voice broke.

"About them or yourself?"

How quickly Georgia had seen through her. Laurel squirmed. Too many *too*s littered the path home.

"It's complicated and risky. I will one day."

"Let me get you that tea while they talk, dear."

Over hot tea and fresh apple cake Georgia Rutabaga shed light on the stark difference between the home's face and core.

"The military marched in and immediately began confiscating the best homes. Making the outside so hideous no one would want to live here assured the best way to keep it. As predicted, they passed us over. The Mabreys, Schluters and several others wish they'd done likewise."

She and the old house had a kinship. Both resembled souls that ached with weary despair.

Her heart longed for something it couldn't have.

Brodie's swollen rebel grays hadn't disguised the truth.

He'd taken her love when it suited him, then discarded her as nothing more than ballast in a pockmarked pirate ship.

Georgia Rutabaga's endless chatter the entire ride back to Redemption grew tiresome. Poor Mr. Rutabaga never had an opening to toss in even an occasional word. Although grateful for the couple's armed escort, Laurel would've preferred more quiet. The day's events required mulling.

The misery Brodie dealt sat heavy in her chest. He'd never accepted her past, never had faith she could change.

She'd needed him to believe in her. And now he might die.

Ollie's grim lines greeted. "It's about dadburned time! Worrying a poor body to death oughta be a crime."

The wolf dog rose from the pallet and bared his teeth.

"Hush, Hannibal. These are friends." Laurel kissed Ollie's cheek. "I couldn't help it. Use your best manners to welcome Mr. and Mrs. Rutabaga. I apologize for Ollie. She's not ordinarily this cantankerous."

"Am too." Ollie pushed her away and held out a hand. "I'm Olivia Applejack b'Dam and I'm right pleased to make your acquaintance. It's not every day my girl brings home guests. Will you be staying for tea and crumpets?"

"I'm afraid not," Alfred quickly got in, "unless Miss James has further needs?"

"You've done more than enough. We'll be fine."

"I don't know, Alfred. I worry about leaving them."

"I insist." Laurel steered them toward the door. "I'll lock up so tight a cockroach couldn't find a crack."

"Think about going home," Georgia whispered in her ear.

By the time the Rutabagas' buggy faded in the distance, Laurel had bolted both doors, slid chairs under the knobs for extra measure, and checked each window latch.

"Hannibal, on guard." She selected the sharpest knife.

Let Taft try to harm them now. Although one disturbing thought niggled: Would the wolf choose Vallens when it came to it?

"Girl, I need you to help these old bones up the stairs if you've finished whatever it is you're doing. Rutabaga is the silliest name I ever heard."

318

Ollie generally didn't ask for help of any sort. Laurel worried about her friend.

The woman hadn't even badgered her with a million questions.

"What's wrong, Ollie? Is it your heart?"

"Just need to lie down for a bit. I just cain't see so well all of a sudden."

The tick of the clock almost drowned out the weak voice. Laurel shouldered the slight frame, taking care not to waken Adeline. Ollie collapsed on the bed. She didn't make a squawk when Laurel removed her shoes and drew up a coverlet.

"Ollie, can I do anything else?"

"Stay with me."

Shallow breathing robbed the room of air. Laurel gasped from the pain of fighting a battle she was sure to lose. She'd lived in dread of this moment since learning of Ollie's poor health. Her head told her she couldn't stall the inevitable, yet her heart wished to believe the motherly friend would live forever.

She thought of fetching Curley, but danger lurked outside their doors. She prayed he'd forgive her.

Tears dampened her cheeks as she curled up beside Ollie and took the thin face between her hands.

"I don't think I told you how much I love you."

"Girl, no need to speak of things we already know. Afraid it's time to part company."

"Please don't die."

"Ain't of a mind to, but ol' Gabriel's tootin' his horn. Purtiest music I ever did hear."

Laurel strangled a sob. "Rest awhile and you'll be fine."

"Mama, I've missed your smile. What's that, Mama?" Ollie's voice became childlike. "Grandpappy, you came."

Chills tumbled end over end. Laurel had heard that when a body neared the end the spirit of loved ones would come carry them home. She smoothed back Ollie's faded spikes, wishing she could go with her.

"I need you a bit longer, Ollie. This world's a cold, forbidding place." Thank goodness Ollie hadn't learned about Taft and Vallens. Laurel had spared her that, at least.

Laurel took the knife and laid it beside her.

Ollie mumbled incoherently.

"Do you need something? Maybe a cup of your brew might get you raring to face another morn."

"Reckon the good Lord put me on this earth for a reason and that was to take care of my girl. You gave an old woman purpose when I had nary. Certainly filled my days with more love than an old crone like me deserved."

She kissed the fragile hand. "We're about equal in the giving department. You saved me when no other would."

"I failed. Tried to hang on 'til I got you with your folks. Promise you'll go to them once I'm gone. And don't be too hard on Yates." Ollie's murmurs grew more faint.

A blessing the woman didn't know about the shambled mess in her heart. It was nothing to share with a dying friend.

The magnitude of an empty life suddenly washed over her.

What would she do? Who would she turn to?

"Shhhh, don't worry. I'll make do."

"Say you'll go to your ma and pa."

A body had to keep a deathbed pledge no matter what. Yet how could she vow it, seeing the impossible nature? Hot tears rose. She had jinxed everyone she ever loved.

"You should rest now, Ollie."

"Not until you promise."

Once the stubborn woman buried her choppers in

something she wouldn't let go, not even in the throes of crossing the dark river. Laurel worked to form words she couldn't fulfill.

"I will. Now save your strength."

"I love you, my beautiful angel girl."

"Wait for me over there. I need someone to welcome me."

Laurel snuggled close and laid her head on Ollie's chest. A death rattle commenced that no amount of prayers could stop. Ollie had begun the journey. Soon the dear woman would rest and be free from pain. Laurel hoped the good Lord would overlook faults and take a liking to the crusty soul. Surely a heart as big as the whole blamed state of Texas would go a long way in atoning for any faltering Ollie did on earth.

"Please, God, she didn't really kill Vallens. And she wouldn't have stolen that money from Taft if there'd been any other way. So open the gates and let her in."

Midnight came and went. In the wee hours when dawn stole into the room Ollie breathed no more.

Laurel clung to the shell of her brave friend's body. Deep sobs wracked her as tears flowed onto the cold, stiff body.

The turning doorknob had Laurel grabbing the knife. She clutched it with both hands. Long blond hair brought relief.

"I thought I heard . . . oh, no, is something wrong with Miss Ollie?"

Laurel lowered the knife, wiping weary eyes.

"She's dead. Her heart played out."

Adeline sank to the floor. "What're we going to do? Two girls alone that everyone threw out with the slop."

"She did love us for a fact."

"Who'll care for us now?"

"We will . . . together."

* * *

Laurel bathed every wrinkle of Ollie's body with loving hands before clothing her in a dress of satin and pearls. Aged tissue paper encased the pale blue finery she found oddly hidden in the bottom of an old trunk Ollie brought with them. A tiny box yielded another piece of the puzzle, for inside lay a gold band. It glimmered through a sudden veil of wetness. Laurel brushed her eyes, slipping the ring on Ollie's finger.

Only a woman who'd loved deeply would guard the treasures all these years.

Laurel prayed the man was worth it.

Brodie's bruised, battered face lingered each time she closed her eyes.

Farewell words haunted every waking moment.

Quit trying to mend things that are better off thrown into a trash heap. I'm not redeemable.

Faded letters tied with gold string she put aside, unable to bear the heartbreak of learning a stranger had spurned someone so precious. She tucked the letters into the pine box. The grave would protect an old, private love.

A blustery day added gloom to the funeral. Little more than a handful of people came to pay their respects. But that was fine. Ollie valued genuine friendship. She would've considered it sacrilege to have the scornful there for the send-off.

Laurel kept a wary eye out for Taft and Vallens, although given the sneakiness of the pair, they'd bide their time. That was their way.

Within the circle of Curley Madison's soft warmth, Laurel found courage to complete the journey she'd begun with Ollie that night in St. Louis. Their paths separated here. Each would have to go forward alone.

Nodding politely to Murphy, Nora, and Jake, Laurel pulled her heavy shawl closer. Adeline's sobs punctured the somber quiet. The poor girl had seen too much grief for someone her age.

"Curley, since we don't have a preacher I think Ollie would like you to say something befitting," Laurel suggested.

The saloon-keep blew his nose and cleared his throat.

"Friends, we're gathered today to mourn the passing of Olivia Applejack b'Dam whom the Lord Almighty saw fit to take."

He paused for a moment, struggling for breath.

"Many of you chose to see a rough, crotchety has-been. Not me. Beneath the layer of salt and vinegar was the finest, most beautiful lady I've ever met. She left a piece of herself within each of us. Ollie imparted wisdom and truth that we might not've wished to hear but had to anyway. Each morsel enriched our lives in ways we never guessed."

A purple and yellow bouquet of prairie flowers, spiderwort, and broom weed clutched in her fist seemed appropriate for Olivia b'Dam, who lived life natural and free, on her own terms.

"If a body's judged by the mark they leave behind, Ollie needn't worry, because hers is wide enough to accommodate the state and have room for Arkansas." Curley's voice quavered. He mopped his eyes with a handkerchief. "Dear Lord, don't get too mad if you catch her swinging on the pearly gates. Having fun is purely her nature. And she's a little on the sassy side, which you'll overlook once you take a shine to her. Amen."

"Hallelujah." Smiling, Laurel sniffled.

Through a haze of tears she winced as dirt covered her friend's coffin. Adeline's hand strayed into hers and she took comfort in the meager offering.

If only she'd done more to relieve the stress on Ollie's heart.

If only she'd stayed instead of going on a fool's errand.

If only she could've taken Ollie's place.

Laurel swallowed a sob, mindful that the woman didn't have anyone left to kill, run off, or hide from.

Murphy hugged her. "Don't blame yourself. She lived on borrowed time. Be grateful we had her as long as we did. Nora and I are here if you need anything whatsoever."

One by one, everyone left except Laurel, Adeline, and Curley.

"I can't leave her. What will I do without Ollie?"

"Follow your dream, child." Curley's arm encircled her. "Just because loved ones pass don't give us call to slink away. Ollie would tell you to leave her to the grave and go on."

The advice stuck with Laurel on the long walk back to an empty life and the task of moving her belongings across the hall.

"Are you sure Miss Ollie's things won't . . . ?"

Adeline fingered the worn dress they'd exchanged for the blue satin, unable to complete the thought.

"Give me the willies?" Laurel kissed the top of the blond head. "I honestly don't know. I can still smell that pipe. On the other hand, it'll seem she's watching over us."

"Like my ma. Sometimes I smell her perfume."

"I surely wouldn't doubt it."

Heaven must've had powerful need of livening up to have left them so bereft.

"Maybe you should close the cafe for a day or two," Curley said, dropping by around sundown.

"Can't afford it." Laurel pushed a strand of hair from her face. "This business is our means, and it helps to keep busy."

Unless Taft had other plans.

REDEMPTION

"But Curley, do you mind staying close?" Anger turned him beet red when she told him about Taft and Vallens.

"Those bastards! I'll set up a bed in the kitchen."

With the cafe locked tight and Curley snoring downstairs, Laurel felt relatively safe . . . from most things.

Ollie's gamine features poked from each shadow while the scent of the pipe swirled in the still air. Fresh grief rose.

Then steamy recollections of a different sort entered the mix to keep her eyes from shutting.

Silvery moon rays scampering through the window—hard muscle sliding over hers—the crooked smile of a shameless rogue—these brought tiny shivers . . . and an ache for tender caresses unlike any other.

Chapter Thirty-one

"I swore I heard that funny little cackle of Miss Ollie's." Adeline set an armload of plates by the bucket. "Hard to believe we buried her yesterday."

Pain between Laurel's shoulder blades reminded her how time dragged. She redoubled her efforts on hardened stew in the bottom of the pot. She'd hid in the kitchen, assigning the girl dining room duty, thinking it might somehow be easier. Not so.

Danger lurked in the moonlight. Eyes watched, waiting.

And where had Hannibal gone?

Odd that he hadn't scratched to get in since Curley let him out.

"Don't you have enough to busy yourself? Don't you have customers to satisfy? Floors to sweep, tables to clear? Some mice traps to set?" She missed Ollie in every way possible.

"That busybody Mrs. Kempshaw's taking her sweet time. She's the last. I've gathered the dishes, wiped tables, and you know we never sweep the floors until all have gone. I don't know nothing about baiting mice traps. Always get my fingers in the darn things." Adeline scooted out a chair and plopped down.

"I apologize for being ill tempered. Guess I'm tired."

"It's all right. Ain't complaining. It's not the saloon."

Laurel flashed a wan smile. "I'm blessed you're here."

"Can I ask something? What kept you from going insane when those men forced you to . . . you know?"

The ugly word filled the space—an unmade bed in an otherwise orderly room that you tried not to notice but couldn't help doing it. This bed had every corner tucked in neatly and still a body couldn't erase the memory of mess and chaos. Hate welled for the man who'd stolen Adeline's innocence, making her a woman before she'd put away her dolls.

"I survived by doing what I had to. Thinking of my family, fresh green fields cleansed by rain—Mama's blueberry pie."

And later, waiting for Brodie's return.

"I prayed for God to strike me dead." Adeline's voice trembled. "I hated when my papa made me drink the potion."

Laurel's head snapped around. "The what?"

"Ain't rightly sure what's in it. Toads innards wouldn't have tasted as bitter." The girl wrinkled her nose. "Made me drink it once a week. Said it'd keep my monthly coming."

Black haw tonic from cotton root bark, maybe. The stuff worked well in preventing babies. Taft forced the horrid liquid down her until a doctor supplied plant seeds from Queen Anne's lace. A spoon with a glass of water each morning spared a child they'd have ripped from her arms. She'd witnessed that misfortune in others.

"He was right on that count."

"Do you suppose it might keep from making babies one day? I mean, when I meet the man I'm going to marry?"

"Don't worry. It has no lasting effects."

Laurel's heart lurched. The wondrous night in Brodie's

arms, the rebel she wished more than anything to grow old with, might have left permanent proof of a love she'd fight to keep.

Even though the father didn't wish to become one with her.

And God forbid should he perish at the end of a rope.

A babe would assure that she kept a piece of him always.

She shook away the thoughts. "You'll give your heart to the man of your dreams and have a houseful of beautiful blond babies."

"If Paw happens to find me, will you let him take me back?"

"I'll kill him first. You have a perfect right to live free from twisted perversions."

"And you? What if those men come?"

"I'll never again be a whore!"

The door into the dining room moved ever so slightly.

Brodie knew every speck of dust and spiderweb in the dark sweat box intimately. It was home. Probably would remain so until the appointed hour.

Deep black water amid the cypress held secrets, but in his lady love's sultry kisses he'd found the lost soul for whom he searched . . . only to leave it scattered among the ruins of broken promises like the moth-eaten rags on a peddler's cart.

Hell and be damned!

He forced aside despair as boots crunched on the rocks littering the stockade. A key grated in the lock. An abrupt glare almost put out eyes that'd seen far too much horror.

"Come along, Shenandoah. Got a visitor."

Georgia clay! He'd begged Laurel to stay away. Another encounter with the raven-haired temptress would drain him. Ahhh, but he'd savor something to carry besides the lavender scrap of lace in the memory bag the general had ripped off.

He stumbled, faint from hunger. The soldier jerked him to his feet. Seconds later, the blue belly shoved him into a room.

"Yates, so we meet again. This time under more, shall we say, favorable circumstances." A hint of a smile twisted the jagged scar into a well-traveled road pitted with deep ruts.

"Fighting a bound man would seem fair-minded only to you."

"You don't scare me."

"That so." Brodie kicked a chair into the wall, relishing Vallens's sudden jump. A quick curl of his foot around the leg flipped the seat upright. He hoped the leisurely drop into it masked his pain. To expose suffering would reveal a chink in the fortress. "I expect you came to gloat."

"How you misjudge me. I wished to inform you of Will Taft's arrival in town. He means to reclaim what's rightfully his."

"Damn you!"

Brodie lunged, driving his full weight into the man. Zeke Vallens staggered against the wall.

"Guard!" Vallens's yell alerted the soldier posted outside.

"Reb, in the corner or I'll shoot your sorry ass."

"Better get him out, Blue Belly." Brodie lounged easily, though he dared anyone to interpret his stare as cordial.

Zeke Vallens retrieved the black hat that had fallen in the scuffle and wedged it on his head. "Good day, Shenandoah."

"Heed my words: Harm Laurel—you and Taft'll answer."

"To whom, pray tell?"

"You'll see. I'd pay attention." Hatred silenced the rumble in his belly. If only it fed a soul's gnawing hunger as well.

The black-hearted devil's smile wobbled a bit as he left.

"Come peaceable, Reb. I wouldn't want to have to call reinforcements." The young soldier cast a wary glance.

What rankled most was leaving Laurel at the mercy of evil. He couldn't protect her. He couldn't soothe her trembling limbs.

Good God, he couldn't even love her like she deserved. Guilt rode like a dark shadow, blotting out the sun.

"Private, do I get a final request before my execution?"

"If it's within reason, I'd suppose."

"How about a letter? Think you could deliver it?"

"I'll see to it, but I'm not sure how soon."

"I'd prefer it happen today. It's imperative."

With it written, Brodie found the metal box a tad less dark than before. Something he'd learned about people in the war let him believe the private would keep his word. With luck the letter would be in the right hands by nightfall.

Even though he might not stick around to see the outcome.

Beyond the stockade walls, Zeke Vallens flipped open a timepiece. Anyway, he'd given Yates something to chew on. The visit might pay off in the event he lost control of the situation. The night would tell whether it'd been profitable.

Plans oftentimes took a volatile twist.

His jaw tightened. The pliable leather fob curled around his hand. He returned the watch and reached inside his somber frock coat to pluck a tintype from his pocket. The face in the small likeness stared into the blackest crevice of a heart the years had turned to stone.

The lady once had the clearest blue gaze. She overlooked the parts no one else could stomach and saw something redeeming.

He'd disappointed her on many occasions, though she never let on.

Damn! He breathed a grateful sigh that she'd never know what despicable things he'd done.

Zeke flipped the tintype to hide the gentle soul's calling, tucked it away, and lowered the brim of his hat.

Panic bubbled, spurring Laurel into action. She threw back the kitchen door and stood nose-to-nose with Florence Kempshaw.

"Why on God's green earth are you eavesdropping?"

Florence stepped back and huffed. "I can smell rotten garbage a mile off. I knew your story didn't quite wash."

"Whatever you think you heard—"

"More'n enough to run you out of town."

Laurel's fist doubled. She yearned to punch the gossip.

"One thing about me, Florence . . . I don't scare."

"We don't need your kind. When I get done, you'll wish you'd stayed in that whorehouse in St. Louie!"

Adeline gasped over Laurel's shoulder, silencing a dare for the woman to take whatever steps deemed appropriate. Baring the secret would disarm its power. But she must consider the girl.

"Every story has two sides. Care to listen?"

"You're not fit to associate with decent, God-fearing folk, and it's my duty to let others know."

"Mrs. Kempshaw, Laurel is the most generous, caring person I've ever known besides my own mother." Adeline's voice quaked.

"You're tainted, too, girlie. Unless we put a stop to it, you'll turn this joint into a billiard parlor behind our backs. I'm not stupid. I know what goes on in those dens of iniquity."

It appeared Redemption's finest would get an earful.

"Since I can't appeal to an obvious lack of compassion, we have nothing further to discuss."

Linda Broday

The woman's thin lips puckered up as if she'd bitten into a green persimmon. "Olivia b'Dam must've been in cahoots. I'll wager she was one of your sort; I could tell by that wild hair. Kept a path hot to that saloon."

Laurel's blood boiled. Ollie hadn't even grown cold in the ground. "Get out of here before I forget the sort of real lady I am."

"And those Yates boys. Praise be you didn't marry and bring them to ruin. I shudder to think how a faithless harlot tried to play them for fools."

"Out! Or I'll snatch you bald." Laurel shoved her.

The beady eyes grew round with fear. But courage returned once she had access to running room.

"You and little missy pack up. No one'll spend another cent in this flea-infested establishment. I'll fix you."

The door slammed against Florence's heel, propelling her onto the sidewalk faster than she intended.

"I should've taken a butcher knife to that old biddy."

Tears welled in Adeline's blue eyes. "I hate her."

"Ah, honey." Laurel pulled her close, smoothing the pale locks. "Don't waste a second on someone who has nothing to do except judge others and delight in spreading poison."

"Will we leave?"

A short while ago she would've. But Ollie had taught her how to build a fire and make a stand.

She prayed those flames didn't heat a bunch of tar for the chicken feathers Florence already gathered to roll them in.

"We're staying." She firmly bolted the door, sliding a chair beneath the knob. "Running is for sissies. Let's finish up so I can tuck you into bed."

"But it might get plenty ugly."

She tucked a long strand behind Adeline's ear. The word that brought shivers went a bit further than ugly.

"My dear, try as I might, I can't foresee the future. I'm rusty in foretelling such. But Ollie warned me never to do anything in haste. Or maybe it was her grandpappy. Don't know about you . . . I'm ready to fight if that's what it takes."

"Will they send me back home?"

"Absolutely not. Get that out of your head. We're a pair. Nothing can separate us. Honey, I swear on a stack of Bibles."

Lord give her strength to keep that promise, for their enemies consisted of a small army.

Where on earth was Hannibal when she needed him?

Swinging toward waiting work, Laurel's toe caught the ridge of an uneven plank. A table's sharp edge drove into her thigh.

Spit and thunder!

Pain shot in both directions at once. She gritted her teeth to silence a sob.

Life always had a damn board sticking out ready to trip a hardworking body. The uphill battle to reach leveling-off ground had beaten the whey out of her. Up was the only visible trail through the forest. She saw no place to rest for a while.

Oh, for the day she'd reach a tiny ledge.

With thoughts going helter-skelter, she jumped at a pounding on the door. Taft and Vallens wouldn't bother announcing themselves; they'd kick the door in. Adeline held a broom at the ready.

"Miss Laurel?" Curley's boom was a relief. "It's me."

"I didn't expect you for another hour or so," she greeted him.

"Whistle Dixie and pass the ammunition! Closed the saloon early. No customers. Worse'n when I ran out of whiskey once."

"Let me guess: They've linked you to my lily-white character."

"Ollie'd whale my hide to bring such a grim face. She claimed a smile lifts a body's spirits faster than wild horses in a stampede." He planted his girth at the kitchen table and raised his feet for Adeline's broom.

"I haven't exactly seen reason to smile."

"I heard the rubbish . . . right before I knocked out two of the gossips' teeth."

Frayed nerves and sorrow ended up in peals of laughter. Adeline and Curley pronounced her a bona fide lunatic.

"You shore have a strange way of showing spunk, girl."

Laurel sobered the next minute, wanting to cry. "I can just hear Ollie, her head cocked to one side, squinting through pipe smoke." She launched into an imitation. " 'Grandpappy always said it's a true test of a feller's fortitude who can ponder how a predicament could be worse. Attacked by a mountain lion on a narrow trail, the man reflects on the good fortune in being better off than if he was gut-shot and left in agony. Best to get the dyin' over with fast. Yessiree.' "

Curley swiped at his eyes. "That woman knew how to live and how to die. Some folks can't do either. Least not well."

"All I ever desired was a quiet place to bury the last six years, start fresh, and live a normal life. Is that greedy?"

"Shoot, a dream isn't anything more than a thirst for something a bit better than a you got." Curley patted the back of her hand. "You're entitled to all the water you can drink. You have a lot of giving inside."

Another knock sounded on the door.

Shaking, she stole quickly behind the saloon-keep. Perhaps they'd come for the tarring and feathering. She snatched Adeline against her. They could do what they wanted with her, but not a blameless child whose only crime was having a depraved father.

Curley flexed his hands before jerking it open.

Murphy leaned on Etta's son Jacob for support. "Madison, I'm relieved to see you. I need a word with Laurel." He met her worried gaze. "In private."

"Sure thing. I take it you know about the newest quagmire?"

"It's why I've come."

Adeline and Curley vanished before Murphy accepted a chair. Tight lines around his mouth signified something awfully important.

"Oh, God, it's Brodie! Mr. Epperson couldn't save him?"

Perspiration dotted her upper lip. The thought of her beloved dangling on a high platform made her skin crawl.

"No, Brodie's still in the stockade. He sent a dispatch tonight. Jacob, will you wait by the buggy? I won't be long."

"You're in no shape to go gallivanting around town." Laurel tried to ignore the unease leapfrogging up her spine.

"Your welfare causes great concern. Vallens paid Brodie a visit earlier, to rattle him, it would appear. I come on my brother's behalf." Murphy reached for her palm. "And I also come in regard to another matter. There's a plague of loose tongues running rampant."

"I must commend Florence. Her news swept faster than news of a gold discovery in California."

"I have a solution to the whole rotten mess."

Chapter Thirty-two

"Marriage! Did you fall and hit your head?" The offer both stunned and dumbfounded Laurel.

"It will silence talk—in addition to providing safety."

"And Nora? Have you forgotten who holds your affections?"

Anguished features couldn't hide Murphy's distress. "You have no one to protect you. It's the only solution."

"A pretty sad excuse for throwing away love. The letter you received from Brodie . . . this ludicrous notion is his."

The man still persisted on tying her to his brother.

Murphy released her hand and slumped. "He can't save you. Guilt does things to an ordinary man. Brodie is much more. In him emotion cuts like a deep river. Us marrying would ease his mind."

A horde of butterflies built a nest in her stomach. The memory of hard, muscled flesh robbed the room of oxygen.

Dear Lord, she'd never use the term ordinary.

The devilish grin made his kisses irresistible, his touch melted the finest steel, and the mere heat of his gaze aroused passion she'd never found in another's arms.

Part of her wished they'd never met. The loss wouldn't be nearly as devastating.

Another part cried to walk those steps one more time.

In a strange way he completed something in her.

She'd manage without him. She had grit. But part of her would never be the same. And she wished to do more than manage.

Damn you, Brodie!

"Your generosity amazes me. I don't see wings sprouting, but you're an angel all the same." Her fingertips grazed Murphy's cheek. "Sacrificing what you and Nora have . . . for me . . . I won't allow it. Ollie, God rest her soul, was fond of reminding me that I'm way past grown. I carry my own burdens these days."

"But—"

Laurel pressed a finger to his lips. "Shhh. Yes, Will Taft frightens me to death." So did getting tarred and feathered, only she didn't add that. "But you know what? They don't have me yet."

"He'll come eventually."

"When he does he'll find I'm tougher than I used to be."

"You won't reconsider, or at least come to the house for tonight?"

A sharp knife, Ollie's old pistol, and a good brain could outsmart a whiskey-soaked brothel owner.

"Go, give Nora a big hug, and tell her how lucky she is."

He got slowly to his feet. "I'd take it personal if anyone hurt you."

That made two of them.

Later, she swore Curley's snores vibrated the cafe. Intruders wouldn't have to use stealth.

Her nerves twisted into bowties.

She wished Taft would hurry so life could assume some semblance of normalcy, whatever that was. For the hundredth time, she touched the knife and pistol, wondering about Hannibal. He could fill some gator's belly.

Adeline poked her head in the open door. "Can you sleep?"

"No need to whisper."

"Mind if I scoot in beside you?"

Laurel threw back the covers, glad for the company. It made her feel braver about what she had to do at daybreak.

Laurel dressed early, taking extra pains with her hair. She leaned near the mirror. An amazing thing had happened since Ollie's passing—seeing her reflection didn't bother her anymore.

Adeline sat up, rubbing her eyes. "I overslept."

"Go back to sleep, honey."

"You can't leave me. You promised." Covers tangled in Adeline's wake. "I'll be good. Please, let me come. I beg you."

"I'd never sneak out and leave you behind."

The brush fell to the dresser as Laurel embraced her. Adeline snuggled into the comfort, gripping tightly. Laurel hadn't the courage to admit she offered no safety or security. She couldn't guarantee they'd keep their home or their lives one more day. Because of her past, trouble would call.

"Why are you dressed up?"

Her chin rested on top of Adeline's golden silk. "I wanted to look stunning before I do battle."

"I wish everyone would let us live in peace. We never did anything. Mrs. Kempshaw is plain ol' mean."

"People fear what they can't understand. We threaten them. It's not so much what we've done that frightens Florence, but what might occur as a result of who we've been." Laurel sat her firmly aside. "Now, young lady, I'm going to fix you and Curley some breakfast. Forget this non-sense about leaving you."

A hot cup of tea did wonders to help organize her speech. Their snoring protector didn't rouse until she set a plate of flapjacks, eggs, and steaming coffee on the table.

"Wherever you think you're going this fine morn will be on my arm." Curley grunted, pulling on his boots.

She untied the apron and grabbed the shawl beside it.

"My errand requires no audience, but thank you anyway."

"Use your noggin, girl. It's foolhardy to go out."

"I'll be back before anyone realizes I'm gone."

Her footsteps pounded the sidewalk. It didn't escape her notice that several women hastily crossed to the other side. She ground her teeth and plowed on. It was fair to say electricity might've snapped her skirts smartly.

Florence Kempshaw's modest residence showed neglect. She was much too busy destroying lives to tend to repairs. Laurel rapped on the weathered entrance.

"You! What gall."

Laurel's foot prevented the door's slam. "I will have a moment of your time."

"Won't spare a second for the likes of you."

"I don't give a rat's hindquarters if you despise the very ground on which I walk. You will hear me out." She pushed past the surly woman. "Shut your mouth or you'll attract flies."

"I'll yell if you hit me."

"Much as I'd delight, I'll restrain . . . unless provoked."

Laurel wore a satisfied smile when she emerged from the long chat. Fire blazed in her chest.

It simply took a poke with a sharp stick to get her back bowed. The good folks of Redemption didn't know who they dealt with. Neither did Taft or Vallens.

* * *

Throughout the day a steady stream of customers kept the eatery open. It heartened her that a few of Redemption's regulars drifted in besides the steamboat and barge crowds.

Moonbeams now trailed through the back window. Laurel adjusted the wick of the oil lamp and counted her blessings. Not a soul came with tar and feathers, thank the Lord.

Perhaps "letting the hide go with the tallow," as Ollie would put it, accomplished something.

Florence had actually listened. And even though the gossip couldn't meet Laurel's eye, Florence showed slight thawing. Her tale of the abduction even sparked a hint of human kindness.

The clock neared ten when sharp knuckles beat on the door. She gripped the knife in her pocket.

Curley lumbered over with his rifle ready. "Who's there?"

"It's me, Arlo." The shout belonged to a worker from the Dry Gulch.

"I told you not to disturb without good cause." He slid the new, heavier bolt Laurel had installed.

"You hafta come quick! Some fellers got liquored up bad. They're breaking glass, furniture, and bones."

"Ladies, I have no choice but to leave you alone. Lock up and don't answer to anyone. I mean it."

They finished straightening for the next day's business. All the while she listened for Hannibal's scratch. The animal's long absence saddened her. He'd be hungry.

Adeline yawned. "I'm beat down to the soles of my feet."

"No use in us both waiting. You go on up, honey."

The ticking of the clock filled the room. The creak of boards above ceased as Adeline settled down. Laurel rested her head in her hands. Brodie filled every corner of her mind. Thoughts of his welfare formed images of the twisting, agonizing kind.

An hour stretched into two, and yet Curley didn't return. Perhaps he figured they'd gone upstairs and didn't wish to wake them. Or . . . the thought of rabble-rousers killing her friend turned her to ice. Losing another would further test her ability to survive. She pondered venturing to the saloon, swiftly rejecting it as unwise. For now she'd stay put.

First checking on Adeline, Laurel lay down fully clothed on Ollie's bed. If trouble called she'd be ready.

It seemed she'd just dozed off when a noise jarred her.

Low whispers.

Wooden planks complained beneath someone's weight.

Intruders lurked in the hallway.

If Curley found a way past the bolts, he'd not come upstairs. Nothing would drive Adeline from bed unless she was ill, and the girl hadn't stirred when Laurel looked in.

The knife slid into place, the pistol into her palm before her feet hit the floor.

A muffled scream froze her midway across the room.

On tiptoes, she peered around the door frame. Shadows moved along the hall in the murky light.

They had Adeline.

Laurel ran after two figures who hauled the kicking form, catching them at the head of the stairs.

"Put her down this instant!"

"Who's gonna make me?" Will Taft whirled.

Laurel shivered into the face that spawned nightmares and dominated daylight hours. She raised her chin a bit to swallow past strangling fear.

"I am."

"What's a scrawny-ass harlot gonna do?"

"Lessons you taught in survival might not work in your favor, Taft." She leveled the pistol at his gut. "I said get your hands off the girl."

"You're full of surprises, Lil."

Adeline jerked free and pasted herself to Laurel's back.

"Vallens, lead the way downstairs. Remember, this six-shooter will put a big hole in your boss should you make one move. I swear to God I'd dearly love to."

Chaos erupted at the bottom of the stairs when Vallens suddenly darted from sight. The man hid, ready to pounce. Taft lowered his hands. His body shielded them. What seemed a smart plan at the onset suddenly didn't look so good.

She shoved metal into his spine. "I'll kill you."

"You sure you know what you're doing, Lil? Don't reckon you ever shot a man before."

"With you it'll be awful easy."

Taft cleared the steps, leaving Laurel on the last one.

"Zeke, why don't you show Lil our trump card?"

The death angel raised the wick on the oil lamp and held it toward a bound, gagged female. A cry sprang from her lips.

"Hannah!"

Taft's hoarse voice pierced the air. "Give me that pea shooter or her brains will spatter the walls."

Laurel's arm sagged. She'd lived her life, but Hannah and Adeline were young.

Taft's fist caught her mouth the moment he took the pistol. She slammed to the floor. Blood wasn't something a person forgot the taste of. Hate crawled from the dark corners of her soul.

"You bastard!"

"What a pity. I went to enormous trouble arranging this little tea party and you haven't the slightest gratitude."

The taunting sneer on the sinister mouth leaned too near.

A waddle of spit hit him squarely, running down the bridge of his nose. The bold impulse earned a kick that brought stars, but seeing the smug veneer slip made it worth the pain.

Her breath came in short gasps. "I have friends."

"Zeke, explain why poor Mr. Madison can't come to her aid."

"Taft took care of him. There was no fight at the saloon. Madison feels a bit poorly at the moment."

She prayed Curley wasn't dead. Outsmarting them was up to her. They'd have hell getting the girls to St. Louis. Taft had better re-think the plan. No swamp scum would soil Hannah and Adeline. Blocking pain that hurt to blink, she stood. He'd have to go through her. A squared jaw dared him.

"No one will pay a red cent to lie with a corpse."

"Silly twit, I have fresh merchandise. You're expendable. In fact, you'll make a prime example for those who think to escape my clutches."

"Except it's a long way to Missouri," she needled.

"We ain't going anywhere." Adeline launched herself onto Taft's back, raking her nails across his face.

Laurel fingered the knife in her pocket, watching Zeke Vallens. If the distraction occupied both him and Taft, she could take them unaware. She had just one chance.

Once she buried the knife in Vallens, could she get the pistol quick enough?

Chapter Thirty-three

Brodie Yates broke formation, spurring the loaned horse into a gallop. If this nag possessed Smokey's long gait, he'd not have doubts circling like vultures. Cold sweat dotted his brow. The half dozen men who ate his dust could sway the odds.

They had to beat Taft and Vallens.

Thanks to the Citizens for Peace, false documents clearing him of all charges made it to General Buell's hands. The general immediately deemed him a free man. Brodie wanted no part of staying in the stockade until morning, and the general had no desire to keep him any longer than necessary.

Sheer terror that they'd be too late booted off the devil's scorn that usually shared his saddle.

This night it would have to find its own way—if it dared.

Laurel was in danger. His gut never lied.

The memory bag Brodie snatched off Buell's desk molded to the warmth of his skin. It still held each treasured item.

Something Murphy said bumped across the ridges of his

conscience. *Never let a woman go who lights up the dark, lonely places of your soul.*

His lady did a damn sight better than merely light up dark corners of a moth-eaten soul. She built a bonfire!

The right choice meant he wouldn't be alone anymore.

Or filled with haunting coldness a flame couldn't touch.

He was anxious to give marriage a whirl. Had to get the begettin' started soon. Eight little ones posed a chore.

First he'd have to talk her into having him. A fellow with nothing but a reputation and a six gun to back it up could have the devil of a time.

Running from every name-seeking fast gun between here and San Francisco wasn't much to ask a woman to share.

. . . Unless? Thoughts of losing Laurel froze his blood.

He bent over the flying mane, leaving the road to cut through the pines.

Though Taft had confiscated Ollie's pistol, Laurel took comfort in her weighted pocket. She focused on the two men. Taft stood nearest, the logical target. She shortened the space until Vallens's black gaze met hers in silent warning.

Spit and thunder! At least she hadn't revealed the knife.

Taft grabbed a handful of Adeline's hair and yanked, pulling her off his back. He held her tightly in a vise. Laurel winced at the girl's cry.

"Leave her alone. She's merely a child."

"You were once. Or has it been so long you forgot? This sassy one's gold hair an' face of an angel'll make me the envy of everyone." Lust glittered in Taft's gaze. "And I can't tell you what treats are in store for your sweet sister. She'll take to whoring. Just like you." He spoke to Vallens. "Load Sis in the wagon and I'll be along directly."

Something human crossed the angel of death's features. "I agreed to locate the two thieves who parted you from your money. The one in the grave ain't no fault of mine. I'm done."

Vallens with a sliver of conscience?

How absurd to think he'd become an ally. Balking could buy an extra favor or two from the good Lord, however.

"I have a forty-five that says different."

The two swapped glares. Taft shifted his weight back and forth. The clock ticked loudly. Vallens didn't back down.

"Threatening women is easier than a grown man. I'm walking out of here, so I reckon you gotta do what you hafta."

Hope plummeted when Vallens moved to leave.

She met the horror in Adeline's blue eyes and nodded slightly, flicking her head toward the dining room. If the girl understood, she'd run the second Laurel made her move.

"I'll pay a bonus, you low-down swindler."

"It takes one to know one. You don't have the kind of money to buy me." The man in funeral attire opened the door. The wolf dog bounded in. "Dog, I told you to stand guard outside."

Would her brief compassion toward Hannibal overcome the wild instincts Vallens encouraged? Hannibal's stare bore no sign of recognition. One didn't have to possess keen insight to know that bared fangs and the bristled neck weren't signs of affection. Sorrow rippled through her.

The wolf dog kept his stance, ignoring the order to retreat.

With Vallens continuing outside she had to make her move.

Gripping the wooden handle, she jerked the knife high.

Hurtling in Taft's direction, she aimed for any part of the

hated enemy. A person would think defending those she loved made it easier to bury a knife into a body. And yet nothing prepared her for the sight of a six-inch blade plunged to the hilt in Taft's arm.

Or the smell of blood swimming up her nostrils.

"You stinking harlot!"

A flash of fleeing nightgown reassured her of Adeline's safety. It was the last she saw of her before Will Taft flung her to the floor and straddled her stomach. She knew the sickening crack of bone. The absence of the sound now was a miracle. Not that it mattered with murder lurking in Taft's eyes.

The fury in the raised fist told her the man would not stop this time. She waited for the pain behind closed eyes.

The blows never came.

Hannibal sprang with a feral growl, more vicious than anything Laurel had ever heard. The animal ripped into the uplifted arm, tossing his head from side to side.

"Zeke, damn you! Get this beast off."

Laurel scrambled into a corner and huddled there.

"I warned you about the animal, Taft."

"Call him off! Name your price."

"I said I won't be bought."

"I'm pleading. Please."

"Just gonna get Dog off. Nothing else."

The wolf dog avoided the foot, sidling in Laurel's direction. She wanted to pound both men into everlasting hell. But she hugged her most unlikely protector, vowing to feed him the biggest piece of meat. Sorrow ebbed back from the gray eyes.

A mangled limb didn't stop Taft. In considerable agony, he rose slowly, pulled out a Colt, and stood over her.

"I've had a gut full of you and this mangy wolf."

The cold barrel touched her forehead. Laurel clenched her teeth. Ollie had better get ready for a visitor.

"Cain't let you do that, Will."

Laurel held her breath. Vallens had pressed his Colt to Taft's left ear, knocking the six-gun from his boss's grip.

"Get outta my way, you chicken-hearted bastard."

"I ain't gonna let you ruin more innocent lives. Your flesh trade stops right here, right now."

"Since when did you suddenly get religion?"

Vallens met Laurel's gaze. "I've watched her, even tested her for sign of weakness. Why would someone work so hard when she could line her pockets with riches? It seems farfetched. I came to admire her courage. Then I got word you killed my daughter to keep me in line. You shouldn't have done that."

"Spare the hymns," Taft spat.

"You're for real, Laurel James. I do believe you'd fight to the death to protect everything you stand for."

Had Ollie reached down to soften the heart of stone? Though barely audible, her reply held grit. "Make no mistake."

"This ain't over, Lil." Taft measured the distance where a man could disappear into the inky night.

"You're wrong about that, you sorry slaver. Go ahead, I'd love for you to run." The soft suggestion carried the deadly hiss of snake rattles. Laurel whirled to find Brodie blocking the doorway. He held a cocked rifle. "Vallens, put down the Colt or I'll make you eat the damn thing."

Laurel wondered if she imagined the lean figure. Yet the heat caressing her face appeared beyond the scope of an apparition's power. Oh, Lord, she hoped he hadn't broken out.

"He's on our—" She never got to finish.

"Drop it, you two-legged jackal." The brittle order meant

Brodie had spied her bruises and meant to make someone pay dearly. "Take a deep breath, because it'll be your last."

"Please, it's not what you think." She tried to diffuse the anger. Murder would for sure earn him the gallows.

"Maybe you don't know that I'm Will Taft and this woman rightfully belongs to me." Taft found his tongue once Zeke Vallens didn't threaten to fit him for earrings.

"Reason enough to shoot you on the spot. Where I come from Will Taft is Cajun for skunk piss." Flinty sparks shot from the rebel. "And you're truly misinformed. No one *owns* Laurel."

Adeline peeked curiously around Brodie's bulk.

"I suppose you'd be Yates," Taft sneered.

"Welcome to Judgment Day, you piece of filth."

Soldiers swarmed through the open back door before anyone could explain the situation, adding more confusion. Laurel threw herself in front of Brodie. She'd not let them take him again, although she hadn't a clue how to prevent it.

"Which one is the Confederate spy, Shenandoah?"

Laurel inhaled sharply. Wouldn't they already know the jail escapee's appearance?

"Sergeant." Vallens pushed Taft forward. "He's your man."

Air slowly left her lungs. She went limp. "Yes, indeed. He's Shenandoah." She leaned into the warmth of Brodie's broad shoulders a moment to banish the chill before running to Hannah. "He'd have murdered us all. The man bound and gagged my poor sister. I'd appreciate a knife to cut her loose."

"They lie." Taft's face mottled with anger. "You had the right man in your stockade all along, you bumbling idiots."

"Private, shackle this man and throw him on a horse."

"Lil, tell 'em who I am. Zeke, tell 'em." He fought the soldiers, losing in the end. "You'll all burn in hell."

Cries of revenge echoed until hoofbeats drowned him. She prayed he'd not convince them for many years, or at least enough time to give Brodie a head start.

Vallens moved lightly toward the night. "Dog, better get moving."

"Hannibal; his name is Hannibal." Laurel braced herself against shooting pain when she helped her sister stand. "I want you to remember that, Mr. Vallens."

"What a fool name. I expect I will, though."

Brodie swung the rifle dead center. "Thought you'd walk out scot-free, Vallens?"

"No." Laurel planted herself in front of the rifle.

"I understand not wanting blood spilled on the kitchen floor, but he isn't leaving. Move out of the way."

"We figured him wrong. Zeke saved my life." She crossed the space to touch the man's arm. "I won't forget it."

The man tipped the brim of his hat. "Hannibal, come."

Man and beast padded off into the star-studded darkness.

"What on earth happened?" Curley held a wet cloth to his head. "One minute I'm headed for the saloon and the next a steam engine slams into my head. Yates, what in saint's name are you doing here? Don't tell me you broke out."

A pair of rebel grays fastened on her and dared her to break free. A crooked grin played across his features.

"General Buell discovered he had the wrong man, thanks to Laurel."

"It's about dadgum time," Curley grumbled.

"Are you truly my sister, Laurel?" Hannah tugged her from one kind of dangerously deep water only to plunge into another.

The moment of reckoning had arrived. She chewed her lip.

"How would you feel? I'd understand it if you hate me."

"Don't be a goose. You can't know how happy I am. And

proud. I want to run home right now and tell everyone that I've found our Laurel."

Brodie threw her an I-told-you-so stare.

"I'll mosey on." Curley eased out. "Maybe I'll go tell Ollie what she missed. Things ain't the same with her gone."

Untangling Hannah from around her neck proved a daunting task, for the sister clung worse than thistle, although she wouldn't have traded it for anything. Well . . . except lying bare as a newborn babe, with the man of her dreams crawling inside and hanging out a do-not-disturb sign.

Only that would have to come later.

"Hannah, Mr. Yates will take you home at daybreak. But promise not to tell a soul about me."

"I can't do that. They have a right to know."

"See?" Brodie rubbed the small of her back. "I'm glad others see the obvious."

"The choice is mine. I'll do it when the time is right."

"Whatever you say, darlin'. You're so tired you can't think clear." Brodie scooped her into his arms. "I say a bed would look mighty welcome."

Tomorrow Laurel would worry about propriety. For now, she loved the beat of his heart next to her ear. She snuggled deeper into the arms wrapped around her. "Adeline, will you make Hannah welcome? I'd appreciate it, dear."

"Consider it done." Then she leaned closer and winked. "I like him. He's the right one for you."

Upstairs, he started for her old room before Laurel realized. "I sleep in Ollie's room now. She died in my arms the night I returned from the stockade."

"So that's what Curley meant by that strange remark."

"Adeline has my room. The girl's afraid of ghosts. I find it peaceful in here with Ollie's spirit."

"She'd better hide her eyes because I intend to love you like you've never seen."

He eased her to the patchwork quilt and made quick work of stripping off his clothing. Then he slowly undressed her, planting kisses on each new patch of exposed skin.

"My stars, Brodie, at this rate daylight will come before we even get down to the best part." She gasped when his tongue meandered down the crevice between her breasts to draw a wet heart on her stomach.

"Complaints so soon, darlin'?" He propped up on an elbow and let a fingertip continue the journey. "We make quite a pair. You're more battered than I am, I do believe. Are you certain you're up to this after your hellish night?"

The last few hours had fled. Laurel brushed back the rebellious hair from his forehead. She prayed they'd never have anything worse than a few scrapes to complain about. Though a breeze blew in from the swamps ruffling the curtains, she felt nothing but the sultry breath feathering across bared flesh.

"I'm positive. I have this need . . ."

"Good, because I was thinking . . . maybe we should start on those eight little ones before we grow too old."

A moan crept from her throat. He touched places no one had charted—dark places that never experienced the thrill of human contact. The gentle man's tender lovemaking brought a mist to her eyes. Redemption hadn't come without sacrifice. It took letting go of preconceived notions and letting ash return to ash. Their souls flourished. And still their love would take constant nurturing to survive.

Light pressure located old scars on the solid body of her warrior. There were fresh ones as well. Those created an ache so deep not a parcel of daylight penetrated.

"Fine wine always tastes better when sipped, precious."

"But . . ."

Her rebuttal got lost. Scandalous pirates had that affect when they pilfered a woman's jewels.

Dampness covering her inner thighs assured he'd have no trouble sliding inside.

She wanted him now.

A patient lady would grind her teeth and wait.

A desperate one wouldn't.

Chapter Thirty-four

Dawn crept silent as a thief into the room. Brodie pushed raven strands from Laurel's face and kissed each bruise. A tic jerked along his jaw. The thought of how close she'd come to dying chilled his bones. He'd littered her life with disappointment and setback and gotten her heart riddled with cracks and holes. His chest constricted.

Brodie lifted her hand and turned it over, marveling at the strength there. He kissed her palm and each fingertip.

"Thank you very much, beautiful Lil."

"For what?"

"Loving me. Letting me love you back. Forgiving me."

"Before Ollie died, I promised not to give up on you."

"I'm sorry you had to deal with burying her alone."

"We don't have a choice in those matters. I'm a big girl."

"I know the tragedy of burying family. Deep loss becomes a part of you. A body never truly stops missing them."

"Even for a little boy forced to become a man too soon."

He quirked an eyebrow. "Murph told you about Mother?"

"Are you mad? I wanted to discover what made you tick."

"Surprised at him. Learn anything else?"

Laurel's satiny curves molded to his large form. Her fingers tangled in fine chest hair. "You're not some big, bad ogre. Compassion and respect comes out of hiding more than suits. I also see how you guard a fervent desire to belong."

"Do tell." Needles of discomfort pricked. He might as well have posted the secrets in *The Jeffersonian*.

"Those qualities most endear you to me. After Ollie died I discovered we don't ever know a person, and perhaps that's the way it's intended. But there's something that intrigues me."

"I can't imagine any tidbit that escaped your notice."

She raised her body and leaned over him, her lush breasts leaving imprints above his heart. He inhaled sharply. His memory bag dangled from her hand. "When I asked about this before you told me it was nothing of much value. Please, can I look?"

Brodie had never revealed the private stash to anyone. Each sentimental treasure revealed something of him— things he'd clutched fiercely when the world slept.

Still, he had to begin trusting. That meant letting the woman he loved into the dark pain. He swallowed hard.

"Be my guest."

She removed Aunt Lucy's letter and opened it.

The gold band glistened in the early morn. A questioning gaze caught his. "My mother's," he murmured.

Laurel placed it tenderly on the letter as though sensing agony. Murphy's lock of hair joined the ring. Brodie held his breath and tried to turn away. The last item held the most significance. Her reaction to it would determine their future. "Oh, my love!" A rush of tears darkened the violet gaze. She cradled the scrap to her heart. "Lace from my skirt. You kept the memento. Putting it in such good company must mean—"

His lungs hurt with the need to breathe.

"I love you. I always have."

"You hid it well. I thought you despised me."

The split lip, compliments of Taft's fist, trembled. He pressed his mouth very lightly to the wound, moved along the jaw line to a dainty earlobe, before placing feathery kisses on her eyelids. She'd suffered too much over the years, something he'd have to live with. If he could. Memories hurt.

"That's because you were set to marry the wrong man."

She groaned. "What a horrible mistake! I didn't love Murphy. I thought it would be the answer."

"You've reason to change your mind?"

He loved the wrinkle in her brow when wheels of thought turned inside her head.

"I realized after the soldiers took you that no one can bring redemption to another. I'm proud of who I am. I don't need to marry anyone to prove I'm good and decent."

"And beautiful and generous to a fault." Brodie shifted onto his side. "You pounded a few things into this lame brain. The stockade took the blinders off. You're right—the past has nothing to do with the future except shape us into the people we are." He squared his jaw. "I was a jackass. I'm sorry. Other than a reputation as a broken-down gunslinger, I'm no prize."

"I never asked for anything more, Brodie."

"You know it eats at a man to be unable to provide."

The dark head turned away. Her husky voice held a quiver. "You think I'm merely an obligation—"

"Darlin', you mean life, death, and the hereafter to me."

He inhaled her fragrance and plunged. "That's why I humbly request your hand in marriage."

Laurel swung back. "Of all the dumb ways to ask!"

"I haven't had much practice. Is that a yes or no?"

Anger and confusion darkened her features. He hadn't a clue whether the roulette wheel would stop on red or black. Hell, he couldn't even tell where the chips had fallen. He just pitched them out. Perhaps it was too late for roots.

"I can't. I truly can't."

Ice water in the place of blood didn't flow too easy. "I've messed up real bad. I just hoped—"

"Hold on, rebel, I'm not finished. I can't vow to love and cherish until we settle some things. First, how do you feel about swapping a Colt for an apron? I warn you, it's a big switch."

A chuckle rose. He kissed the sweet, honey mouth. A fingertip traced the curve of a bruised cheek.

"I feel a bunch of emotions, but none faintly resembles the excitement of gunplay and fast draws. What else?"

"I'm afraid."

"Makes two of us, darlin'. We'll face fear together."

"What assurance do I have that you'll not up and leave on me?"

"The word of a Johnny Reb. Does that mean anything?"

"What about the ugly whispers? Can you face those?"

"They best not let me hear 'em." He itched to give the gossips a dose of the Brodie Remedy.

"Gossip is hard to silence. They may run us out of town."

"Let's get married right now, this very day."

"*Spit and thunder,* you're not in the least hurry!"

"I'll make an honest woman of you. My name hanging on the end of yours will solve most problems. They'll think twice before opening their big mouths," he growled. At

Linda Broday

least folks would know who looked out for her. "Anything else?"

Sweet Jezzie, he prayed not. Her naked body was doing things beyond his control. No telling what would happen if he denied the urge much longer. He inched a finger up and down her long legs in sensual circles. He yearned to fill every lonely nook and cranny with his love.

"Just one more thing. This honest woman business . . . I can't build a life on lies."

"It's about time you went home." The crooked grin came from the place where old memories died and new ones were born. "To make it perfectly clear . . . you're accepting my proposal?"

"Aye, aye, Sir Pirate." Laurel ruffled the hair on his neck and drew him near. Her throaty whisper made him tremble, a little thing he predicted would never change. "I love you, Brodie Yates. Don't you be forgetting it."

"I'm sure you'll remind me a few thousand times."

"We've spent a lifetime thinking of what might have been. I prefer focusing on bright tomorrows, not to mention moonlit nights, we'll share."

"Ummmm, moon mist! Knew that scent was familiar."

Laurel slid from beneath the nuzzling assault of her neck.

"You said that was the musky aroma of moonbeams bathing an aroused woman. Impossible in broad daylight."

He massaged the tips of her breasts between forefinger and thumb. "You certain?"

"Adeline . . . Hannah . . ." Breathless words trailed away.

"They can wait."

Several hours later Laurel wiggled into the saddle atop Smokey. Adeline and Hannah rode buggy style. A horde of flutters whipped her stomach into froth.

"Thought you learned what happens to little girls who

insist on rubbing a man the right way." Snake rattles on the felt hat hissed. Brodie looped the reins around the horn and wrapped her in the security of his arms.

"What will I say to them?"

"The truth. Quit worrying."

Miles passed until at last they wound down the lane through tall sycamore and pine. Rounding the last bend, she glimpsed the house. The two girls climbed from the buggy. Blue Boy abandoned the porch, racing for her.

"Blue, I've brought someone special. This is Brodie."

"Hey, fella." Brodie rubbed the dog's droopy ears.

"Everyone, look who I found!" Hannah raced inside.

A woman shielded her eyes from the sun. Laurel slipped a palm inside Brodie's.

"Saints be praised! Hannah, you gave us such a fright when you disappeared. I saw it happening all over again."

"Two men abducted me, but Laurel fought them. It's her, Mama."

"Laurel? Our Laurel?"

Brodie gave a reassuring squeeze.

"It's me, Mama."

"Hannah, get your papa from the barn." Wetness streamed down the aged face. Mary James gathered her lost daughter close. "I can't believe it, child."

"Many nights I laid awake, my soul dying bit by bit, willing myself back here. Now I am."

"Baby girl, rest on my shoulder. Soak up all the love I saved special for you. Everything's right as rain now."

Long-deprived senses soaked the aroma of vanilla and fresh baked bread. She had come home. She snuggled into the soft haven, barely aware of footsteps.

"Laurel?"

Strain lingered in her father's question. Dread lodged like a week-old biscuit in her throat. She pulled herself from her mother's arms. Where had Brodie gone? She couldn't face stern disapproval alone. He'd disappeared into the sea of faces.

Raising her chin, she met him honestly. "I'm home, Papa."

Ben James hugged her. "All these years and here you are." The stripes of the bibbed overalls blurred.

They accepted her just as Ollie had vowed. So far.

"Your face, child. What happened?" Work-roughened fingers touched her wet cheek.

"It's a long story, Papa. A wise woman once said a person without scars never fought for anything they believed in. I'm happy to say I'm home because I stood fast and won."

"You should've seen my sister," Hannah seconded. "Without her courage, I'd be bound for Missouri."

Laurel spotted her love, standing apart from the rest wearing a lopsided smile. She pulled him forward. "This is Brodie Yates. He asked me to marry him. And show Adeline Cade a warm welcome. Our family just got larger."

"Lordy! Not only do we get our Laurel back, but we have another son. And a new daughter, to boot." Ben slapped Brodie's back. "Thank you for watching over my little girl."

"Don't give me credit. Miss Olivia Applejack b'Dam had the honor, Mr. James."

"Plain old Ben, that's what everyone calls me. That Olivia sure has a fanciful name. I'll have to ride back and meet her."

Hotness lurked behind Laurel's lids. She lived up to the promise. "Ollie's a little busy polishing a halo and trying to be as good an angel in heaven as she was on earth. We laid her to rest a few days ago."

"I would like to have known her," Mary murmured.

"She's watching and grinning from ear to ear."

Brodie draped an arm around her. "That she is."

"Hey, Sis. Glad you found the way back," Quaid said.

"Us, too," chimed the rest of her siblings.

"I'm waiting for that long story, girl. Let's go inside."

"I'll make some lemonade." Mary James rushed up the porch.

A hand prevented Laurel from following. She couldn't conceal panic in the gaze she favored Brodie with. The shaky footing wouldn't become solid without his help. He couldn't back out.

"Aren't you coming?"

He brushed her jaw. "I have some business in Jefferson while you visit with your folks. Don't worry, I'm not about to let you out of my sight for long."

"Is it wise? The general might believe Taft."

"Not a chance. Shoot, those fake documents almost convinced me." The soft kiss held desire and promise. "An hour or two won't allow me to get into too much trouble."

"I can't bear us to part. Silly of me, huh?"

"I'm glad. I'll bring a surprise."

"Something sneaky up your sleeve?"

"Who, me? I'll never tell." Grinning, he untied Smokey.

Keeping an anxious eye out the window, she bared the whole ugly story since that fateful day, including how Ollie helped her escape. Hannah filled in the ending, which gave the shady lane Laurel's undivided attention. He should've returned.

"You should've left that low-down scum to us. We'd teach him what happens when you hurt a James," Jeremiah proclaimed.

"I hope he has to live with nasty pigs," Millie said.

Mary James held Laurel's hand as if afraid she'd disappear.

Ben James blew into a faded kerchief. "I failed my duty."

Through a misty haze, she stared at the love surrounding

her. Grief had aged her father and mother beyond rightful years. She despised Taft more for that than anything.

"Stop blaming yourself, Papa. The man is getting his due. What happened was unfortunate. Can we go back and undo it? Not a chance." A glance encompassed them all. "Hope that I'd see you again sustained me through all the dark times. And yet, shame kept me away after Ollie freed me. I was afraid you'd think badly of me."

"Don't be ashamed of anything, Sis." Rafe's voice broke.

"Amen!" Blue Boy's pitiful howl appeared to add agreement.

Darkness hovered in the sky when Laurel heard a horse's hooves. A dignified stranger riding abreast drew frowns. Perhaps the man had turned down the lane by mistake. Then she saw the big appaloosa.

She flew into Brodie's arms the minute he swung from the saddle, not caring that people watched. Worrying about proper things tuckered a body. She'd learned not to waste good time. Folks would think what they wished anyway.

This man was hers.

No reason to hide a love she'd almost lost.

"You're back."

Her pulse raced with need reflected in the rebel grays. He planted a long kiss, letting her know he could assume a pirate's plundering duties in the wink of an eye. Her knees went weak. She leaned against Smokey for support when he released her to reach into his saddlebag for a mysterious bundle.

"Did you bring a guest?"

A tall, reedlike man in a frock coat tied his horse.

"Reverend Thompson has agreed to wed us tonight. I didn't think you'd fuss, having the ceremony with your family."

"Tonight? I somehow pictured myself in a grand gown."

"What's going on?" Ben rose from his favorite roost, wood shavings falling from his lap.

"A wedding, Papa."

Mary James beamed. "Land's sakes! This calls for a feast. Don't know what I'll scratch up befitting the occasion, but I'll scare up something. Girls, come and help me throw it together."

The women hurried into the house, chattering like magpies.

"Reverend, I don't entertain often, but I'm a real good listener. Ever whittle?" Her father offered a chair.

Laurel's attention never wavered from Brodie.

He was a rogue.

And a scoundrel.

But the man kept a length of lace next to his heart.

"Darn Ollie! She couldn't have waited just a few more days." Unshed tears clogged her throat. She plucked at the string securing the package he clutched. "It would make this perfect."

"I don't have the power to bring her back." His husky voice cracked. "But I did fetch something else."

"The preacher and whatever that is you're holding."

"Always mean what I say and say what I mean." Unspoken promises clung heavy in the swamp breeze.

Deliriously happy, Laurel floated. "Fork over that gift or I'll sic Blue Boy on you."

Brodie's twinkle shifted. "He's mighty vicious, all right."

Accepting his elbow, Laurel navigated the steps in a trance, unable to take her eyes from his face. Each line, each crevice, told of the many roads he'd traveled to get where he was.

"Still waters run deep," Ollie had once remarked.

Laurel couldn't wait to begin exploring things she'd only begun to learn.

Brodie poked his head in the midst of a lot of pots and pans banging. "Mrs. James, I'd be obliged if you'd suggest a place for a moment's privacy."

"Use my bedroom, son. It's safest from interruption."

"I'll show you." Laurel took his hand.

Safe from prying eyes, he placed the gift in her hands. She ripped off the brown paper. Rich folds of a beautiful dress unfurled. Thickness rose in her throat.

"My darling husband, you truly amaze me."

"Every bride should have a wedding gown. You don't mind it being lavender? The color brought us together."

"Mind?" The purple satin brushed her cheek as whispery soft as baby's breath. She blinked back tears. He'd given her something truly meaningful. The past was behind them at last and they had nothing ahead to fear.

"I hope . . . does it bring back bad memories?"

"That you selected lavender means more than you'll know."

The wedding gown slid to the bed as her arms went around his neck.

Hand in hand, they stood before the reverend. The man stronger than the mightiest storm, taller than a swamp-water cypress, who moved heaven and earth to set her world straight, stole her thoughts.

Through a brilliant mist, she watched Brodie shake the gold band from the pouch inside his shirt. She didn't mind the imperfect fit.

"I pronounce you man and wife."

Fiery passion in the kiss sealed the union. He swept her up into his arms, her feet dangling amid yards of lavender and lace. Albeit a bit scarred, she'd found her soul mate.

Blue Boy's howls nudged them back to earth. Scowls emphasized Brodie's craggy features before he put her down.

Brodie rubbed the hound's ears. "You belong to her, but you have to learn to share. I love her, too."

Epilogue

Brodie settled into the living quarters above the cafe while a new house took shape on land adjoining Murphy's.

The parade of nameless faces no longer tormented him. Allowing love into his heart freed him.

"What'll happen to me?" Adeline's mouth had trembled.

Both he and Laurel assured her she'd always have a bed under their roof, no matter what.

Florence Kempshaw dropped by to eat a big helping of humble pie. The rest of the town followed suit, which brought relief. The devil take anyone who harmed her. They'd deal with him first and find it a pretty big chore.

"I'm anxious to hear what prompted you from running her out of town to smoking the peace pipe," he had inquired casually of Florence.

"She risked death to keep Vallens and Taft from taking those girls, and stood up and fought to stay when it would've been easier to leave," Florence had answered.

His gorgeous wife abruptly captured his wandering attention.

"Are you ready?" Laurel held a bouquet of purple pansies.

"For anything, darlin'. Let me grab my hat."

The flowers added flair to Olivia Applejack b'Dam's bleak grave. He missed the jabs the woman delighted in poking him with now and again. She'd grown on him before he ever realized he wanted her to. Ollie thought she could paint over the crust so no one would see the size of her heart. She'd fooled him for a while—until he peeled aside the layers.

A cool wind blew raven tendrils across Laurel's face. He held her tight, brushing them back to dry the tears. He blinked hard when she knelt to adjust the pansies.

"I did it, Ollie. I went home. You were right about my family. I also think you pegged Brodie for the handsome rebel he is. We're married now. I miss hearing your cackle, but you probably know that, too."

Brodie's heart ached with loss left by his mother, Aunt Lucy, and Ollie. The palm he laid on Laurel's bowed head shook.

"Her spirit lives with us, darlin'." He sniffed the air. A swallow stuck on the way down. "I swear, if it's not smoke from that damn corncob pipe."

Laurel smiled up through misty eyes and drawled, "My grandpappy always said, 'Girl, ain't nothing to dying. It's the living that takes talent.'"

All of a sudden, the breeze ceased. Not a leaf, a blade of grass, or a ripple of air moved. Amid the hush, a red bird landed on one of the flowers she'd brought. It chattered, scolding.

"Great Johnny Reb! Ollie always insisted on the last word."

"That she did." Laurel accepted his hand and came into his arms. "Ollie b'Dam, you try to behave yourself and mind your manners up there. Don't try the good Lord's patience with all those righteous sayings."

Arm in arm, they strolled for the cafe just as a strange horse and rider galloped from the woods and into town.

Brodie tensed.

"Who could that be?" Laurel shivered, as if sensing danger.

"The only thing you should worry that pretty head about is the lusty lover who'll be in your bed come sundown and taming his wild streak." He tweaked her nose.

"A pure waste of time. I like him exactly as he is."

The man sized them up. Brodie pushed back the felt hat, releasing the rattle's hiss. He returned the hard, piercing stare, noting the twin ammunition belts crossing the stranger's chest and the pistols at his hip.

"Lookin' for a feller. Goes by the name Shenandoah."

Laurel sucked in a sharp breath but kept silent.

"Rumor has it the army took him to the stockade in Jefferson to be hanged. Others claim he headed east to St. Louis. Mentioned something about the Black Garter."

"Obliged."

Unease gripped the air until the stranger rode past the saloon without a glance and disappeared into the woods.

Laurel let out pent-up air. "I thought for a minute you yearned to do something rash."

"Can't go around shooting strangers. What would our eight children think of their paw?"

"That he's the keeper of their mother's heart?"

"Absolutely. But they'll be more seekers come this way. My dear Mrs. Yates, think you can handle life with an ex-hired gun?"

"Strange question, seeing who you bedded up with."

"You're a lavender-eyed vixen, you know that? Had to seine through a bunch of ugly rocks to find the right stone. Mighty glad I did, too." He flashed a crooked grin, winked, and dropped the old hat onto her dark head.

"I declare, Brodie, you need to brush up on sweet-talking a lady." The rattles hissed when she brushed the lock of hair from his forehead.

"Don't have any call to practice now. You're mine."

Promising secrets peeked around the edge of her smile. Lush hips filled his hands. He nibbled gently on a mouth that fit perfectly against the curve of his. Her lips knew him and didn't hold any slights that might've occurred against him. A sight better than he deserved. Brodie moved to the pulse in the hollow of her throat before she pushed him away, laughing.

"You may just change you mind." Laurel crooked a finger to follow, which he'd blindly do to the ends of the earth. "Come, my love. I want to find out which apron fits best."

"Now, darlin' . . ."

He discovered how adept she'd gotten at dodging glares.

Damnation! She paid them less mind than a pesky fly. She at least swatted at those. But Lord, did those curves sway when she moved.

"Everything comes with a price. Ollie once tried to convince me we're all rare jewels that need polishing. I would say we're both gold nuggets."

Call it passion, call it lust, or call it fulfilling a dream—his soul was no longer lost. He'd discovered it in Redemption, where it was born.

THE COWBOY
WHO CAME CALLING
LINDA BRODAY

Glory Day has found the man who promises to solve all her troubles. Then an interfering stranger literally comes between her and the outlaw she plans to bring in for the reward money. And she accidentally shoots him! Worse, Luke McClain is no ordinary cowboy; he is an extraordinary lawman and a true gentleman to boot.

While Glory doctors his wounds, Luke humors her ailing mother and seems determined to help save her father from jail and her family farm from ruin. What is a woman to do with such a meddlesome admirer? After one kiss, Glory realizes she *has* collared the correct man: She'll rope him into hanging his saddle next to hers for life.

Knight on the Texas Plains
Linda Broday

Duel McClain is no knight in shining armor—he is a drifter who prides himself on having no responsibilities.   But a poker game thrusts him into the role of father to an abandoned baby, and then a condemned woman stumbles up to his campfire.   The fugitive beauty aims to keep him at shotgun's length, but obvious maternal instincts belie her fierce demeanor.   And she and the baby are clearly made for each other. Worse, the innocent infant and the alleged murderess open Duel's heart, make him long for the love of a real family. And the only way to have that will be to slay the demons of the past.

Windfall
CINDY HOLBY

1864: Jake awakens from months of unconsciousness with his body healed, but his mind full of unanswerable questions. Is there a woman waiting somewhere for him? A family? A place he belongs? Shannon walks away from her abusive father and the only home she's ever known. Can a soldier with no past be the future she's prayed for? Grace tries to be brave when the need to capture a traitor rips her lover from her arms. Will it take even more courage to face him again now that his seed has blossomed within her? Jenny's grandfather's beloved ranch becomes a haven for all those she holds dear, but now the greed of one underhanded land baron threatens everything they've worked for. How can she keep the vision of her murdered parents alive for the generations to come?

The CHASE
LYNSAY SANDS

Seonaid Dunbar was trained as a Scottish warrior, but fleeing to an abbey would be preferable to whacking Blake Sherwell with her sword—which she'll happily do before wedding the man. No, she'll not walk weakly to the slaughter, dutifully pledge troth to anyone the English court calls "Angel." Fair hair and eyes as blue as the heavens hardly prove a man's worth. And there are many ways to elude a devilish suitor, even one that King Henry orders her to wed. No, the next Countess of Sherwell is not sitting in her castle as Blake thought: embroidering, peacefully waiting for him to arrive. She is fleeing to a new stronghold and readying her defenses. This battle will require all weapons—if he ever catches her. And the chase is about to begin.